IDENTIFIED

John Wilander

Cover design: Lance Buckley, lancebuckley.com
Identified logo: Peter Karlsson, Svarteld Form & Foto AB, svarteld.com
Author portrait: Christopher Michel, christophermichel.com

ISBN: 979-8-9850254-0-8 (hardcover)
ISBN: 979-8-9850254-2-2 (paperback)

Twitter: @johnwilander
hackerfiction.net

CHAPTER ONE

Find Me

Those fuckers.

West paced in his mom's living room, spitting invectives. Those fuckers had gone after her, not him.

His dues were paid, fifteen years for a teenage hack. But the government wanted more, probably because of his mom's persistent campaigning for his release.

He had been at the hospital again this morning and failed again to talk her out of her fatalistic plan. She just wanted to go home and continue her life.

Should he talk to a lawyer? Or a journalist? Or at least to someone at her workplace who might be able to attest to her tobacco-free life?

Nah, the only one he knew who'd be willing and capable of putting up a fight against G20S was Melissa.

Find me. She wouldn't have said that if she didn't mean it. Whatever she left me with has to contain enough information.

He got a notepad and a pencil and listed the breadcrumbs.

Melissa trail:
 Runa (weird name)
 Santa Cruz
 Pacific Avenue
 Her note
 C Weed
 Cookies (something dream)
 Boyfriend broke up

He needed to search for these things online to see if anything came up. But using the internet would be like talking straight to G20S.

I have to fly under Timothy's radar. Gosh, it's been a long time since I did this.

He needed to fool the government's filters by hiding his real search inside enough bland searches. *Bland* meant all the things a computer nerd who'd been away from society for fifteen years would search for.

He jotted down what came to mind.

Normal search activity:
*   *G20S (should make them proud)*
*   *Food in San Francisco*
*   *Public transportation*
*   *China (superpower nowadays?)*
*   *The president*
*   *Games*
*   *Music*
*   *TV series*
*   *Movies*
*   *Online dating*
*   *Pron (you sorry ass)*
*   *Programming languages*
*   *Smartphones to Tiles*
*   *The Tiling protocol*
*   *Tech companies*
*   *DEFCON*
*   *Climate change*
*   *California drought*
*   *Weed legal?*
*   *Ongoing wars*
*   *Trendy clothes*

He drew a graph of how to go from searching for food in San Francisco, through seafood and restaurants with ocean views, to his real goal of searching for Santa Cruz things.

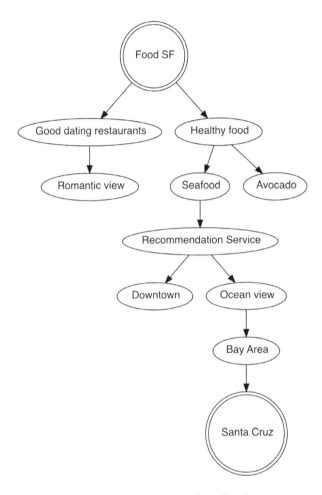

Timothy might be back to question me before this day is over.

He worked his way through the graph, typing search queries on his Tile. Apparently Santa Cruz had opted out of the latest anti-crime surveillance program. They even had a slogan for it: "Be Yourself in Santa Cruz." That was probably why Melissa picked it.

Nothing else stood out. No events, nothing special about Pacific Avenue.

Next up was the name Runa. With a specific query like that, he'd better fake a typo.

He listed words with just one mistyped or missing character away from "Runa."

Run
RNA
Tuna
Rune
Rung
Runs

Tuna's a good one. T and R keys right next to each other.

He followed his second search graph, starting with the California drought situation and going through desalination plants and ocean waste to tuna.

Misspelling *tuna* as *runa* gave him a Wikipedia search hit.

Runa or Rúna (ancient Scandinavian) is a Nordic given name used for females. Both Runa and its male forms, "Rune" and "Runar," stem from the word *runa*, which means letter or secret wisdom. The oldest reference to the name can be found in an 11th-century runic inscription. Runa is also a Japanese given name for females, meaning secret lore.

A Nordic or Japanese name related to secret messages or knowledge. And Melissa had something called Swedish Dream Cookies, right? That's two references to the Nordics.

Day turned to evening as he found out that marijuana had indeed been legal in California for many years, and he continued on to places to buy it and tapped his way to info on the C Weed coffee shop, where they had met. He even went into cookie recipes including the dream variety, only to find nothing. Hours at the screen and not a single concrete lead on where to find Melissa, not a single step closer to getting his mom that surgery.

He went upstairs and threw himself on his bed like he used to do as a teenager. This was where he had lain figuring out the details of his earliest hacks.

The later stuff, including the NSA hack, he and Melissa had done from her place since she had her own apartment. Her dad had rented it for her when it got too intense between them.

He wondered how her relationship with her latest boyfriend had been. Did that guy get to call her Liz?

Find me. Find me. What am I missing?

The note with the coordinates for C Weed he'd gotten through his mom lay on the bedside table. He had at least been able to decipher that one.

When you decide you want to start connecting dots again, find me. That's what she said.

Or had he not really deciphered the note? Maybe there was more to it?

The note is laser printed.

He shot up from the bed, went downstairs to get one of his mom's many pairs of reading glasses, and then trudged back up again to his mom's walk-in closet. He closed the door and pulled up a beautiful sea wallpaper on his Tile to inspect Melissa's note in blue light.

The glasses magnified well enough for him to find what he was looking for—small yellow dots in a strict, logical pattern. These were tracking codes that color laser printers had used since the 1990s to stop forgery of documents and paper money.

How on earth am I going to decode this? Searching for a spec on this format will trigger the G20S filters immediately.

He copied the pattern onto a piece of paper while trying to come up with a plan.

He scribbled on his notepad.

What I want:
    printer dots
    printer code
    printer watermark

How to hide:
    printer dot...s per inch
    printer co...lor
    printer wat...t comparison

Dots *and* code *are too broad. Gotta go with* watermark.

He searched for "printer wat" on his Tile, made sure "printer watermark" popped up among the suggested search completions, then added the remaining characters in "printer watt comparison" to make sure G20S didn't know what he was up to.

He checked the browser's cache, and there it was—a preloaded web-page called "Printer Watermark Obfuscation Redux."

The page provided a legend for how the printer watermark worked, and he applied it to the first set of dots on Melissa's note.

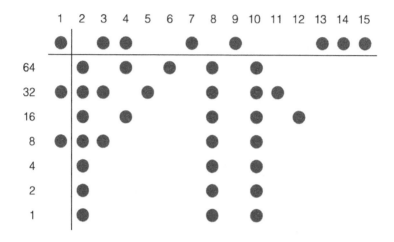

He started to decode the rows.

```
101010101001000000
110100101101000000
```

I'm going to have to get a Unicode spec to convert these.

As the tip of his pencil jumped from dot to dot to double-check the ones, he got the urge to actually *connect the dots*.

He did, and something emerged.

Runes! So that's the Runa clue.

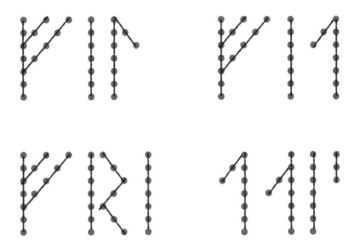

A rune translation table was available in his mom's old print version of Encyclopedia Britannica, and he deciphered the message:

Velvet Fridays

We got this, Mom.

Chapter Two

Members Only

West dared not search for "Velvet Fridays" online and instead meticulously scouted The Mission and surrounding neighborhoods in San Francisco for days, reading streetside displays and asking locals for cool places to go on Fridays. He worried he might be watched somehow, but it was an emotional reconnect with the city he used to enjoy as a teenager as well as an exposé of new technology in everyday use.

A lot of people were wearing minute, transparent earpieces, and by the look on their faces, it gave them tranquility. Probably noise cancellation. But the city was far from as noisy as he remembered it, with almost exclusively electric cars and buses in the streets. He had heard a few drones, which were mildly annoying, but he quite enjoyed the sound of the city, the buzz of life.

On Thursday, he finally struck gold. A lilac velvet flag reading "Fridays" hung outside what looked like a club entrance. This had to be it.

The entrance door was made of tinted glass and a chrome metal frame.

He approached and leaned forward to get a glimpse of the inside, with his hand shielding his eyes from the daylight. The instant his hand touched the glass, the whole door lit up with a display. He jerked back.

The display's content had a retro cyberpunk tone to it. Green font on black background and floating images from movies like *Bladerunner* and *Tron*.

Unrecognized ID. Access denied.

He glanced at his orange identity band, which clearly was active. A segment of the display opened a video stream with a woman looking straight at him. She had spiky orange hair and smeared, multicolor makeup.

She chewed and swallowed something before speaking. "Excuse me, we can't confirm your membership."

"I'm not a member. But I'd like to come to the club tomorrow night."

"The club?"

"Yeah. Velvet Fridays."

"Velvet Fridays is a hackathon."

"Oh."

She sighed. "Are you at all into programming?"

"I used to be."

A glimpse of interest in her eyes. "Which languages?"

"C, C++, JavaScript, assembly."

"Old school. Got any repos we can look at?"

"I haven't been coding for years."

"No code, no member."

West closed his eyes and flipped his head back to face the sky.

"Or you solve one of the membership challenges," she said. "Check to the left."

On the door, there was now a list of programming challenges.

```
..oo0  Membership Challenges  0oo..
..oo0       PoC || GTFO       0oo..


0. Code a quine (self-replicating program)
that prints out its own source code. Must
be shorter than the current leader.

1. Code a polyglot (single file that runs
as different things) in any three of these
formats:
     Forth | JavaScript
     Swift | Go
     Rust  | Swirl
     HEIF  | Shell script
     WebP  | Python

2. Solve the P versus NP problem.
```

West smiled. P versus NP was one of the Millennium Prize Problems. A rusty hacker like himself was unlikely to crack it in one day when no one had in fifty years.

"Can I see the scoreboard for the quine, please?" he said as he scribbled down the challenges on his notepad. The screen changed without the woman moving. "Thanks. Do I submit my code to you?"

"Mhm. We do care for anonymity, so use whatever medium you think we can handle."

"Paper?"

"Eh, sure."

The display faded out. Did he stand any chance at all of refining one of those quines? In a single day? People had probably spent weeks just to shave off a single character here and there. But he had to find Melissa and figure this whole thing out about his mom.

The polyglot seemed more reasonable. Just read up on the specs and start hacking. But three formats at once? It wouldn't be listed as a challenge if it wasn't as hard as the quines.

Can I hack the challenge itself? Is there a flaw I can exploit?

His mind wandered as he slowly walked down the street. Wasn't there an old prank with quines? He smiled.

It's worth a shot.

He turned around and went back to the glass door. It again lit up as he touched it, and the woman looked a bit surprised. "You?"

"Yeah. I think I have a solution for the quine challenge." He tore off a sheet of his notepad and held it up. A traditional mail slot opened to the right of the door. He slipped in the piece of paper and saw the woman on the video stream pick it up.

"It's empty," she said.

"Exactly. The program is empty and prints out nothing. Voilà, the shortest possible quine."

She gave him a naughty smile. "It appears we have a bug in our challenge description. It should of course say *non-empty* quine." There were a few seconds of silence. "But that's cool."

Chapter Three

ID bb8a2a6fc1ccd229a0a7b66ac42f97ef

"I knew you'd find me," a voice said behind him.

West swiveled around in his chair. It was Melissa, his old girlfriend.

"I trust you've changed your mind, then," she added.

The sensation of seeing her after all these years was still jolting.

She was wearing two T-shirts—the outer about his size, which meant severely oversized for her. It featured a whacky, colorful pattern that looked like fragments of a city landscape in the style of cubism. Over one of her arms was a folded denim jacket.

She looked around. West did too. No one at the hackathon was watching them.

He got up and hugged her.

"My mom's sick," he said while holding on.

"Let's not talk here," she whispered, wriggling out of his embrace. She pointed at the handheld device connected to his monitor. "That's not your own, right?"

"No, they lent me a smartphone."

"Tile."

"Right. Sorry." He got his own Tile out of his pocket. "I turned mine off before I got here. Government issue," he said with a frown and sat down again.

She took out and held open a sack slightly larger than his palm. It was made from a dark glittery fabric. Her eyes moved back and forth between his government Tile and the sack.

He dropped his Tile in.

Melissa pulled back the sleeve of his sweater with her pinky and revealed his identity band. Her brief touch triggered its orange glow.

"Got it a few days ago, straight from some Agent Timothy who's assigned to my case," he said, looking at it.

She nodded at the mesh pouch and sealed it as soon as West got his band inside.

They left through a back door. The San Francisco summer evening was cool. There was a smelly garbage container beside the door and poor lighting.

"Did you use your GPI when you searched for me?" Melissa asked interrogatively.

GPI meant Global Personal Identity: his ID band. Of course he had used it. It was the only way to get access to the internet. He told her about all the precautions he had taken to obscure his online searches.

"AI is able to glean context out of almost any group of words these days," she said. "They even offer it as a service called Context Search. Did you have surgery in prison?"

"What?"

"Surgery."

"I had appendicitis a few years in."

"Those few years probably coincided with the Surveillance on Probation and Parole Act, SOPPA."

She tapped a few times on her Tile and put it against his stomach about navel high. It chirped, and she held up the screen for him to read.

bb8a2a6fc1ccd229a0a7b66ac42f97ef

"That's you," she said. "Felons are implanted with an RFID chip so the government can track them in public spaces, especially ones released on parole. Political compromise to not get mandatory facial recognition in cities. Only people convicted after the enaction were supposed to get the implants, but rumors say prisons have created excuses to do it to all their inmates. They get paid for each implant."

West's right hand palpated the area around his belly button. There was no trace of a chip or rigid implant.

Melissa got another glittery sack out of her pocket and a roll of surgical tape. "Cover your navel. I believe it's a criminal offense to obscure the signal, but no one told you you're chipped."

Criminal offense.

He accepted the pouch and rolled its metal mesh fabric between his fingers. It rattled gently. The woven strands felt cold against his stomach, and he wondered how much hair would be pulled out when he ripped this tape off.

When he looked up, Melissa had taken her huge, outer T-shirt off.

"Wear this too." She handed him the tee. "I don't trust that they aren't using facial recognition here in the city."

Gosh, she was skinny, fighter skinny, like a flyweight boxer. She put on her jacket. He squinted in the dim light. It looked like she had mismatched tack buttons on her breast pockets.

"You don't need this yourself?" he said as his head popped through the neck of the cubist T-shirt.

She just smiled and handed him a black facemask with ear straps. "The one thing fucking Covid did for us was normalize these. Let's head to the lab."

They walked several blocks without talking. The surgical tape around his navel stretched and pulled every time he turned around to look for signs of surveillance, finding none.

Cameras were right in your face in prison, a deterrent.

They entered what looked like a regular apartment building and took the stairs. West got his mask off as they ascended. Melissa used a physical key to unlock and open a door on the third floor.

"The Survivors," she said with an inward gesture.

CHAPTER FOUR

The Survivors

Three people in the dimly lit apartment looked at West, two of them getting up from a couch close to the entrance and the third sitting at a computer screen further in. Two women and a man, all younger than he.

West pulled a hand through his hair.

Melissa nudged him in, closed the door, and introduced her buddies one by one.

First, the sole man in the group. "Jitterbug: hardware tinkerer and maker deluxe. Indulges in hacking challenges." He was a good-looking Black guy in his midtwenties, neat haircut, trimmed beard, black shirt, khaki slacks, and shiny shoes. No big muscles, but fit.

Melissa looked at Jitterbug. "West here got into Velvet by submitting an empty quine. Get it?"

"Empt... Ooo." Jitterbug nodded approvingly.

Melissa looked back at West. "In addition to loving a smart hack, Jit believes in God Almighty and thinks we should all stop swearing."

"My mom would approve," West said.

Melissa turned to one of the two women, a blonde with an asymmetric haircut. "Kiss: social engineer extraordinaire. Needs to up her feminist game, but always helpful when it comes to dating."

Kiss wore a tank top and denim overalls. Her face reminded West of some British pop star. He guessed she was about thirty.

"Did you two exchange jeans buttons by any chance?" West said, looking back and forth between Kiss and Melissa.

Kiss pulled out the straps of her overalls and looked at the buttons. "We did."

"We can analyze the buttons later," Melissa said with a smile.

"Last but not least, here's BestBye."

A petite woman with what looked like Japanese heritage got up from her office chair.

"She can get on your nerves, but she's the smartest hacker I've ever met. A control freak like myself. She hacked my boyfriend once, which I'll never forgive her for, but we're cool."

BestBye had skinny jeans, ballerina flats, and a worn-out blue T-shirt with its neckline cut off just enough to show a Japanese character tattooed under her left collarbone. She looked very young, but her posture said otherwise, especially with the reserved look she gave West.

Melissa pointed her thumb toward him. "Y'all, this is West, famous NSA hacker and the best pattern matcher I've ever worked with."

West blushed. "Hi!" he said, one hand waving and the other safely in his pocket. "I should say up front I'm not a hacker anymore. I haven't been allowed to touch tech stuff for fifteen years."

"Old school hacker, you are," Kiss said in what sounded like the voice of Yoda from Star Wars.

"If he's no longer a hacker, then why is he here?" BestBye asked Melissa.

"He's plenty smart and someone I trust."

"So you say," BestBye replied.

They all fell silent. He looked around. The place was full of gadgets—cables, gaming equipment, old keyboards, and what were probably Tiles in various sizes.

The left side of the room had windows covered by blinds and a long desk with four large monitors. It reminded him of LAN parties in the good ol' days.

The corner to the left of him had a huge screen facing the middle of the room. To the right were two armchairs and the L-shaped couch where Kiss and Jitterbug had been sitting. The coffee table in between had an empty snack bag of something called Flamin' Shokra.

"Do you have any reason of your own to be here?"

He looked up. It was BestBye asking.

"My mom," he said in a low voice. "The G20S, which I looked up, and it's some joint security agency for the G20 countries."

"Trust me, we know G20S," Melissa said patronizingly.

"Okay. Well, they have evidence of my mom smoking, and now her insurance won't cover surgery for a life-threatening condition. It's just that she's never smoked in her life. They framed her."

"Why would they do that?" Kiss asked.

Jitterbug gave her a meaningful look. "You surprised, sis?"

"That's just speculation," BestBye blurted. "Maybe your mom did smoke. People do all sorts of things they don't want to tell their kids about."

"You don't know my mom." West's voice was louder now.

"Don't let BestBye get to you," Melissa interjected. "She has no filters. I believe you. It's a known thing; false evidence on the blockchain."

"Blockchain?"

"Mhm. The G20S has the right to collect any data they want on you as long as it's put on a blockchain tied to your GPI and replicated so it cannot be changed afterward. They've merged in social security numbers, driver's licenses, voter registration, you name it. Everything *you* is on the G20S blockchain."

Kiss pointed toward the back of the room. "We've got a pot of coffee. You want?"

"Yes, please," West said.

Soon enough he held a mug in his hand and had picked the corner spot on the couch. "I'm rusty on this stuff, but you're saying the blockchain found its way into government use? That's one for the history ledger." He blew steam off the top of the mug.

Melissa nodded from her armchair.

"How do they produce false evidence?" West asked.

"We don't know yet," Melissa said, leaning back while holding on to both armrests. "But your mom is not the first case, not by a long shot."

West lit up. "Can we prove she's being framed?"

Melissa shrugged. "The inside of G20S systems is going to get you a whole lot closer."

"You have access?"

"Not yet. But it's why we're all here; that's the goal of the Survivors—take down the Global Personal Identity system." She made a gesture toward the rest of the team.

Jitterbug gave him a curious smile, and Kiss nodded behind her coffee mug. BestBye was inspecting her fingernails.

They're going after the big guys just like Melissa and I did.

West took a deep breath. "I need to fix this for my mom."

"I saw her a couple of times on the news, campaigning for your release," Melissa said. "Placards saying 'NSA was wrong, my boy was right. God knows.' That kind of stuff. I guess G20S ain't too happy about it."

"She always told me God promised her to get me out, quoting the Bible. 'I will never leave you nor forsake you.' I tried to talk her out of it to not get herself into trouble."

"Seems she's in a shitload of trouble now." Melissa fished out her Tile and spoke as she flipped through something on the screen. "If you want to hang out with us, we have a few Survivor rules. Three to be exact." She beamed her Tile's content to the big screen in the corner behind her.

1. **Sharing Is Caring.** Share vulnerabilities or exploits with the team on SurvivorNet but never disclose them to anyone on the outside.

2. **No Killing.** Hacking can risk lives. Don't get anyone killed.

Killing?

3. **No Romance.** Survivors don't date other Survivors.

The last rule had nothing to do with hacking. It felt strange given his and Melissa's past.

He realized the others waited for him to say something. "I really shouldn't hack stuff anymore," he started off. "I'm on parole and something they call Internet Restriction. If they catch me breaking into computers again, I'm finished."

So why did you track down Melissa? Now you look like a fool.

Melissa replied in a tone of reason. "We get that you're on parole. No one here is risk-free. We're all going down if this fails."

"Seems pretty stupid to come here if you're not going to hack things," BestBye added.

"Give the man a break," Kiss shot back. "He just did fifteen and his mom is dying."

"Sitting at home won't save her," BestBye said as she walked over to her monitor by the long desk, sat down, and started scrolling through something.

She's right.

He let his thumb glide over the glazed, hot side of his mug. Coffee was so much better out in the free world. "I'll do my best," he heard himself say.

"Good enough for me," Melissa responded, cutting it short. "By Monday you need to have drafted two fake identities for yourself. Backstory, personality, the lot. We need to generate data that looks like a plausible past, and the more detailed input, the better."

"Are we hacking my identity?"

"We aren't able to hack the GPI bands," Melissa said. "But there is a different kind of band we are able to hack." She walked over to the entrance and shrugged a glossy nylon jacket in place. "You're headed for a little accident."

Chapter Five

West's New Identities

"A hit. Or maybe a hit and run if the car owner is stupid. We've all done it," Melissa said with a hand gesture toward the others in the lab.

West was speechless. He'd been wondering all weekend what this thing was. A car crash was not a little accident.

Melissa leaned forward in her armchair. "The only way we know of to create a new GPI for a person is to get them an emergency ID at a hospital. ID-less patients in critical condition are issued a temporary GPI—wristband and all—to track them through the healthcare system. Hospitals must do it that way for liability reasons. So we stage a car accident, you go to the hospital, get one of those temp IDs, and leave before they can get your real ID."

How have they figured all this out?

"That sounds dangerous," West said.

"It's not easy to get hit by modern cars," Melissa replied, leaning back again and tapping the armrests. "At low speeds, you really have to jump it. But we're not shooting for real injury."

"Still sounds dangerous. How can I use multiple IDs? My face and fingerprints won't change."

He had done as he'd been told and created two alternate identities: Bruce Silver, an incarnation of one of his duties in prison, cooking; and Jonathan Ash, an old-school sound technician built around a teenage hobby of his, music.

"Undercover agents need to have multiple IDs that match the same body so G20S made that possible," Melissa replied. "When the system hits multiple IDs for a single face, fingerprint, or whatever they have recorded on the individual, it picks one at random to not create traces for those undercover agents. Regular people just have one ID."

"But we're not regular people." It was BestBye from over at the desk.

"Of course we are." Kiss rolled her office chair a few inches away from BestBye.

"We're not. Everyone in this room is a lot smarter than the average American." BestBye turned to him. "Except you, West. I don't know whether or not you're smart yet. But let's assume you are for the sake of argument."

"You're such an asshole, Best," Kiss said, shaking her head.

"A smart asshole."

"Please, you two." Melissa held up her palms above the chair's headrest. "Getting back to West's IDs. You can create as many fake ones as you like, but you need two that you rehearse the shit out of to nail them when we're out and about. That's your Bruce and Jonathan. You've met Runa, she is one of mine. If one of these fake IDs gets exposed in any kind of hacking, you have to kill them. You can't just abandon them."

"Let me know if you need any help in that department," BestBye said. "It's fun coming up with causes of death."

Kiss turned her chair toward West instead of BestBye. "There's one more thing about the car accident. You have to end up in a police investigation," she said. "Otherwise, your temporary ID won't carry over to G20S. As soon as the police have grabbed your temp ID, we just hack the hospital and populate their database with new data whenever you need to create yourself a new citizen in the GPI system. Everything automatically syncs."

It was a neat hack. But still, bloody hell. Staging a car accident?

West drew a deep breath and felt a small sting of pain under his belly button, where Jitterbug's veterinarian friend had removed the small, pill-shaped parole chip from his soft tissue. In that same place was now a barbell piercing made of translucent Teflon to hang the chip off of whenever he needed to be identifiable and keep G20S from getting suspicious.

"Where?" West said. "Where will we stage the accident?"

"We can't do it here in the Bay Area because then you'll run the risk of running into a nurse or physician who recognizes you afterward. I can't tell you more because you need to be confused to pull it off."

"I have to notify my parole officer if I'm going out of state. And I have to come up with an excuse for Mom."

"Your parole officer won't know. Jit has some cool stuff for dealing with G20S surveillance." She tilted her head toward the other armchair. "Tell him about your gyro hack, Q."

"I thought you had given up homophobic Bond movies," Jitterbug said, raising his eyebrows.

"I skip the bad parts."

Jitterbug turned to West. "She tried to have us call her M." He rolled his eyes. "Gyro hack. Here's the thing. The G20S uses geolocation and sensors in your 'gubment' Tile to monitor you. So, if you bring it on our little road trip, you're bust. But if you just leave it at home, the gyroscope in it will not behave like the Tile is being used, and that's going to raise suspicion."

Jitterbug got up, walked over to a box along the wall, and fished out a black, extended, and sturdy handle with fittings the size of a Tile.

"Wait, don't tell me," West said, straightening himself up. "They're called … selfie sticks! Hottest thing when I went to prison."

"It's a gimbal stabilizer made to shoot video Steadicam-style, but I've modded it into a motion simulator. You leave your Tile in this at your mom's and it'll report to G20S that you are walking around, lying in bed reading, or pinching a loaf."

No Tile on the trip means I can't stay in touch with Mom.

Melissa stood up. "Let's get cracking. We've got car hit training and a long ride ahead of us."

CHAPTER SIX

G20S: Mixed Reality

"I don't know what to make of this, sir." Agent Timothy's direct was pointing toward two screens on the desk—one with a set of data from the monitoring of West's Tile, the other with a map featuring two dots.

Timothy looked back and forth between the screens, then straightened and massaged the front of his neck, checking that his shave was still good.

"The system picked up the subject at these two spots," the direct said, pointing at the map. "But the Tile says he's at home with his mom."

"Picked up how? Chip or GPI?"

"Neither. It says 'model matching,' so I assume they had some model of the subject built when he was an inmate. I know prisons record walk patterns."

"Model matching is unreliable. Only a few states even use it for public space surveillance. Apparently Nebraska is one."

Timothy's direct gave the edge of the desk a push and rolled backward a few inches to stretch his legs out. "I can't believe we've only had GPI for, what is it now, five years? How did we do our jobs before? And it was a close vote too."

"Not a day goes by when I don't thank the don't-take-my-guns nutjobs. Always remember this: Whatever political adversary you face, get 'em bundled up with the gun lobby, and you've got the Democratic votes on your side. They don't know it, but the NRA did save this country."

The direct chuckled.

Timothy grabbed his paper cup and disappointedly noted that he was out of coffee. "I'll check in on the mom's house."

Chapter Seven

One Hit Wounder

The two-day road trip to wherever the Survivors were taking West could have been a treat. But he was blindfolded and suffered badly from motion sickness. They stopped a few times to charge the car, which at least allowed him to move, but Melissa insisted on bagging his whole head and telling concerned people at the charging stations that he was on a surprise birthday trip.

In addition to the nausea, he worried about his mom. Sure, he had decided to take action and she'd been totally fine with him going on a hiking trip, but he was nowhere close to figuring out how she was framed. Getting a fake identity was just one step of the way. Every day that passed was another day without her surgery.

Melissa, Kiss, and Jitterbug spent the trip mostly listening to music and reading, taking turns being the car's designated operator. BestBye had stayed behind since they staged her accident in the same city they were taking West to.

Jitterbug cranked up the volume on the car stereo. "I love NuMo. We should go discoing while we're there."

It sounded like a mix of electronica and slowed-down disco.

Melissa talked over the loud music. "We'll stage your accident in a specific district to get you to a clinic where we have access to the computer system. We also want to avoid BestBye's hospital. If multiple emergency patients disappear from the same clinic, they'll have to report it to the state, whereas one-offs typically are silenced."

Hours passed as West heard the countryside soundscape turn into suburbs and further into a city buzz before they parked.

His blindfold was finally removed, and he found himself in a hotel room, blinds shut. Melissa made him promise to not try to figure out where he was while they scouted the spot for the hit.

Alone, he sat down on the bouncy bed. The room featured a stained wooden desk with mirrors above it, a humming mini fridge, a TV with a scanner on the side labeled "GPI or Axxxess," and a large poster of a Ford Model T with its picture frame slightly tilted.

He nudged the frame until it was perfectly level.

Hacking a hospital and getting a fake identity. Illegal for sure.

There would be no turning back if he went through with this, no having paid his dues.

NuMo and Ford. I'm pretty sure where we are. I wonder if that game developer train ride to San Francisco is still a thing?

•

Next morning, West's blindfold back on, Melissa and the others brought West to what he pictured as a small, rural street based on the sounds and the low speed of their car.

Melissa described the scene to him. "It's a sunny summer afternoon, in the low eighties. Kiss is waiting at the crossing up the street, and she will let us know when a suitable car is coming. We're on Lauder Street in a single-family-home area in Detroit."

Bingo.

"They have anti-crime cameras downtown and in poorer neighborhoods, just so you know. Down the street, under some trees are two parked cars on the right side. You crouch and face the street through the gap between those cars. The car to jump will approach from the left. Speed limit here is twenty-five."

West tried to match the picture Melissa just painted to what he knew he had to do. He had practiced thoroughly on a clunker at an isolated spot back in California—jump a reasonably slow-moving car, kick the side of it with a steel-toe shoe to generate a bang, tumble over the hood, and pretend to get hurt badly.

Melissa's Tile buzzed. "Kiss says incoming car. West, you ready?"

He heard the car door open beside him and felt Melissa's fingers slide in under his blindfold and remove it. The only response he got out of his body was "Fuck."

He stumbled onto the sidewalk. The low-hanging morning sun struck his eyes like knives.

Did she say left or right?

He shielded his eyes. Before him was a lane of neat lawns with attached brick-and-mortar houses. The street was at ease. He could see the cluster of trees ahead. They looked sparser than he had imagined.

He hid between the two parked cars, trying to recall Melissa's directions. A brown, Beetle-like car approached from the left—speed reasonable.

Three, two, one.

His timing was accurate. Right foot into the side of the car, just behind the front light. Bam!

He folded his upper body over the hood and started his rolling motion. The car's automatic brakes kicked in, quickly slowing it down, and its proactive security system popped the hood an inch to become more flexible.

As West's left foot lifted off the ground, it hit the front-facing tread of the tire and was pulled down by the friction of the moving wheel. The pull stopped his forward motion, and instead of his body rolling over the hood, his head hit the far right of the front window and his hip snapped the side mirror.

The car had already stopped before West was completely still. On the ground, in a haze, he saw Melissa running toward him.

His hand instinctively moved to the left side of his head. The last thing he remembered was the sensation of warm blood on his fingers.

CHAPTER EIGHT

Botsford Hospital

Kiss heard screams and noises down Lauder Street. Her hands clasped her stomach. The cries sounded more real than they should for a faked accident.

Soon thereafter, the Survivors' car picked her up. Jitterbug looked haggard in the operator seat.

"What the fuck just happened? Is he hurt?" she yelled as she got in.

"Wait." Jitterbug gave the car instructions to park along McNichols with a visual down Lauder. "I couldn't see properly, but I think he's hurt. It went awry. I saw blood."

"We have to help him."

"Melissa stayed behind to make sure an ambulance picks him up. You and I are to follow that ambulance."

It didn't take long for paramedics to show up. Emergency service vehicles travelled the streets fast now that self-driving cars automatically gave way.

The ambulance carrying West came back to the crossing and took a left.

"Shouldn't it go the other way?" Jitterbug cried as the ambulance passed them. Jitterbug's hands trembled as he grabbed the steering wheel, ready to drive it manually.

"Just go," Kiss said. "I'll figure out where it's going."

Jitterbug took control of the vehicle and violently began their pursuit of the ambulance. The car's safety alerts went off, and he hit "Emergency" on the mid console screen to shut it up.

Normally an emergency override would be directly reported to local traffic police, but they had hacked the car's communication bus and filtered out any such messages. Now they only had to worry about being reported by cameras and other vehicles, including the ambulance, but they couldn't afford to lose track of West.

The ambulance passed the bridge over the freeway, went further west, and took a turn onto M-5. Miles passed in the wrong direction. Finally, an exit.

"We're headed for Botsford," Kiss said.

"Isn't that where BestBye got her ID?"

"I don't know why they didn't go to Sinai. This is more than three times the distance."

"I think I saw blood."

"You told me."

There were pros and cons to the situation. They knew Botsford well from BestBye's case, both physically and computer-wise with back doors already planted into the medical record system. But this would become the second stolen emergency ID from this hospital and would probably not go unnoticed by management and thus G20S.

Jitterbug let the car park as soon as West's ambulance had disappeared into the building. He landed his head on the steering wheel, closed his eyes, and let out a groan.

Kiss reached out from the back seat and put her hand on his shoulder. "We can't help West if we're freaking out. Let's just do this like we always would. Okay?"

They sat quietly for half a minute, collecting themselves.

Kiss used their digital back door to enter the Botsford system and started tracing changes to medical records with a filter for "G20SEMID"—the keyword for emergency IDs. Soon enough, she got a hit. Someone was creating a record for West.

```
G20SEMID No existing GPI available
G20SEMID New emergency patient ID
G20SEMID Male
G20SEMID 30-40 years (estimate)
G20SEMID Caucasian
```

"Okay, they've got him set up. Caucasian race and all. Although I think West said his father is from India." She got her seatbelt off. "What happens if you're multiracial? I bet GPI makes you pick one. Such BS."

Jitterbug gave a puff of a laugh, half gleeful, half nervous. "I once changed my GPI race to 'Gay' just to see the look on the faces at airport security."

"That's awesome. What did they say?"

"Nothing. They don't want to tell people all the detailed info they have access to. But they sure took a good look at me."

More data came through Kiss's filter.

```
G20SEMID Fingerprint hash
    8655b12c1424c835e68d7fd479172d87
    b66d67b8368a207b927e9867fe630732
    89c129058185109c7ed9d1f8d5d52e9e
    124f71271a5f161d0fdcc5914136e042

G20SEMID Retina hash
    240e6314195ccdf0d161f5a17217f421
    e9e25d5d8f1d9de7c901581850921c98
    237036ef7689e729b702a8638b76d66b
    78d271974df7d86e538c4241c21b5568

G20SEMID Emergency SSN
    386-E2-1256
```

"Got the hashes." She added the emergency social security number to her search filter to keep following West.

"I need to find a restroom," Jitterbug said. "You want something while I'm out?"

"I'm dying for a coffee."

"No milk or sugar?"

"Correct. Once black, never go back."

"Mind your Ps and Qs. What's with the lewd jokes anyway?"

"Sorry. It's from my previous life. I told you that."

CHAPTER NINE

Shuffle

Kiss pulled up the digital blueprints of Botsford Hospital and reviewed how they got BestBye out last time.

Something moved in the log trace for West's emergency ID.

She stared at the screen. This couldn't be data for West. Had she made a mistake when she added his temporary SSN to the filter? Quick check. Of course not.

She texted Melissa, who'd been asking repeatedly for an update.

> Concussion, possible
> traumatic brain injury :((

Da fuck?

> That's what the log says.
> I don't know what to do.

Had to deal with the police.
I'm getting a car, headed to
Sinai.

> No. We're at Botsford.

???

> That's where they took him.

> The police will come. Some
> old man sat watching in
> his house and told the
> police that West jumped
> the car.

Kiss looked up. There was a police car parking to the left of the emergency room's pedestrian entrance. She opened the window and got her Tile out to take a photo just as two officers got out of the vehicle—a woman of average height and a tall man with a short red beard. Both wore black clothes, and law enforcement gear sat snugly around their waists.

She sent the photo to Melissa.

> That's them all right. That
> beard. One of you needs to
> get inside now and make
> sure they don't identify
> West.

> J!t is getting coffee.

> Then it's you.

Kiss reviewed the blueprints. It should be possible to sneak in through the ambulance entrance and go to a storage room for the vending machines close to reception. Hopefully, she could hear any conversation between the police and the receptionists from there.

She got out of the car and had a good look around. Three surveillance cameras were visible around the parking lot. They probably shouldn't stay here much longer.

Another ambulance came in as she got close to the building. She dashed into the garage behind it and hid until the interior doors swung open to let the new patient in. Just as the electric openers let go, she took a leap diagonally to the storage room door on the left.

She grabbed the handlebar. The room was locked.

No time to think it over. She had to find somewhere to hide; hide and listen.

The last person following the new patient went through a wide pair of doors on the right-hand side, twenty feet in. The noise of life-saving activities filled the hallway as the doors remained open a few seconds with an electric buzz.

The police probably wouldn't handle a potential crime matter in the public waiting room. Maybe here in the corridor? Or in Security's room to the left?

There was a vacant bed right across from the storage room. She jumped over, got up on the bed, and pulled the blanket over her body and face. The fabric clung to her forehead as it sucked up sweat.

"Officers, let's stand over here. We don't want to block the hallway," a calm male voice said, coming closer to Kiss's position.

"Thank you for taking the time. We can see you're busy."

"Well, a nearby emergency hospital received a bomb threat and is currently sending all acute patients to us and two other clinics, so we're barely keeping up."

"We heard about the bomb."

"Of course. What can I help you with today, officers?"

"We believe you received a male patient fifteen minutes ago or so. He was in a car accident and hit his head. Midthirties. We have reason to believe the accident was staged, probably insurance fraud, and we would like to know his identity."

"I'll have to scan your police IDs for our audit logs before I can check the system."

Kiss heard two beeps.

"Hey, Tile, give me the identity of emergency patients within the last half hour. Male. Thirty to forty years old. Head or brain trauma."

Nothing was said for a few seconds.

"We have one such patient. Identity unknown."

"Unknown?"

"Either the patient has lost their wristband, had it stolen, or took it off."

"Can't you ID him through fingerprints?"

"We need authorization before we can retrieve GPIs from finger-prints or retina scans. In emergencies, that's not a priority."

"I see. But we are authorized. Can we see him?"

"He's unconscious. But I just flagged his temporary ID for you, so you'll be able to import the data later for your investigation, no worries."

"He doesn't have to be conscious for us to get a fingerprint."

"Understood. I doubt we allow that, though." There was a pause. "But let me double-check."

Kiss's breathing intensified under the blanket. If West got identified, it could spell disaster for him. They were so close to getting him out of his GPI jail, they just couldn't fail him now. Could she take down the whole hospital's IT system? Maybe another bomb threat? Nah, it would risk the lives of all the patients, including West.

A minute passed before the person from the hospital came back.

"I'm afraid the patient is going into surgery right now. You'll have to wait at least an hour to get a fingerprint scan."

"Oh. We can't wait here for that long. Let's just get a copy of that temporary ID for now. Here, just read it to my Tile."

"386-E2-1256."

"Thank you. And can you make sure he doesn't leave until we see him?"

"He's not going anywhere."

"Perfect. Just making sure. Thanks so much for taking the time."

Kiss heard the police officers leave. She stayed put and contacted Melissa.

> Inside. The police asked for West. They couldn't ID him because of surgery. We have an hour.

Do you know where he is? Can we get him out?

> No and no.

Why?

> He's in fucking surgery.

If the police find out who he is it's game over.

The police scanned my
Runa GPI at the scene and
can link it to his real one.

o.0 I'll figure something out.

Someone stopped by Kiss's bed. "Hey, who left a patient in the freaking corridor?"

Kiss activated all her muscles while frozen still. Her pulse caused audible fluctuations in her breathing.

"Who what?" someone replied from down the hallway.

Kiss saw the silhouette of a hand close to her head. The fingers grabbed the blanket and started pulling.

A high-pitched, ear-piercing beep announced another ambulance on its way in. The hand on Kiss's blanket released its hold.

Shortly after, a new emergency patient was rolled in. The medical team stopped close to Kiss's bed to brief the trauma physician on duty. Apparently, they were short on care units.

A woman went through the details quickly. "Male, about thirty, head trauma, stable but unconscious."

Kiss gently lifted the side of her blanket to look. The new trauma patient lay just a few inches from her. She forced herself not to look at his head.

There were traces of blood on the man's clothes. She slid out her hand and moved it toward the man's bed. Her index finger pulled back the sleeve of his sweater and revealed his GPI band. She released the band's metal stud from its hole and snagged the band just a second before the man was moved into the emergency space.

Five minutes later, she was back in the car with Jitterbug. She fired up the filtered view of the hospital's medical records.

"I just made sure Botsford received a second ID-less trauma patient."

"Come again?"

"Hold on, I got this."

She worked feverishly for ten minutes.

"There." She dropped her Tile in her lap, threw herself back in the seat, and closed her eyes. "Sorry for going silent. The police are going to scan West's fingerprints when he gets out of surgery, and we can't let that happen. So I stole the GPI band from another male patient and switched West's emergency ID with his in the database. Now they'll scan the second guy's fingerprints."

"Doesn't that mean the second guy will be the one who ends up in an investigation and gets imported into G20S systems?"

"He will. Unless I switch back after the police get those fingerprints. Please remind me." She flashed her friend a smile.

•

The Survivors successfully duped the police and risked one more day with West in the hospital to let the health professionals keep track of his vitals while the team made sure to get the full list of supplies for his treatment and steal plenty of it.

West was in a haze the first twenty-four hours on the car ride back. He kept mumbling about how his mom would never let him go on a hiking trip again.

Melissa used the time to hack his temporary GPI and connect it with the two alternate identities he had developed—Bruce Silver and Jonathan Ash.

"There you go," she said. "Now you need to decide whether you're Jon or Bruce before we get you to the clinic in Salt Lake City. We'll stay there for a night or two."

"I feel like shit. Can't I just be myself and you do the talking?"

"From now on, you will never be yourself again in any public space or online, unless you have to in order to keep G20S happy."

He groaned. "I'll be Bruce. No, Jon. I'll be Jon."

She fired off a couple of commands and ran a test scan of West's GPI band. "Hi, Jonathan."

Melissa started talking to all of them while she looked out the window at stretches of summery Wyoming landscape. "We need to get going on our real mission. BestBye texted me yesterday. She has confirmed the names and affiliations of the three agents she spotted outside the G20S meeting in New York City last month. They're from Canada, Mexico, and Brazil. We need a human target as entry point to the GPI system."

CHAPTER TEN

Bugger Off

"He was here, that agent," his mom said, lingering on the last step of the staircase as she came down to welcome him.

West had just entered the house after the trip back from Detroit and dropped his bag on the floor. His head was a blitz. Had G20S been here?

"I …" He grabbed the nearest hook of the coatrack on the wall and closed his eyes. His other hand fumbled in the air for something to hold on to.

The next thing he knew he was sitting on the couch, his mom holding his hand. She was panting as if after a workout.

"What happened to you?" she said frantically. Her free hand touched the edge of the wound dressing sticking out from underneath his beanie.

He tilted his head away from her an inch. "I fell during the hike. Nothing serious. We went to the hospital to play it safe. That's just to protect from infection. What was it that you were saying?"

"Falling and hitting your head. When will we get a break?"

"It's really okay, Mom. The agent. What about the agent?"

"A day after you left the city, he came here. The one with the ginger hair."

Timothy.

There was accusation in her voice, but West couldn't tell if it was aimed at him or the unwelcome guest.

"Did he enter the house?"

"Not this time. My courtesy ended when they served me that concoction of tobacco lies. I told him to ask his questions right there on the porch."

"What did he …"

"I told him he could call you if he wanted to know where you are."

West gritted his teeth.

"Which I believe he did, several times, because I heard your phone buzz in your room. I figured you had left it behind on purpose. Being reachable all the time is a nuisance."

"Thank you, Mom. I'm sorry you have to go through this."

•

Headaches and inflammation rode West for the next three weeks as he recovered from surgery. He visited the lab on days when he was feeling better and was given a training set to get back into lock picking—something he used to be pretty good at.

His mom probably understood that he hadn't told her the truth about the injury, but she didn't bring it up and insisted on taking him to Carmel-by-the-Sea as soon as he was fit enough. The beach down there was her favorite place on earth, and she had taken him every summer—as a kid, as a teenager, even his last summer in freedom.

Seeing his mom by the steering wheel of a car going 65 mph south on CA 101 and not actually driving the thing blew his mind. He'd been in an automated vehicle a few times by now, starting right at his release going home, but it was still amazing.

They got parked in Carmel and carried their foldable chairs and beach tent toward a nice spot.

The sensation enveloped West—padding through the warm sand, hearing the waves roll and crash, and the smell of the ocean mixed with the scent of waffles from people eating ice cream from the nearby stand. He thought about the power of tradition. Going here so many times together had created an experience beyond the mere presence of the place.

He had to stop himself from weeping as they finally got settled and his mom poured them both a cup of coffee from her thermos and pulled out their true-to-tradition two-pound box of strawberries. This was what freedom was about.

"Back when you were small, I used to carry everything myself, and I couldn't sit down for more than one minute without you chasing seagulls or wandering off to talk to strangers."

"You never told me I used to harass people."

"We haven't had much chance to talk as adults, now have we? But you were very sweet."

West reached for a strawberry and looked around at the other beach-goers. Lots of kids, some people with dogs, and beautiful youth. "I think I lost that in prison. Zero interest in talking to strangers now."

"You were a bit of a double nature actually. You could play by yourself for hours and didn't really need anyone to be happy, not even me. But then you had that explorer mode when you'd go asking people about their cars and computers. And names; you always asked for their names, then proudly stated your own."

West remembered how he had convinced Melissa they should use their real names instead of handles as hackers. "We should be proud of what we do," he had said.

"Maybe I got the explorer mode from Dad. Have you heard from him?"

"Not a word. I have his email address and made sure he knew about your situation all along, but he hasn't written back in years now. I don't feel like …"

"Don't worry about it, Mom. I rarely think of him."

Her hand landed on his forearm lying on the armrest. They looked at each other.

"Whatever happens, I want you to know that I'm always on your side," she said.

She squeezed his arm gently before letting it go and gazing at the infinite blue in front of them. "Did I ever tell you I got so worried about you the first few years of your sentence that I started singing your lullaby again, on my own?" She chuckled. "Crazy old lady." She started singing quietly. "Lullaby and good night …"

West filled in the next line spontaneously.

She had continued to sing "Brahms's Lullaby" until he was old enough to remember the lyrics. Such a beautiful melody.

"You should join a choir," she said. "Singing on my own made me realize I had to talk to people who actually understood what you and Melissa had done, why you did it. I know now that what you did was important. Important for people without power, for people like me. The Bible says: 'Remember the prisoners as if chained with them—those who are mistreated—since you yourselves are in the body also.'"

"I wouldn't paint our hack in righteous colors. Not anymore," he said.

"Remember that young man you told me about all those years ago?" his mom said. "The young man who tried to give people access to research?"

"Aaron Swartz," he said.

Of course he remembered. Aaron, Edward, and Chelsea were the reasons he and Melissa had embarked on their hack against the NSA.

Aaron had committed suicide when faced with thirty-five years in prison for trying to release tax-funded research papers to the public. Then NSA contractor Edward Snowden had disclosed vast US surveillance on a global scale and had to flee to Russia to escape decades in prison, and intelligence analyst Chelsea Manning had been sentenced to thirty-five years in prison for leaking footage of US military wrongdoings in Iraq and Afghanistan through WikiLeaks. All within less than a year.

His mom gave him a serious look. "I read about Aaron, and I think they are trying to get to you just like they did with him. They hate that I got you out of prison. I could see it in their eyes when they came to me in the hospital. If they can't have you locked up, they want us to spend all our savings on some advanced surgery no one's ever heard of. I'm not going to give them that. I always knew there would be a price to pay to get my son back. If this is the price, I'll pay it, not you. That college fund is for your future, not for my worn-out body."

West couldn't stop the tears. They'd been fighting over this on and off ever since she got denied by her insurance company. She just wouldn't let him help her.

"I know you want to help me, and I love you for it," she said. "But you have a whole life to catch up with. We're going to get you your college degree, we're going to celebrate Thanksgiving like never before, and we're going to see Europe, just like we said."

He pulled himself together. "And Japan," he added.

"And Japan."

Chapter Eleven

Survivor Kit

"You look like a new man, man!" Jitterbug said and gave West a powerful hug.

West was out of his misery and off antibiotics. Half an inch of hair had grown back where the surgeon shaved it off, and he hadn't suffered a headache in two days.

Jitterbug had texted that he had a surprise in store, and West could see over his friend's shoulder a bunch of things laid out on the lab's coffee table, including a brand-new Tile, similar to Melissa's.

"Okay, Jon-Bruce," Jitterbug said, releasing his embrace. "I know you have a meeting with your parole officer later, so let's cheer you up. This is your hacking gear or, as we like to call it, your Survivor Kit."

He pointed at the new Tile. "This is your best friend. I've set it up for you, so now it has the team's encrypted knowledge base covering every known computer device, integrated chip, and named algorithm since the 1970s. You never know when you need to hack some marvelous ol' piece of digital equipment. As for the Tile itself, we use this model because it comes with a couple of useful extras for construction workers, engineers, and property managers. The LED flashlight is brighter, and you can switch it to red for low-light conditions. The camera has an infrared sensor for heat, and these"—he held up two short cables that could connect to the Tile—"turn your Tile into a multimeter for electrical stuff." He launched an app on the Tile. "We also have our own little app to jam Wi-Fi networks with."

"Don't." It was BestBye.

Jitterbug smiled and looked over his shoulder before turning back to West. "Let's demo that some other day. Now, what do Survivors always carry other than their Tiles? First, the Faraday pouch, or F pouch. You already have one. Keep antenna-equipped things in it, such as your Tile or ID band, when you need to go unnoticed or discuss super sensitive things in person. Speaking of unnoticed, we've got these."

He held up a small ziplock bag with what looked like penny-sized peels of skin. At the bottom of the bag was a tube the size of one-time-use toothpaste. "Thin latex caps you glue onto your fingertips to provide fake but working fingerprints. You should make custom ones for your alternate IDs. God always knows who you are, but others don't have to."

Jitterbug picked up what looked like a minute USB flash drive. "The OmniPort thumb drive. Or the 'Bunny' as Kiss calls it. This can perform tons of exploits over a direct connection. If you get access to someone's device, pop this in and you're often golden. It only has two settings." He showed West a switch on the side labeled "Shell/Die."

"OmniPort replaced USB, right?" West asked.

"USB is still around, but yeah. Next, the rogue network plug." Jitterbug showed him a white wall plug without a cable. "Fits most electric outlets, scans for existing networks and mimics them. Also sets up a server for you to talk to it."

"Like the old Pineapple?"

"On the button."

Next, Jitterbug held up a credit-card-size pouch with flat metal instruments in it. "These have not changed much since you were active."

"Lock picks."

"Mhm. And physical locks haven't changed much either, as you saw in my collection." He chuckled.

Jitterbug sorted his way through the remaining things. "Let's see, we've got a multitool here and a glass fiber knife. Ah, the chemistry section. Superglue is a must." He pointed to a small tube. "But this last thing." In his hand was a small, unlabeled spray canister.

"Pepper spray?"

"You may think, but it's not. This is Dee N' A, a product invented by a biotech whiz kid in the UK. It's a soup of DNA samples, synthesized based on the Anonymous Biometric Archive. Did Melissa tell you about the archive?"

"I did not," Melissa said from over in her corner.

Jitterbug got excited. "Buddy, this'll blow your mind. About five years ago, the EFF disrupted law enforcement's abuse of DNA evidence."

"That EFF?" EFF was short for Electronic Frontier Foundation, a digital rights organization.

"Alive and kicking, my friend."

"That's the first good news I've heard since my release."

"Right on. Anywho, you know those sloppy investigations that relied solely on DNA instead of proper police work?"

West nodded.

"The EFF killed that malpractice with the Anonymous Biometric Archive. Now anyone can anonymously file their DNA profile and high-resolution images of their fingerprints and retina patterns to the EFF, who makes the data publicly available. This gives everyone in the database plausible deniability for any accusations involving just DNA or fingerprints."

"Oh my."

"Right? People started doing it en masse when they realized that you got away with it. Why leave yourself open to framing?"

"Don't people need to use their fingerprint to log in ... Oh, wait, that still works because the database is large enough and anonymous?"

"Spot on. Anyway, Dee N' A uses random samples from the archive, so one of these cans has a lot of people's genetics in it. Always keep it on you, and make sure to reduce the statistical chance of G20S matching your DNA with any one of your fake IDs, should Jonathan or Bruce end up in an investigation."

"Is it legal?"

"Dee N' A is banned in the US and many other countries, but instructions on how to make it leaked long before the legal process caught up. We buy it from a local biotech hacker in Oakland."

"Oakland. Do they still call it Smokeland?"

"Pothead." It was BestBye again.

"Don't worry about her. Things just pop out of her mouth sometimes. That's it. With this kit, you can hack the planet."

CHAPTER TWELVE

Just Give Me a Glance

West woke up gloomy.

Yesterday's meeting with his parole officer had left him tossing and turning all night. "We suspect this is you," she had said and showed him a photo of himself with the bag over his head at one of the charging stations along the way to Detroit. Admitting it was him would have been a direct violation of his terms, so he had to lie. But how had they detected him? He hadn't been wearing his GPI band or the chip or carried his Tile on that trip.

Then she had asked about his head wound even though he wore a beanie. Another lie.

The interview had ended with her methodically reminding him of all the virtues in life he had yet to achieve—college education, a nice job, and a family of his own, or at least the prospect of one—all in the plan she had created for him before his release.

He looked at the bedroom walls around him. His mom had kept his room just like he left it a decade and a half ago. There were two framed posters—one of the rapper Drake in a half-unbuttoned brown shirt from the *Take Care* album and one of Avicii behind his turntables looking out over a huge, dancing audience. Above the foot of the bed was his black acoustic guitar hanging in a strap off a brass hook, and above his head was a pinned sheet of paper featuring a handwritten copy of the Hacker Manifesto. He turned his head around just enough to read the last two paragraphs.

> Yes, I am a criminal. My crime is that of curiosity.
> My crime is that of judging people by what they
> say and think, not what they look like. My crime is

that of outsmarting you, something that you will never forgive me for.

I am a hacker, and this is my manifesto. You may stop this individual, but you can't stop us all ... After all, we're all alike.

It was a remnant of his life without a criminal record, without a parole officer.

The walk to the lab featured autumn leaves baking in the dry air. October was waiting—waiting for Halloween, waiting for Thanksgiving, waiting for rain.

He stopped outside the lab's door. The other locks in this building were GPI controlled, but Melissa had chosen physical keys for the lab, probably for a reason. He unlocked the door with the key copy Jitterbug had given him and entered.

"Gaaaah!" Kiss let out a yell, eyes wide. She was standing against the back wall staring at Jitterbug, who was shooting a video of her with his Tile. Melissa lay on the couch reading something, and BestBye was hammering away on her keyboard by the long desk.

"You can do it, girl," Jitterbug shouted to Kiss, counting down with his fingers.

"Fuck." Kiss squatted and rubbed her eyelids.

"Good job, except for the abhorrent swearing."

"What's up?" West said, trying not to leak his mood.

"Oh, hi," Jitterbug replied, looking back at him. "We're trying to get half a minute's shot without her blinking."

"Shot of what?"

"Man, you really were in a cloud when we were planning this, weren't you? She's wearing semi-reflective lenses that go all the way to the side of her eyeballs."

Jitterbug started a slow-mo playback on his Tile to show West. Kiss's eyes had a reflective, oily coating. Zoomed in really far, West could see himself by the entrance, bent like in a convex mirror at a funhouse. The resolution was astounding.

"We hope to glean the passcode off someone entering the G20S branch I scouted out in Vancouver. By the old art gallery. We know the exact curvature of the lenses, so we can flatten out the final video."

"Why not reflective sunglasses?" West asked.

"Too Hollywood. Say we get inside. At some point they'll find out and start investigating. They'll see us on their surveillance cameras, and reflective glasses will raise suspicion. But hey, your question reminds me of my anti-X-ray glasses. They're rad. You gotta see this stuff."

Jitterbug fetched a pair of ordinary-looking sunglasses with thick arms. He was giddy as a child. "X-ray surveillance cameras make it hard to conceal your eyes with just dark glasses, and eyes are great identifiers for anyone who wants to track you. Check these out."

West got the glasses on. "They're opaque."

"Spot on. They're made of low-heat emittance, opaque pieces of glass. You can't see through them at all, which means X-ray cameras can't see your eyes. Now watch this."

West suddenly saw a video stream displayed on the back of the lenses. He moved his head, and the camera image followed flawlessly.

Jitterbug explained. "The frames have video cameras on both sides to produce a stereo image with sense of depth. They're good enough for orientation and moving at pretty high speeds. The video blends regular and infrared if light gets low."

West turned to Kiss. "The important question is, do I look cool or cheesy in them?"

"A little bit of both."

Jitterbug gave West the case for the glasses. "We all have a pair. You can keep them."

"Thanks." He removed the glasses. "Won't we have a better chance if there are two of us in the shot? I mean with the reflective lenses. Two different angles and whatnot. Kiss and I can do it together, like a couple on vacation in Vancouver." His heart picked up speed. "Or like friends."

Kiss tilted her head to the side. "Sure, we can do it together."

The two of them did a couple of trial runs, and he enjoyed every minute of it. They would be holding each other by the waist. Feeling her warmth, hearing her raunchy jokes; it all made him feel good. That damn parole officer couldn't live West's life for him.

Melissa looked up from her Tile for the first time since West came in. "I was going to send just Kiss and BestBye to Vancouver." She gave West a lazy look. "BestBye has intel on how to compromise Canadian G20S. We need to get her inside that office complex."

"Intel?"

"Yeah. Says it's better we don't know exactly what she's up to, should she get captured on the inside. I trust her. Sometimes you need to go solo."

I thought sharing was caring.

West looked at BestBye. She was scrolling through something on her screen, seemingly not paying attention. He was in no position to question any of this—Melissa's judgment, BestBye's intel or intentions, or Vancouver as a target.

As if sensing his thoughts, Melissa called for everyone's attention and beamed a news article onto the big screen. "Apparently, we're not the only ones targeting Pelletier."

Breaking: Fight Over G20S Leadership

North America is next in turn to lead the global security organization G20S as Europe's two-year term comes to an end. The USA, widely expected to support Canada's candidate, Commander Emelie Pelletier, instead put forward its own contender, Dr. Akiko Kawasaki, Thursday morning.

This unprecedented battle for power means the council will invoke Section 3.2 with an anonymous vote among the member countries late February next year. Sources say Kawasaki has already begun her campaign to sway the vote in her favor, whereas Pelletier has yet to engage in this unexpected challenge for the top spot.

The only thing still certain is that G20S will appoint its first woman as leader.

This article's sources are GPI-validated.

"Kawasaki keeps touching my lifeline," Melissa mumbled.

West hadn't thought about Dr. Kawasaki in many years. She had been on the receiving end of his and Melissa's hack. Not as a target but as an up-and-coming employee who happened to be in charge of security updates to NSA's hardware security modules at the time.

"You've been in contact with her?" he asked.

"Two weeks after you went in, she invited me for coffee. Just the two of us, to talk things over. I didn't go, but she kept making contact. Eventually, she broke into my apartment in the middle of the night, sliced up my couch with a fucking sword, and told me I was being watched twenty-four seven."

"Fucking hell, Melissa. You never told us that," Kiss said, half in question, half in awe.

"I'm telling you now."

"You think she's upset about your release?" Kiss asked in West's direction.

Melissa didn't give him a chance to reply. "Bet my life she's tapping into his parole surveillance. She's not the type to let go. Anyway, the three of you go to Canada. I'll stay behind with Jit in San Francisco and provide ground support."

"Staying behind because of a date, sis?" Kiss asked her in a suggestive tone.

BestBye finally spoke, without turning from her monitor. "Meeting a man is what Melissa is trying *not* to do. In Vancouver, that is."

Melissa didn't respond to BestBye's comment. Instead, her eyes were back on her Tile, flipping her thumb forcefully on the screen.

"You lost me there, Best." Kiss sounded genuinely confused.

BestBye kept talking into her screen. "Her last boyfriend moved to Vancouver after she broke up with him because of her promise to West. They're not on good terms."

Everyone but BestBye looked at Melissa for a reaction. West took a step back.

Melissa slowly lifted her stare from her Tile to BestBye. "Best, why do you always poke around in shit that's none of your business?"

"I keep track of things. You know that. He's a major risk."

"Just because you like celibacy doesn't mean we all should stay single."

"I don't like celibacy; I just dislike bodily fluids. Your choice of boyfriend was poor. I approve of you staying away from him."

Jitterbug sighed and looked at West. "Here we go again."

Melissa's face reddened, but her tone was still controlled. "Best, can you at least look at me when we're talking."

BestBye spun around in her office chair, and Melissa continued. "He's cool. I told you he's fucking cool."

"No, he's not," BestBye snapped back. "He used to work for the agency, which you failed to tell us about. And he lied to you about his social media accounts."

"You hacked his Tile to find those things out, yet you conditioned your own membership with us on that we never dig up *your* background. You don't find that a little peculiar?"

"I chose to not be a public figure. If you don't like it, you can kick me out. It's your team."

Melissa drew a long breath, held it with her eyes closed, then let it out audibly. "No one's being kicked out, Best. We accepted you, and I stand by that decision. I just wish you'd show some respect for someone other than yourself."

"He was using you. By the way, he still has your contact details. I know because I still own his Tile." BestBye turned to her screen again.

Kiss took a step in between the combatants. "We don't have to talk about your reasons for not going to Vancouver, Melissa. Sorry for stirring this up. You and Jit stay here. The rest of us should get packed."

Chapter Thirteen

Silver Skagit Road

Kiss, BestBye, and West decided to avoid Canadian border control, which meant using the only reasonably close uncontrolled border crossing—the Silver Skagit Road through the Cascade Mountains.

BestBye traveled as her self-proclaimed "cheesy" alternative ID Svecia Jarlsberg—a goth punk girl in studded black leather and contrast-heavy makeup, inspired by Lisbeth Salander from *The Girl with the Dragon Tattoo*. Kiss used her Amber Love ID—a red-haired retired adult actress. She wore a beautiful red wig. West stuck with Jonathan Ash.

They rented gasoline motorcycles outside Seattle and rode inland. Every piece of the journey was a marvel of freedom for West: riding his own vehicle, the wind against his body, and the autonomy of deciding where to go and how fast.

A small ferry carried them to a set of picturesque floating cabins on the lake called Ross Lake Resort, and after a night's sleep, the resort staff took them on a motorboat to Hozomeen Campground on the east side of the lake. The water actually stretched into Canada, but the resort was only allowed to cross the border by boat with guests who had preregistered with Canadian authorities, and authorities were what the Survivors were trying to avoid.

A mere two and a half miles north of the campground lay the border, and the way there was the Silver Skagit Road.

The North Cascades surrounding them were as breathtaking as they were desolate. Snow-clad mountaintops rose in the distance; pine trees in green and larches in yellow and gold paved the gravel road.

Not long after they got moving, Kiss raised her hand and slowed down. They came to a stop and took off their helmets.

Kiss took her wig off too and scratched her scalp, cursing. She looked back at BestBye and West. "Do you see what I see?"

West squinted as far ahead as he could. "I see a structure. I think."

"Not just any structure. It's not supposed to be there, but I believe that is a G20S self-service border control station, monitored twenty-four seven."

"Can't we just go around it?" West asked.

"Uh-uh. Traps. If you try to cross the border illegally, traps will spray you with a radioactive liquid that won't wash away for months. They claim it doesn't affect your health." Kiss snickered.

BestBye broke in. "Same thing at the Mexican border. Much cheaper than a wall."

"We should have crossed over the lake," Kiss said with a sigh. "That station will require GPI, a bunch of scans, and a video interview with border control before the gate opens." She got out a thermos and poured herself a coffee.

BestBye dismounted her ride. "There is nothing else to do but figure out how this thing works and hack it. I'll take the lead on this because you're too flimsy and, West, you have yet to prove yourself." She left no room for objection. "The station has to talk to G20S for the GPI scans. Satellite or cellular you think?"

Kiss shook her head slowly while swallowing a mouthful of java, then checked her Tile in its bike mount. "I haven't had cellular service since we got to the resort, so I'd say satellite."

West looked at his own Tile.

No service. What if Mom gets worse?

"The control system for all those sensors has to be a full-fledged operating system," BestBye said.

"Which means the G20S-flavored BSD."

West wanted to chip in. "There has to be an interface or a way to connect to the system. Locally I mean, a local network for G20S staff to connect to when they're out here."

BestBye side-eyed him up and down as if inspecting his clothes. "That's easy to check." She pulled out a foldable, directional Yagi-Uda antenna and connected it to her Tile. "I need line of sight."

They went closer to get a good visual of the small building between the thick fir trees. BestBye pointed the antenna toward the station and started a scan as they all watched her screen.

Two Wi-Fi networks popped up—G20SWiFiSecure and G20SWiFi-Emergency.

"Shoot!" BestBye directed the antenna away from the border station and yanked the cable out of her Tile. "I forgot about emergency networks."

"Are you saying you haven't shut that shit off?" Kiss burst out. She noted West's confusion. "G20S is required to have open hot spots for safety reasons, and all Tiles are preconfigured to automatically connect if they don't have a cellular or known Wi-Fi connection. If our Tiles connect, G20S will know someone's here."

West got help from Kiss to check the emergency configuration on his Tile, which Jitterbug had already turned off.

BestBye sifted through her Wi-Fi logs. "Nope. I'm good. But that emergency network may be our way in."

West and Kiss again gathered to look at her screen.

"Hello, Cisco, my old friend. US configuration. Multi-antenna. That hot spot is ancient."

"As in known holes?" West asked.

"G20S usually doesn't run with known vulnerabilities, but you never know out here. G20SWiFiSecure looks modern. Let's go through what our knowledge base has on these two pieces of network equipment."

"Two of us is enough for that," Kiss said. "I'm going for the layer below. I'll scout around to see if the station has any other tech stuff worth considering. And no, I won't trigger any traps."

Two hours passed, and the sun started its slow descent.

BestBye went through all exploits they had on old Cisco Wi-Fi equipment as well as known vulnerabilities for the standard authentication protocol that the secure network used.

West went through numerous hacker community documents on G20S systems in search of what they could expect of the emergency network.

BestBye summarized what they had once Kiss was back.

"We have two half-plausible exploits against the old emergency network and zilch on the secure network. No weak spots in the surroundings according to you. Bad odds."

Kiss pinched the bridge of her nose. "If we're going to try to hack the emergency network with those exploits, we have to minimize the time for G20S to react. How much time do we give ourselves? And what do we do if that time runs out?"

"Five minutes," West said.

BestBye looked at him. "Are you pulling that from your behind, or do you have a rationale?"

"From my ass."

Kiss looked at them. "Five it is. No results and we pull back to the campground. Let's do this."

They gathered around BestBye's Tile with the antenna. She flipped through her open tabs, the last two with the exploits lined up for execution, and got ready to connect.

"Stop," West said louder than he intended. "Go back to the second tab."

"That's just one of the Wi-Fi logs I checked before. I'll close it."

"No, please let me see."

BestBye opened tab two. She had unintentionally left it dumping whatever her device saw on the Wi-Fi frequencies.

"Look. Something is communicating over the emergency network." West pointed at unreadable lines of network data. "Shouldn't all the internal G20S stuff be on the secure network?"

"Happens all the time," Kiss said. "They install some crufty old equipment that can't communicate with modern, secure connections. So they hook it up to the open network. Get done, go home."

"Crufty old equipment sounds like a weak link." West's pulse sped up.

"Except we don't have a clue what it is." BestBye looked at him as if he was stupid.

"Do you mind if I have a closer look at the logs?" he said.

BestBye looked at him for two seconds, then handed him her Tile. He sat down cross-legged in the dirt, pulled out his pencil and notepad, and started scrutinizing the Wi-Fi logs.

He'd been at it for fifteen minutes when he burst out with, "Check this out!"

His index finger went back and forth between two lines on the screen. "These two are almost exactly the same, right?"

"Almost exactly is not a thing," BestBye mumbled. But she looked intrigued.

The first line was:

```
UFdSMDg5MTg4NjE5NDE0MA==
```

And the second line was:

UFdSMDg5MTg4NjE5NDIwMA==

As they were talking, the log on BestBye's screen spat out a new set of data, containing a third, similar line.

UFdSMDg5MTg4NjE5NDI2MA==

West continued. "That right there is either an encryption flaw or un-encrypted data. Proper encryption never repeats itself in a predictable manner."

"Is this why Melissa calls you a pattern matcher?" Kiss touched the tip of his nose with her index finger. He blushed.

"How did you spot that?" BestBye sounded skeptical as she grabbed her Tile. "It looks Base64-encoded." A terminal command later and she had decoded the three similar lines.

```
PWR0891886194140
PWR0891886194200
PWR0891886194260
```

"The numbers increase by sixty," said Kiss.
"Maybe a minute?"
The log received a fourth line.

```
PWR0891886194320
```

"Something is firing once a minute. The right half has to be a time-stamp." BestBye extracted the last ten digits and converted them into human-readable time. It was today's date and the current time.

West eyed the left half. "The rest is consistently PWR089."

"Power?" Kiss suggested. "Maybe it's some power backup system re-porting its battery status once every minute? Like, Power at 89%."

"Backup power out here sounds wise. Power outages must be part of the threat model." The others agreed with him. "I wonder what happens when that message says zero?"

Kiss and BestBye smiled.

"Can we inject a fake power status message?" Kiss said.

BestBye was already processing the attack setup. "We have to race this thing. Our fake message has to reach the main system right before the legitimate message is sent. Otherwise, the timestamp won't match and we might cause an error condition."

They synchronized the Tile's time with the station's Wi-Fi clock and successfully predicted ten messages in a row, character for character.

The sun cast longer shadows, and the temperature slowly fell as they made the necessary calculations for how to race the message.

"You two with good eyesight, what's the distance to the station?" BestBye asked.

Kiss picked up a pebble and swung her arm as if preparing a throw. "Conservatively, two hundred yards. But my best guess would be around a hundred and fifty."

"Let's go with two hundred." BestBye tapped away on her Tile's calculator. "Wi-Fi signals travel through air at roughly two-thirds of the speed of light. Two hundred yards at two-thirds of light speed means we see the status messages on my Tile one microsecond after the Wi-Fi router does. It will take one microsecond for a fake message to reach the router from here. That means we need to send our fake message three microseconds before we see the legitimate one."

She wrote a script that would send messages with zero instead of 89, once a minute, racing the real messages by three microseconds, and got ready to execute it.

Kiss put her hand on West's shoulder. "What if the thing goes into some alarm mode?"

BestBye replied before he had a chance to say something. "We disconnect and go to the campground, as you said." Her voice was unswerving. "It's getting dark."

Kiss and West looked at each other.

BestBye activated the script.

CHAPTER FOURTEEN

G20S: Warrantless

"I knew they'd serve me a shit sandwich, and the spineless muppet behind this won't even show his face!" Agent Timothy had taken off his ginger wig, and sweat beads were forming on his shaven head. His direct listened to the rant in silence, sound echoing in the bunker-like, screen-filled room where they handled the surveillance of Timothy's five assigned subjects.

West's government Tile hadn't moved for three days. This time, Timothy hadn't asked the old lady nicely. He had applied for the necessary search warrant and been shut down by some faceless superior at the agency, for reasons unknown.

"How am I supposed to do my job if backseat drivers second-guess me?" No response from the direct.

Timothy wiped his scalp with his hand and looked at his wet palm. His voice got more bearable. "I joined the agency twenty-five years ago. Did I ever tell you that?"

His direct nodded and waited for the rest.

"I was destined for military intelligence but got a nice offer from the CIA. My memory probably deceives me, but it seems things were much easier back then, clear-cut. We had a few good years with the NSA and Five Eyes."

What Timothy didn't tell his direct was that there was further reason for his frustration. He had received a formal warning from Human Resources over the health insurance stunt he had pulled on West's mom. Someone was after his ass.

CHAPTER FIFTEEN

Power Move

Bestbye, Kiss, and West stood in a frozen pose in the middle of the North Cascades National Park, right by the International Boundary between the USA and Canada, waiting for something to happen as BestBye's script counted down to the first fake message send.

Off it went. Nothing happened.

A minute went by, and a new fake message was fired.

Another minute, another message.

Still nothing, at least nothing detectable.

"Pee, I need to," Kiss said, heading off into the woods.

"Timing issue. That's the usual suspect in racy hacks," BestBye reasoned with herself.

"You think we're too slow?"

"Or too fast. Either way, our power message is not being accepted by the receiver."

She adjusted her script to fire four microseconds earlier. No changes in the Wi-Fi logs. The system kept chugging along.

By the time Kiss got back, they had tried to send messages later too. Still nothing.

"I had a thought while I was peeing."

"Did you wash your hands?" BestBye asked her so sternly that West flinched.

"Yes, mom."

"Okay. What you got?"

"I thought, what's left at zero?"

"Are you thinking rounding errors?"

"No, no. Not that complicated. I mean, what's left at zero battery power? Nothing, right?"

BestBye nodded. "Mhm."

"By then, all precautions, alarms, what have you, should have already happened. The station simply doesn't have any battery backup at that point. Any low-power adjustments must happen before it reaches zero. That's how I would have written the code, anyway."

West followed her line of thought. "So you're saying our fake messages should gradually step the power percentage down in a more plausible fashion?"

"Correctamundo."

"You are not all boobs after all," BestBye mumbled.

Kiss squashed her chest into BestBye's face while shaking her butt. "You like 'em."

"Get off me," BestBye yelled, pushing Kiss away.

After an awkward minute in silence, BestBye pulled herself together and hammered out the script that would take them from 89% to 1%, one percentage point a minute. "Worst case, one hour and twenty-eight minutes until we can call it."

She hit "execute," and the script started firing messages again.

"We might as well eat while we wait."

The resort had prepared sandwiches for them, and West had asked for bacon on his.

"If you keep eating that much processed meat, you're going to die young," BestBye told him with her mouth full.

"Veggie stuff seems really good these days," he replied, "but I can't help myself. Fifteen years without bacon."

"Those years might turn out to save you from premature death."

"When you put it that way, Best, totally worth it," Kiss said.

Hunger taken care of, the three of them admired the beauty of the nature in the lingering daylight. They agreed it was a shame so few Americans got to see the northwestern parts of the country.

West had almost fallen into a slumber when there was a sound from the station—*ka-chunk*—as if a mechanical switch had just moved.

Kiss stood up and gazed toward the building in the pale sunset. Silver Skagit Road was peaceful.

BestBye checked the Wi-Fi logs. "My script just sent out the fake 25% message, and there's lots of traffic on the secure network. Nothing special on the emergency one."

"Maybe it's a controlled shutdown of something?"

"Shhhh! Listen." West's eyesight was not as good as Kiss's, but he was sure he heard something.

A soothing wind made its way through the thick mix of conifers and broadleaf trees, but somewhere in the general direction of the border control station there was a faint electronic beep.

"You hear that?" he whispered. The others nodded. "Shit's happening."

The beep stopped.

"Now what?" West realized he kind of expected the women to have a plan.

"Secure Wi-Fi network is back to normal," BestBye said, looking at her Tile. "G20S is probably looking at this as we speak. Either we stabilize my script at twenty-something and wait for a few hours to reduce the risks, or we try to cross now."

Kiss added a third option. "Or we keep lowering the power to see if more things happen."

"Could work," BestBye mumbled. "But a remote operator might start looking into this any minute, and they'll see our fake status messages in the logs. Constantly a fake one from us and then one from the real system. That's gonna look suspicious."

"You're saying we go now?" West asked.

"We've fiddled too much to stick around, that's what I'm saying."

West's heartbeat reflected the raised adrenaline in his bloodstream.

Kiss held up her hands. "Hey, we shouldn't risk all three on the first attempt to cross. One of us should go alone, pass from this side, and then try to hold the gates open from the other side to let the others through on the bikes. That should minimize exposure."

"Who gets to be the probe?" BestBye asked.

"I can do it," West said.

"You sure?" Kiss said, eyebrows raised. "That thing might challenge you to prove your identity. You don't have too much experience with modern interfaces."

"Regular people are supposed to work this out, right?"

She pouted her lower lip and wobbled her head from side to side. "A little clumsiness might make it more believable. Go slowly, read all instructions, and wear fingerprint protection. And we should all wear Jit's anti-X-ray glasses so they don't get retina shots."

West had been wanting to use the glasses ever since Jitterbug's demo at the lab. He got them on, and the infrared blend made him see much better in the low light.

BestBye looked at them. "Turn off your Tiles and GPI bands and put them in your F pouches. They'll be recording us."

They lined up and walked their bikes in silence toward the border station.

The wordless tension and sound of gravel under his feet gave him a flashback from his prison friend Jeremy's funeral march. Jeremy had known that no family of his would be willing to pay for his funeral services, so he had spent the time after his cancer diagnosis building a casket for himself dubbed "The Bomb Shell." Four well-behaved inmates had been allowed to carry Jeremy in it to the prison gates, where the county took over. West had walked first that time too.

Kiss and BestBye stopped halfway, and he walked the last stretch alone.

CHAPTER SIXTEEN

The Privileged Mr. Singh

Details of the border station unfolded as he got closer. The gateway to Canada was an arch with a sign on top—"International Boundary, G20S Border Control"—large enough for small trucks to pass under. He could not see through any part of it, so he assumed there were gates shut further in. The left side of the building was wider and had a door. Two surveillance cameras were visible on the front wall, and right off the corner of the building there was a wooden box on a waist-high post. The box had a slanted top, and its glass front showed two shelves of books on the inside.

West kept rolling his bike forward at a slow but steady pace as he entered the passage under the arch. A large display on the left inner wall came to life, lighting up the cave-like space.

A male voice assistant greeted him, along with subtitles on the screen.

Welcome to the international boundary
between Canada and the United States
of America. You are entering from the
US side. Please provide your Global
Personal Identity.

Bienvenue à la frontière internationale
entre le Canada et les États-Unis.
Vous vous apprêtez à entrer depuis les
États-Unis. Veuillez présenter votre
Identifiant Internationnal.

Bienvenidos a la frontera internacional
entre Canadá y los Estados Unidos de
America. Usted está ingresando del
lado de los Estados Unidos. Por favor,
presente su Identificación Global
Personal.

There were touch buttons for all the G20 languages. The last button read "Emergency/Urgence/Emergencia."

He looked back toward his teammates, but the light from the screen affected the glasses' low-light vision.

He chose English and pressed "Emergency."

Emergency border crossing is only
allowed in an emergency. Please confirm
that you do not possess or cannot use a
Global Personal ID.

West confirmed.

Please confirm that this is an
emergency.

Lie number two.

A photo will be taken since you do not
possess or cannot use a Global Personal
ID. Please face the camera to your
right.

West turned his head, and a circle of white LEDs lit up around a camera lens to the right of the display. Jit's glasses adjusted to the new light condition.

Please remove your sunglasses.

Fuck.

He looked to see if there were any other options available. None.

The voice repeated the message.

```
Please remove your sunglasses.
```

If G20S wasn't already watching him live, they soon would be.

He had to get out of here. All three of them had to. It would take the bikes an hour and a half to reach Canadian civilization, and the agency would surely try to intercept them if it got notified of a breach.

```
Please remove your sunglasses. If
you are unable to comply, please say
"emergency" now.
```

West let out a sigh.

"E…" He stopped himself.

Get your shit together, man.

He shoved his index finger into the side of his mouth to hamper normal tongue movement and lowered his voice as much as he could. "Emergency."

```
Emergency border passing acknowledged.
You are required to report to the
nearest G20S or police station as soon
as the emergency is over.
```

A red rotating warning light turned on, and the gates to Canada opened to his right.

He started pushing his bike toward the gates when, in the corner of his eye, he saw the big display go pitch black.

He stopped. In the upper left of the screen appeared a green command line prompt, and someone, or something, started typing.

```
station442$ scp
mr_singh@g20s.bc.ca:privEscalate.c .

station442$ clang -o privEsc
privEscalate.c
```

What the?

Someone with username "mr_singh" was controlling the station re-motely, and "privEscalate" sounded like privilege escalation, which was a well-known hacker term. Was someone *hacking* the station?

He quickly started his motorcycle to get the others' attention without using his voice, rested the bike on its kickstand, moved in front of its headlight, and started waving frantically.

The "mr_singh" account was working at full speed, hammering away commands.

He heard Kiss's and BestBye's engines start, straddled his bike, drove through the gates, and pulled to the right.

As he looked back, the gates started closing.

Kiss and BestBye were closing in on the building. With only his toes reaching the ground, he pushed his bike backward toward the right gate door to see if he could trigger a safety sensor.

At least one of the bikes behind him hit maximum thrust, and its headlight jolted into the air as it reared.

The closing gate did not stop because of his wheel. Instead, it pushed his bike sideways. Kiss charged through the opening so close that the drag almost made him fall. The next bike would hit him if he stayed where he was. His hand released the clutch, and he rolled forward.

The sound of BestBye's bike resounded in the space under the arch. West's instincts told him her handlebar would be too wide and hit the closing doors. She was going to crash.

At an immense speed, BestBye's front wheel came through the nar-row gap several inches up in the air.

Just as the wheel passed the doors, it flicked ninety degrees, which meant the handlebar was now vertical. BestBye's elbows touched the doors as she shot through the narrowing slit.

West felt sick. What the fuck were they doing?

Moments later he realized his comrades had just continued, full speed ahead, and rightly so. They had to get out of the woods and disappear into civilization.

Chapter Seventeen

All About That Kiss, No Trouble

It was a beautiful October Tuesday in a vibrant Vancouver, with people hunting for lunch spots and tourists here and there. West stood waiting at the meeting spot Kiss had picked, marveling at a movie teaser running in a nearby window. The star was Carrie Fisher.

Kiss had calculated three individual routes from the end of Silver Skagit Road to Vancouver using an escape route app she had created as a high school project when digging into the classic Traveling Salesperson Problem.

West's path had included a night in Harrison Hot Springs before commuting downtown on the West Coast Express.

Kiss knitted her brows as she walked up to him at their rendezvous spot. "No sign of Best?"

West shook his head. "You think something happened? No reply in the chat, right?"

"She doesn't play games."

"I guess the fallback is to come back here at noon tomorrow? Rinse and repeat."

She started fiddling with her Tile. "We have to update Melissa and Jitterbug."

West's eyes wandered back to the movie teaser running on repeat. He asked his Tile how old Carrie Fisher was.

"Carrie Fisher, famous actress, writer, and comedian, died December 27, 2016, at the age of sixty."

"That's sad," he said to himself.

Kiss looked up from her Tile. "You into Star Wars?"

"I like Star Wars, but the teaser there says it's a new movie with Carrie Fisher. Don't know what's up with that since she's dead."

"Oh, that's pretty popular. They create digital models of dead actors based on old movies and then animate them in new ones."

"Is that legal?"

"Money rules. The movie makers share revenue with the actor's descendants. Living actors hate it. Always cheaper to animate with a classic face than to pay for flesh and blood. In porn they offer it on-demand so you can get actor X with body Y."

She got back to tapping her message to Melissa and Jitterbug.

"We could go watch the movie," West said.

Kiss looked at him for a second, then scanned the street around them. "Not in the mood. Let's get a room."

They found a unisex public restroom where West helped Kiss dye her hair copper red so she wouldn't have to wear the itchy wig anymore. She looked stunning with wet hair.

Kiss rented an apartment for three nights with the option to extend through the week. The place felt like a bland hotel room—kitchen utensils mostly untouched and walls filled with old movie posters in cheap frames. West got worked up about a misspelled title, *Scavanger Hunt*, in the corner of one of the posters, for which he earned a laugh from Kiss.

They lay on the king-size bed for half an hour, flipping through the news on their Tiles, before Kiss turned on some background music and sparked up a conversation.

"Have you watched any of my porn movies?"

West couldn't tell if she was in her Amber character or if she was joking. He decided to play it cool. "No."

"Did you watch porn in prison?"

"Not allowed."

"I guess you do now, though."

"I didn't know where to get porn when I got out. Things have changed."

"Did you get an Axxxess Card?"

"A what?"

"Axxxess with triple x."

"I saw that by the TV in Detroit. Is that a porn thing?"

"One of the few things Americans just wouldn't accept with GPI was having to identify themselves to watch porn. So people who can afford it buy an Axxxess Card with their GPI and then use the card to get access without logging in. It made porn profitable again, which is kind of funny. I doubt Axxxess Cards are as anonymous as they say. Anyway, I wasn't Amber back then if you decide to dig up my old porn stuff."

This meant she was talking about her real self. "So who were you?"

"I'm not going to tell you that!"

"Why did you do porn?"

"You better not be judging me."

"I'm not. I'm genuinely curious."

"There's no future in Juneau unless your parents buy you a fishing vessel."

"You're from Alaska?"

"Yeah. Beautiful, boring Juneau." She looked at the ceiling. "Rich kids go to college down in Washington or California. The rest have to fund their own way out. Tough ones have the military. Others do girl- or boyfriend-for-hire. I did the 'fresh amateur' porn thing. You do a handful of clips, then either step it up with fetishes or exit with whatever money you haven't spent on partying."

"Did you step it up?"

"I find your lack of faith disturbing," she said with her deepest possible voice. "I did interracial—which is total racist bullshit but paid well—then I went and worked at a brothel for a while."

"Do the others on the team know?"

"Melissa knows. It's why I joined her team. Once GPI was enforced, there was a massive leak of sex workers' real identities. Got really ugly with harassment and doxing. Banks downgraded my credit score, and insurance companies either refused me service altogether or bumped the premium to where I couldn't afford it. As if their staff had not been watching porn five nights a week. Fucking hypocrites. I've paid for healthcare out of pocket ever since."

They fell silent and listened to the music. Moral judgment mixed itself with affection and wonder in West's head. Kiss was mesmerizing.

CHAPTER EIGHTEEN

The Shot

Twelve sharp the day after, West and Kiss found BestBye sitting at the rendezvous spot, fiddling with a Rubik's Snake. She no longer looked like Lisbeth Salander and took her time before looking up at them.

"Do you know these snakes can be twisted into almost seven trillion different shapes?" she said.

"Is that counting mirror images?" West replied.

"Of course not."

They beamed the third apartment e-key to BestBye's Tile as they picked up coffee and then went separate ways. With all three finally in the living room, Kiss and West were eager to hear what had happened to their teammate.

"I was driving my designated route, got bored on the highway, and started tapping through the bike's options. Turns out it had a freaking streaming music feature which constantly scanned for networks. My bike had all those bells and whistles yours didn't. I assumed it had revealed itself to the emergency Wi-Fi at the border station. Plenty of wilderness around, so I dumped the bike along with my clothes and stayed off the radar for a day."

"Do you think they've connected the bike to Svecia?"

"I paid for fuel with her GPI back in Washington, so they probably connected her to the bike's media feature there. Either way, I set Svecia up to die at a seedy place in Seattle whenever we're confident her passing won't stir up an investigation. The report will say death by suffocation during erotic asphyxiation. Now I'm operating as Miniona."

"I hate Miniona," Kiss muttered.

West had heard about Miniona Styx. It was BestBye's self-proclaimed impersonation of her mother, and it wasn't a loving one. Miniona was a bitch.

They spent the next day between eleven a.m. and one p.m. around the gallery entrance Jitterbug had scouted to look for good targets to glean a passcode off of and to get a sense of the space. It had rained in the morning, but now the sun was out and the air had a pungent smell of autumn turning into winter.

Vancouver Art Gallery was situated by Robson Square, or rather the other way around, given their respective ages. The square was a great public space built mostly in concrete but with sections of stairs creating levels and closeness, and huge raised containers with trees and plants softened the visual impression. In front of the gallery there was a plaza and then a grand set of stairs up to the entrance, guarded by a majestic stone lion on each side.

The gallery building itself was a former courthouse with four thick pillars holding up the angled roof in the center piece. West identified the capitals as Ionic, something he remembered from art class. He wanted to say something about it to Kiss but feared he'd be wrong and get corrected by BestBye.

Several people entered and left the building, some of them picking up lunch in a box. There was a slot in the wall fitting Jitterbug's description, where people entered their codes. Very few looked over their shoulder before doing so.

West wanted to write a text to his mom but remembered he didn't have his government Tile and that he was abroad. Jitterbug had offered to take his government Tile out for walks back in San Francisco to make its sensor patterns more believable, but Melissa didn't want to introduce the Survivors to his mom. Instead, West had just left the Tile in its gimbal stabilizer on his nightstand, just like last time he was out of state.

Back at the apartment, Kiss was weary as they summarized their findings outside the gallery. "It's worth a try, but it looks really tricky to get the right angle and see the keypad inside that hole in the wall. Plus, we have to scan the public GPI profile of whoever we get the code from."

BestBye leveraged help from Melissa to urge them on, which meant the next day they sat basking in the midday sun by the pillar closest to the agency's entrance. This time Kiss and West wore their reflective contact lenses.

West kept track of people passing to the left and BestBye to the right. The first hungry G20S employees floated down the stairs.

Not long thereafter, Kiss said, "Hey, Jon, I want a photo of you and me with the square in the background."

His heartbeat quickened. That line was the cue.

They casually got into position. BestBye took a few stills and complained about their postures. "Shoulders back, chest out. Be proud." West assumed it was her impersonated mom talking, but she was also adjusting their angles to make sure the reflections were right.

A minute or two passed. It was getting awkward. Then Kiss spoke.

"Hey, take a video shot, Miniona. I wanna tell the world how much I love Jon."

Love wasn't in the script. West swallowed. BestBye did a thumbs-up and started recording. West kept his eyes open.

Kiss talked into the camera. "Hi there! We're on our Vancouver trip, and I just wanna say how much I love you, Jon." She turned to him and gave him a kiss on the lips.

West got into a haze and missed the rest of the scene. He had forgotten the cushion effect of lips touching and the intimacy of another person's breath.

Chapter Nineteen

Kiss IRL

They stayed in character but went separate ways as soon as they had left the square. Back at the apartment, West desperately wanted to catch up. "Did we get a good shot?"

"I sure hope so. Best, get it on the screen. And yes, I've disabled its Wi-Fi."

BestBye connected her Tile to the display in the room and streamed the wefie video. He looked stupid and zoned out in it. But at least he had kept his eyes open. Apparently, Kiss had been talking to the camera for another twenty seconds after the kiss.

BestBye zoomed in on Kiss's left eye. It had a crisp reflection of an agent walking swiftly, scanning her GPI band, and entering her code on what looked like a full-size keyboard fit into a recess in the wall. The woman had a bob cut, chestnut hair so perfect it looked like a wig.

"Holy smokes, that looks like the photos you showed us of Commander Pelletier in New York," West said.

"That's what her GPI's public profile said too." BestBye showed Pelletier's particulars on the screen. "Should work as a username."

"Isn't it a little risky to target the bigwig?"

"A wig will be absolutely necessary, but Pelletier is pretty close to me body-wise, so I'm happy with the choice."

"You're going in as a double?"

"I brake for nobody."

"Oh, I love you, Best," Kiss blurted, only to note West's confusion and explain herself. "Best loves to pull *Spaceballs* quotes to contrast my Star Wars fandom." She tilted her head and blinked intensely at BestBye.

"I can switch to Jar Jar Binks if you like," BestBye replied.

"Not taking the bait. We caught the big fish, and I call for drinks." Kiss asked her Tile to play "Sweet Little Sister" by Skid Row and got her jacket on.

BestBye rolled her eyes and disconnected from the display. "I'll start editing the video while you drink."

"What kind of beer do you like, West?" Kiss asked on her way out.

"I don't know."

•

Kiss got back with two bags of beers and snacks enough to skip dinner. She fetched a stack of fleece blankets from a cupboard and nodded for West to join her on the balcony.

The air outside was nippy. Two Adirondack chairs invited them to sit and watch the sun set over the rooftops.

Kiss put two beer cans and glasses on the small table between them, rolled herself up in double blankets, and used the tip of her lab key to hit little dimples into the top of her can.

West stared dumbfounded at the scene as he was getting comfortable.

She looked up at him. "You don't knock your beer?"

"We mostly drank out of bottles."

"You must have missed the craft beer revolution. Here, take this." She handed him the knocked beer.

He cracked it open with a satisfying sound and started pouring.

"Pour on the side," she instructed him. "You don't want foam on ale."

He tilted his glass.

She smiled. "You know nothing, Jon Snow."

"That reference I know. *Game of Thrones*."

The beer was citrusy and on the verge of boozy. It didn't take long for the ethanol to induce relaxation and an appreciation for being in another country, far, far away from the indignity and isolation that had stamped half of his life.

"I don't know much about you," he said, leaning back. "What's your story?"

"Whoa." She mouthed her ale. "What a question."

"You can ask *me* anything."

She chuckled. "So that you can ask *me* anything? It's a trap! What do you wanna know, man?"

"I don't know. How you got into computers and hacking?"

"Easy. I was twelve when the whole girl code-camp thingy took off. From code I started reading about jailbreaks, credit card heists, car hacks. I got bitten by breaking things logically instead of physically. Plus, it was fun when rich capitalists got their pants pulled down by teenagers."

They traded old hacker stories long enough to get them to their second beer. Kiss filled him in on some mind-blowing hacks of late and all the election manipulation that democracies were struggling with.

"So you went straight into hacking?" West asked, circling back to her background.

"There was this boy who was really in love with me, and he was into password cracking and wacky challenges like typing on the keyboard behind your back. We broke up when he understood I was smarter than him." Kiss shook her head lightly. "An idiot move, but then again, my relationships all end badly."

"Do you have a boyfriend now?" His heart took an extra beat.

"Hell no. I have two go-to guys if I need sex. But I really should get serious someday. I want a kid. Not necessarily a family and all that, but a kid."

Kids. Parenting. How many steps removed am I from being a father and singing lullabies?

She looked at him. "Do you think I'd be a good mom?"

"Why wouldn't you?"

She turned her gaze to the cityscape and fell quiet for a while. "A mom should be dependable and grounded. I'm too … flimsy." She put down her beer glass and pulled the arms of her sweater down over her hands. "I don't know why I'm telling you that though. Are you still into Melissa? You seemed a little bothered when her past boyfriend came up."

Had he been bothered? Maybe. No one but his mom had asked him about his feelings for Melissa.

"I don't get it," Kiss continued, looking at the semi-lit sky. "I get that you two had a teenage dream and made a deal, but why break up with Jeff only to half ghost you? She's miserable now."

I'll be there when you get out, was the last thing Melissa had said to him before his time behind bars. They had both been put on trial all those years ago, and throughout the legal proceedings, West had valiantly taken responsibility for crafting the security exploit and for writing the payload that corrupted the NSA's databases. The prosecutor could only prove that Melissa had played a minor role, so West did the years while Melissa got probation.

When they met at C Weed in Santa Cruz after his release, she had lived up to the deal by dumping her boyfriend just a few days prior. She had wanted West the hacker back. He had wanted West the teenager back.

He felt a sting of guilt. He should have told Melissa she didn't have to do this. It was a stupid deal anyway.

"Melissa and I couldn't get back together even if we wanted to."

Kiss rolled her head sideways against the high back of the chair, turning to him. "Because of the stupid Survivor rules?"

He nodded.

She turned toward the sunset again. "If Melissa wants to get involved with you, I'm fine with that. She freaking makes the rules."

"How did the two of you meet?" West asked.

"Melissa? She spots all her team members at Velvet. I went to San Francisco after I got thrown out of the brothel."

"Thrown out? What happened?"

"A lot of things happened."

West slowly swallowed a mouthful of beer and waited.

"When I started working there, I was just out of a bad breakup—a *bad* breakup. Weeping in public places—that kind of breakup. I didn't feel sexy for anyone, let alone complete strangers. But those sisters I worked with there really got me back on track. They helped me build up my confidence. First in my sexuality, then about being smart." She shivered in the cold air. "Man, talking about sex work makes me want to smoke."

"Please don't. Reminds me of prison."

"Fuck, I keep forgetting you've been to prison for fifteen years. You're the one who should be talking about how you got your life back."

"I don't know that I have."

"Long journey, huh?"

"Yeah. I don't know what a good life looks like. I'm happy being with my mom and you, but just being happy feels insufficient. It's like I'm supposed to do more, be more."

"I think you're doing great. I totally expected a hardened ex-convict when Melissa started talking about you, but you're not."

"I was in a medium-security prison. Lots of hardened people in there, but I guess my fallback has always been to stick to myself."

"Just let me know if you want time alone."

"Not at all. I like being with you." He nabbed his glass from the top and rotated it on the table. There was only a mouthful left, and before he knew it the glass was empty. "It sounds nuts, but prison was so much easier. It was just about the rules—sticking to the rules, knowing the rules. Out here it's so … open ended."

"I'm bad with rules. Rules are what got me at the brothel eventually."

"With the customers?"

"No, no. Partying rules were easy. But management was very strict about relationships between us sisters. I'd decided brothel life wasn't for me and called the owner to let her know I was headed out by the end of the month. That was all cool, but when she found me sitting in the bar chatting with two sisters about it, she got furious and gave me one hour to pack my stuff and leave. The rule is you don't influence others to quit. I remember standing outside with all my shit in bags. I didn't even get a chance to say goodbye."

"Wow."

"Sums it up."

West reached for a third beer under the table and duly knocked it with his lab key. "I think you'd be a wonderful mom," he said.

"Well, thank you." She raised her glass. "I just need to find the right man, a dependable, grounded man."

•

Kiss and West were hungover and not ready to roll until late afternoon the day after. By then, BestBye had a good video render of Commander Pelletier's code entry, adjusted from the curved visuals from the lenses.

"Get over here, losers," she yelled as she put the video on a loop on the big screen.

"You can't really see what she's typing." Kiss squinted. "The keyboard is fitted too far into the wall."

"That is true. But I have a plan," BestBye said. "We have the position of her arm and hand relative to the slot in the wall, and she enters the code with just one hand. The rest is down to her finger and muscle movements. Look at her arm."

West looked at the clip as it looped. Pelletier wore a slim-fit, denim shirt with folded sleeves. You could see the fine muscle movements of her right forearm as she typed in her code.

BestBye showed her own forearm as she moved her fingers. "I've already recorded my own muscle movements for all five fingers and the arm in the same angle as Pelletier's. You two do the same, and we'll be able to model finger-to-muscle synchronization and work out which fingers she moves in that clip."

Three painstaking hours later, BestBye had an estimate. "Pelletier performs seven keystrokes in a circle. The only thing we can't deduce is how far she stretches her fingers, so we have two plausible character sets—U J N B G T Y and 7 U J H G T 6. And a less likely third one—Y H B V F R T."

CHAPTER TWENTY

QWERTY

Early Sunday morning, two and a half hours before sunrise, both Robson Square and the Vancouver Art Gallery plaza were deserted. The ground had a layer of autumn leaves made mushy and slippery by a night rain that hadn't quite made up its mind to stop.

BestBye wore a bob cut wig, a denim shirt with folded sleeves, and the right makeup. She had practiced Pelletier's stride, and they had crafted a fake GPI setup with Pelletier's public profile. This was as close to being Emilie Pelletier as she could get with the information and time available.

The stone lions watched her as she climbed the stairs to the art gallery. She tried to look confident and at home, since cameras were surely watching. Her GPI band emitted a pulse of azure blue light as it delivered Pelletier's public profile and made the keypad slot in the wall open and light up.

There was a keyboard in there, full-sized just like she had predicted. It was fitted deep inside the wall, which meant that Pelletier had probably been typing on the lower keys, or plausible character set number two in their model. But the keys had no labels. They weren't even laid out as a regular keyboard with a space bar and such. It was just a matrix of square white keys.

This wasn't a password thing with characters; it was a pure pattern-based code system.

She bit her lower lip. Hesitating at the keypad would look suspicious on camera; turning on her heels and leaving would look worse.

How quickly could she visualize the characters of a qwerty keyboard in her head and map them to the unlabeled keys in front of her? Would it be easier with her eyes closed?

A small screen above the keys came to life as she moved her hand closer.

Welcome, Commander Pelletier! Please
enter your passcode.

She lowered her right hand at the exact same distance from the right edge of the slot as Pelletier had, closed her eyes, and gently typed 7 U J H G T 6 as if a qwerty keyboard were under her fingertips. She slowly opened her eyes again.

Wrong passcode. Two tries left.

She closed her eyes again, tried the U J N B G T Y pattern, and squinted at the screen.

Wrong passcode. One try left. Note that
you will be blocked from entry if you
fail this time.

She knew that with the third passcode from the set she would have covered all the plausible ones—plausible to whatever degree of certainty they had. But the third was also the least likely one.

Had she been sloppy the first two times? Maybe it was wiser to try the first one again, the one she really believed in?

No, the plan was there for a reason.

She sucked in her upper lip. It tasted salty.

She adjusted her right arm ever so slightly and let the third passcode flow through years of experience using qwerty keyboards, onto the faceless keys under her fingers.

She opened her eyes after several seconds.

According to our records, you are
already inside the building.

Please choose one option:

```
( ) Report this as an error or potential
breach.
( ) Report this as you failing to badge out
earlier.
```

She had gotten the code right, but Pelletier was inside, at freaking five in the morning, on a Sunday.

BestBye's instinct was to not pick an option at all. She could wait outside for Pelletier to leave the building and then enter without hassle now that she knew the code. But that would be in daylight with people around. And not picking any of the options in front of her might default to an alarm. Not good.

"Report this as an error" was a clear escalation. Not good either.

She tapped the second option, acting as if Pelletier had tailgated someone out hours earlier.

```
This is the first time you've failed
to badge out. Your superior will be
notified the third time you fail to
badge out.
```

There was a click sound to her left; the entrance door was unlocked.

CHAPTER TWENTY-ONE

Do You Dare Explore the Dungeon?

Behind the agency door was a narrow entrance. On the left wall was a flush keyboard and a screen just like the one outside. The screen said "Welcome, Commander Pelletier. Three other employees are in the building at this time."

About ten feet in, to the right, was a door with the label "Gallery" on it. Straight ahead was a corridor, lit all the way down. Two doors on the left had gender binary restrooms, and then the corridor took what looked like a forty-five-degree turn to the left.

BestBye passed the bend of the corridor. The right side turned into a glass-walled, curtain-hidden, triangular meeting room labeled "Roy." The opposite side had evenly spaced office doors with name tags. She moved closer to read them. Neither of them carried Emilie Pelletier's name.

The meeting room was empty and the door slightly open.

The corridor continued and bent back forty-five degrees. On the left, more offices, larger, judging by the distance between them. No Pelletier name tag. On the right was a door labeled "Brodeur (Situation)."

The corridor came to a T.

To the left was a new corridor with office doors on one side and a meeting room named "Sawchuk" on the other. To the right was a dead end with only one door across from her: "Belfour (Docs)."

Bingo. She pushed the Belfour door lever. Locked.

A steel-framed touch screen came to life above the handle. It displayed a keypad with the digits zero to nine in random order.

BestBye checked the screen surface for fingerprints and grease, but there were no discernible patterns. It wouldn't have mattered anyway since the random order of digits indicated that this was a code lock with a changing pad layout.

The question was, did the order change every time it lit up or only after each *use*?

She took a photo of the digit layout, waited for it to dim without touching it, and woke it up again by pushing the door lever. The numbers were laid out the same way.

She looked for a mechanical fallback—a hidden keyhole, a sliding cap, or some minute button. There was a slot on the bottom of the frame, just under the display. It didn't feel large enough for a key though, rather the tip of a screwdriver.

The pin on her multitool fit in the slot, and she pivoted it gently. The whole lock house cracked open with the thin display hinged at the top. She looked down the hall and listened for a moment. No signs of anyone nearby.

Underneath the lock house was a circuit board with a transparent cover, two AAA batteries, and an LED flashing green every five seconds. There was also a minute written instruction.

```
Replace batteries when the light is
flashing red or there is no flash at
all. You will be notified when the
power is low or when the lock has had
too many failed code entries. See full
documentation for instructions on how to
set up notifications.
```

Using a piece of wire, she drained the left battery of power in place in the lock. The LED started flashing red.

She quickly fitted the lock's display back on and dashed to the Roy meeting room to hide, leaving its door ajar to be able to hear activity in the corridor.

A motion detector turned on the lights. She froze. No sounds.

The detector was placed right above the doorway, and BestBye recognized it as the ultrasonic type. She kicked off her shoes, got up on a chair, covered the detector with her wig, and turned off the lights manually. The light from the corridor bled in through cracks in the curtains.

The room was a perfect right triangle. The left wall had a big screen, and in the middle was a wooden, triangular conference table with rounded corners, probably custom made for the room. The black chairs around it were faux leather and well used. The far corner, back toward the gallery entrance, was narrow and the space was wasted except for a small fridge.

Within half a minute, someone came out of a room close by, either the situation room or one of the offices on the opposite side of it.

BestBye heard faint pop music playing. The person walked straight to the Docs room and fiddled around for a while, probably replacing the batteries. She heard five beeps as the person entered the code to check the functionality of the lock.

A door closed, and the pop music disappeared.

She hurried back to the locked Docs door and took a thermal image of the display with her Tile's camera. Five warm areas. Overlaid with her previous photo of the display, the warm spots were on 2, 6, 5, 1, 8. The eight was clearly the warmest, i.e., the last digit entered. The others were less certain.

Worst case, she was down to twenty-four tries. Not good enough.

How could she make the thermal print clearer? Could she cool it down and have the person enter the code again?

Back in the meeting room, she checked the fridge. It was full of bottled water. She soaked one of her socks and cooled the display for a minute before executing the battery drain procedure again.

This time the pop music person muttered loudly as he arrived. "These bloody locks." It was a man with an Indian English accent.

She heard the five beeps again.

A few minutes went by with the music still playing. She shook her head in frustration. The thermal imprint was surely gone by now.

Finally, the Indian guy went back into his office, and the pop music died. She snuck out of the meeting room, only to find that the Docs room scene had changed.

She chuckled quietly. The man had used a thick book to block the door from closing, and there was a sign on it.

Lock broken. Keeps draining the batteries. I'll contact Maintenance.

/Singh (Oct 14)

Five minutes later, she had what she wanted from the Docs room. This was it. She just needed to get out safely.

As she picked up the wig from the meeting room and put her wet sock back on, she heard humming from back at the T junction. The sound was getting closer quickly.

She moved toward the exit and took the last forty-five-degree bend. To her right was the women's restroom, which would allow her to silently disappear for a few minutes. The exit door fifteen feet ahead would make more noise and required a few seconds to badge out, but it meant freedom.

The hum got stronger. It was a melody from some recent earworm, but she couldn't recall which. She gently snuck into the restroom and locked herself inside one of the stalls.

Twenty seconds went by. The restroom door swung open, and the humming filled the space. High heels on stone floor accentuated the steps as they came closer. Whoever it was, the person chose the stall closest to the exit.

BestBye could hear every detail through the four-inch gaps between the stall walls and the floor. Pants or skirt unzipping, silk lining and cotton panties against shaved legs, pee against porcelain. Then a resounding fart.

"Bless you!" BestBye burst.

"Sorry, I didn't realize someone was in here," came from the other stall.

BestBye heard the woman tear off toilet paper, wipe herself, and flush before the heels headed for the basins. A faucet started pouring.

"Who's in here anyway?"

BestBye watched the woman's shadow move under her stall door.

She had to respond. "Hey, can I get some privacy here, please?"

A pause. "Of course." The click-clack went toward the exit. "I guess I can just check the badge logs instead."

The restroom door opened and shut. Silence. Complete silence. BestBye stayed put for exactly five minutes.

When she opened her stall door, there was a woman facing her in a frozen pose right by the exit door. It was Commander Emilie Pelletier. She had opened and closed the exit door, but never left.

BestBye jerked backward like a wounded animal.

Pelletier broke her pose and moved closer to get a good look at

BestBye. "Sorry. I didn't mean to startle you like that. But we're a security agency after all. Can't afford privacy here. Who are you?"

"I'm Miniona, Miniona Styx."

"What a peculiar name. I don't believe we've met. As a matter of fact, I know we haven't met. Mind if I scan your GPI?"

BestBye did mind profusely, but that wasn't an option. She extended her wristbanded arm.

Pelletier instructed her Tile to scan and pointed it at BestBye. The wristband lit up, and the commander browsed through the information she received. Her eyebrows furrowed. "What the? Let me try that again," the commander said, moving her own left wrist with her GPI band to her back.

The re-scan didn't make Pelletier any happier. "This thing is broken." She lowered her Tile and instead eyed BestBye up and down. "Nice shirt. I see you have access to the Docs room."

The blue binder BestBye had taken was pressed tightly under her left arm.

Pelletier continued. "Who do you work for?"

The office door name tags BestBye had seen earlier flickered in her memory. Randomly picking one of the names would be a huge risk. It might not be a manager at all, or it might turn out to be one of Pelletier's directs. "I'm pretty new here, but I believe I'm not supposed to tell you who I work for before I do a disclosure check."

Pelletier's eyes darkened as she put on a fake smile. "You are perfectly right, Miss Styx. I will instead go check the online directory. I suggest you do your disclosure check so we can have a little chat. I'm Commander Emilie Pelletier—disclosed on everything." She extended her right hand.

BestBye anxiously pointed toward the basin. "I have to wash my hands first."

The commander pursed her lips and looked as if she had been made fun of. Within seconds she had left the restroom.

CHAPTER TWENTY-TWO

The Blue Binder

It had been a daring escape from Vancouver.

BestBye had gone straight for a fake commuter crossing to the US exclave peninsula Point Roberts, where Miniona Styx's holier-than-thou attitude paid off in convincing the guards of her rights to cross. Then a hitchhike to Juneau helped by truck operators being so bored sitting in automated vehicles that catching a ride had become easy, and finally a flight back to California.

Kiss and West had driven back to the US under made-up Canadian IDs.

It felt like West had been gone for a month once he got back home and hugged his mom. She had been happy to see him too. No agent had knocked on her door this time, and his government Tile had stayed in place, untouched. There was light at the end of this tunnel.

Now all five of the Survivors sat around the lab's coffee table as Best-Bye told the story of the break-in and her close encounter with Pelletier.

"I'm glad you got out in one piece. That's some serious heist shit," Melissa said with satisfaction in her voice. "But you're leaving out the most important thing—*what* did you steal?"

BestBye sipped her sencha tea. "A binder with high-octane stuff. I photographed and OCRed the contents into a file, then burned the paper original. The file is on SurvivorNet, still encrypted."

Everybody waited for her to continue.

"Why work hard when others have already done the work for you?" She shared the decryption key. "I give you G20S Canada's latest pentest report."

A pentest, or penetration test, was a paid attempt at breaking into computer systems to find any holes before real criminals did.

Jitterbug got a wide grin on his face and started mini clapping his hands rapidly. "This calls for an appletini—Mr. Robot style."

"All, let's keep the goal in mind as we go through this," Melissa said. "There's going to be a ton of juicy stuff in here, but we're looking for a way to take down GPI."

"And for how they framed my mom," West put in.

"Sure," Melissa said with a quick nod.

The Survivors dug into the report like a pack of coyotes. Two hours went by with spontaneous comments, scribbling of notes, and several what-the-fucks.

The first real gold nugget was the calendar system.

"The whole fucking G20S has a shared calendar," Melissa said.

"Can we cut down on the swearing, please?" Jitterbug pleaded. "I'm trying to work."

"How's it broken?" BestBye asked Melissa.

"You can access any employee's calendar with a timing attack. If the first character doesn't match the person's calendar password, it fails immediately, but if the first character is correct and the second isn't, it takes a tiiiny bit longer to fail. So you can search for the password one character at a time, movie style."

The second piece of gold they struck was a type of security problem West knew about. "I thought I'd seen the last one of these—SQL injection. You can't make this shit up."

It meant injection of commands to a database to exfiltrate data, write new data, or even execute code.

"I saw that one," Jitterbug said. "Goes to some central documentation server, right?"

"The pentesters snagged a copy of the agency's budget. That's how you prove your worth."

Jitterbug and West spent a full day weaponizing the SQL vulnerability to run their own code. This meant they were now behind G20S's firewalls.

Meanwhile, Kiss and Melissa used the injection to pull down actual documents from the database.

They were just about to wrap up for the day when Kiss held up her

Tile. "West, you got to see this. I found docs on how to remotely log in to automated border control stations. Brings back memories, huh?"

West's eyes grew. "That may have been what that Mr. Singh used when he closed the gates on us." He moved over. "I remember the station number."

They logged in to Border Station 442 and checked the command line history. It was all there, step by step.

Singh had first killed the voice and text interface for crossing the border. That was when the border station's screen had gone black.

Next, he had downloaded a privilege escalation exploit, compiled it, and ran it to get administrative access to the whole station—a so-called *root* account.

These new access rights had given Singh the power to override the emergency passage and close the gates. Apparently, he had also reactivated the cameras and sensors that had been shut off due to the faked low battery power.

"See if the camera files are available in the station's storage," Kiss said.

They found video clips of Kiss and BestBye crossing the border. None of them were identifiable, but their bikes were. Seeing BestBye's death-defying squeeze through the closing gates made them realize how close a call it had been.

West had a look at the compilation step in Singh's command line history.

```
station442$ clang -o privEsc
privEscalate.c
```

"Jit, check this out," he said.

Jitterbug squinted at West's screen.

West gave him a clue. "It's a BSD system."

"Oh, the database server we just hacked is BSD too. You're saying this Mr. Singh has an exploit for G20S's own servers?"

"I bet they have not reported the vulnerability to the BSD project. It's a zero day."

They downloaded Singh's border station exploit to the G20S SQL server and escalated their privileges there. They now didn't just have an account behind the firewalls, they had a root account.

CHAPTER TWENTY-THREE

The GPI Blockchain

Forty-eight hours of hacking with occasional sleep got Jitterbug and West all the way from root on the document server to one of Canada's local replicas of US GPI blockchains. West was happy to have at least one other team member help him try to figure what had been done to his mom.

On West's screen was now a form field asking for which identity to show the blockchain entries for.

He entered his mom's full name and address and hovered his index finger over the Submit button. Once he pressed down, he would know everything G20S had collected on her, things she might not want him to know, things she might want to protect him from or didn't even know herself.

He looked at Jitterbug with his finger still in the air.

His friend nodded slowly. "This is what you came here for, buddy. I'll look away, and you tell me if it's okay to read."

West pressed down.

The screen filled with a grid of personal information. The upper left corner was his mom's most recent registered event.

```
Event: Refused to assist Agent Jim
Timothy in learning the whereabouts of
her son, West William Wilder.

Justification for collection:
Noncooperative regarding person on parole.
```

He felt the familiar prickle of tears forming under his eyelids as he read further through the entries on his mom. It was a testament to her determination and persistence in getting him out of prison. Her public appearances as well as closed-room conversations with federal representatives were documented in detail. In between those entries was on display the level of access G20S had to people's private lives. Medications his mom had used, bank statements, insurance details, approved credit, and travel documents.

"You can look," he said quietly to Jitterbug.

Jitterbug briefly put his arm around him.

West searched for "smoking" and got a single hit.

Event: Subject smoking tobacco.

Justification for collection: Anti-fraud, insurance, Social Security, Medicaid.

The entry had a screenshot from his mom's social media account with a photo of her smoking a cigarette and joking about how stupid it was.

"This has to be forged. She would never joke about such a thing."

"I just realized you probably never heard of deepfakes," Jitterbug said.

"Huh?"

"They became popular about ten years ago in political smear campaigns and fake celebrity porn. You replace the face or body with someone else's in photos and videos."

Melissa overheard the conversation and sat down beside West, looking at his screen. "Fake entries, doctored photos. There are a number of cases where people claim to have been framed or that blockchain entries about them were wrong. The question is how the US government adds those entries back in time since blockchain technology and replication is supposed to prevent tampering."

She shared a file with West. "This file has info on the cases of framing I'm talking about. Media reports with names, residential info, professions, age, and what the people were accused of. If you can find them on the blockchain, you can cross-reference and look for traces of how US G20S does it."

West browsed the file. Several cases turned out to be similar to his mother's with either tobacco or marijuana smoking deemed to be insurance fraud. A few cases were accusations of colluding with the enemy for low-ranked people in the armed forces. A handful were people losing their property because of alleged illegal contracts.

The two things all the cases had in common were that the accused were common people and that the media sided with the government because of the strong evidence on the blockchain.

He and Jitterbug managed to match several of the media reports with blockchains and downloaded the chains for a closer look.

Sure enough, the surveillance entries supporting the accusations were all there, and the hashes were valid.

As West went through the chains, he noted they all had kind of swirly, colorful images interspersed between readable entries.

"Do we know what these are?" he asked.

"That's G20S's classified, encrypted information," Jitterbug said. "They are required to put it on the blockchain for it to hold up in court, but you need keys to decrypt it. The images serve as visual integrity—a unique image per classified entry. Just an encrypted blob didn't fly with the public. But it's the hash of the image that really counts. They made the hashing tool public for transparency." He used air quotes for the last word.

West scrolled back and forth on one of the downloaded blockchains, and a handful of swirly images passed by. He checked the other chains, and they all had the images.

"How come G20S has so much classified information on all these people?"

"It costs G20S nothing to store the data," Melissa said. "Many of those entries are probably classified because …" She lowered her voice, pretending to be someone else. "We don't want to tell you we know this, but we'll dig it up in ten years when we need to take you down."

West scrolled through his mom's chain again, then stopped at one of her swirly image entries. "I've seen this one before. I've seen this exact image on one of the other blockchains."

"Well, they all look kind of similar."

West frantically scrolled through the images on the other victims' chains in search of what he had seen.

"There it is. Look at it." He beamed from his Tile to the big screen, jolted up from the couch, and pointed back and forth between two wavy, mostly red images.

"I'll be darned." Jitterbug did a slow clap.

West was too worked up to indulge in Jitterbug's praise.

"Why does a …" He checked his Tile for the profession of the second person. "A bartender. Why does a bartender in Chicago have a classified image entry that's an exact copy of an image on my mom's chain? These images are supposed to be unique. Right? That's what you said, Jit?"

Jitterbug nodded.

West's find piqued BestBye's interest, and she got up to have a close look at the two images on the screen. "They *look* the same, but I bet there's a difference. Diff them."

West ran a bit-by-bit diff. Sure enough, there was a difference: a single pixel with a different shade of red.

"I guess that solves the mystery," BestBye said as she went back to her desk. "Still, a cool find."

West sat silent. The intention was for regular people to interpret these images as distinct, unique entries, not for a computer expert to tell them apart through a differing pixel.

This is sloppy. There's something wrong here.

He ran the proprietary, officially sanctioned hashing tool on both images to make sure they produced the two different hashes that were on the blockchain. They did.

He opened the image from his mom's chain in an image editor. It was a Portable Network Graphics file, or PNG. He changed the one differing pixel to make it an exact match of the other image, saved the file, and ran the hash algorithm again.

Its hash value hadn't changed.

"Hey, I got something. I changed the pixel on my mom's chain to make the two images *truly* identical, but the hashes don't match. Two identical images should produce the same hash, but they don't."

West changed the pixel to pitch black instead of red and hashed the file again. The hash value *still* stayed the same.

"Check the metadata," Jitterbug suggested.

West opened the file in a hex editor.

Author
    G20S USA, California branch.

Description
xrDG9DLtoUb0OoCIlIfPTLMLEiVDwwX9
6EX5mqpSrJjgnioOw1FNmlgix61ZXOe4
U1PPX51X0SUZm1exQAtoPCEqM3a4xc8a
nqxRFVHmxH9Dnklby1cqSNlRLK6SDHqT
YUDPaI33f1Yf74Ge1Ks074at1FL7kADI

Software
G20S PNG encoder.

Comment
qItC6lONrcBM8q5MHtxqxWByJLRTXtHE
W9We1RbZz6jed8RKlKp6SvxQqyEBjL12
F2r9T8O9Nd0veFVbiV6XjJp7Bo3Y6eY9
pR2aYRTbxkDmNk52sqrqsKvdOG36HoSD
t05bPaqczAxtOxM8AO0kgbZu6FuJoGyq

p0DSRN2rUhJ9jn4JcbTXKkp5r0r1eELD
DrvEkMONoz0APXlnSDP4Z6qu7sS71zHu
YvafOwFlzLRrzakxZxrH1f87mQQfxxDs
ZIIAMJVCvy3RNloctLvU5g8YLDyIHlfN
gx38SSulO8Xiu8PcUhVbSsF57mDyE2PN

rl6Q7IfbfzHLlVVU1WrCfvpAYevf25Cu
14LOBLqLbyVRDBByyg8GbzRl7hK91eVC
VpoRiMegJWZb63Yi2gqIzTfTXtctp3W7
9dv9stFjR74JUajXEocbPfzRr4E2JF2i
vSZF5pLMDB3KuztR3IBjdNeKqNDew9Kc

"Holy moly, both the Description and the Comment sections look like crypto text. Is this public info?"

"No one but G20S and courts have access to these files. You are allowed to *see* your blockchain and validate the entries but not look inside the files. We're the first ones outside of G20S looking at this."

West pulled up the metadata of a few other swirly images. They all had unique five-line descriptions and comments of varying sizes, none of them readable to a human.

He mumbled to Jitterbug. "The descriptions are fixed in size. Could they be crypto keys? Or a salt? And the comment is the payload?"

"Storing the crypto text and the key in the same file sounds stupid."

"With a military mindset, availability often trumps confidentiality," BestBye said. "This info is not sensitive for G20S, it's sensitive for the individual. If you split crypto text and keys, you run the risk of getting out of sync and losing all this precious surveillance data. That's worst case for them."

Jitterbug shrugged. "Try decrypting your mom's classified image metadata with all the symmetric crypto algorithms we know of and see what we get."

An hour later, they got a hit on one of West's mom's image entries. NGE2, or Next Generation Encryption Two, had decrypted the image comment section into plain English.

Event: Subject involved in extramarital affair.

Justification for collection: Moral character, inheritance, cause of conflict.

"What da fuck? My mom has never been married."

If there was any doubt as to the truth about his mom's smoking habits, this was as clear as it could get. This was the truth in plain lies.

They decrypted image metadata from all the other victims' blockchains and found classified entries for black market payments, drug abuse, dealings with countries under embargo, domestic violence, prolonged use of strong medication, hospitalization for mental instability, and involvement in extremist organizations.

"A freaking menu of character assassinations."

Melissa stood looking at a few of the entries on the big screen and shook her head. "Looks like G20S is sprinkling these out slowly but surely as time goes by, to always have something on every potential threat. You make a misstep, they reveal one of these, and you've lost whatever you were fighting for. The government isn't framing people when needed; we are all pre-framed."

West landed his right fist in his left palm. "We have the scandal we are looking for, Melissa. This'll clear my mom's name and get her the nano surgery. How do we get this in front of the public?"

"We don't. Not yet." Melissa stood still as a rock.

"What do you mean? This is what we set out to do."

"This is what *you* set out to do."

CHAPTER TWENTY-FOUR

Fight to the Death

West still held his right fist in his left palm, staring at Melissa. No one said a word. Ambient noise came from the fans in the lab's computers. BestBye's office chair squeaked as she swiveled slowly to watch the standoff.

"My mom needs surgery," he said with his voice breaking up on the last syllable.

Melissa took a breath. "I know. But the mission is to take control over GPI. Compromise the whole thing so that they have to dismantle it. A scandal about false evidence will not get us there. We'll get some new legal protections here in the US, but the identity system will remain."

Tears were welling up in West's eyes. He tilted his head. "She is dying."

Melissa was tearing up too and said nothing.

"We have root access," Jitterbug said. "Let's hack Canada's GPI signing keys and start corrupting entries. That'll show the world we have control. This could be done in a jiffy."

Melissa turned to Jitterbug and regained her composure. "I have no doubt we can go from our current level of access to actually compromising Canada's entry point into the GPI system," she said. "But it's not that easy, as I found out while digging through that document server." She got a foreboding look on her face. "Hacking a single security agency is not enough. The GPI system was built to withstand war."

She started fiddling with getting some document up on the big screen.

West raised his voice. "Melissa, listen to yourself. You're telling me we can't save my mom because it doesn't fit in with your plan? What happened to you?"

She turned halfway toward him, stopped, and closed her eyes. "I …" She pursed her lips hard. "I wanted you on this team to take on the global surveillance machine. That is what this team is about. You added your own goal, and I agree it's worthy and noble, but we must not play our cards before we have a full hand. G20S will come at us with all they've got—legally, digitally, and physically. We've got one shot."

West got up. He looked at the others. Melissa by the big screen, which now displayed something titled "Technical Task Order 1104," BestBye at her desk looking indifferent, Kiss fidgeting by the other end of the couch looking at him and slowly shaking her head, and Jitterbug sitting down with eyes closed and his nose and forehead leaning against clasped hands.

West dropped his Survivor Tile and lab key on the coffee table, grabbed his jacket, and left.

CHAPTER TWENTY-FIVE

Sacrifice

"Mom, I got us help."

She was watching him get his jacket off from her favorite spot on the couch, book in hand, with the reading lamp shining gold on her partly silver, partly chestnut hair. She must have been dozing.

"What's that you said?" she asked.

West walked into the living room. "I know how the agents did it, how they made it look like you'd been smoking."

"How?"

"It's something called a blockchain." He stopped at the coffee table.

"No, I mean how did you get help?"

He rubbed his palms slowly against the side of his jeans and wet his lips. "I …"

He sat down at the other end of the L-shaped sofa and leaned forward. "I asked Melissa."

She tilted her head to the side, silently questioning him like he was a little boy lying about having done his homework.

"How did they do it?" she eventually asked sternly.

West explained the pre-frame exploit. He didn't outright say Melissa refused to help but said she had a plan for how and when to disseminate the information and now wasn't the time.

"It's better you're not part of any public scandal," his mom said. "I doubt your parole allows you to poke at the government."

"I'll stay out of it. But given that you will get justice eventually, will you now allow me to use my college fund to pay for your surgery?"

She looked at him sideways.

"We can't live like this, Mom." He pressed his lips together, and the fine muscle under his left eye twitched. "I can't live like this. I can't wait for death like some price to pay or dark fate I must accept. You have to let me help you."

They sat quietly for several moments. West rocked back and forth with his hands clasped between his knees. The tension between the two of them slowly faded.

"We should accept help from and give support to each other," his mom recited quietly. "That's what they said during sermon this past Sunday."

West nodded and let a tear slip out. He moved over and put an arm around his mother. "I'm thirty-four, and I'm not sure I want to spend years studying anyway," he said. "What I *do* know is I want to help you. It's my turn."

He knew this was hard for her, not just because it was a lot of money or because the money was his. It was hard being the recipient of sacrifice and generosity. Her role had always been the caretaker.

"If we can't get them to yield, I'll sell the house and pay you back," she said with emphasis.

West buried his face on her shoulder and held her tight. "Thank you."

•

West had a good night's sleep and made breakfast for them both. At eight thirty he was done eating and heard his mom's alarm go off. She'd be headed for church in an hour. Perhaps he should join her? She'd love that.

The alarm kept beeping. He went upstairs to her bedroom. She was lying on her side, facing him with a calm, relaxed look. He turned the alarm off.

"Hey, Mom," he whispered.

He nudged her shoulder.

"Mom."

He pushed her shoulder gently backward. She rolled over on her back. Her head sagged.

"Mom!"

He leaned in close, falling to his knees. She wasn't breathing. She wasn't breathing!

He got up, burst out of her room and into his, and grabbed the Tile sitting in its stabilizer.

His thumb trembled as it tapped the glass surface.

"Nine-one-one, what is your emergency?"

"My mother."

"Where is your mother?"

"At home. She's in bed."

"I have your location, and you are West Wilder, correct?"

"We were going to go to Japan."

"What is your mom's emergency?"

"She's not breathing."

A convulsion jerked his upper body forward, and vomit splashed on the bedside table in front of him. His left hand shot out against the tabletop to stop himself from toppling over.

"An ambulance is on its way. Do you know CPR, sir?"

West slowly removed the Tile from his ear. The dispatcher's voice came through thin and high-pitched. "Please make sure the door is open to your house. If you know CPR, please perform it while you wait. Help will be there shortly, okay?"

The next thing he knew, he was back on his knees beside his mom's bed. He tried to perform CPR, only to find blood in her mouth. Iron-tasting blood.

So this was how it would end.

He carefully wiped the blood off her lips with his shirt. Her drooping face looked calm, and her hand was only slightly colder than his.

Tears rolled over his cheeks. He hugged her, landing his chin on her shoulder and embracing her remaining warmth before it was all gone.

He started rocking them both gently while singing in the faintest of voices.

Lullaby and good night …

Chapter Twenty-Six

Ashes

The majestic waters of the Pacific Ocean accepted West's mom's ashes off the coast of Carmel-by-the-Sea a week and a half later. Early November was a beauty. The air was cool, and a humpback whale breached with impressive splashing nearby.

He was going to throw in some strawberries for her to take on the journey, but it felt a little weird. She would probably have preferred he eat them.

Farewell, Mother. You were the best. I'm sorry I made you end up here. I'll make it right somehow. You didn't deserve this. I will always remember how you took care of me, and I will carry with me your kindness and your sense of right and wrong.

He read John 10:27–29 from his mom's Bible, stood silent for a while as the ash flakes dispersed between the waves, then nodded to the captain of the boat that he was done.

On their way back to port, he felt as if a window was closing in his life. Many opportunities and possibilities had been cut off, and only a few remained.

San Francisco was getting ready for dinner when he got back to the city. His funeral jacket weighed heavy on his shoulders as he walked up the stairs to his new home. He had fled to a rental apartment a couple of days after his mom's passing, fled the pain and memories and presence of death. Hired help was now cleaning up the house, stashing boxes in a storage unit, and applying fresh paint to the walls in preparation for the market.

He blipped his GPI band to unlock the apartment door.

It was already unlocked.

CHAPTER TWENTY-SEVEN

What Kind of Fool

West's brain desperately worked through the possibilities. Could it be a lock error? Or had he forgotten to lock the door? Had the property manager been here? Or the police? It could be a break-in.

He put his ear to the door. Not a sound except his own amped-up breathing.

He turned on audio recording on his government Tile, dimmed its screen, and slowly opened the door, peering inside as the angle widened.

The apartment was dark. Streetlights below his kitchen window rendered yellow lines along the blinds; that was it.

He tapped on his Tile's smart home controls to turn on the lights. It responded with a warning sign and the word *Disconnected*. He reached for the manual light switch just inside the entrance. It clicked under his fingers, back and forth, back and forth. No light.

The Tile's flashlight would have to guide him.

He noticed something standing on his kitchen table—a slender object a few inches tall, almost like a piece of art, a little sculpture.

As he moved closer, he realized it was Jitterbug's Tile motion simulator. It was placed over the corner of a printed letter.

```
Mr. Wilder, welcome home.

My job the last two and half months has
been to make sure you are living up to the
conditions of your release and that you
don't threaten G20S in any capacity. That's
an assignment I'm overqualified for. It
```

should be easy, but much to my chagrin, I seem to be set up for failure.

I will figure out who or what is protecting you and crack it wide open. Meanwhile, my recommendation is you take advantage of the sliver of a chance you have left at leading an honest life. I have dirt on you, enough to get you back where you belong.

Oh, and what kind of fool do you think falls for this gadget here?

Yours, Agent Timothy

PS. You want to check your fuse box.

I also need to check my own blockchain.

CHAPTER TWENTY-EIGHT

Melissa IRL

West stood outside the door to Velvet Fridays with his jacket under his left arm to expose Melissa's anti-surveillance T-shirt. He wore his face mask, his government Tile was at home on the coffee table, and he had just put on his GPI band, having carried it here in its F pouch. The winter evening chill made him shiver.

He had no means of contacting Melissa without the Survivor Tile, and he didn't dare go straight to the lab in case he was being followed.

Realizing he didn't even have someone to text after reading Agent Timothy's letter had been like a cold hand gripping his inside.

He rubbed the back of his neck with his free hand before reaching out to touch the interactive door.

It lit up, and the woman with spiky orange hair on the screen seemed to recognize him, or maybe she had help from facial recognition. She had a book in her hand.

"You still need a lender?" she said as the door opened.

He spent two hours at the hackathon, not really getting anything done but looking over his shoulders, expecting Timothy to show up at any moment or one of the other participants to start asking him questions.

So much time seemed to have passed since last he was here. The rows of desks with geeks hunched over hardware and software projects had really made an impression on him then. Now all he could see were the GPI bands around their wrists.

If these people didn't know any better or chose to ignore it, the rest of the population was truly and utterly fucked. Should any one of these techies ever go up against the government, the US G20S would just reveal one or two pieces of evidence on their blockchain and take them to the gallows; problem solved.

He still had no idea what Timothy meant in his letter. Was someone really helping West on the inside? Could it be Melissa?

His lender Tile buzzed.

**Go to Infidel Castro
at 18th/Castro. /Runa**

•

Infidel Castro was a Cubano place smelling heavenly of roasted pork and melted cheese. Inside, there was loud music playing, and West suspected Melissa saw that as a feature. The high walls had wooden shelves with full-size Spitting Image bobbleheads of old political leaders, including Fidel himself. The menu had sandwiches with names like Bay of Pigs, Smoking Gun, Panama Pineapple, and Raked Forest.

West scanned the seating area in search of Melissa but couldn't find her.

He sat down at a small, square table by the right wall and ordered a Just Say No sandwich through the interactive menu on the table. He was about to blip his GPI band when Melissa showed up out of nowhere, sat down across the table, snatched the menu, and added an order of Basket of Deplorables veggie chips and water. She paid for them both.

As she put the menu away, she stretched over the table and dropped a pair of earphones in front of West. Same as in Santa Cruz.

He looked at her before putting them in his ears. The noisy music was instantly dampened.

"How you doing?" Melissa said, looking around. He heard her clearly even though she was keeping her voice down.

"Mom's dead," he responded, sinking an inch into his chair.

She looked at him in shock and disbelief, then moved to the side of the table enough to lean over and hug him. A long rescuing hug.

"I'm so sorry," she whispered. "For all of it."

It felt like a storm coming to rest in his stomach, something settling or cooling off.

They stayed silent in each other's arms until a serving robot rolled up with Melissa's chips and two large glasses of water.

Melissa got back in her chair, wiped tears from her eyes, and pushed the basket of snacks to the middle of the table.

West told her what had happened, from finding his mom in her bed through the funeral. But he left out Timothy's letter without really knowing why.

She said she thought the sea burial was a beautiful thing to do for his mom and that she wanted to avenge her.

"How's Kiss and the others?" he asked.

"I left them at a bar when I went to check on Velvet. They'd love it if you showed up."

"Now we've got time at least," West said.

"You say we," she smiled ephemerally.

West had some chips. "It still beats me how they managed to even build a *global* identity system. What about east and west? Are they friends now?"

"Anything international is shared: passport info, flight tickets, Interpol, that kind of stuff. But deeper data is kept in the old spheres. Five Eyes for instance."

West remembered Five Eyes. It was an intelligence alliance between Australia, Canada, New Zealand, the UK, and the US with roots in World War II.

"EU shares within its bubble," Melissa continued. "Russia controls its Commonwealth, and China is an island."

"Can people just read up on this stuff online?"

"Nope. But I'm still friends with Robert. You remember him, right? Swedish hacker who gave us info on those hardware security modules."

West had a vague recollection of someone named Robert. "Did he get caught up in the NSA aftermath?"

She shook her head. "Kept his info public through talks, so there wasn't much to go on. Nowadays he's helping Sweden defend against digital threats. He keeps me informed on the politics of GPI."

West got his Cubano from the rolling robot. He was still amazed at how nimble and quiet such machines were. This one was branded "Servidude."

He had a couple of bites before noting that Melissa had gone silent, mulling something. He gave her time.

"I wanted to circle back to Santa Cruz," she eventually mumbled, biting her thumbnail.

"What about it?"

"I did a bad job of explaining why I do this." She loosened her thumb from her mouth and shifted in her chair. "I wasn't ready to talk to you about what really happened to me during all those years. The rest of the team barely knows either."

He swallowed a piece of bread. "I won't tell anyone."

Melissa put her elbows on the table and put one hand in the other like paper covers rock. "Did I ever tell you about my father?"

"I met him a couple of times. Physician, right?"

"Tragic man. Not career-wise, but as a human. He hates women. Or at least he thinks women are lesser than men." She lifted her head and put both her hands around her water glass. "He seriously lectured me on why men are superior to women on anything involving math, logic, engineering."

"You're super smart, you know that."

"He doesn't give a shit. I'm a girl, and girls don't do tech."

"Just ignore him."

"It doesn't work that way. Not with him, not with someone you've been dependent on for so long. He told me over and over that I would never find someone again after you disappeared. He even pulled some biological shit on me, told me that a woman's fertility declines after the age of twenty-seven and that I should act accordingly."

West was about to mention that there were other ways to get pregnant but snapped out of it. "That's awful."

She had a sip of water and nodded before returning the glass to the table, keeping it cradled in her hands. She looked sideways around the place. "It got so bad that I decided to get my tubes tied. I wasn't planning on having kids anyway, so why keep the subject alive?"

"Did you?"

She looked at him. "Get sterilized?"

"Yeah."

"I got away from him instead. Said I would go to nursing school but then did computer science."

"Nice. Where?"

"Couldn't go to Stanford because Dad would stalk me and find out, and I couldn't go to MIT because of what they did to Aaron, so I went to Carnegie Mellon. They were totally cool. Helped me rig a fake admission to the undergraduate nursing program at the university. Apparently, I wasn't the only student faking my choice of education to satisfy pesky parents."

West remembered how he and Melissa often dreamt of life at some technical institute back when they were together. No parents, lots of weed, and all-night hacking.

"I was there for four years and was headed for a PhD. But then came GPI, and all schools had to merge student IDs with real IDs. My fake nursing school enrollment triggered some procedure where they sent out a physical letter to my parents. Imagine that—a paper letter. My dad went ballistic and sued CMU. I got kicked out as part of the process and never even got my master's degree."

"What the fuck?"

"Mhm. It was his final play to get me out of tech." She sat back. "Some got it worse, though. There was a Harvard student who committed suicide after his parents were notified their tuition money had gone to social studies instead of law school."

"That's heartbreaking. *Dead Poets Society*."

Melissa nodded. "Some parents exercise that kind of power over their kids. So I decided that if I can't get my degree and that young man can't live because he prefers social sciences over law, I can at least make sure young people have a way to escape their parents' tyranny in the future. GPI has gotta go."

They sat silently for a while. West thought about how *his* dad had left the scene before he could remember. What a dreadful thing it must be to fear a parent.

Melissa's chin dropped, and her upper body slumped. "One more thing," she said. "All those years ..." She lifted her head just enough to meet his eyes under her eyebrows. "I feel like shit about not visiting you in prison. You took fifteen years for me and for the people of this world." Her eyes were welling up. "You properly ruined a huge portion of your life for a greater cause, and I love you for that."

A tear rolled down West's cheek. It was his turn to reach over and hug his old girlfriend.

"We'll fix this," he said. "We'll fix it all this time."

CHAPTER TWENTY-NINE

Technical Task Order 1104

GPI TECHNICAL TASK ORDER 1104
CONCEPT OF OPERATIONS FOR THE KEY
MANAGEMENT SERVICE,
GLOBAL PERSONAL IDENTITY

Version 1.4 A001

900 Elkridge Landing Rd Linthicum
Maryland 21090

1 Scope

This document presents the concept of
operations (CONOP) for the G20 Security
Agency (G20S) Global Personal Identity
(GPI) Key Management Service (KMS).

2 Executive Summary

2.1 Goal
The goal of the Global Personal Identity
(GPI) system is to provide secure, robust,
fast, and up-to-date identity information
on any person residing in or visiting a G20
member country or a participating nonmember

country. The identities are managed to
support data collection for intelligence,
criminal investigations, taxation, et
cetera. It has no single point of failure,
and it builds on established cryptographic
standards.

2.2 The Central Key Pair

The service has a public/private crypto
key pair, created and refreshed jointly
through a threshold crypto system (see
2.4). Communication clients such as
member countries, participating nonmember
countries, and all legs of these countries'
governments and agencies are called nodes.
All nodes in the system know the public key
of the service and trust any certificates
signed by its corresponding private key.

2.3 Acceptable Risk Level

The acceptable risk level is set to 3
(three) simultaneously compromised member
countries by the G20S Board of Directors,
meaning the system should tolerate and
automatically recover unless an adversary
is able to simultaneously compromise the
GPI service of 3 (three) member countries.

2.4 The Threshold Crypto System

The GPI's private key is divided into
10 (ten) shares that can produce partial
digital signatures. The G8 countries—
Canada, France, Germany, Italy, Japan,
Russia, the United Kingdom, and the United
States—are permanently granted one share
each. The remaining two shares are cycled
on an annual schedule among the remaining
twelve G20 members.

The process of computing a full signature
from partial signatures is basically an
interpolation.

The cryptography scheme uses key share
refreshing. Countries periodically compute
new shares from old ones in collaboration,
without disclosing the service's private
key to any one country.

Distribution of trust is done through
threshold cryptography, and the GPI system
employs a (10, 3) configuration. It allows
10 (ten) countries to share the ability to
perform cryptographic operations so that
any 3 (three) countries can perform this
operation jointly, whereas it is impossible
for at most 2 (two) countries to do so,
even by collusion.

2.5 Backup
The various blockchains used in conjunction
with GPI provide backup by the nature of
being replicated.

However, only a fraction of incoming data
connected to GPI ends up on blockchains,
specifically data legally required to be
stored in that manner and data that might
be needed in legal processes.

The rest of the data poses a significant
backup challenge. The backup must have the
means to reinstate events as they occurred
to make G20S intelligence algorithms
reproduce the same results. Additionally,
the backup must be instantly available to
be useful in a real-time failure scenario.

Only the US offered to fund such a massive
live backup system and hosts it on behalf
of G20S in an undisclosed location. It
manages a complete 30 (thirty) day rolling
backup of the global G20S data feed. Also,
see technical note 1.

"Three countries, not one, and exhaust a thirty-day backup," Melissa
said, leaning against the lab's long desk, noting that West had finished
reading the document. "We compromise GPI by hacking two more
countries' security agencies and feed the system corrupt data for a month.
Then we own it."

They had gone to the lab to pick up West's Survivor Tile, and Melissa
had insisted that he read the doc. The others weren't here; he and Melissa
were alone in a non-public space for the first time since their teens.

"Are you sure this time?" she asked.

"I've promised myself never to go to prison again. I was alone the last
four years in there. Had one friend for the first eleven," he said. "Jeremy.
He was in for having blown things up. Not terrorist stuff. He never killed
anyone. Bank vaults and armored cars. He loved talking about the tech-
nicalities."

"There are a lot of things worth blowing up."

West paused. "Jeremy never got out. He died in there."

"I'm sorry."

"I'm just saying I'm taking a hell of a risk. We all are. What's the deal
with BestBye?"

"I trust her."

"She doesn't trust me."

"Takes a little time. She'll come around."

West let his head fall back against the couch's headrest. He looked
around. The lab was barely lit, which pronounced the LEDs from all the
powered equipment.

"Her parents are rich and famous," Melissa said. "But we don't know
who they are. Best's asocial side caused some harm to the family's reputation, and she detached herself. Her parents don't want to deal with
a loose cannon creating gossip. I think she sees them like once a year."

"Is that her beef with GPI?"

"The hard link to her family? Yeah, she hates celebrity chains."

"What about the others?"

"Kiss and Jit were pretty upset when you left. I got an earful from Kiss."

West caught himself smiling for a second.

"And you?" he said.

She put her hands on the edge of the desk and rubbed her chin against her left shoulder. "I already told you I want you on the team and that I'm sorry for the whole enchilada: for your mom, for saying we couldn't save her yet, and for your time in prison."

"I should say I'm sorry about Jeff," he said.

Her face frowned in the dim light.

"Our deal was stupid," he added. "You should get back with him."

She sighed. "That's not on you."

West swallowed.

"Shit, I don't want to be sad on a Friday," she said abruptly, taking a few steps toward the door. "The next GPI target is Brazil. Let's go see if the others are still at the bar."

Chapter Thirty

Party Like a Pro

It was a Monday in early November and the lab was filled with the smell of pumpkin spice from Jitterbug's humongous coffee mug.

"We have a Brazilian Casanova on our hands," Melissa declared from her favorite position, leaning against the desk, with West, Kiss, and Jitterbug in the soft seating area and BestBye by her screen.

Melissa beamed a portrait photo of a handsome man with perfect teeth, intense eyes behind trendy glasses, and a bloodred handkerchief loosely tied around his neck, tail ends drooping below the knot.

"Mr. Espinoza—another one of the agents Best spotted in New York City. He works on the right stuff within ABIN or Agência Brasileira de Inteligência, the Brazilian Intelligence Agency, part of G20S."

She flipped the big screen to a calendar view. The Vancouver pentest report had provided them with every G20S employee's calendar, including Mr. Espinoza's.

"In here are his work meetings and business trips, but it's also full of nighttime pleasures. Clubs and parties, passphrases for VIP entrance to concerts and exhibits. And lots of female names."

"Hey, look, he's a ProPartyer," Kiss said.

West scanned the screen content and spotted the word *ProParty* on the coming Friday. "What's that?" He bit his lower lip.

I could have searched for it.

"You pay to virtually tag along to a party, streamed live to you. You see what the partyer sees, hear what they hear. Hugely popular, especially if they have sex."

"You mean pick-ups?"

"Everyone has to consent and gets a share of the pay. People without a ProParty account are blurred, but there are whole clubs where you have to be a ProPartyer so the stream can be blur-free."

West was about to say something about this voyeurism. It wasn't porn. It wasn't a reality show either. It was reality.

Kiss didn't wait for his comment. "It's not just partying though. You can join celebrities during workouts or up on stage at concerts. It used to be open, but that got ugly with live beatings and vandalism, so now it's curated." She pulled up her Tile. "I wonder what this guy's ProParty name is?"

Melissa filtered the calendar to get a summary of Espinoza's ProParty events for the last year. "I don't have a ProStream account, but I'm guessing you have one, Kiss?"

"You bet," she replied in a puff.

BestBye muttered something but didn't engage.

Kiss logged in to the ProParty service and imported Espinoza's party calendar events as a search query and got tons of hits. "We need more than his dates. What are we guessing here? Hetero and premium price?"

"His home address is in Brasília," BestBye said from her seat, sifting through data on her own screen. "Often flies business to São Paulo but coach to Rio de Janeiro."

"Business up front, party in the back," West said. Melissa chuckled.

"Rio de Janeiro," Kiss spelled out as she typed in a new ProParty search. "Here we go: 3,904 heterosexual, male, premium accounts in Rio. They won't let me query that many from one location, so I'll have to do multihoming."

Painstakingly, they pretended to come from ten different cities in the US to fetch the event history of all the accounts and matched them with Espinoza's party schedule both back and forward in time.

"Gotcha. His handle is SecretionAgent."

"Same kind of humor as you, West," Jitterbug said, leaning over.

Kiss looked through the profile info. "About five hundred people pay to see him on a regular night. Not bad."

"You should follow this prick on his Friday night escapade and see what you get." Melissa scoffed. "Maybe you'll see some contents of his Tile, what apps he uses, that sort of thing."

"Sure. I can bring one guest. Who is open-minded enough to watch Espinoza fuck?"

"Pervert," BestBye mumbled.

"I am," West said. "I mean, I want to see what this ProParty thing is."

•

Weekdays meant contractor work for every Survivor but West. He had been wondering how they paid their bills, but hearing what they charged for their pentesting services made him realize it was a well-funded operation Melissa was running here. Their specialty apparently involved physical-entry hacking, which brought back memories of his break-in at SafeNet.

He kept himself busy with lock picking and an online course in a new programming language, but something kept bubbling up in his mind—checking his own blockchain. He hadn't told anyone about Timothy's visit.

None of the misdoings he'd seen planted on the others' chains would work for the time he'd been locked up, so whatever dirt Timothy had put there must be for the last few months. Drugs probably. But then why was West still out? If G20S could produce proof that would hold up in court, they could just take him now.

Maybe the sole reason was to make him worry, keep him on his toes. It was like those speed cameras in the UK he'd read about long ago. Three out of four are just empty shells but "work" anyway.

It's about how we change by mere threats.

•

Friday evening came, and West found himself in Kiss's apartment ready to ProParty with Mr. Espinoza.

Kiss wore fraying sweatpants and a green hoodie that read "Crypto, it means Cryptography."

On her messy desk was a 3D-printed figurine that looked like her, naked. West couldn't help but stare at it.

She noticed. "You have to scan your body and upload a model if you're going to do any kind of serious online dating," she said. "Once I had it, I figured I'd print it." She walked to the kitchen, still talking. "The latest is you have to model your brain too so people can date your virtual self before actually interacting with you. Brain modeling is just endless questions and images and video clips to measure your reactions and behavior." She got some things from her fridge. "Pretty creepy if you ask me, and I'm sure G20S taps into that shit, but it sure sped up matching once they started doing virtual-to-virtual."

As much as West hated asking about yet another part of modern life, current-day dating was something he'd love to understand.

Kiss kept talking into her fridge. "They let your brain model date other brain models virtually to create a shortlist of potentially good dates for you. It's like you're dating twenty-four seven."

"You're pretty leet with the dating business, huh?"

"Winnow the hunks from the Hanks, you must."

They prepared snacks together and sat down in recliners beside each other with stereo projection glasses and noise-canceling headphones on.

SecretionAgent logged on timely and spoke directly to his followers. "Hello, mah friends. How are you?"

It was a strange sensation to hear his voice recorded from the position of his ears, and at the same time see what he saw. The realism was stunning.

"Inglês?" one of his followers responded instantly in the chat room.

"Yes. Tonight, I have two English-speaking party members. But I also have a very special gift for all of you."

"Moreno?" Another text response.

"Brunettes, sure. But it's something else I want to tell you. I have not had sex or masturbated for three days. Three fucking days! So tonight, you will see a big load from the agent."

The chat room poured with praise.

West felt disgusted at first. Then he felt sorry for himself. Masturbation was all the sex he had known for his entire adult life.

"First let's do some coke," the agent continued.

As if reading his mind, Kiss spoke from the other chair. "Cocaine has been legal in all of South America since a few years back."

It felt strangely out of context to hear her voice intercept the video stream. He adjusted the projection image to see-through and glanced at her. She was fully focused on the stream.

Over the next hour and a half, Mr. Espinoza had two huge lines of cocaine and two cocktails—a Hurricane and what sounded like a Kye Pirinja. The bars he visited both had a Caribbean theme, and the women at these places were mostly in their early twenties with tasteful makeup and sexy, skintight clothing. Many of them recognized Espinoza. He got kisses and suggestive whispers.

Maybe these girls are in it for the money? I wonder what Kiss is paying for us to watch?

West could not believe how real the experience was. Several tiny cameras in the ProPartyer's glasses recorded what Espinoza saw and interpolated the stereo image to replicate the perspective from the pupils. When someone looked into Espinoza's eyes, they looked into all his followers' eyes too.

Of course, West didn't get the scent of the girls' perfume, the warmth of their cheeks, or the pressure from their boobs against his chest. But still.

The chat room was bubbling. Apparently, a couple of the girls had been on the show before, and the followers were discussing how great the sex had been.

"Are we getting anything useful out of this?" he asked.

"Now we know he likes rum-based drinks."

"True."

As if I knew there was rum in those.

West was getting turned on. The service was working. If Kiss looked at him now, she'd see he was getting a hard-on. Would she feel sorry for him?

She's done porn. She knows what a hard-on is.

Out of nowhere, West felt real, physical lips kissing him. He removed his goggles and found Kiss getting comfortable on his lap.

"I don't care that you used to be Melissa's boyfriend."

CHAPTER THIRTY-ONE

The Snowman

West woke up several hours later. Kiss was still asleep. It was late in the morning, judging by the daylight that leaked through the blinds.

He lay thinking about the sex they'd had. He had of course come too fast. What a joke of a thirty-four-year-old man he was.

He heard something. High-pitched hissing noises. They came from where they sat yesterday. He took a few limp steps over to the chairs and picked up his headphones. The stream was still on!

He put his glasses on too and sat down.

Mr. Espinoza was in a self-driving car in what looked like central Rio, still in his party clothes. The chat room only contained West and Kiss.

Espinoza got out in a crossing and waited for the car to leave before walking casually toward a white, cubic, three-story building. Its windows had a green tint to filter the sun. The sign on the wall read Polícia Civil.

The agent was met with respect and familiarity by the officer in reception. A click sounded, and Espinoza entered an unlabeled door where a corridor led him to the right side of the building. He exited to a small parking lot, walked on the shady side, and arrived at another cubic building labeled Polícia Militar. Inside was an officer behind a desk, reading on her Tile.

She looked up at Espinoza with a serious expression. "Você está atrasado."

Espinoza just passed by her into a small corridor. After almost reaching the end, he held up his GPI band to a large screen displaying the military police's logo on the left wall.

A speaker said, "Bem-vindo, Agente Espinoza," and the screen changed to a picturesque scene of a smiling snowman outside a cottage.

The snowman had a pair of skis leaning on its right shoulder and a red scarf like the handkerchief around Espinoza's neck on the photo Melissa had shown him. The cottage was built out of dark wood. Espinoza looked steadily at the image for a few seconds.

Then he turned, and what had looked like the end of the corridor slid open and revealed a passageway with a staircase. He headed up and entered a large meeting room.

The men and women around the table looked up at him. He apologized for being late and sat down.

A woman's voice with an American accent started talking while he was still fiddling with his chair. "As I was just about to say, I'm grateful for the chance to meet you, Saturday and all. The United States would look favorably on Brazil's support for my candidacy."

Espinoza's field of view changed from the vicinity of his seat to the speaker across the table. It was an Asian American woman in her late forties or early fifties with strands of gray in her black hair and a skin tone that implied lack of direct sunlight or habitual use of sunscreen.

The woman continued. "Commander Pelletier is a very capable person, but we think at this juncture, US leadership is more appropriate."

Suddenly, the woman's eyes fixated on West's, or rather Espinoza's. "Those are not video-recording glasses, are they? This meeting is off the record, might I remind you," the woman said.

"Dr. Kawasaki, dese are ordinary prescription glasses," Agent Espinoza replied.

West's projection image suddenly disappeared.

"Are you fucking crazy?"

His eyes adjusted to the dim light in the room. Kiss stood in front of him wearing nothing but underwear.

"If he sees that someone is exploiting the fact that he forgot to terminate the stream, he will hunt that account down. *My* account, you idiot." Her breasts swayed as she gesticulated. In her right hand was the computer rig's wall plug.

"I'm sorry." West pulled himself together. "Won't our accounts stay logged in now that you've just killed the computer?"

"The best thing we can hope for is my account turning idle before he notices. That way he might think we left last night." She walked over to the bed and put a T-shirt on. "Well, did you at least get any useful information?"

"Espinoza looked at a picture of a snowman right before the door opened. I tried to see if it was a challenge or some watermark thing."

Kiss's eyes grew. "It's probably a pass thought. You have to draw the image."

"A pass thought?"

"Brain waves. You're shown a specific image, and your brain emits a unique pattern. A revokable biometric password. Come on, you have to draw. Now."

"To show him or what?"

Kiss dug through a desk drawer. "We steal that pass thought and log in as him of course. Somehow." Kiss gave him a stylus, apparently for his Tile.

"Do you have pencil and paper?"

"You are old-school."

Chapter Thirty-Two

Humanoid Invasion

"We find out what ski goggles Espinoza uses, fit a duplicate pair with some equipment, do a switcheroo"—Jitterbug's hands moved as if doing a magic trick—"and scan his brainwaves."

They were discussing how to record Espinoza's pass thought to access his account and hack into G20S Brazil. The reason for the idea with the ski goggles was an upcoming trip to Tahoe in the Brazilian's calendar.

Kiss's arms were hanging down the sides of her armchair by the lab's coffee table. "It's at a convenient distance, but he'll notice if we switch them. Custom settings, software, what have you."

Jitterbug threw his hands up. "So we figure out a way to sneak a brain scanner into *his* pair."

Kiss wasn't convinced. "We won't be able to connect to them without his account."

"The ski trip is in three days. Even if we fail, we at least get to see some snow," Jitterbug pleaded.

"Speaking of snow." West pointed at the lab's big screen, where his sketch was on display. "There's also the part of actually showing him the snowman to trigger the pass thought."

"I have an idea for that part." It was BestBye.

She switched the big screen to a promotional picture from the Lake Tahoe ski resort, which read "Free* ski lifts."

"That asterisk isn't a snowflake," she said. "They show you ads in your goggles as you ascend. We just hack the ad system, render a nice version of your clumsy sketch, and show it to Espinoza in his goggles."

Melissa was on her way out and grabbed a worn-out gym bag that read "Kick Like a Girl."

"Did you stick with kung fu?" West asked.

"I'd whip yo' ass," she replied before turning to Kiss. "They're right. Tahoe's what we've got. We still haven't figured out where to actually log in with his pass thought anyway." She checked the door viewer and left the lab.

Jitterbug did a quick drumroll with his index fingers on the coffee table. "Someone, please do a photo search for Mr. Espinoza wearing ski goggles. I'm gonna build me a brain scanner."

West joined Kiss and BestBye for the photo hunt. They found ski photos on social networks all right, but none of them detailed enough to tell which brand and model of goggles Espinoza wore.

"Who is he traveling with?" BestBye asked as if the others would know. "It seems to be the same woman on many of these ski trips."

"Didn't his calendar say Elsa? Some college friend I think, based on the photo comments." Kiss highlighted a couple of examples.

"Let's find out who she is and dig through her photos too."

Elsa Peskow had plenty of ski photos posted, and after some search wrangling, they stared at a photo of Mr. Espinoza in profile looking at gorgeous mountain scenery, bathing in low sunlight. He was leaning forward, shoulders resting on his ski poles. They zoomed in, and on the side of his ski goggles—Eyes OTG.

BestBye asked her Tile for details, and the voice assistant came back with the answer.

"Eyes OTG is a Chilean brand of ski goggles. OTG means Over the Glasses, which allows customers to wear regular glasses underneath. Eyes OTG runs Humanoid, has a built-in camera, and supports Humanoid add-ons such as augmented-reality engines for downhill games."

•

Jitterbug ordered a pair of Eyes OTG and brought in the whole box the morning after.

"West, you wanna join me in the Shaq?"

There wasn't really space for two people in the lab's walk-in closet, so West had to sit halfway into the main room. The Shaq's back wall was covered from floor to ceiling with plastic drawer organizers full of resistors, integrated circuits, capacitors, diodes, and larger parts. To the left was a narrow desk with a soldering station, a desk lamp, a large rectangular magnifying glass fitted on a movable arm, and video-capturing equipment. Above the desk was a poster with lavish lettering that read "With God, All Things are Possible. —Matt. 19:26."

Jitterbug had also ordered a pair of stereo cameras that connected to the goggles for 3D video capture of your skiing. "Every certified peripheral has specific permissions, approved by the Humanoid Consortium," he said. "My brain wave recorder needs power and a way to send data to our server. So I thought we'd repurpose these cameras."

A couple of hours of soldering and mumbling ensued. Jitterbug had obviously done this kind of Humanoid repurposing before.

"Now the part Kiss thinks will beat us: authorization. Espinoza's goggles are logged in with his Humanoid account, and he has to authorize any new peripherals. We don't have his credentials, so we won't be able to just install the brain wave recorder on his goggles. However, there was something that made me buy exactly this pair of stereo cameras."

He held up the cameras' branded box and pointed to a feature blurb on the front. "Check bullet point three."

West read it out loud. "Ready to Use. Accredited Humanoid dealers can install these cameras for you."

"What does that tell you?" Jitterbug asked, pointing both index fingers at West.

"That there's a way for dealers to install peripherals without access to the customer's account?"

"Bang on target. It's called Pre-Auth."

Jitterbug pulled up a photo on his Tile, featuring a black handheld scanner unit designed like a handgun, apparently made to scan Humanoid base units. It had a numeric pad and a small screen on top.

"I've been wanting one of these for years. They're proprietary and only issued to accredited dealers," he said. "If we were to scan Espinoza's goggles with one of these, we'd get a four-digit PIN code on that display there, and that code would allow us to connect the stereo cameras, soon to be a brain scanner, to Espinoza's goggles."

"Four digits should be brute-forceable," West said.

"That's the spirit!"

•

A day and a half later, Kiss, Melissa, and BestBye were watching a movie in the lab's main room. Tomorrow, Agent Espinoza would hit the slopes in Tahoe, with or without them.

West and Jitterbug were still defeated by the Humanoid Pre-Auth code.

They had successfully recreated the wireless communication that the proprietary scanners sent out and gotten the goggles to *receive* PIN codes.

Their initial plan was to brute force it until they got the right PIN, but the goggles blocked code entries for twenty-four hours after five failed attempts. At that pace, it would take them almost three years to find the right code for Espinoza's goggles.

The movie ended and the rest of the team went home. Kiss had left West and Jitterbug in the Shaq with a mildly sarcastic, "Let us know if the trip is still on."

The lab was silent except for the ever-present fan noise.

Jitterbug looked at him. "I don't often pray when I hack, but I think we're at a point where we need a little divine inspiration. You pray?"

"Not really. Mom does. Or did."

Jitterbug folded his hands and closed his eyes. "Lord of all the earth, You hold the universe in Your hands. You have created all things large and small with intricate beauty and life. We seek Your wisdom and help as we try to hack these goggles in pursuit of salvation for the people who suffer under G20S. You are our Savior, our friend, and our hope. Amen."

Peace lingered. West felt good.

"I take it you go to church," he said to Jitterbug.

"I do. Rainbow Church is my new home after I had to leave my old community."

"*Had* to leave?"

"I'm from Cincinnati, Ohio. Got my family there, and my old church. But I had to leave it all behind."

West could sense grief. "What took you to SF?"

"It's a great place for gay people, so I don't mind living here. But I left because of some community members. I used to be African Union Baptist, and homosexuality is still hard to deal with for them. It's a 'don't ask, don't tell' kind of thing. I used to attend service as myself and do clubbing and dating as a made-up guy called Chad. It all worked fine until the government enforced GPI and my online identity was merged with my real ID. Some members of the church went on a witch hunt, scouring gay dating sites and social media for what they called fallen angels."

West rolled his shoulders. "What happened?"

Jitterbug sniffled. "They waited for me outside a club and beat me down like a dog."

"Oh, man."

West hugged his friend, and they sat folded over into each other's arms for a good while.

West felt Jitterbug's chin move against his shoulder as he spoke in a soft tone. "It's long gone. But that's why I left, and that's why I fight for people's right to keep secrets. There are so many out there willing to ruin your life because of their view of what love and life should be like. Now I'm part of the Rainbow Church in the city. God always finds a way."

They sat back up. Jitterbug dried his eyes and nodded toward the screen, where their Humanoid PIN code hack was still waiting for that divine inspiration.

"Let's go over this thing one more time," he said.

On the screen was the re-symbolicated, disassembled source code of the goggles' PIN verification. They had gone through it at least ten times in search of a bug to exploit.

The block mechanism was no more than eleven lines.

```
let result = authenticate(peripheral, pin);
if (result == WRONG_PIN) {
    numberOfTries++;
    storeSynchronized(numberOfTries);
    if (numberOfTries < 5) {
        callback(NEW_TRY);
    } else {
        start24HourBlock();
        callback(BLOCKED_24H);
    }
} else {
    callback(CORRECT_PIN);
}
```

"The goggles send the PIN code to the authenticate function. We've convinced ourselves that there are no bugs there," Jitterbug said, resting his head on a balled-up hand under his chin.

"Right. Then the result is immediately checked," West said. "If it was a failed attempt, it increases the fail counter and stores it."

"Then comes the check for max number of tries. I can hear how I'm repeating myself. Less than five means regular fail. Five or more means twenty-four-hour block. We don't seem to be able to make the number of tries be negative."

"And we've checked that the twenty-four-hour time function is sound with time zones and all."

"Correct." Jitterbug closed his eyes. "But there was something you said just now."

"Failed attempt? Increases counter? Time zones?"

"No, it was something about checked."

"That the result is immediately checked?"

"Yes, the word *immediately*. There's a race condition here, right?" Jitterbug's eyes grew. "There is a microscopic time gap where the goggles have decided that the PIN was wrong, but they have not yet increased the fail counter."

West nodded. But how to exploit it? The two of them mulled it over in silence.

Then West put his hand on Jitterbug's shoulder. "We cut power to the processor right before it increases the counter."

"For realz. You're a freakin' genius, you are."

An hour later they had a stable exploit and texted the others triumphantly.

Tahoe is on! We have to reboot the module for every PIN we try, which takes 540 milliseconds. On average, we need 5,000 tries to brute force a four-digit PIN. 5,000 tries times 540 milliseconds equals 45 minutes. Worst case would be trying all 10,000 possible PINs which means ninety minutes. Give us an hour and a half with Espinoza's goggles and we pwn them.

CHAPTER THIRTY-THREE

Close Encounters

The crystal-blue water of Lake Tahoe rested in a giant mountain nest powdered in snow and decorated with pine trees. Kiss, Jitterbug, and West arrived in wonder at the Main Lodge by the foot of Mt. Rose just after nine o'clock in the morning.

"I'm gonna miss the chance to go down some of those slopes," Melissa had said when she announced that she and BestBye would stay behind and focus on where to replay the pass thought to log in to Espinoza's account.

West gazed at the mountaintop. He vaguely remembered the feeling in your feet and ankles after wearing ski boots a full day.

"Let's rent gear and start looking for Pinjo," Kiss said.

Pinjo was the decided-upon codename for Agent Espinoza. They would be on the lookout in two spots—West at Winters Creek Lodge and the other two by the Main Lodge.

West managed to find a seat outside the restaurant and sat down for his watch, with just one of his earphones in. To his right, there was a robot arm neatly storing people's skis in a rack. According to instructions on a sign, you scanned your GPI when you handed the robot your skis and then again to get them back.

He noted that the pegs that kept the skis in place in the rack were slightly bent outward on the far side, indicating that the bot was probably off calibration by a few millimeters.

Machines still don't do what we want them to do, just what we tell them.

An hour and a half passed without a sign of their target.

West started worrying that he wouldn't recognize the agent in ski goggles. It was time for a bathroom break. He sat down in one of the stalls, got out his Tile, and started flicking through photos from the past few weeks. So much had happened.

He stopped at a photo of Kiss.

I can't believe I had sex with her.

The heater in the restroom switched off, and as the fans came to a halt, he could hear he was not alone. Two or three stalls away there was someone. A rhythmic sound of clothes moving. Was someone jerking off in there? Or having sex?

He tried to not listen, but it was impossible. Instead, he got out of his stall in a calm manner. Meanwhile, the person, alone or not, hit the apex with a few grunts.

A toilet flushed, and a stall door swung open at the far corner of the room. West stared at himself in the mirror, making sure he showed no meaningful smile, no blush, no nothing.

He turned his eyes slightly to the left to greet the approaching man in the mirror.

It was Agent Espinoza. No glasses but the same bloodred handkerchief around the neck. Or wait, this handkerchief had embroidery. But it was Espinoza all right.

West stopped rubbing his hands. The faucet poured over his wrists.

Espinoza spoke. "Girls are sexy when dey ski. You agree?"

Accent spot on. West nodded.

The agent chuckled. "Don't tell me you don't rip one off in de men's room every now and den."

Espinoza barely washed his hands and instead dampened a paper towel and pressed it over his eyelids like a cooling mask. He let his thumb and index finger roll over his eyeballs.

"Mah eyes dry up," he uttered under the towel.

A few seconds passed. The agent lifted the towel, threw it away, and looked at himself in the mirror before heading out.

West stood staring into the mirror.

He dried his hands and followed suit. Espinoza's friend Elsa waited outside the lodge, and the two started to ski slowly toward the Blazing Zephyr lift. West got his earpieces in and discreetly took a photo with his Tile and distributed it to Kiss and Jitterbug before following on his skis.

"Did you interact with him?" Kiss's voice asked.

"Yes," West mumbled.

"Would he recognize you within an hour?"

"Yes."

"Does he have the right ski goggles?"

Fuck.

He increased his speed to catch up with the agent and turned around shortly after he passed him, only to feel his right ski shoot out at an angle and his upper body heading straight for ground level.

He tumbled over and spat out snow.

"You need help?" It was Elsa, who had stopped to check on him.

"No thanks, I'm good."

Espinoza stood alongside her, looking upslope. West couldn't believe it. After all the work he and Jitterbug had done to fit the brain scanner into a pair of Eyes OTG, the broad strap on Espinoza's goggles read "Z" with a tilted swoosh on each side like Saturn's rings. The side of the plastic read "Kea." These goggles weren't even Over the Glasses.

Espinoza gave a nod upward and started moving. Elsa followed.

West got up and brushed the snow off his jacket before sharing his discovery with the others.

Jitterbug commented less than half a minute later. "Zion Kea. They come in two sizes. Can you measure them?"

West looked uphill. Espinoza and Elsa were getting into a lift chair. He dashed up and got in line. Nine people between him and his target.

Two chairs between us. I won't be able to keep up downhill.

West got in with three others and sat down on the far right side. The seats were heated.

Before they even began to move, his rented goggles started playing a commercial for something called "Bundle Dating." A cheerful voiceover said, "Did you know most people are considered 10–20% more attractive when they are among friends? There's no I in team and no single in bundle. Build your bundle today and start dating at a higher level. Wink either eye twice to get started."

An automated safety rod was slowly lowered toward their laps.

West ducked beneath the bar and jolted out of the chair. "I got it!" he shouted as he dodged an angry lift guard and headed out of the crowd, back toward the Winters Creek Lodge.

He almost bumped into a guy as he opened the door to the lodge's men's room. The trash bin was half full. He poured the used paper towels on the floor. There it was—Espinoza's face mask. It still had wrinkles from where the agent had massaged his eyes and a stretched line where it had arched his nose. West took measurements with his Tile and sent it to Jitterbug along with a brief explanation of what it was.

Jitterbug concluded that the glasses on the agent's head had to be size large.

Soon enough they got Kiss's report from the on-site store. "They haven't even heard of the brand."

There was silence for a while.

"One of you needs to break his goggles," said Jitterbug.

Chapter Thirty-Four

Bunny Time

"What?" Kiss replied.

"If we break his, he'll buy new ones from what's available," Jitterbug replied. "And I can buy a duplicate pair and make the scanner fit."

"I'll do it," West said.

She'll be impressed.

"No one's physically engaging with Pinjo," Kiss burst out. "You said you need on average forty-five minutes to brute force the PIN. That should be enough time to also make the scanner fit on his Zions."

"Risky," Jitterbug mumbled.

"You think *that's* risky?"

The matter was settled; Jitterbug would have to hack the PIN and change the shape of the scanner at the same time.

•

West, still at Winters Creek, spotted Espinoza and Elsa dropping off their ski wear in the designated lobby area and entering the restaurant almost two hours later. He sent a message to the others.

> Pinjo's goggles are hanging in plain sight here in the lobby.
>
> I saw a maintenance room we can use.

Kiss arrived first. She distracted the guy watching people's clothes and gear with a hilarious story about snowboarding and how she had misunderstood the term *Goofy*. Meanwhile, West snatched the agent's goggles.

Soon enough, West and Jitterbug were in the maintenance room.

Jitterbug got the agent's goggles on to have a look at the heads-up display. "Shoot. It's syncing images for his account." Jitterbug took the goggles off, and his face wrinkled up in a grimace. "It'll slow us down with that thing eating CPU cycles in the background."

"Can we make the sync fail?"

Jitterbug looked at him. "I suppose I could just kill his network module for a while."

Forty minutes went by. Kiss texted West.

> Got it working yet? Pinjo and his gal just got their coffee. You've got 10 more minutes.

> We've got everything fitted but still no luck with the PIN. I'll join you. J!t doesn't need me here.

West found Kiss just outside the archway between the lobby and the restaurant. They made sure not to look at each other.

"Can you distract them to give Jit a little more time?" he whispered.

"Maybe. Check to the left." Kiss nodded discreetly inward in the direction of a small counter in dark wood. "See that? The hostess uses some kind of tablet Tile." Kiss pulled out her OmniPort drive from her left pocket. "Bunny time."

West saw Kiss's thumb flip the drive's switch to "Die."

The restaurant's hostess was talking to a couple of guests. "Just one more minute. They're getting your table ready. How was your day so far?" Not long thereafter she took her tablet under her arm and escorted the guests into the restaurant.

Kiss slowly moved up to the ebony-stained counter and squatted as she swung around to the back of it.

West saw the charger stand for the tablet move on the countertop as Kiss fiddled with its cables.

Kiss got back to him by the entrance right before the hostess came back. The hostess put her tablet flat on the countertop, not in the charger.

Kiss walked up to her with a smile. "Hi! What's the waiting time right now?"

"Welcome! We can get you a table pretty much right away. For how many?" She grabbed the tablet.

"I'll have to go get my girlfriend first. You don't need to hold a table for us. Just checking." Kiss glanced at the tablet. "You know those should be charged as often as possible, right? You get better battery life that way."

"Oh, I did not know that. Thank you." The hostess flipped it up and connected it. "There we go."

It took the restaurant staff fifteen minutes to reboot the system and resurrect all the guests' tabs after Kiss's Bunny killed the tablet. Espinoza got furious over at his table and demanded to be checked out first.

West texted Jitterbug.

He'll be out in a minute.

Still no luck with the PIN.

Shit.

I wouldn't put it that way,
but yeah.

Espinoza succeeded in cutting the line, paid, and went to pick up his stuff. His voice blared in the lobby's hallway. "Where the fuck are mah goggles?"

Chapter Thirty-Five

I Can Read Your Thoughts, Mr. Espinoza

The young man in charge answered Espinoza sheepishly. "I'm sorry, sir. We will try to find them for you. But we cannot be responsible for any equipment you leave here."

"I'd like to see de manager."

"Absolutely." The man was just about to call his boss when she entered through an office door in the back.

She went straight up to Espinoza. "What seems to be the problem, sir?"

"I left mah stuff here just like everybody else. I come back and mah goggles are gone. Dis boy here has no clue where dey went."

"Sorry, are these yours?" It was Jitterbug. He held the agent's ski goggles in his right hand. "I must have taken them by mistake."

Espinoza struggled to wind down his anger as he snatched the goggles out of Jitterbug's hand. He held them in front of his eyes for a couple of seconds. "De fucking thing is not done syncing."

He turned to the clerk and his manager. "You two should do a better job protecting other people's property."

The agent and Elsa left. West, Jitterbug, and Kiss stood looking at each other, positioned separately in the lobby. They had reached the final stretch of capturing a Brazilian G20S agent's pass thought. All the gear to record and transfer Espinoza's brain waves was in place, hidden inside his goggles, and preauthorized with a brute-forced vendor PIN.

Outside, Jitterbug told them in a low voice, "You two can ski so you play a couple and get him to see the snowman. BestBye's compromise of the advertisement system is ready."

West watched Kiss getting dressed.

They didn't say anything to each other as they caught up with and followed Elsa and Espinoza to the main lift from Winters Creek, but managed to get right behind them in line.

"Can we join you?" Kiss asked Espinoza in a sugarcoated voice. Her smile was a winner.

"Beautiful ladies are always welcome." Espinoza showed some teeth too, making sure to sit directly next to Kiss, with Elsa to the far left.

West felt a drop of sweat building up on his upper lip. The ad stream they would inject into the system would start with a real commercial for South American tourism to catch Espinoza's attention and then a fake one featuring the snowman.

A minute up the lift, Kiss nodded to him. He triggered BestBye's hack and could see the tourism ad roll on the inside of his own goggles. They were now at countdown, thirty seconds until the snowman would show up.

West leaned forward to check in on the agent. He wasn't wearing his goggles.

West poked Kiss's waist with his elbow while pointing at his own eyes.

She turned around and fired off another of her gorgeous smiles. "Would you like me to take a photo of you two?" She pulled her glove off and held her hand out to Espinoza as if to receive his Tile.

Twenty seconds to go.

"Yes, please," Elsa replied and gave her Tile the voice command "Câmera" as she stretched across Espinoza's lap to give it to Kiss.

Fifteen seconds.

"You should wear your goggles, man," Kiss said as she framed the perfect picture on the screen in her hands.

"You think so? I hate dos ads." Espinoza looked at his goggles in his hands. Seven seconds.

"Hey, it's a skiing photo, right?"

Espinoza put them on.

West saw the South America ad end as Kiss took three rapid photos.

The snowman ad made the agent freeze for a second, or so it seemed. A moment in time recorded as neural oscillations from Agent Espinoza's frontal lobe.

West pressed a key on his Tile to save the exact timestamp.

Chapter Thirty-Six

Make Amends

They didn't dare stay in Tahoe for the night, which meant a late drive back to the Bay Area. The car's automation did a good job of managing the wintery roads while the three Survivors rejoiced in their success.

"I hope the recording really unlocks his account," West said to Kiss, with whom he shared the back seat.

"Tonight, I don't care. We did a damn fine job. You did a damn fine job," she said, giving him a nod.

"I got lucky with the snowman."

"The only thing I know about luck is that the more I practice, the luckier I get," Jitterbug said from the front.

Lucky or not, West felt good. Vancouver had been so much of Best-Bye's show, whereas this thing he had taken major part in. He hadn't even left California, which meant he wouldn't have to lie to his parole officer in two weeks.

Or wait, he'd been to Vancouver since the last time he saw her. His guts churned. At least he wasn't the only one lying in those meetings.

"Did the two of you check your blockchains?" he asked his car mates.

"I did," Jitterbug said from the front. "Not as much there on my faith and church as I suspected. More political stuff, like records of every voter call I've ever made and movements I've supported for queers and home-less people."

West looked at Kiss.

"Uh-uh," she said. "Don't doomscroll your own past. I claim the right to forget."

"You mean the right to be forgotten?"

The EU case where a Spanish man won the right to be erased from web searches had just been settled as West and Melissa went on trial for their NSA hack. He remembered it as a profound victory for the little guy.

"Nope," Kiss said. "The right to forget. Life is miserable enough as it is. I don't want to be reminded of old shitty decisions or screwups or shitposts. People change and cope. Have you heard of data decay?"

West shook his head.

I don't even know what shitposts are.

"Data decay makes all your messages and social media posts degrade over time and eventually go away, like human memory. If you periodically go read your old email, it stays fresh, but if you haven't touched it in years, you just get a summary and eventually nothing. Man, don't look at your blockchain. Live your life."

She was right. Fretting over what fabricated data points might be on his blockchain was what Timothy wanted him to do. Otherwise, he wouldn't have said anything. Actually reading it might be worse, like knowing about a medical condition that can end your life at any moment.

They stopped for burgers at the scenic In-N-Out in the old gold rush city Placerville just as the sun set over the Sierra Nevada foothills.

"What are you two doing for Thanksgiving?" he asked the others as they lingered, eating gratuitous fries.

"Annual dinner for the homeless," Jitterbug proclaimed. "Five thousand meals, lots of work, lots of love. You should come, both of you."

"Juneau for me, and it's going to be effing cold," Kiss said.

•

The smell of roasted turkey, mashed potatoes, and gravy seeped in through the poor window seals in West's apartment. Probably through the walls too. It was the fourth Thursday of November, and everyone was celebrating.

He sat at his kitchen table in silence, recalling Agent Timothy's words: "I have dirt on you" and "I will figure out who or what is protecting you."

He really should stop thinking about it.

The "who" or "what" was protecting him was more puzzling than the kompromat, though. Who on the inside would do that, and why? If there was a "what" that was protecting him, it could simply be his fake IDs. He probably caused all kinds of weird mismatches in US G20S data collection. They had managed to detect him with a bag over his head, so they clearly had a multipronged surveillance machine on his tail.

He looked at the entrance door to his apartment. Melissa could help him get a good lock with physical keys. Why hadn't he told her about Agent Timothy's intrusion?

Another puff of Thanksgiving scent reached his nostrils. Soon his neighbors would all be stuffing themselves to the brim in the company of loved ones. Well, there was no guarantee of love. Melissa hadn't seemed happy about seeing her parents, and BestBye had muttered sullenly about New York.

He was alone, but he had much to be thankful for this past year: his mom's fight and sacrifice, his release, his new friends, and the fact that he had money to spare after selling his mom's house.

His late prison buddy Jeremy spoke about life on the inside early on: "We do have days in here when everyone isn't plotting against you. Thanksgiving is one of them." It wasn't just peaceful in prison during the holiday season but also a comparative feast in food. Real pecan pie. "Then comes Christmas and New Year's and another notch on the wall," Jeremy had continued.

West had counted his years by pencil.

He got his prison notebook out from the drawer in his bedside table and opened it at random about a third in.

Things to do when I get out:
1. Eat good food.
2. Have sex.
3. Go to Hawaii.
4. Do something good for people.

The first three were superficial things the other inmates would go on about. He remembered how writing those points felt dishonest, as if he wrote them for someone else. There had always been the fear of someone digging through your stuff and exploiting any perceived weaknesses. The fourth was honest but so utterly vague.

Sitting here didn't get him closer to any of the items on the list or any other goals in life.

He picked up his jacket, got his shoes on, and exited. His mom would have wanted him to do something about item number four on that list, and the homeless people in line at Jitterbug's church deserved pie. Real pecan pie.

•

After toiling away for four hours with Jitterbug and his community, and seeing the thankful, unpolished smiles of so many humans who had come up short in the lottery of life, West's hands had burn marks, his feet had blisters, and his mind had peace.

They sat down to eat together with the other church members.

"People need to be empathetic," Jitterbug said, looking into the distance. "It makes us whole. Working like this is a gift."

"I remember when I was a kid, Mom used to tell me that giving is more gratifying than being given to. I didn't believe her." West pondered.

"Did you see many of the homeless have GPI bands?"

"I did."

"That's fairly recent. It was pushed as an equality thing, but you knew what was behind it when police started harassing the ones without."

"Some of them asked me if they should scan it."

"I've made sure we don't. So what if a homeless person snags a double meal every now and then?"

West knew what it was like to never get to decide for yourself what to eat or how much.

"Oh, did you see the news dump today?" Jitterbug asked, fishing up his Tile from his pocket.

West shook his head, mouth full of green beans.

"Amendment," Jitterbug muttered as he beamed over a news article to West.

Amended Peaceful Assembly

In a landmark proposal to Congress, the Republican Party today made good on their promise to push for regulation of political protesting. The GOP wants carrying your GPI to be mandatory for a public assembly of more than fifty people to be considered peaceful.

The First Amendment to the United States Constitution — adopted in 1791 — prevents the government from making laws which regulate the right to peaceably assemble or the right to peacefully protest.

"The tension around political protests has historically led to violence, looting, and chaos, and the perpetrators have often escaped justice by wearing masks or otherwise obscuring their faces. The First Amendment guarantees the right to peaceful assembly. We think law enforcement's ability to identify and arrest criminals who are not peaceful will support the guarantee of the First Amendment," said Republican Speaker of the House, Dick Johnson.

This article's sources are GPI-validated.

Chapter Thirty-Seven

Wilshire Grand

Monday morning. The big screen in the lab featured photos of the beautiful Wilshire Grand skyscraper in Los Angeles. Brazil's Consulate General resided in one of its office suites.

While West and the others were in Tahoe, BestBye and Melissa had done a deep dive into how G20S agents operate outside their own countries in search of the right spot to replay Espinoza's pass thought.

G20 countries were required to offer maximum-security network connections at all their embassies and consulates so that summits were possible in all major cities with no delay in communications back to the representatives' countries.

BestBye explained the floor layout of the majestic building to Kiss, Jitterbug, and West.

"Ground to floor 2 have meeting rooms, a ballroom, and retail with two luxury clothing stores and a large coffee shop. Floors 3 through 29 are the building's office space. Brazil's consulate is on floor 28. Hotel rooms are between floor 31 and 69, with the lobby and sky bar all the way up on floor 70. Restaurants on floors 71 and 72, and finally a rooftop pool."

Melissa nodded with a tight expression. "We need an excuse to scout floor 28."

"I did a search on businesses in the building. Law firms, model agencies, consultancies, startups, and a few other consulates."

"We could apply for a job, a couple of us," West suggested. "Maybe there's a startup there looking for some hacking talent."

"Or we could hit up one of those model agencies." Kiss pouted her lips.

"Nah, you can't lose enough weight in time," BestBye said.

"Excuse me?"

"Hey. We're hackers, not women longing to be part of some patriarchal bullshit," Melissa said, pulling out her Tile. "I like West's idea. Best, Kiss, and I start working on our cover letters. West and Jit, you make a plan for scouting the general premises."

"Okay, boss." Kiss rolled her eyes.

•

Melissa, BestBye, and Kiss sent their résumés to a startup in personal protection called Proté-J. The description included "active defense," which was code for offensive hacking.

Not revealing their relationship, they passed phone screening and got the hiring manager to schedule them for onsite interviews, all on the same day, December 5th.

CHAPTER THIRTY-EIGHT

The Grand Scheme

The drive down from San Francisco to Los Angeles helped West shake off his recent dreary meeting with his parole officer. They had spent significant time on the passing of his mom with an undertone of "See what you've done here, West." The next meeting would be in early February with Christmas and New Year in between. He wondered if he should spend those, too, with Jitterbug and his church.

They parked, or rather, the car parked itself in North Hollywood, and the team took the subway, getting off at 7th and Metro.

At over a thousand feet, the Wilshire Grand Center cut through west downtown like a blade. The sun had risen an hour ago and glimmered on the building's high-performance glass and slender metal seams. In the skyscraper's ground-level lobby, an enormous Christmas tree stretched toward the glass ceiling. Video adverts for upcoming events moved on the lower half of the lobby's glass walls.

Jitterbug and West scouted both the public ground level and the hotel lobby on the top floor while the others got interviewed.

Early afternoon, the whole team met in a booth at the sky bar. West ordered ale from a San Diego brewery for himself and Kiss and got a "Not bad, Jon Snow" stamp of approval.

Melissa raised a dirty dry martini. "A toast to ourselves."

"As no one else is likely to concern themselves with our welfare." Jitterbug finished her sentence.

Melissa grimaced as the fiery liquid trickled down her throat. "What do we have?"

BestBye went first. "The Brazilian consulate's badging system uses

GPI plus optical RFID, which requires line of sight. I don't think that's a viable way in."

"I'd rather not do a break-in with any risk of people still inside the offices," Melissa said. "For all we know, the consulate may be staffed twenty-four seven."

West was eager to tell them what he and Jitterbug had found. "The lobby elevators skip the office floors, so we can't use *them* to get to the consulate. But if we need access to any of the special floors—the basement and floors 55 and 72—we found a trick for the fingerprint reader." He put on a clever face. "I tailgated a staff guy who used his thumbprint to go to the basement. Halfway down, I discreetly pressed floor 55."

"No new fingerprint scan needed?" Melissa guessed.

"You got it," Jitterbug said. "After someone with access authenticates, as long as the elevator is still in motion, you can go to *any* restricted floor."

"Nice. The office elevators at the north entrance had a fingerprint system too. Probably the same flawed one. I tried to access the basement and floor 30 through the stairs, but they end up at locked doors."

West reacted. "Thirty was missing from the building layout, right?" he said. "I remember it wasn't in the description BestBye gave, but I thought it was a silly off-by-one."

BestBye pulled up the Wilshire Grand document on her Tile and checked her notes. "You're technically correct, West. The best kind of correct."

"Probably a mechanical floor," Melissa speculated as she took on her martini again. "Modern skyscrapers have sturdy cores with struts stretching out to the walls to keep the whole thing stable. Called outriggers. You saw them in the office space during our interviews this morning, right?" She looked at Kiss and BestBye. "They cut diagonally through two or more floors, and those floors are often used for central plumbing, elevator machine rooms, window washing equipment, that sorta stuff."

Kiss was intrigued. "How come you know about skyscraper mechanical floors?"

"Property maintenance training for a part-time job in Pittsburgh." Melissa twisted her martini glass back and forth between thumb and index finger, and her eyes started wandering as if she were processing something. "I might have a plan for how to get into the consulate without a badge. Those struts go through gaps in the floor, with rubber fittings to allow for movement. That means there's physical access from floor 30 to the offices on floor 28. We just need to figure out how to clear the office spaces on 29 and 28."

"What about a good old fire alarm?" West suggested.

"Maybe. It would have to be on floor 29. Skyscrapers have high-rated firewalls and special rules for evacuation. Only people on the affected floors and the floors immediately above and below are required to get out."

"I assume you know that from training too." Jitterbug smiled.

"Mhm."

BestBye put her Tile between them on the table. "I took a photo of the small elevator lobby on floor 28 when I was checking out the consulate's badging system. Looks like a regular fire alarm pull station. It has a plastic stopper cover with a horn. You won't go unnoticed if you open it."

Melissa shook her head slowly. "Even if one of you triggers it after I get to floor 30, it's going to take me time to get into the consulate, find and log in to the G20S system with the pass thought, and get back out. They'll have the false alarm figured out before I'm done."

"How about a real fire?" Kiss looked disturbingly excited.

"Yeah, what could possibly go wrong?" Melissa said with a smirk. "But what about a real fire *drill*? If they have one planned, maybe we can reschedule it."

It took the team an hour to figure out how to retrieve Wilshire Grand's internal calendar through the public event calendar on the hotel's website. A slight alteration to the query made it show the whole thing, instead of just the coming month.

Jitterbug searched it. "They do have a fire drill scheduled. In almost a year."

"Changing it in the calendar would be easy," Melissa said. "But no fire trucks will come unless we also change it on the fire department's side. It needs to be the real deal to give me enough time inside the consulate."

Kiss put her hands together in a clap. "Jit, check who set up the calendar event."

Jitterbug pulled up the details. "Looks like it was sent by a Captain Pence of the Los Angeles Fire Department, Station 3."

Kiss got earbuds in and asked her Tile to call the Wilshire Grand reception.

"Human, please. … No, human, please." She rolled her eyes.

"Good afternoon, Christy. This is Carla Westin, secretary of Captain

Pence of the Los Angeles Fire Department, Station 3. How are you today?"

Polite phrases were exchanged.

"We have a fire drill scheduled for the Wilshire Grand on Monday, November 25th next year, correct?"

The other side seemed to confirm.

"Exactly. There are some new regulations under Los Angeles Fire Code, chapter six, that go into effect at the start of the new year, and unfortunately the last drill we had with you did not cover all the inspections needed for compliance for high-rise office spaces. We can get you a one-month exception, but after that we're unfortunately looking at liability issues on your part. We are so sorry for not noting this earlier, and Captain Pence has told me to be extra flexible in finding a date and time that works for you to get this drill rescheduled for January. If you can provide us with three options, we will do our best to accommodate."

Kiss went silent for a while, listening closely, and scribbled down three dates on her Tile.

"Thank you so much for your cooperation. Again, Captain Pence and his department are so sorry for this inconvenience. If it's any comfort to you, I can say you are not alone. Nine other high-rise buildings are in a similar situation downtown."

A few more courtesies and the call was over.

West was stoked. "Wow."

"One more to go." Kiss initiated another call.

"Human, please."

"Hi! This is Christy Morse calling you from Wilshire Grand Center, the executive office. May I speak with Captain Pence, please?"

A respectful greeting later, she moved right ahead. "We have a fire drill scheduled for the Wilshire Grand Center November 25th next year, correct? … We are expecting VVIP guests to one of our office floors in February, and the Department of Homeland Security has requested we do a fire drill before that since it was more than two years ago we had our last one. Would it be possible for your department to reschedule for January? I do realize this is short notice."

Kiss explained the sensitive nature of the visit and that she could not share further details. "Thank you, Captain Pence, I appreciate it. We have three preferred dates."

A short negotiation followed.

"Yes, you can just go ahead and reschedule, and I'll accept the invite on our end as confirmation. Thank you so much for making this work, Captain Pence. On behalf of the whole Wilshire Grand, I'd like to wish you a Merry Christmas and a Happy New Year. Again, thank you."

Kiss started a repeated refresh of the calendar view on the Wilshire Grand webpage. Three minutes later, the event change came in from Captain Pence's office, and reception accepted it right away.

"Yay, we get the holidays off. January seventh, shit is going down."

CHAPTER THIRTY-NINE

G20S: A Call from Canada

"Dr. Kawasaki, you have a call from Canada over the Five Eyes link." The ops guy looked nervous.

"Is that stuff still in use?" She followed him to the operations room and grabbed the wired phone device. "Kawasaki speaking."

"Dear Dr. Kawasaki, this is Commander Pelletier with Canadian G20S. Sorry to bother you. How are you this afternoon?"

"I'm doing well, very well indeed. And you?"

"Decent, but not quite as neat as I'd like it."

Kawasaki smiled. They weren't using video after all. "Why are you not using a GPI connection?" she said. "I have no way of knowing who I'm talking to."

"Well, the Five Eyes link isn't exactly unauthenticated. But I can send you a signed message as an out-of-band confirmation."

Dr. Kawasaki waited in silence for Pelletier's ping to arrive.

"Okay, proceed," she told the Canadian.

Pelletier exhaled audibly before speaking. "We're in a, should I say, sticky situation, and I'd rather not make this official G20S business. That's why I opted for a more restricted channel. We had an incident almost two months ago, an intrusion, a physical intrusion."

"You mean a break-in?"

"Yes. Some internal documents were stolen, and we have been on an arduous hunt for the perpetrator ever since—a woman identified as Svecia Jarlsberg. She falsely stated her name as Miniona Styx. She's an American citizen, but we're having trouble finding her. Her G20S data is sparse and restricted."

"Are you saying it's taken you two months to find a woman you know the GPI of? It seems you should have been more focused on your duties than on your career."

"I'm sorry?"

"I trust you can handle a simple thief. Why are you contacting me on this matter?"

"I do realize it sounds odd, and again, sorry for bothering you. At first, we handled this as a domestic investigation, but this woman's records are restricted in a way that I frankly don't understand. It's almost as if she's under US G20S protection or maybe has a covert ID. We can't get a normal hit on her in any system. This has led us to believe we might be looking at … counterintelligence."

Kawasaki wrinkled her nose. "From us?"

"I hope not. And I'm not pointing any fingers. We just need help in figuring this out. All instances within your organization have pointed upward when asked, so now I'm calling you."

"I see. Can you share with me what you have on her? Photos, queries you've made, and what she stole?"

"I'm afraid we can't disclose what she stole, but the rest I can get to you within the hour. Do you mind if we keep this between us?"

"I'm a professional, not a whistleblower."

Chapter Forty

Self-Signed

Melissa had given herself a margin of ninety minutes to get to the skyscraper's mechanical floor before the ten thirty fire drill.

She wore a stolen light beige uniform with the Wilshire Grand logo on the back and carried a large toolbox. In it she had a bunch of tools and gear that any HVAC technician would bring.

The toolbox also held her Survivor Kit, a mesh nylon skull mask, a neck pouch with wet wipes, and a small bottle of Super Lube oil. At the bottom was Jitterbug's device to reproduce Agent Espinoza's pass thought.

Her opportunity to piggyback on someone in the elevator presented itself at 09:18.

"Happy New Year," said the short, chubby man wearing the same beige uniform as she. He waved her into the elevator on the ground floor, and Melissa noted that he was already authenticated to go to the basement. She pressed 30 on the touch screen. The hack worked; no new fingerprint scan was needed.

"You're actually supposed to put your thumb on there even though I already did." The man smiled and pointed at the fingerprint reader. The elevator doors shut, and they started to move down. "I know it doesn't require it when a coworker has already pressed that thing, but Robertson says we should do it anyway." He put one hand over the other on his belly. "You new here?"

"Yes." She moved her toolbox to her left hand and reached out to shake his hand. "I'm Beth. Nice to meet you." She had created the HVAC engineer Bethany Hill to not burn one of her permanent fake IDs.

"Hi, Beth! I'm Carl." The skin of his hand was thick and dry. "Why don't you join us for morning coffee? That's where I'm headed." The elevator slowed down as it reached the basement.

"I really should go check the vent up on 30. Thank you, though."

"Your loss."

The doors opened, and Carl took a step out, then turned around.

He put his foot in the doorway to stop the elevator from closing. "Hey, since you're new and all, can you just do the thumb thing for me, please? I see you're going to a restricted floor."

"Sure. But I don't recall registering my fingerprint." She pushed her thumb onto the glass surface on the left of the keypad. An LED strip blinked red.

"Try your other thumb."

Red again.

"I guess you'll have to join me after all. Robertson will get you set up in no time."

Ten minutes later, she found herself put away in a small, windowless office. The manager—tall Mr. Robertson—obviously didn't recognize her as a new hire, and things went sour from there. Through the wall, she heard the chubby man Carl and Mr. Robertson debate whether they should call the cops or Wilshire management.

Carl was furious. "This could be a fucking burglary. She was headed for floor 30."

"Calm down. She's wearing company clothes. Where did she get those from you suppose, huh? This could all be a misunderstanding."

"She probably stole the clothes."

"Nonsense. And what's so interesting about the mechanical floor? It's not like we have money there."

"What if she's an arsonist?"

"Carl. I'll take care of this. Go have coffee with the others. They're halfway through the break."

There was some mumbling, and things calmed down. She checked her Tile—sixty minutes to the fire drill and no carrier service.

They hadn't bothered locking the door to the office she was in since you could unlock it from the inside. Could she run for it? The manager would notice for sure, and she'd be no closer to floor 30. Was violence an option? Nah, there had to be another way.

She looked around. In the back of the room was a small desk with a laptop computer, an office chair, and a used coffee mug. On the floor stood her toolbox and an empty trash can. Mounted on the right wall, about seven feet up, there was a Wi-Fi router.

She got the rogue network plug out of her Survivor Kit and put it in one of the power outlets under the desk. It detected three protected Wi-Fi networks, and the strongest signal by far was for a network called WilshGra_302. She configured the plug to broadcast a password-protected Wi-Fi hot spot with the same network name.

There was no visible power cable going to the wall-mounted router. No external antennas either. Its front panel was easy to remove. Underneath was a power LED, two Phillips screws securing a lid, and a sticker with regulatory information.

She carefully unscrewed the lid. The whole electronic package came out of its plastic socket with just a power cord tethering it to the wall. She cut its power.

"Now we wait," she said to herself as she put her ear to the wall.

Soon enough, the manager sputtered a few invectives on the other side and connected his PC to her hot spot. Her rogue network plug received the Wi-Fi password "LakersForever8."

He would not be happy unless her plug actually gave him network access, so she plugged the Wi-Fi router back in and connected the rogue plug to it using the "LakersForever8" password. With this, she could create a bridge so that Robertson's computer got access too, *through* her equipment.

Her data detectors started looking at what Robertson's computer was doing on the network. Fifteen encrypted web sessions, a few software update checks, and an encrypted chat protocol. The chat was connected directly to an IP address, so the server couldn't be using a proper security certificate.

She made her network plug intercept the chat with a self-signed certificate using the exact same organization details as the chat server. This would prompt Robertson about a bad certificate. He might not accept it, but if he did, she could see all messages going back and forth.

A connection was initiated. Melissa held her breath. Connection terminated.

Another connection came in. Again, terminated. Robertson was clicking "Deny" in the chat's security warning.

A third connection ... and he accepted.

Melissa exhaled. "When accept is the only way to get the work done."
The transcript of a chat between Robertson and someone else came
alive on her Tile's screen.

You there?

What happened?

> I lost connection. First the
> Wi-Fi, then a warning in the
> chat program.

> Anyway. Seems OK now.

> I've got her here in Yolanda's
> office.

Bethany Hill according
to the GPI logs from
the entrance. No LAPD
records.

Did she say anything about
why she's here?

> Something about a vent. I
> can ask properly.

Please do. The only thing
that comes to mind is last
week's issue. But that was
hotel, not office.

> I'll go check.

There was movement on the other side of the wall. Melissa's eyes immediately went to the Wi-Fi module, which was hanging by its power
cable.

She shoved the electronics in place without the screws and snapped the cover back on. A second later, Robertson opened the door. He stopped in the doorway, holding the handle.

"What did you say you were here to work on again?"

"The vent up on floor 30. You had a problem with your fresh air ventilation in the hotel part, and I'm here to make sure the office floors don't have the same issue."

The manager sighed, looking irritated and relieved at the same time. "Why didn't you say so? And why the hell did you say you were employed here when you're not? We could have avoided this whole mess."

Melissa started sobbing. With all the tension, it wasn't hard to fake a few tears. "I'm very uncomfortable with men I don't know. Especially in confined spaces like an elevator. He started asking questions, and I just made shit up. I just wanted to get on with my work."

"Hey now, we'll straighten this out. If I can just get the contact details of your employer and double-check things, I'll get you started."

She theatrically pulled herself together. "Can I just use the restroom first?"

"Of course."

Melissa still had a faint Wi-Fi connection to her plug from inside the restroom and texted Kiss instructions to expect a call from Robertson and to convince him that Beth was there on a legitimate work order.

Kiss worked her magic, and next thing Melissa knew, the elevator stopped on floor 30. She was escorted in by Robertson himself.

It was a noisy space due to ducts, fans, and elevator motors. The ceiling height was at least double compared to the other floors Melissa had visited. She couldn't help but look at the outriggers—sets of majestic twin struts shooting up through the floor at a sixty-degree angle on each side and attached to the outer walls about halfway to the ceiling.

Robertson showed her around haphazardly.

"Call me if you need anything," he said as the quick tour ended. "You play nice up here, okay? We've got security cameras." He glanced toward the ceiling.

Melissa had already noted the cameras, especially the fact that the backside of a rack of computer network equipment was at a bad angle for them.

Chapter Forty-One

G20S: I Have an Identity for You

"Happy New Year, Pelletier, this is Dr. Kawasaki speaking."

"Nice to finally hear back from you. How are you?"

"Fine," Kawasaki said. "Your pings have not gone unnoticed. I have an identity for you, and it's neither Svecia Jarlsberg nor Miniona Styx. The woman who broke into your office space is Tsukiko Kawasaki."

She was taking a huge risk handing over a real US citizen's identity. But this had to stop, so she had made sure the ID would match the documentation the Canadians had on their intruder, and she had also made sure Tsukiko could not be found for questioning. As a bonus, it would keep Pelletier busy.

"A namesake," Pelletier commented.

"Kawasaki is a popular family name. I'm sending you our records on Tsukiko. Call me back when you have confirmed the identity."

"Do you know where she is? We need to question her."

"Sorry, I do not have time to run this investigation for you."

Chapter Forty-Two

Brazilian Haxx

Melissa walked around the mechanical floor on her own to get a good look at the metal struts. No one watching the camera feed could blame her for being amazed by these enormous pieces of engineering.

Between the struts and the wall was a triangular space about eight feet high and five feet long. The gap between the floor and the outrigger was fitted with an accordion seal. Probably fire-retardant rubber. Whatever damage she would have to do to get through it would be the least likely to be detected here on the outer side.

She estimated the width between the concrete slab and the strut to be seven or eight inches and instinctively put her hands on her butt cheeks. The cloth of her beige uniform glided over the synthetic, compressive leggings she wore underneath.

She could see the whole building sway in the wind by just watching the rubber expansion joint. It moved slowly like a giant lung.

She fiddled around until 10:25. Fire drills were no exact science, and the alarm could go off any minute now. There was enough HVAC equipment close by the networking rack for an excuse to work there a few minutes. She slowly got herself to the bad camera angle.

The thick door on the back of the rack was comprised of water-chilled coils. She gently opened it enough to get her hand in between the server and the lowest switch. Her fingers found the temperature sensor she had noted from the front, and it was easy to remove from its clip. She pulled it back and let it hang loose outside the rack.

Now she just had to wait for the LA Fire Department.

She plugged her ears in anticipation of the alarm. The wintery daylight made its way down the body of the high-rise and blended with the light of the mechanical room's fluorescent lamps.

Eeek, eeek. Melissa jolted. The alarm sound was very loud even with earplugs. This was it.

She lit her lighter and put the flame under the hanging temperature sensor. The rack's heat protection triggered within seconds, and the network's power supply shut down.

The security cameras would continue to work, but now they had nowhere to send their data. Everything they saw her do would be lost in time. "Like tears in rain," she said to herself as she clipped the temperature sensor back in place.

A few swift strides and she was at the outrigger. The accordion seal was thick and leathery. It was glued to the concrete slab but not to the outriggers. Still, there was absolutely not enough space for both her and the rubber in the narrow gap.

The opening in the slab was perpendicular to the floor, whereas the struts penetrated at an angle, which meant there would be an edge to pass before the gap would widen.

She made pilot holes in the seal with a hand drill, then widened them to about an inch with a wire cutter to be able to work it with a small reciprocating saw. The alarm kept blaring, and sweat dripped from her brow onto the industrial material she was cutting with muscle power.

Finally, she could remove the slice of rubber and look below with her Tile's flashlight. Less than ten inches down was an array of soundproof ceiling tiles.

The fire drill was fifteen minutes in. She lifted the closest soundproof tile up and put it aside. Below was someone's desk. No sign of movement.

She stripped to her workout clothes and wrapped the necessary tools and her neck pouch in her uniform before dropping it through the hole. It landed with a thump. No intruder alarm, at least no audible one.

She hid the toolbox, lubricated the butt of her leggings and the tips of her sports bra using the Super Lube, wiped her hands, put on work gloves and the skull mask, and gently clamped the brain wave emitter between her teeth.

The gap was so narrow that her buttocks had to be hand-pressed down, bit by bit. Excruciating pain ripped through her body as the rugged concrete edge pressed hard into her flesh. The movements of the building forced her to time her squeezes to when the gap was the largest. In between, the gap pushed her intestines to the sides. The plastic of Jitterbug's brain wave emitter crackled as she involuntarily bit down on it.

Inch by inch, she got through and dropped onto the desk below, easing her landing like a cat. This was the office of the startup they had interviewed for. On this floor, the outriggers went straight through the middle of the office space. Several computers were left unlocked, coffee maker on, whiteboards with notes on client assignments and customer training.

Security cameras were evenly spaced along the inner wall. Most likely, they used the skyscraper's network, which was dead. Regardless, unless she made a mess, no one would ever review the video recordings with her in them.

She got a chair onto the desk, wiped the concrete opening above, sprayed it with Dee N' A, and fitted the cut-out rubber seal and the soundproof tile back in place. Beads of sweat seeped through her nylon mask.

She crossed to the other side of the struts and found a flush handle in the floor. She pulled, and a heavy, two-inch-thick floor tile opened, struts continuing underneath. At the end there was another rubber seal. She let the tools work their magic once again.

The slide on top of the struts was easier than hanging off the slab, but the pain of another encounter with concrete against her butt was almost unbearable. She let out a whimper as she pushed through, again wiped the rugged edge, and closed the hole. She was inside Brazil's consulate.

The inner wall featured a huge consulate seal—a light blue circle with the Crux star constellation on top of a five-pointed star in alternating yellow and green with a red edge. Below it, a light blue ribbon read *República Federativa do Brasil 15 de Novembro de 1889* in gold letters. This was some sort of lockdown area.

To her left was a row of offices. One of the name tags read ABIN/ G20S. The door was locked and used physical keys. These people knew not to trust GPI locks.

She was just about to pull out her lock picks when she realized that traveling agents can't be walking around with keys for these offices. The consulate had to have the key.

She exited the office corridor and blocked its door with a replica of the FIFA World Cup trophy she found in a bookshelf. The space on the other side was open, segmented with five-foot wood panels plus an additional two feet of vertical glass on top.

Melissa searched under desks and in drawers. No keys. But under a table way in the back, together with various forms for visas and passports, she found a small safe with a number pad. She squatted and pulled the handle.

Locked, of course.

She could afford a few minutes to try to find the code since she knew the list of the most popular PIN codes by heart, and they gave her a pretty high chance of getting it right.

```
1234, 1111, 0000, 1212, 7777, 1004,
2000, 4444, 2222, 6969, 9999, 3333,
5555, 6666, 1122, 1313, 8888, 4321,
2001, 1010
```

No luck. She needed context, a distinctly Brazilian four-digit number.

A smile passed across her face as she remembered the consulate seal on the wall.

1889. Nope.

15th of November. 1115, 1511. The display still told her she was wrong. It would come down to picking the ABIN/G20S door lock after all.

As she was about to return the FIFA trophy to its shelf, she had one more hunch about the safe's PIN code. She hated being defeated by non-hackers. One more try.

Back at the safe, she entered 8068, the statistically *least* common four-digit PIN humans choose. The small electrical motors hummed as they pulled back the steel bolts and the safe opened. Someone at the consulate had tried to be smart.

Sure enough, she found the key.

The ABIN/G20S room was small and looked almost unused. No personal belongings and no signs of activity, just a wooden desk with a comfy black chair. Behind it, a window covered in thick privacy film, dimming the daylight to an eerie glow. On the desk was a large, curved screen, which lit up as she approached. Its networking icon indicated it was online, just as expected. These systems switched to whatever was available.

She sat down and put Jitterbug's brain wave emitter on the desk. Her pulse increased as she made her Tile output Espinoza's public GPI profile. An image of a snowman emerged on the screen, and a voice assistant greeted her—"Bem-vindo, Agente Espinoza."

Chapter Forty-Three

Keys to the Thiefdom

It was late Sunday, and BestBye was headed to the lab. She had stayed for the Anime Los Angeles convention after Melissa's successful consulate hack last week. Now she was asked to go check in on things. Probably for the best. Melissa had her reasons to be paranoid.

BestBye took the stairs as she always did. Cardio.

There was a note on the lab's door.

PLEASE RETURN THE KEYS TO THE LANDLORD ASAP. THANKS!

She froze her position so as to not make any sounds.

Was it a prank? Had they been thrown out? Or compromised?

She quietly walked up to the door and put her ear to it. There were sounds inside. Furniture moving around and a muffled female voice saying, "This place is clean. They wouldn't leave anything behind."

Whoever she was, she didn't sound like Melissa or Kiss. Then a male voice. "I'll have someone do a proper search. Detectors and all that."

The woman again, this time much closer to the door. "Sounds good. Let's go. We've got to report back on these pranksters."

BestBye dashed up the staircase to the floor above, hiding with pulse and adrenaline as company. As the apartment door opened, she slid her Tile slightly off the edge of one of the steps, just enough to give its wide-angle camera a chance to capture what happened below.

The woman and man came out, both in black suits. She in a baseball cap with an emblem BestBye had never seen before and no hair visible beneath it; he had blonde, ginger-tinted hair. They closed the door and locked it. They had keys.

The man removed the landlord's note. "Why haven't we banned physical keys already?"

They entered the elevator and left.

BestBye waited exactly five minutes, then walked down, checked for sounds inside, and unlocked the door. The inside looked different, bathing in sunlight. The intruders had opened the blinds, something the Survivors would never do.

There was not a single piece of technical equipment left; the big screen, her own rig, everything was gone. Only dust marks on the desks from screens and cables. It didn't look like there had been a traditional break-in though. No mess, nothing broken.

No need to look further. She had to get out of the building *now*.

It would be too risky to leave through the main entrance. Instead, she took to the back-street emergency exit. It had a set of metal fire stairs zigzagging their way down the backside façade of the building, squeaking as she descended.

The exit discharge to the street was through an extendable accordion ladder. She pulled the lever, and the scissor joints let out a high-pitched complaint as gravity did its job.

With just a few ladder steps remaining, she noticed a man approaching from her left. Dark complexion, pitch-black hair, maybe dyed, late thirties. He wore a khaki, double-breasted trench coat and appeared not quite adjusted to the winter temperature.

"Tsukiko Kawasaki?" the man said. "I'm Bala Singh." He extended his right hand well before it was possible to shake it.

BestBye began a ferocious ascent. Singh rushed toward her but not fast enough to reach her from the ground. He started climbing after her.

As soon as BestBye got to the landing above, she grabbed the crank to pull up the scissor ladder. Singh's added weight made it extremely heavy to turn. After two full revolutions of the crank, she could hear the man swearing below her. His coat was stuck in one of the closing joints, and the thick cotton wouldn't move or tear.

Singh started to undo his breast buttons one-handedly. With her full body weight, she managed to get the crank moving again, effectively decreasing the distance between her and Singh but also decreasing the distance between the steps of the ladder.

Singh had wriggled the coat halfway off his shoulders when two pieces of steel squeezed his left pinky. He let out a scream of absolute pain.

BestBye pushed the crank another half inch. The cry below intensified. She released the ladder with the lever, shooting her wounded opponent to the ground.

"That was a red choice." The voice was familiar, and close.

BestBye glanced over her shoulder. Haircut and posture produced an instant match in BestBye's memory—it was Commander Pelletier. She stood just a few feet behind her on the landing. "You need to make another choice, Tsukiko. Either red again and go up against a G20S commander, decorated for her skills in close combat, or a green choice and come with that same commander for a chat."

Neither of the two women moved. Below, Singh bemoaned his injury.

•

BestBye was handcuffed for the two-hour transport to an East Bay office space. They dropped off Singh at a hospital on the way.

BestBye kept trying to figure out why Pelletier and Singh called her by her sister's name. Could it be some misguided face recognition?

Tsukiko shouldn't be hard to locate as opposed to herself with her multiple identities and the flag in G20S's databases for secret identity.

Pelletier guided her detainee into an unused open-space area, and they sat down on either side of a regular desk. No time was wasted on small talk.

"Why did you break into our offices in Vancouver?" Pelletier asked.

"I don't know what you're talking about," BestBye replied monotonously.

Pelletier burst into a sarcastic chuckle, leaning back in her chair. "We know you're working with the director of US G20 Security, and we know you are related to someone important in the US government. Given your family name and what Mr. Singh has been able to find out, we think you're the niece of Dr. Kawasaki."

BestBye didn't respond, but her heart was racing. Pelletier and Singh had her mixed up with her sister, but they were close enough.

Pelletier continued. "You either help us figure out what Dr. Kawasaki is up to, or you come with us for prosecution back in Canada."

"You know nothing about me. What is it you want?"

"You broke into our offices and stole a security report. We want to know why, who you're working for, and where the report is now."

"If you press charges, you'll get nothing but trouble."

"I'm used to trouble."

The room went silent for several minutes as BestBye was given a chance to think it through.

Pelletier got a message on her Tile. With a swift move, she pulled a GPI wristband out of her pocket. "Wear this," she told BestBye. "You will be Grace Oshiro from here on. We're taking a government plane to Vancouver."

CHAPTER FORTY-FOUR

Compromised

Three days earlier.

•

Melissa's daring hack at the Brazilian Consulate lingered with the Survivors as they took a few days off from each other. Jitterbug had work to do at a homeless shelter, Kiss went to see friends in Nevada, BestBye stayed in Los Angeles to attend an anime convention, and Melissa healed her buttocks.

It was also a new year, and West was getting up early with the intention to make it a habit. He had shaved off half an hour per day, and by Friday he was up at seven with his mind set on watching some of the videos from the recently held Chaos Communication Congress in Germany.

He got fresh bags of coffee beans in his delivery locker on Thursdays and went down to get it. Inside the bag, on top of the beans, there was a piece of paper about the size of a label, with a strange message:

```
https://[FEDC:BA98:7654:3210:FEDC:-
BA98:7654:3210]:443/khjpgsdfi.html

Leaf PK SHA3-256
  09234807e4af85f17c66b48ee3bca89d
  ffd1f1233659f9f940a2b17b0b8c6bc5

Password:
  incorrectHorseBatteryStaple
```

Waaat? This is hacker catnip.

It was a link to a webpage called "khjpgsdfi.html." "Leaf PK" probably referred to "leaf public key." There was a hash of that key and a password.

This meant that whoever created this note wanted the reader to visit the link and be able to check that the server connection was not intercepted.

Could this be an ad from the coffee company? Geeks were caffeine targets, but this felt far out.

He copied the link and the hash with his Tile camera and downloaded the webpage. The server's public key matched the hash.

He loaded the file in a cleanroom browser window without network access and entered the password. A message was revealed.

```
How can a vendor that serves almost half
the market have "great" coffee? Great
means exceptional, outstanding, better
than the rest. At Luw4k Coffee, we give
you great coffee. Make it count! Visit
luw4k.coffee/gr8 for 10% off your next
purchase.
```

Damn, these ad people are smart.

He resorted to grinding beans and putting them to work in his coffee maker. As the first sip of fresh brew hit his tastebuds, he scrolled through what he had set out to do today—check out the talks from Chaos Communication Congress.

There was an interesting one on Wi-Fi hacking under the title "Why Fi When You Can Scry?" and a talk by a hacker who had hacked a microbrewery to change a beer recipe to her liking entitled "All Your Barley Are Belong to Us."

But the talk titled "Seeing is Believing, Not Knowing" really caught his attention. The presenters had de-anonymized decades of pixelated or blurred media photos of whistleblowers, arrested celebrities, and people under threat. Same thing for protected voices on radio, which historically had been anonymized through audio phase shifting, pitching, and layering, none of which resisted modern reversing.

He paused the video and thought about the underlying message. It was profound; what is considered secure today will inevitably be broken by the ever-increasing capacity of computers and artificial intelligence.

But there was something more that percolated in the back of his

mind. What was it? He closed his eyes, sifting through what the conference speakers had just said.

What you see is not all you get.

He opened his eyes again. Could there be something more to the
piece of paper in the coffee bag? Or in the encrypted webpage? Or in
the coffee ad?

Back at the browser tab, he read the Luw4k Coffee advertisement
again. He highlighted the text to move it over to an editor. Just as he hit
the shortcut for copy, he saw something. There seemed to be whitespace
characters trailing the end of the message.

He pasted the string into his editor and put the caret at the end of the
sentence, after "… off your next purchase." By tapping the right and left
arrow keys he could step through several invisible characters, some wider
than a regular space, some with no width at all.

He wrote a script to reveal all invisible characters with their character
codes.

```
How\u2061 can\u2063 a\u2060 vendor\
u2061 that\u2061 is serving over half
the market have "great" coffee? Great
means exceptional, outstanding, better
than the rest. At Luw4k Coffee, we give
you great coffee. Make it count! Visit
luw4k.coffee/gr8 for 10% off your next
purchase.\u2067\u2061\u2062\u2062\u2060\
u2064\u2060\u2061\u2060\u2061\u2061\
u2066\u2063
```

There were in total eighteen hidden characters, all between the codes
\u2060 and \u2067.

This has to be an encoded message.

He extracted the invisible character codes in the three reasonable
ways you could interpret them—all four digits, the last two digits, and
just the last digit.

```
2061 2063 2060 2061 2061 2067
2061 2062 2062 2060 2064 2060
2061 2060 2061 2061 2066 2063
```

```
61 63 60 61 61 67
61 62 62 60 64 60
61 60 61 61 66 63

1 3 0 1 1 7
1 2 2 0 4 0
1 0 1 1 6 3
```

The Unicode table indeed listed the four-digit characters as invisible. But they didn't make sense. They had names like "invisible plus," "right-to-left isolate," and "function application."

The numbers 60 through 67 in the ASCII character table produced "=?<==C=>>@<=<==B?" in decimal and "ac'aagabbd'a'aafc" in hexadecimal.

He took a mouthful of his now lukewarm coffee, swallowed, and leaned back in his chair, looking at the ceiling.

How would I place an invisible message in there? What's the trick?

He jolted back to normal sitting position and looked at his extracted string of single digits: 1 3 0 1 1 7 1 2 2 0 4 0 1 0 1 1 6 3.

All between zero and seven. Is this octal?

Octal encoding was rare and ancient, but the ASCII character table for three-digit octal numbers 101 through 132 represented the Latin characters *A* to *Z* and 141 to 172 represented *a* to *z*. Space was 040. He grouped his string of single digits into segments of three and decoded them.

A grin emerged on his face.

```
130   117   122   040   101   163
 X     O     R           A     s
```

The character *A* had been used by hackers for decades, and this hidden message was an instruction for him to mangle either the crypto text or the password with the logical function eXclusive OR and a set of As.

He did as instructed and was soon looking at a very different message on the saved webpage.

```
Hey, West! This file is self-contained.
By replying to the question here, you
```

will prove that you are indeed West, and
the rest of the document will decrypt.

Where did you store your passwords as a
19-year-old?

A prompt was blinking in the empty input field below.
*Who wrote this? I never told anyone where I stored my passwords. Am I
being tricked into revealing something here?*
Those old passwords were useless now.
He reluctantly entered the correct answer to the question.

In a power strip

As soon as he hit the last character, a second message was revealed.

Hey, West! This is Melissa. You're
probably wondering how I know about your
old password stash. You told me once
when you were high.

The Survivors have been compromised.

His pulse jumped from the adrenaline rush.

Cannot tell you how. It is extremely
important that you don't talk to anyone
about it, not even the other members.
I'm reaching out to y'all individually.

Our adversary will understand that
we've figured it out and start a search.
Therefore we need to leave the country as
soon as possible. We will travel separately
tomorrow, Friday, and meet a.s.a.p. in Room
207, Econo Lodge & Suites near the port of
Corpus Christi, Texas.

Texas? How's that gonna help?

Travel light. Your route:

1. Fly as Bruce to Las Vegas.

2. Hitchhike to Henderson.

3. Pick up a used Hyundai waiting for Jonathan Ash at HH rental.

4. Stream the UK version of the documentary *Shoah* on the car's entertainment system. The player will crash and take its geo position reporter with it. (It uses a 16-bit signed integer for counting seconds, and the movie is over 32,767 seconds long.) This means you can drive untracked.

5. Drive to Corpus Christi through Albuquerque and Lubbock.

If I don't see you in Texas, I will reach out eventually. Could be months ... or years.

Take care.

He dropped his Tile on the table, took three long steps into his bedroom, and tugged open his closet. Friday wasn't tomorrow, it was today.

Chapter Forty-Five

A Quantum Leap

Friday had turned to night when West entered room 207 at the Econo Lodge in Corpus Christi. His eyes were tired of watching the road, and his body was ready for bed.

Kiss, Melissa, and Jitterbug were in the room. They looked relieved to see him.

He put down his nylon duffle bag. "I thought I would be the last one here. Where's BestBye?"

Kiss and Jitterbug looked at Melissa in silence. She pulled out her Tile. "Tiles off and in F pouches. I wanted everyone here before we talk."

Melissa looked at them one by one as they complied, then drew a deep breath before talking.

"The four of us got our emergency IDs at different hospitals." They nodded. "I put hooks in place to notify me if ever the associated medical records were touched again. Up until last week, no one ever changed our records. Zero. But six days ago, there was a series of updates to BestBye's files."

"Did something happen to her?"

"That I don't know. But a bunch of Detroit Police Department data on Best was synced to the hospital's database. According to that data, the police started an investigation two months ago, by request from a certain Commander Pelletier, Canadian G20S."

"Oh my God," Kiss uttered.

"The new files contain BestBye's real name, Tsukiko Kawasaki. Turns out she is one of two daughters of Akira and Miyako Kawasaki—the famous venture capitalist family in New York."

Kiss's face tightened. "Are you sure? That would make her worth billions."

Melissa brought out a small stack of papers from her backpack and put them on a side table. "I tried to figure out a way to double-check, and I came up with this." She handed them the paper at the top of the stack. It was one of the hospital's photos of BestBye, with an inset zoom of her Kanji tattoo.

"That's *Tsuki*, moon, as in Tsukiko. Tattoos are apparently still stigmatized in Japan, so the fact that she has it is probably just another fuck-you to her parents."

West squinted. "This data sync could be G20S playing us somehow."

"It could, but that wouldn't change much. Pelletier's investigation has led her to Best's medical records, which may uncover how we all got our fake IDs." She gave West a worried look. "Especially yours, since you, too, ended up at Botsford Hospital."

West felt the side of his head.

"The tattoo isn't the only thing," Melissa said, rubbing the tip of her nose. "There was a metadata value added to Best's photos. Recognize this?" She gave them the next paper, and it had a set of seemingly random characters. West had never seen the string before.

"No one?" Melissa asked. She cleared her throat. "Trivia question, who's the most famous Detroit figure in the public sector?"

"Current or historic?" Jitterbug asked.

"Current."

"Wasn't there a Detroit judge appointed to the Supreme Court?"

Melissa nodded. "Her name is Ann Claire Jones. It wasn't too hard to find the names of her family members. Botsford didn't have their records, so I used the Sinai-Grace hack we set up for your accident, West. I found Jones's son among their medical records, including a photo." Melissa paused. "What do you think I found inside the photo file?"

Jitterbug raised his shoulders and turned his palms up. "The same metadata value as the one added to BestBye's?"

Melissa pulled in air to say something but swallowed and covered her mouth.

West could see her cheek muscles move. "What's going on?" he asked.

Melissa was getting misty-eyed. "I believe the metadata implies that the person is or is closely related to someone high up in the US government."

"But you just said BestBye was from a VC family."

She wiped her eyes before reaching for the remaining papers in her stack. "Check the Kawasaki family tree," she said, handing over papers with printed photos of BestBye, Akira Kawasaki, and Dr. Kawasaki.

A tear rolled down Melissa's cheek. "I believe BestBye is the niece of Dr. Akiko Kawasaki, head of the US G20S."

The room fell silent. Jitterbug slumped in his seat with a distant stare. Kiss had a solemn look on her face. Melissa dried her eyes to no avail.

Eventually Kiss spoke her mind, in no particular direction. "A mole. That's why Best knew what to do in Vancouver. This is why it was so easy. We're fucked."

Melissa folded her arms. "I take full responsibility. Maybe I didn't want to see it. I was the one who accepted Best's solo plan. I trusted her like I trust you. Given Dr. Kawasaki's efforts to beat Pelletier and get elected director of G20S, I think Kawasaki used us to hack the Canadian G20S."

West got up and put his arms around Melissa. She kept her arms interlocked but leaned in. He moved back a few inches, holding on to her shoulders.

"Where is BestBye now?" he asked.

"I don't know. I got us out of California as soon as I found out. We have one more day before the anime event is over and Best is supposed to be back in San Francisco."

West let go of Melissa and turned so he could see all of them. "With US G20S on our tail, Texas is no better than California."

Melissa nodded, drying her eyes with the arm of her sweater. "We will start by going to Cuba."

"Cuba?" Kiss cocked her head to the side.

Jitterbug threw his hands up. "What's the plan here? To live the rest of our lives in exile?"

"Cuba hasn't adopted GPI," Melissa said. "That'll give us a chance to stay under the radar until we've figured out what our next target is."

Jitterbug jerked his head back, talking to the ceiling. "Next target? Are you going to continue the war on G20S? They're going to find us and either kill us on the spot or just shove us into a detention camp, and we'll never get out."

No one said anything for several moments. West was running on empty after the long-haul travel.

He took a deep breath and looked at Jitterbug and Kiss. "If we are fucked, our only play is to follow through, take down GPI, and get our lives back." He turned to Melissa. "That's what you're saying, right?"

She nodded, both in confirmation of what he said and in appreciation of his support.

"The G20S knows all of our plans," Jitterbug pleaded. "They have BestBye."

"BestBye doesn't know everything," Melissa said, putting proper pressure behind her voice again. "I've kept a few things to myself."

"So much for trust," Kiss burst out. "What exactly have you not been telling us?"

"I'll share once we get to Cuba."

"No, damn it." Kiss got up. "You share with us now. We're not kids." She looked at Jitterbug and got a loyal nod back.

"We are four hackers," Kiss continued, "betrayed by a member of our own team who turns out to be a relative of the enemy. One of us is on parole from federal prison. You're suggesting we flee our home country. What you got, Melissa?"

The room brewed in silence. West saw Melissa contemplating.

Eventually, she replied in a low voice. "I'll share with you what I know. Then we need to continue as a team."

She leaned her hip against the side table where she'd kept the stack of printouts. "The amount of data the major spheres within G20S have on people is vast beyond imagination. No computer system in the world has the capacity to keep up with the stream of *new* data, let alone analyze it together with *historical* data. So why are they collecting it, you may ask?"

She pointed at West. "West and I asked ourselves that very same question a decade and a half ago about the NSA's databases, and the answer is still the same. It has always been a bet on the future, a bet that one day they *will* have the capacity to go back through all the data and deduce swaths of knowledge about every individual one of us. All of our secrets, fears, and unknowns are in that data, ready to be used to manipulate, oppress, and mind-fuck us all."

She picked up the paper with the photo of Dr. Kawasaki, flipped it to the backside, and drew a simple X-Y diagram with a hockey stick curve. "Quantum computing—a global race for quantum supremacy with no clear winner ..." She added a vertical line in the diagram right before the sharp upward bend. "... yet."

She threw the pen down on the paper. "The US branch of G20S is secretly lobbying our government to allow them to process the GPI data set as soon as they have enough quantum computing power, without telling the rest of the world. This would provide the United States with a modern advantage equal to the atomic bomb."

"How do you know about this?" West asked.

"The EFF found out through leaks in DC and made a deal with me two years ago. Their job is to educate the current administration and monitor the legal aspects. Meanwhile, I am to form a team of independent hackers and produce proof that GPI data can be manipulated without G20S noticing. That's the linchpin we're betting on. If we get the EFF that, they will be able to push Washington to make the right decisions."

Jitterbug squeezed his eyes shut. "Are we doing this on behalf of the EFF?"

"We're independent and doing it on behalf of the human race. If America pulls this one on China and Russia, we're likely facing warlike consequences."

CHAPTER FORTY-SIX

G20S: Fly Together

BestBye had spent three days in Vancouver helping Mr. Singh patch security holes described in the stolen pentest report. It was a card she decided to play without admitting to any guilt. Hopefully, it would let enough time pass for things to work out.

One of the issues they had fixed was the calendar exposure. Singh was warming up to her, quite impressed with her skills.

She looked around at her confinement and wondered for how much longer they'd keep her here. It was a windowless 200-square-foot room with a small couch and TV area, a breakfast nook in the corner where she and Singh did their work, and a small bathroom with a shower. With no access to daylight, she had started to lose track of time.

"I get it that you want to fix your shit," she said to Singh, "but why these crazy ideas about Dr. Kawasaki? And is it worth the abduction of an American citizen?"

Singh sipped water from a bottle, his bandaged pinky pointing out. He asked his Tile for the latest news on G20S, handed it to BestBye, and folded his arms across his chest.

Alleged Intrusion at Canadian G20S

According to validated sources, Canadian G20S experienced an intrusion in October of last year and has engaged in a coverup ever since.

A security compromise of G20S operations would be devastating news for an organization that has banked all of its reputation on the safety and integrity of its digital systems. Other G20 members are already asking for an investigation into these allegations.

"This is a smear campaign orchestrated by people opposed to my candidacy," says Canadian G20S representative Commander Emelie Pelletier, who was slated to take over global G20S leadership until Dr. Akiko Kawasaki of US G20S was announced as a contender around the time of the alleged security incident.

"I'm not surprised by infighting," says independent intelligence expert Doyen Savant. "Smear campaign or not, the self-declared 'unpolitical' G20S is wielding so much power these days that politics are inevitable, in all its shapes and forms."

This article's sources are GPI-validated.

There was a sudden burst in the corridor outside BestBye's room. Shattered glass clattered against the wall and floor.

The door to their room flung open, and three soldiers with US Special Forces badges barged in, bringing with them a gust of ice-cold outdoor air. Mr. Singh was pushed aside by two of the soldiers as the third one asked BestBye to state her name.

"Grace Oshiro."

"You sure? We are told Tsukiko Kawasaki would be here."

One of the other soldiers held up a Tile to BestBye's face. The Tile chirped. "It's her all right."

•

"You could have come a little earlier," BestBye told her aunt, who was sitting across a little table between their seats on the US government aircraft.

"You could have gotten a little less caught," the director of US G20S replied, blinking her eyes slowly.

BestBye looked out the window. The lights of Vancouver were disappearing quickly underneath them, and soon there would be nothing to see outside except for the dimly lit wing of the plane and the reflection of flashing navigation lights.

She had played her part and stayed silent ever since her aunt's men smashed their way into Canadian G20S and got her out. Her relationship to the top US official was no longer a secret, but their *companionship* still was.

Kawasaki drew a long breath through her nose to call for attention. "What did Pelletier ask? What do they know?"

"They figured out we're family, but they think …"

"Your sister was one of the few stunts I could pull."

"You should have told me."

"I told you many things, including not to go after Brazil."

"It got you closer to your goal."

The two of them agreed quietly.

"I had to get rid of Timothy today," Kawasaki said without joy. "Should have done it long ago. I hope he doesn't try to retaliate."

"He was at the lab."

"Mhm. Helping Pelletier."

The seatbelt lights switched off, and Dr. Kawasaki got up and opened the overhead bin. She got a sheathed Japanese sword out and leaned it against her chair.

"I can't believe you still travel with that thing," BestBye said.

Her aunt glanced at her between her stretched-up arms, got out an unopened bottle of Canadian whisky, dropped it on her seat, and stowed the sword again.

The sword was her aunt's "brown M&Ms." Like any other federal agent, she was permitted to travel armed while on duty. Long ago, she had gone through the hassle of getting her katana defined as a service weapon, and she always provided supporting documentation before attempting to board. If the sword was ever questioned in security or by onboard staff, she knew they had not read her documents, and she would refuse to board the aircraft before a security inspection had been done.

BestBye had read the rules on service weapons. Agents were required to keep them in their immediate control and to practice alcohol abstinence.

Kawasaki went to fetch a glass and two ice cubes from a nearby cabinet. She got the bottle from the seat and cracked it open as she sat down. A generous pour and a swirl of the glass later, she had what she wanted.

"I'm starting to doubt this Pelletier takedown," she said, savoring the beverage. "Maybe I could support her and get the job done anyway?"

"Politics," BestBye spat out.

"Domestically, it *is* politics. Internationally, it's war. I doubt the other superpowers will be facing any internal resistance to deploy QC powers once they have them. That's Pelletier's big flaw—she doesn't see the big picture."

Kawasaki downed the rest of the whisky in one gulp. "Fucking Canadians thinking we should all be nice to each other. Something tipped Melissa off before Pelletier and Timothy got to your lab, and since she didn't alert *you* …"

She expected a confirmation, and BestBye provided it.

"… she probably knows at least as much as Pelletier does about you and me. She won't give up," BestBye said, knowing it was true.

"Oh, I know, and she's figuring this out in excellent ways. I have always doubted the other member countries' ability to protect the shared crypto system."

"Might as well let her do a third country as long as you don't let thirty days pass," BestBye said.

"I worry that …" Kawasaki tilted her glass to make the ice cubes swing along the curved perimeter.

"What?" BestBye asked.

"Melissa doesn't know about Technical Note 1. I worry we'll only be strengthening it."

BestBye's heart jumped. She didn't know about Technical Note 1 either.

CHAPTER FORTY-SEVEN

G20S: WTF

Dr. Kawasaki had been expecting this call, and the use of the Five Eyes voice link was a sure giveaway.

"What the fuck, Kawasaki? What the fuck are you doing?"

"Commander Pelletier, how do you do?"

"The woman you took from our custody yesterday, the woman who broke into our office space and stole classified documentation, she is your niece. How do you think that truth will go down in the press?"

"Fighting truth with lies is not going to help you. Besides, this custody of yours was initiated by an illegal apprehension of a US citizen on US soil."

"Because you refused to help us!"

"I'll take that as admission of guilt."

"If you think you can persuade me to back off as candidate, you're fooling yourself," Pelletier said forcefully. "We're still working on finding the source of the leak on the Vancouver break-in. If it was you or anyone taking orders from you, shit is going to get real."

The call ended abruptly. Dr. Kawasaki leaned back in her chair and let out a huge sigh as if she'd been holding in air throughout the argument. It still amazed her how badass she could be in the heat of the moment.

She reached out for the tablet Tile on her desk, launched the web browser, and reloaded the search page for cabins for sale by Deep Creek Lake.

CHAPTER FORTY-EIGHT

Technical Note 1

Melissa's escape route took them from Corpus Christi to Galveston to Mexico before going on a cargo ship to Havana.

The Cuban capital was bustling with tourism. Relations with the US were complicated, as Cuba refused to adopt GPI, but the Caribbean weather and the allure of a different lifestyle kept a stream of Americans and dollars flowing.

West, Jitterbug, and Kiss spent two days marveling at being in freakin' Cuba and indulging in mojitos, cigars, and local craft beers. It felt as if they were clinging on to their last days of freedom. Kiss even convinced them to take salsa lessons.

West was amazed by the easygoing Cuban people and started dreaming of Kiss and him staying here. *Just leave it all behind*, he kept telling himself. Easy for him to say, he *had* nothing behind.

Melissa didn't partake. Instead, she powered through days of research into their next target.

Eventually she pulled the team together.

"You should be sober enough to actually be helpful in a few hours," she said, yawning. "Fuck, I'm tired. I want you to start looking into Italian G20S operations."

"Italian?" Jitterbug asked.

"Yes, Italy is our best bet. We must leave the American continent and go for something outside BestBye's list from the New York meeting. By the way, our access to the G20S calendar has been shut off, so we won't be able to do that kind of research anymore."

"You think that's BestBye's work?"

"Probably. Anyway, investigate Italy. I'm going to go full-on Klono-pin. See y'all in eight hours."

Melissa closed the door to the bedroom behind her, and Jitterbug went back to snoring in his recliner.

West considered taking a nap, too, when Kiss reached over and whispered in his ear. "Wanna bust a nut?"

The last time he'd heard such slang was in prison.

She let her hand slide gently over his chest down to his navel, stopping where his piercing protruded from under his shirt and circling her index finger around it. "I was going to get it on myself, but since the others are asleep, I figured we could go win-win."

Minutes later they paired under the shower nozzle. Her skin was slippery in the pouring water. West looked down at his hands following her curving contours. He kissed her shoulder and neck while she let her thigh gently massage him hard.

She guided him into her, then lifted his chin with both hands. Their eyes met just an inch apart, and West was jolted by the intensity of the moment. Kiss held steady. "I want to look into your eyes when you come."

"Condom?"

"I know my periods. Don't worry."

•

Melissa massaged the back of her neck as she walked to the bathroom after her chemical sleep. She yelled from inside before even closing the door. "Hey, West, your underwear is on top of Kiss's in here. Is there something you two want to tell me?"

"I showered before West," Kiss quickly shouted back from the living room. "What are you suggesting?"

"Nothing. Except it's *your* underwear on top of West's."

Everyone was silent, not a word from the living room, neither movements nor sounds from the bathroom. West searched his memory eight hours back. Melissa was right—it was Kiss's panties on top of his shorts.

The next thing they heard was Melissa talking to herself. "Fuck."

West waited a few seconds. "What's up?" he asked in the direction of the bathroom.

Melissa replied as she closed the door. "Nothing. I just got an unexpected text … and a news link. I'll post in the chat room."

They got the link, and West read the article.

The Mythical Technical Note 1

The security of G20S is shrouded in secrecy and has given rise to its fair share of conspiracy theories and urban myths. Our favorites include a crypto back door stored in an actual golden key and an offline backup on the moon.

But today, for the first time, trustworthy information has surfaced on what's been discussed as "Technical Note 1," or TN1, in the information security community for half a decade.

It is a layer of G20S redundancy or cyber resilience as some would have it.

"Technical Note 1 exists, and it's a safety measure which guarantees G20S's ability to continuously deliver its identity services despite any adverse cyber events," a person familiar with the matter says.

More shocking to some is where this measure resides.

"Russia is the largest country in the world in terms of size, and a key partner within G20S. We're proud of the unique security the Russian government has offered," *Wired*'s source continued.

We've reached out to Russian G20S officials and will update this article if we hear back.

This article's sources are GPI-validated.

Melissa opened the bathroom door and stuck out her head. "That *Wired* piece just changed our plans. No Italy. Our third and last target is Russia. Hack Russian G20S and figure out what this TN1 thing really is. I have a Swedish hacker friend who might be able to help us."

CHAPTER FORTY-NINE

Nord Stream

Stockholm in late January was not a pretty sight. Brown slush splashed on pedestrians as cars drove the narrow streets. Then overnight, that same slush froze, creating treacherous ice tracks for commuters. Still, West was blown away by being in Europe, this old world with its deep ties to the history of the United States of America. How he wished his mom had gotten a chance to go too.

Facial recognition was apparently illegal at bars and clubs in Sweden, and Melissa's friend had instructed them to make their way to the classic Man in the Moon pub in Vasastan.

Glasses specific to each variety of beer hung above the busy bartenders, and the air smelled of garlic from the place's most popular dish—moules frites. They got a beverage each and sat down at a thick wooden table.

Jitterbug looked out the window, where streetlights reflected off wet surfaces. "They say summer is beautiful here."

"It better be," West lamented. "Aren't the Nordics supposed to be the happiest people on earth? Has to be the drinking."

Kiss tasted her Belgian Ale. "BestBye would have pointed out to you that the upper middle class is less happy in the Nordics than in the US because 'happiest in the world' is achieved by relative happiness for the less fortunate, not for people like us." She smiled and shook her head. "I kind of miss her."

The entrance to the pub was at an angle on the corner of the building. A full-bodied man in his seventies entered. He stopped a few feet in, raked glittering water drops off his coat and scarf, and made a friendly gesture to the bartender. Melissa waved him over as soon as he spotted them.

He unbuttoned his coat and removed his fogged-up glasses. Silver stubble covered the lower half of his face and down his neck. "Happy MLK Day!" he burst out. "What's up, Melissa? Long time no see." A wide smile defined his appearance.

She hugged her old friend. "Everyone, this is Robert—Swedish hacker legend. Robert, meet the Survivors." Everyone said hello. "How are things for you, Rob?"

"Pretty good, pretty good. Still working, still buying expensive guitars."

"Old men and their guitars. Rob and I go way back. He's been involved in internet standards, worked heavily on cyber defense for Sweden, done forensics, set up hacker competitions, you name it. I trust him 99%."

"Ha. Trust is good, control is better, PGP is best. We haven't seen each other in a very long time, so let's verify." Robert's smile struck again.

Robert and Melissa typed on their Tiles and scribbled sets of alphanumeric characters on napkins for a good five minutes before nodding to each other.

Robert insisted he would take the subway while the others finished their beers and then walked to his consultancy office. An hour later, they sat down by his combined kitchen and conference room table, and he brought out a bottle of pinot noir "to warm up your limbs."

Melissa looked around with approval. The place was filled with sci-fi memorabilia and old computer games. "This is what I'd like the lab to look like when we rebuild it."

The others nodded.

She continued. "Before we left Cuba, I asked Rob if he could help us find a Russian target. Preferably someone of mutual interest. He's not going to risk his precious motherland, but more than once has he been able to provide me with hardcore information on Russian tech."

Robert laughed childishly. "Come on. Not hardcore."

"Always the bashful one. What you got for me?"

"In fact, I do happen to have some interesting intel. There's this Russian woman, Fedosia Pogodina. Do you know about Nord Stream?"

The Survivors shook their heads.

"Nord Stream is a subsea natural gas pipeline from Russia to Germany. It was very controversial when built around 2010 because Russia had used its supply of gas in political conflicts many times. But Germany needed alternatives to coal and nuclear power."

He got up and sketched a rough map of Northern Europe on a large, wall-mounted whiteboard. He added a dashed line that started at the border between what he labeled as Russia and Finland, passed east of Sweden and Denmark on its way south, and ended up on Germany's northern coastline.

West realized he hadn't looked at a map of where they were. For all he knew, Robert could be making that geography up.

"This is where the pipe lies," Robert continued. "As you can see, or maybe you can't see, but it goes through Finnish, Swedish, and Danish waters, which means those countries have interests to protect, and they all want a slice of the pie. Fedosia Pogodina officially manages Nord Stream's business in Finland, Sweden, and Denmark." He took a sip of his wine. "This involves political connections with the governments as well as more practical issues on the use of ports for maintenance."

"I'm curious why you say she *officially* manages."

"Thank you, miss?"

"Kiss."

"Thank you, Kiss. I'm terrible with names. Yes, there is a reason why I say officially. At the time the pipeline was built, 80% of all international Russian internet traffic passed through Sweden, making it an ideal wiretapping point. The NSA made a deal with the Swedish intelligence agency, FRA, decades ago to get this wiretap data. You probably know about this from the old Snowden leaks."

Robert took a gulp from his glass. "Mmm. I love this wine." He was getting excited. "Russia of course knew about this well before Snowden told the public, and so there was another undisclosed purpose of the Nord Stream pipeline—it carries a subsea internet cable connection to Russia's European exclave Kaliningrad, bypassing Sweden and the FRA."

He added a pipeline fork off to Kaliningrad on his map. "This exclave is the base for Russian electronic warfare in Europe."

"That's a pretty strategic spot," West said.

"You bet. Russia grabbed Kaliningrad from Germany after World War II. Russians of course fear wiretapping of the new underwater cables, and US submarines have been reported in the area. Which is why Pogodina is such an interesting figure. She is also a Russian G20S agent, managing the integrity of Russian internet traffic through the Baltic Sea." Robert looked triumphant.

Jitterbug had big eyes. "I came here with midlevel expectations, and you pull a Cold War-to-G20S connection on me. That *is* hardcore, man."

Melissa was eager to get down to business. "I assume in here lies our mutual interest. We hack Pogodina together, the Survivors get a Russian G20S connection, you help the FRA. And the sad irony is that we help your government tap into ordinary Russians' internet traffic."

"Something like that. In fact, the FRA recently received a top-level request for certain Russian intel that they'd like to respond to."

Melissa's eyes narrowed. "Can you tell us what?"

He smiled. "Not really. But I've asked the FRA to send me everything they have on Pogodina by tomorrow morning."

It was getting late. Robert set up small desks for his guests while West and the others let a second bottle of wine make its way into their bloodstreams. Eventually they got ready for bed.

The place's large basement was fitted with two full bathrooms and bunk beds for when Robert and his team were in crunch mode. Now the four Survivors lay there in the dark except for blue-and-green LEDs blinking from a server rack in the corner. The air down here was cold.

Kiss started to chat with Jitterbug in the bunk below. "Gosh, we're pretty far from home right now. Being on the run like this makes you feel small. I miss San Francisco."

"I miss my church," he replied. "I even had a date lined up when we left. A really nice guy, works at MOMA."

West thought of what lay ahead. Freaking Russia—the world's largest country. Melissa had said all along that they did not want to go after any of the superpowers. Now they were, and at a geopolitical level.

CHAPTER FIFTY

Kungsgatan 79

"Wakey-wakey. You feel that smell? I've got Swedish coffee for you."

"Robert, you don't feel smells, you just smell." Melissa bowed her head to not hit West's bunk above as she sat up.

She looked down into the mug she was handed. "Damn, is this coffee or crude oil?"

"It's called Skånerost."

"Sconeh rawst," she echoed.

The four Americans got dressed and headed up to the ground floor. Two of Robert's team members were preparing breakfast for themselves and nodded a greeting to the guests.

As soon as the Survivors sat down, Robert beamed a fly-by rendering of an old but beautiful inner city building onto the big screen. "Pogodina's offices, Kungsgatan 79, on the downtown island of Kungsholmen. At walking distance from Swedish government buildings across the bridge and reasonably close to the Russian Embassy, which is located on the same island."

Kungsgatan 79 was a wedge-shaped building. It pointed into a street crossing and had round balconies for each floor, bending from side to side at the edge. The façade was cream with a tint of pink, and the roof was made of black metal sheets.

"A tower room, it has," Kiss's Yoda voice threw in. "Good for villains, it is."

Robert gave her a nod. "We believe Pogodina uses the tower room for some meetings, but her office is one floor below. She has calls with Moscow on Mondays, Wednesdays, and Fridays—eight in the morning, always on time, and always alone. The FRA knows about these calls because they see the cellular connections through surveillance equipment they've set up close by. But after about a year's worth of attempts to wiretap, they still know nothing of what is said since it's encrypted voice over IP."

Melissa looked intrigued. "Still, Pogodina is using the regular cellular network."

"Yeah. Russia decided long ago they cannot trust Western technologies and that they need their own security layer on top. That way they can use available infrastructure and still protect themselves. Speaking of which, a 4096-byte high-entropy file is always sent in email to Pogodina only minutes after those phone calls. The FRA thinks it contains rolling, encrypted access keys and that the phone call itself is involved in the handshake."

"How well guarded is the building?" Melissa was moving into top gear.

"No human guards that we know of. That would be weird for a gas pipe company. But I assume they have reasonable physical security. The lights in the office rarely go off before eight in the evening."

"Do they own the building?"

"No. They rent parts of the top floor and the tower room. There are four other businesses. Let me see." Robert fiddled with his Tile. "From the ground floor and up: Beauty and Health Team, Urban Recording Studio, Lead Data & IT, and another music studio called Backyard. The rest of the building, except for Nord Stream, is comprised of private apartments."

Melissa processed the information quickly. "This might come down to crypto hacking if they truly use end-to-end crypto, but physical security and network equipment are always weak points. Let's start by learning who runs those other businesses, when people come and go, what the building's data network infrastructure looks like, and what's up with physical security for the top floors."

West inserted himself into the conversation. "Hey, I've had this elevator trick in the back of my head ever since LA."

Everyone in the room looked at him, and he hesitated briefly before continuing. "We connect to the elevator's floor buttons and trigger a micro camera when the elevator goes to the particular floors we're interested in. That way we will know exactly who goes up or down from the Russian offices."

"Sounds like you're installing it," Melissa said.

"Can you install it, please?" Kiss corrected her.

"Can you install it, pretty please, with sugar on top?"

West looked at them both and nodded.

First time solo.

CHAPTER FIFTY-ONE

Elevated

Installing the camera meant that West needed access to the building and time alone in the elevator.

He managed to get an appointment for an introduction to the Backyard studio in the afternoon and was given the code for general building access.

The elevator was a centrally located, early 1900s birdcage model with a staircase spiraling around it. It had an ornate, black steel frame with a woven steel mesh as walls. West opened the door and pushed aside the zigzag safety door.

The inside had a wooden panel a couple of inches wide with vertically aligned buttons labeled "K" for basement, "B" for ground floor, and "2" through "5" in a metal frame. Buttons K, B, and 5 had the most wear.

Below the metal frame was a modern GPI scanner bolted onto the wood. A sticker on it said it was for people who lived here to conveniently go to their floor. He shook his head.

An aesthetic violation of this beautiful piece of engineering, sprinkled with everyday surveillance.

His plan was to connect a wireless controller to the buttons to turn on a hidden micro camera when someone went to or from the top floor. But the screwheads for the panel were covered by tamper evident destructive seals with a logo.

I can't risk Pogodina seeing broken seals.

He hit 4 to where the studio was located and kept working the problem as he ascended. Above the set of buttons was a registration label covered in plexiglass, and in its upper right corner there were circular stickers stacked on top of each other with a hand-written date in the center. His Tile translated the top sticker's text as "Next planned main-tenance."

He peeled it off.

Oops, I guess maintenance service is seven months overdue.

The guy who greeted him in the Backyard studio didn't seem overly bothered by the missing elevator service when West brought it up. Nei-ther did his coworker in the back of the room.

"Hey, you don't want to take on that kind of liability," West said. "It's very old machinery."

"This is Sweden. We don't sue each other here," the guy said with a kind smile.

"Come on. It doesn't look professional. When you step into an an-tique thing like that, you're already alert. Then you see it's not properly maintained."

"Okay, have a coffee, and I'll call the chairman of the … what do you call it? Hey, what is bostadsrättsförening in English?"

The woman in the back of the room chuckled. "Are you asking me?"

"Whatever. Have a coffee, and I'll call the owner."

By the time they had gone over the studio equipment and pricing, the guy got a call back. The elevator would be serviced the next day.

•

West was back at Robert's office by five in the afternoon and found a box of Korean food waiting for him.

Robert was eager to share what they had on the building.

"It's formally named Drabanten 12, was built 1907–08 and has two addresses—Kungsgatan 79 and Kungsholmsgatan 14. There are street-facing entrances on both sides leading to a joint inner entrance."

Robert displayed a street-level photo on the big screen.

"The ground floor is split level, which is where you find the Beauty and Health Team, owned by two sisters—Ebba and Alice Vennmo—and open between noon and seven p.m."

"I went there." Jitterbug looked fondly at his fingernails. "They do manicure, pedicure, makeup, and the whole gamut of hair services. Staffed by two women and three men today. Free Wi-Fi called 'BHT' with password 'BeautyAndTheBest,' camel-cased."

Melissa did a thumbs-up. "Wi-Fi access is great. That means we can work the building without leaving a cellular trace."

"Speaking of Wi-Fi," West said, "at the top of the building there's a network called 'Dragunov,' which sounds Russian. My Tile saw it when I used the elevator."

One of Robert's team members—a woman in sports clothes and running shoes—commented from over by the coffee maker. "It's pronounced de-rah-goo-noff. Classic Russian sniper rifle." Her voice was a bit nasally.

She turned around to face the American guests, flashing a smile over her steaming coffee mug. "I used to be a sniper in the Norwegian special forces."

Robert and the Survivors looked at each other. Guns.

Melissa didn't want to linger on the subject. "West, what did you learn at the Backyard studio?"

"They offer evening sessions and are fully booked for the week, so there's people there until late."

"Kiss, did you find anything interesting in the neighborhood?"

"I did. There's a tech company called Creuna—customer experience something—on the corner of Kungsholmsgatan and Pipersgatan."

Her Swedish pronunciation made Robert laugh.

"Hey, man, I'm trying. Anyway, the wedge-shaped building where Pogodina works kind of points at Creuna's office, and tomorrow night Creuna hosts a developer meetup. I bet I can sneak in, get roof access, and be able to look into Pogodina's office through a good lens. If I place a repeater outside Creuna's entrance, I'll be able to access the 'BHT' network from up there and stream to you what I see."

"That's a good start," Melissa said. "But there's going to be rain, so prepare for some fun under the sky."

•

Robert had prepared West and Jitterbug for an early rise to be on site when the elevator was to be serviced. "Swedish handymen take pride in arriving and leaving early," he said with a tired look.

The two Survivors stood a few yards apart outside the wedge-shaped building at five minutes to seven. Stockholmers rushed by on the sidewalks with one gloved hand holding together the collar of their coats and the other holding a paper mug of quickly cooling coffee.

The elevator service minibus parked itself in the designated service spot at seven sharp. Out came a woman in her thirties. She opened the back doors and pulled out a black-and-blue plastic toolbox. Jitterbug took a few steps away while West approached the woman casually.

"Good morning! You're here for the elevator, right?"

The woman looked at him, probably surprised to be greeted in English. "Yes?"

"My name is Bruce. I live here. Can I help you carry anything?"

"No thanks, I can manage."

"Got it. I'll hold the door for you."

West followed her to the inner entrance and took the stairs one floor up.

Sounds traveled well in the stone staircase, and he could glimpse down through the steel-mesh shaft. The main power feed to the elevator was turned off, and the woman began her inspection. She inspected the door's electric lock and the zigzag gate before opening her toolbox.

West sent a message to Jitterbug on the outside.

Let's do this.

West could barely hear the minibus's alarm from outside, but the service woman's Tile buzzed almost instantly. Within seconds she was headed out in long strides, and he rushed down.

Her toolbox was neatly organized. He heard his own breathing as he searched through the layers of gear. Custom and regular screwdrivers, a multimeter, various pliers, a can of WD-40.

A disappointed grimace came over him as he found them: a sheet of tamper seals, not a roll.

Stealing the whole sheet would be unwise. Could he cut off just a row? No scissors. And if he peeled off the seals, they would stick to something and break if he tried to move them. He felt his pockets and found the "Next planned maintenance" elevator sticker he had peeled off yesterday.

Sticker on sticker should work.

Carefully, he lifted two circular tamper seals off the sheet and placed them on the maintenance sticker.

As he stood up, he heard the woman's voice behind him.

"Va fan gör du?"

West whirled around. "Wow, you startled me. Sorry! I'm just so childishly interested in elevators. That's why I offered you help back there. I was just on my way out and saw your stuff. Sorry. I just had a quick look." West blabbered on as he stepped out of the cage. "Are those Security Torx drivers? I guess that's standard in elevators, huh?"

She gave him the stink eye. "Get out of here."

CHAPTER FIFTY-TWO

G20S: Candlewood Suites

BestBye was lying on her back on a firm hotel bed just minutes away from the classic NSA headquarters at Fort Meade, Maryland. On the bed beside her lay her sister Tsukiko, swearing over a game on her Tile.

Candlewood Suites army hotel was an anonymous four-story brick building offering few things beyond a cafeteria, a good gym, and spacious rooms with kitchenettes and work desks. That and isolation from the January cold outside. This was where Dr. Kawasaki was hiding the siblings from Pelletier and Timothy. BestBye at least got to work with her aunt, whereas her sister was forced to waste her time.

Tsukiko dropped her Tile on the bed with a sigh. "It's still weird that you're helping Auntie."

"I'm helping the country."

"But you don't care about the country. Especially not the government."

"I care about defense. I told Auntie it was wrong to pull you into this."

"Glad I could help. Plus, I don't have to work. I miss New York though."

"Liberty Bagels."

"Mhm."

Tsukiko picked up her Tile and started gaming again.

"Need extra lives?" BestBye asked.

"No, I'm good."

"I got you three this morning."

"I know."

BestBye looked into the ceiling. Russia as a target was daunting. She had discussed going after superpowers enough times with Melissa to know that the leader of the Survivors wouldn't be happy about the venture but that she'd take the bait given the circumstances.

None of the Survivors knew Russian, so Melissa would do all she could to pull it off remotely like they had with Brazil. That was why she had taken the team to Sweden.

BestBye had asked her aunt twice about Technical Note 1, to no effect.

Chapter Fifty-Three

The Woman on the Roof

Kiss had to hack the waiting list for the meetup at Creuna to get herself a seat.

Tonight's topic was Sweden's 260+ year old Public Access to Information and Secrecy Act and its role in a digitized society. The audience was exclusively preppy Swedes in their thirties. The clothing trend seemed to be cashmere dusters. Not a lot of T-shirts.

The climbing harness Kiss wore underneath her pants chewed into her skin as she sat through two forty-minute talks.

When the organizers announced the mandatory pizza break, she snuck under the thick black cloth which isolated the temporary classroom setup from the empty open-office space behind.

She took the stairs up and went as far as she could. Here the slope of the roof showed along the outer wall. This had to be the uppermost floor.

There was a server room, and past it three storage rooms, the first of which had old marketing material and abandoned PCs from a bygone era.

The next one featured holiday decorations and years of archived accounting, and the third storage room was almost empty except for a broken, foldable chair. It was probably where they kept extra furniture for events like the ongoing meetup. In the corner was a short metal staircase leading to a locked door with a sign that read: "Obehöriga äga ej tillträde" and an iconic stop hand.

Just as she got her lock picks out, she got a message from West.

Are you on the roof?

Not yet, darling.

:)

I'm ready to go in and do
my camera install. No one
has entered the building
for the last 10 minutes.

Just a sec and I can keep an
eye on the street for you.

I don't want to miss the
opportunity. Just keep a
lookout as soon as you get
in place. Thx.

"Hallå?"

Kiss swept around. A young man stood in the door opening. Long hair, black hoodie with what looked like a metal band logo.

"Oh, hi! Sorry, I don't speak Swedish well yet." She shot out her right hand and approached the guy. "I'm Amber."

"Hey. Are you new here or something?" He shook her hand.

"Yes. Yes, I am. I wanted to see if there are some more chairs. Fully packed tonight, huh?"

"It usually is. I don't recognize you. Who do you work for?"

"I work on the UI design team. And you?"

"I work there too."

Kiss cursed inaudibly.

The guy continued. "I did hear about a new hire this week, but her name is Sophia, I believe."

"Ha-ha. That's me all right. I go by my middle name—I'm Sophia Amber Love."

"Okay, I'm Oscar." He stretched to look past her shoulder. "Looks like you're out of luck with the chairs."

"Yeah, there's just this broken one. I'll see if I can fix it. Nice meeting you."

Oscar left, and Kiss had a decision to make. Pretend to repair the chair for a while to keep the theater going, or head straight for the lock picks? She looked at her Tile—incoming text from West.

**I'll unscrew the elevator
panel now.**

Five minutes later, she had picked the lock and the ice-cold wind outside hit her face. The rain had stopped, and the night was beautifully dark with Stockholm's skyline glistening in the wetness.

Her foot skidded forward on the wet metal, and she grabbed the doorframe to regain balance. An aluminum ladder fixed to the roof provided the means to escalate for the daring personnel who maintained these roofs. Kiss clipped her safety rope to the lowest ladder step and began her ascent.

The ridge of the roof was two feet wide and had safety rings to clip onto. She squatted to reduce the terrifying effect of the wind and inched her way to the end of the building, where she got a view into the lit windows of the tower room of Kungsgatan 79.

A few steps more and she could report back to West—no one close to the two street entrances.

She brought out her video binoculars and streamed what she saw to the team at Robert's office.

"I see a circular office with three privacy screens attached to separate desks. Pogodina sits at what would be the tip of the wedge. She's drinking tea and talking to another middle-aged woman. Two pocket-size Tiles on her desk and a big screen. Her desktop computer has a privacy filter, so I can't tell what's on the screen, but the logo says … MCST. Spiral staircase up to the tower room. I only see the reflected light from below up there, but it looks like a library."

Melissa came through in Kiss's earpiece. "Check the surrounding roof. I want to see if it's feasible to get access to the tower from there."

"You forgot to say please," Kiss said, slowly panning the two sides.

"Switch to infrared," Melissa commanded, ignoring Kiss's request for courtesy. "Maybe we can see the building's exit to the roof. It should leak more heat."

Kiss flipped the switch, and the binoculars adjusted for the light environment. "You're lucky the rain has stopped."

Melissa used Kiss like a remote control. "Pan to the left. Good. Down a little," she mumbled as the video stream slowly scanned the roof. "Wait. What's that? Right by that triangular façade piece."

Kiss moved the binoculars and paused. The heat image got sharper. "Yeah, what is that?"

"That's a human on top of the roof, crouching."

CHAPTER FIFTY-FOUR

The Only Way Is Up

Melissa got up in a jolt. A freeze frame from Kiss's binoculars was still up on the big screen.

"I'm going up there," she yelled as she dashed down the stairs to the basement. "I'm getting my climbing equipment. Jit, you'll be my belayer."

It was past eight in the evening, and the rain was returning when they arrived on Kungsholmen in Robert's car.

In between Kungsgatan 77 and 79 was a single-floor structure about twenty-five feet wide, effectively creating a gap leading to the decked-over backyard. The building with Pogodina's office had windows and balconies in the gap, facing east but barely visible in the night.

Kiss gave an update from her rooftop. "I think the person crouching is still on the roof, but it's really hard to see in the drizzle. Pogodina is still in her office."

West joined the voice chat. "Elevator rigged. I found a spot down the street where I can keep an eye on the entrance."

Melissa was clad in black, head covered by her nylon skull mask with cutouts for her X-ray glasses and an integrated lavalier microphone. On her hip was a chalk bag containing her Tile and the Survivors' basic gear.

A downspout on the left side made it easy for Melissa and Jitterbug to get up on the roof of the gap building. Using a mini drone borrowed from Robert, Jitterbug flew Melissa's rope to the top balcony and clipped it onto the rails with a carabiner.

Gusts of wind carrying sheets of more and more intense rain hit Melissa and the building as she worked her way from one slippery balcony to the next. The glasses weren't coping well with raindrops. "Sunny

California tech," she muttered as her muscles pushed and pulled her body upward.

The top balcony was open air, and its table and chairs were covered in white tarps waiting for spring. The apartment windows were dark.

She got over the rails, squatted, and looked up at the edge of the roof. It looked like an upward-pointing chevron from the side and was slanted at roughly forty degrees with only a few inches of overhang.

She would have to get up another six feet to be able to reach it. From there, she knew from fly-over footage that the apartment to which this balcony belonged had a covered roof patio on the inner side, which should provide a safe path to the wedge corner and over to Kungsholms-gatan and the crouching figure.

If she could somehow open this balcony door slightly, she could insert climber's chockstones above its hinges and on top between the door and the frame to create a ladder.

She stretched over the plastic sheet covering the furniture and put her ear against the wet, ice-cold window. Not a sound. The glass showed no signs of alarm sensors.

Hesitation crept up as she got her flat pry bar out.

"West, go check the top, easternmost apartment for me," she whispered into her microphone. "I need to know if anyone's home before I pry open this balcony door. If someone *is* home, keep them occupied for a minute. And hurry. It's fucking freezing out here."

West whispered back to her about a minute thereafter. "I'm at the top floor, east. Only one apartment door here. You ready?"

"You bet."

Melissa could hear the faint sound of a doorbell inside the apartment; her pry bar was at the ready right by the balcony door's bolt. Another ring. A third.

A dim light came on inside.

West had left his microphone on so that Melissa could follow what happened on his end. "Good evening, madam," he said. "So sorry to bother you at this late hour. I don't know if you've noticed, but we've had some issues with the elevator lately."

Melissa put pressure on the pry bar. The doorframe squeaked and let go of the bolt.

West kept stalling the lady.

Melissa quickly got the four chockstones fitted and shut the door again. "West, I'm done out here."

She could hear him wrap up the conversation as she hid in the corner of the balcony.

It didn't take long before the balcony door's blinds turned, and an old lady looked out into the night. She must have felt the cold air.

The apartment went dark again.

Melissa snapped climbing steps onto the chockstones' wire loops and got moving. The wooden door and frame were not happy with the pressure and pull, but nothing broke.

Stretching up, she got her left arm over the angled roof. The surface was wet but had reasonable friction. Her hand searched for something to hold on to. Small ridges held the sheets of metal together.

She stretched further to get her eyes above the edge. The patio opening was there all right. She got both hands on the roof and slowly shifted balance to match the slanting angle. Her legs were bent in a position that would allow her to spring upward.

She whispered into the microphone. "Hey, Jit, loosen the safety rope. I think the friction is sufficient to not slide off the roof if I can get my feet onto the surface quick enough. But I have to jump the last bit. I'm anchored to the balcony door, so if I slide off, I'll come in a swing from the inner side, hopefully not hitting the wall too hard."

"Godspeed."

Like a cat ready to leap forward and catch its prey, Melissa got every limb in order.

She thrust herself upward.

Her hips got level with the roof, and in a clockwise motion she swung her lower body to the left and plunged her torso forward. Her sternum hit one of the metal ridges, and pain signals cascaded through her body.

She started to slide downward. Her limbs fought for purchase—left arm maximizing its contact surface while her right hand tried to grip the roof's edge. The edge was too thick.

Her feet passed the roof's lower end and hit an obstacle. She stopped.

Whatever was holding her feet felt wobbly. She bent her head slowly to have a look. It was the rain gutter.

The light came on inside at the patio to her left. Someone, probably the lady, started fiddling with the patio door. Melissa turned her face away and lay still to blend in with the black roof.

"Hallå?" the lady called into the night. The voice was weak. "Hallåå?" The door closed again.

Melissa heaved herself up, toes pushing down on the gutter.

Two minutes of painful crawling over the ridges later, she grabbed the metal fence of the patio.

From this point it was comparatively easy to get to the corner of the building. She bent down as she got closer and texted Kiss instead of using voice.

> I believe I'm right across. Is the person still there?

Too much rain. Can't see through infrared.

> Shit. The last you saw, just one person, right?

No, I think I saw two.
Just kidding.

> F U. Tower room dark and Pogodina still in her office?

Yup.

> I see a rope fixed to the safety ladder on the Kungsgatan side, and it stretches over to the other side. I believe this is what that person used to get to the hiding spot.

Melissa launched the camera view on her Tile, then lay down just below the ridge of the roof and nudged her Tile over the edge to let the camera see the other side. The crouching figure was there, barely visible. They wore a mask and held a lit-up Tile in their hand.

CHAPTER FIFTY-FIVE

Blind Trust

Melissa zoomed in on the figure until the bright, tilted rectangle of their Tile took up a third of her screen. At this zoom level, the camera image was shaking significantly. Her Tile highlighted the bright object, and Melissa tapped it, making the camera lock onto it and stabilize the image.

She zoomed one level further and started recording.

A minute later, she opened the video take in an editor, flattened the tilted recording of the remote screen, and fiddled with contrast until the screen's content emerged from the bright background. The crouching figure was chatting in Russian with someone called Mikhail.

Melissa's Tile translated the message log.

Pogodina *is* our plan!

You know what I mean.

This is our best shot. If the window is open we know we can trust the insider.

Code could be wrong.

Sure. Then I have my exit plan.

These people were after the same target as they were.

Melissa exchanged her Tile for her glass fiber knife, took a deep breath, and raised her torso over the ridge. She waved over her head. The figure below flinched and covered their Tile.

"Don't do anything foolish," Melissa said promptly. "Talk to me. What are you doing up here?"

Not a word in response.

Melissa pointed toward the tower room, forearm moving like a metronome. "Either you help me get in there too, or none of us gets in."

The two watched each other. There was a long pause.

"I'm not alone," Melissa added.

"Who are you?" The stranger's voice was hard to pinpoint, but Melissa guessed female. The slight accent was probably Russian.

"We don't need to know each other to do this," Melissa replied. "Whoever you tell me you are is going to be a lie, and you can assume the same with me."

"You can call me Naturelle."

"I'm Runa. What is your plan?"

Naturelle was silent. She looked down toward the edge of the roof and then lit up her Tile again, this time screen facing away from Melissa.

"How are you going to get in?" Melissa asked again.

Naturelle fiddled with her Tile.

"Oh, you're just sitting on a roof in ice rain for no reason at all?" Melissa waved her glass fiber knife until Naturelle paid attention. She put its blade against Naturelle's safety rope. "I can offer you a more permanent chill up here."

Naturelle looked down at her screen again, reading rather than typing this time, then spoke. "A window will be unlocked, and the intruder alarm will be off. That's how I get in."

"Who's helping you?" Melissa asked.

"What are you going to steal?" Naturelle countered.

"Once I'm in, I'll figure out my next move."

Naturelle checked the time. "Another hour and we should be good to go."

Melissa put away the knife and texted Kiss.

Still up there, right?

Freezing my ass off.

I'll buy you hot chocolate
afterward.

Bourbon.

I struck a deal with the
crouching tiger. Might get
messy. One hour till we go
in.

A deal? You trust no one.

I don't. But we need this.
Stay put.

Please.

The freezing sheets of rain tormented the three women up on the roofs. Melissa and Naturelle kept an eye on each other as well as the lights from the circular office space below the black tower.

The hour passed, and Kiss notified the team. "Pogodina and her co-worker are heading out."

The office went dark. Naturelle ascended by pulling her rope. Melissa took a step closer to the tower, making sure she didn't turn her back on Naturelle.

"Hey," Naturelle uttered in a sibilant whisper. "The lights in the office are controlled by passive infrared motion sensors. I need to disable them before I heat up. So I go first."

The roof-mounted ladder was close enough to the tower to let them stretch out and set foot on the tower's fringe just below the closest set of windows.

The unlocked window opened inward. Melissa stayed close behind to make sure she wasn't shut out. Naturelle turned around and made a gesture to keep quiet.

They snuck in and closed the window. The smell of old books with leather spines, oiled wood, and thick carpets reached Melissa together with the warmth of being inside. Her rubber soles squeaked as she stepped down on the hardwood floor. Naturelle turned on a red headlamp, and Melissa flipped her Tile to its red flashlight setting and got her wet X-ray glasses off, as they were fogging up.

Out of Naturelle's bag came a microfiber towel. She dried herself quickly, handed it over to Melissa, and disappeared down the narrow, bow-shaped staircase into the office below. Melissa heard movement and saw the flicker of red light for a while before Naturelle waved her down.

The circular office was smaller than she had anticipated, around thirty feet in diameter. The stairs followed the curved wall and were supported by a square, ornamented pillar. To the right of the pillar, under the stairs, was the office entrance.

Naturelle was occupied with what looked like a Wi-Fi router on top of a low bookshelf.

Melissa decided to start at Pogodina's desk.

The centerpiece was a monitor connected to a slim desktop computer—both branded MCST and in sleep mode. She snapped a photo of the PC's exact model. Other electric things were a pair of augmented-reality glasses, wireless charging for a Tile, and a local backup station.

Just as she was going to look underneath the desk, she saw a red light approaching quickly from the right.

Out of instinct, she dropped her Tile and raised her forearms to protect her head as Naturelle's fist came raging in. The impact was strong enough to pierce her guard and hit her chin. The pain came raging in.

Melissa's body automatically circled to face her opponent and got into fighting position, away from the desk, right foot forward.

Both masked women remained silent. Melissa tasted blood in her mouth.

The red headlamp made it hard for Melissa to see the outline of Naturelle, but the twisting movement was clear. A high kick was coming in.

Melissa pivoted her right foot with its heel forward, squatted until her butt almost touched the floor, and spun her body 180 degrees in the drop. A foot swept closely above her head as she put her left hand forward and her right hand on the floor to start a low spinning sweep kick. She hit Naturelle's inner ankle hard.

The trajectory of the red headlamp ended with a thump on Pogodina's desk. Not a whimper from Naturelle.

Melissa got up. "You think this is wise, huh?" Her voice was strained but not loud. "Just bring me all you got, shithead."

Heavy breathing came from beneath the red lamp, again at standing height. Naturelle's voice was low in pitch. "We either fight or you tell me why you're here."

"Fight." Melissa tightened her fists.

"I have an exit plan if I get caught in here. Do you?" Naturelle said.

"I'll figure it out. You're asking me to share information with a person I found hiding on the roof. And you have no way of telling if I lie to you. Whatever we say to each other is useless."

"You keep saying that."

There was a long pause. Melissa considered taking out the woman and being done with it.

Naturelle spoke again. "Let's find some common ground. Maybe we can build trust that way. What's the first thing you think of when I say Morris?"

"What do you mean, first thing?"

"I mean exactly that. What is the first thing you think of when I say Morris?"

"The Morris worm."

"Now you."

"What me?"

"You ask me."

Melissa was skeptical, but she did see what Naturelle was going for. "Explain a buffer overflow attack."

"You overflow a buffer of memory and overwrite a pointer, preferably a code pointer. My turn. Who coined the term *boring crypto*?"

"Dan Bernstein." If this was to convince her that Naturelle was a hacker, she'd have to drill deeper into technical stuff. "How many bits would you lose if you cast a long to a short?" she asked.

"You lose 19 bits."

"Incorrect." Melissa pulled back her right fist, ready to shoot it forward.

"I know. But we're testing each other, right? So 64 minus 16 equals 48 bits. You lose 48 bits. My turn again. Who took down the NSA's databases sixteen years ago?"

The question jolted Melissa out of the tense situation and into a swirl of flash memories. The batteries, the Arabic character for "peace be upon him," and the trial against West.

"You know or you don't?" Naturelle asked behind her nylon mask.

"West Wilder."

"One more. There was one more hacker."

Was Naturelle trolling her?

"We can drop that one." Naturelle sounded almost jovial. "You trust me now?"

The Russian had more or less proved she was a security professional, maybe even a hacker. The fact that they had broken into this office indicated she was a lunatic and a vigilante like Melissa herself, or some secret service agent.

Melissa reasoned audibly. "This is not about trust, it's about risk. Risks and tradeoffs." She picked up her Tile from the floor and felt her throbbing chin. "I'm taking the risk."

"Good. So let's be honest about why we're here."

"You first."

Chapter Fifty-Six

Pogodina's Office

Naturelle leaned on Pogodina's desk and removed her red lamp from her head as a gesture of peace. "For starters …"

"Wait. These walls have ears."

Melissa made her Tile output loud white noise and put it on Pogodina's desk. She waved to Naturelle to follow as she sat down on the floor. Naturelle brought her lamp with her.

"Are you here on government business?" she whispered to Naturelle.

"No, I'm not helping any government. I'm here for my people. My goal is to get certain information on Russian digital communications."

"That's vague."

"We do this in steps. Your turn," Naturelle said defiantly.

"No government ties."

"You know this is Nord Stream's office, right?"

"Mhm."

"The company deals with more than gas pipes. They also facilitate Russian internet communication with Kaliningrad. We need access to the stream."

"Why?"

Naturelle shook her head and pointed at Melissa.

Melissa stared at the masked person in front of her. "We—yes, I have a team too—we want access to Nord Stream computers and their connection to Moscow."

Naturelle sniffled. "Do you know what you're up against?"

Melissa didn't, but admitting it would sound weak.

"We don't have time to go through all of this here," Naturelle said.

"You need the same thing as I do if you're going to get anywhere close to Russian G20S."

"I didn't say anything about Russian G20S."

"Me neither."

She handed Melissa a small, battery-charged circuit board with a JTAG plug on a flat cable hanging off it. "Find the microLED driver chip in Pogodina's monitor and connect this to the JTAG right next to it while I take care of the Wi-Fi."

Melissa never got a chance to argue. She got up to inspect Pogodina's equipment. The MCST monitor was razor thin with all its logic in a bulge at the lower back. She laid it facedown and unscrewed the back with her multitool.

The monitor's driver chip and its adjacent JTAG socket were easily spotted, and she connected the circuit board Naturelle had handed her.

West's voice came in through her earpiece. "Pogodina is in the elevator, going up. You have a minute to get out, tops."

"Naturelle." Melissa gave her voice as much tone as she dared. The red light swiveled at the other side of the round room. "Pogodina is coming. My team has a camera in the elevator."

"Put the monitor back up and tell me exactly when she leaves the elevator. I have to enable the alarm and light sensor." Naturelle moved to the entrance door.

Melissa spoke to West as she reassembled the monitor. "Tell me when she leaves the elevator."

She saw Naturelle enter the first digits of the code on the alarm keypad, then wait with her right index finger on the last digit and her other hand pinching the corner of the piece of tape she had covered the light sensor with.

West came back in her ear. "She's out."

Melissa signaled to Naturelle and dashed toward the stairs to the tower room where they had entered.

A twenty-second alarm activation countdown started on the display as soon as Naturelle pushed the last code digit: 20, 19, 18, 17, 16, 15 … Melissa heard footsteps outside the door. She stopped at the end of the stairs, turned off her Tile's light, and leaned over the railing to see what happened below. Naturelle's headlamp barely lit the scene.

11, 10, 9 ... There was an audible blip from the outside badge reader. 8 ... The electric door lock buzzed. 7 ... Naturelle kicked a box of napkins lying on a chair down on the floor by the entrance, ripped the tape off the IR sensor, and swept behind the ornamented pillar. No more red light.

The office lights came on. Melissa was temporarily blinded but counted the seconds to keep track of the alarm activation. 5 ...

If Pogodina looked at the alarm display now, she would see the activation countdown and understand that someone had just enabled it.

4 ... Melissa squinted down. Pogodina was looking at the box of napkins.

3 ... Pogodina knelt and picked up the box. 2 ... She took another step in—1—and turned her head to the alarm panel just as its beep started blaring through the office, out into the hallway.

Pogodina closed the door and disabled the alarm. She walked over to her desk and pulled out a drawer. Her body froze. Slowly, her left hand adjusted the angle of the MCST monitor.

Then, in an explosive move, she drew a gun and pointed it straight at the pillar under the stairs. Melissa instinctively withdrew into safety and could no longer see what was happening.

From the floor below came Pogodina's sharp albeit calm voice, speaking in Russian. Naturelle replied in short bursts. Melissa instructed her Tile to translate live for her.

> Government business?
> Pfft. Take off that stupid
> mask.

> Whoever you are, you
> better have a damn good
> explanation for this.

> I do. We're here to make
> sure this subsidiary follows
> protocol.

The second voice was Naturelle's. Was she a Russian official after all?

The escape route out the window should be fast enough. The Russian voices below continued.

You must be joking. By
breaking in?

You will find no breakage. I
got in through the door.

Prove it. What's the alarm
code?

999332.

Fuck this nonsense. Why
wasn't I notified?

So you could tidy things up?
That's not how this works.

I've got nothing to hide. Do
you have any credentials?

Be my guest.

The translation prompt on Melissa's Tile stood still as the room below went silent for a while. She heard the familiar blip of a GPI scan.

Ministry of Internal Affairs.
You people make me sick.
And Kaliningrad? Why
would they send someone
from that shit hole?

Watch what you say, Agent.

Which branch?

Economic crime.

Fine. I need to contact my
superiors about this.

No worries. I'm done here
anyway.

You're not going to just
walk out of here. You will
go with me to the embassy
and stay there until this is
straightened out.

Shortly thereafter, the two Russian-speaking women wrapped up and left. As soon as Melissa heard the door close, she ran down the stairs and up to the alarm keypad.

9-9-9-3-3-2; alarm disabled.

She reused Naturelle's tape to cover the occupancy sensor for the lights.

Naturelle had not ratted her out, and she had said earlier that she had an "exit plan if I get caught." Maybe the story Naturelle pulled on Pogodina *was* the exit plan?

West updated the team on Pogodina and a younger woman going down in the elevator. Melissa responded that she wasn't going to waste this chance to dig through the Russian G20S office.

Twenty minutes later, she concluded that the place was strikingly clean of intel. Not even the garbage can or the two suitcases she found contained anything of interest.

She went back to check one more time around Pogodina's desk, and just as she was about to start spraying the place with Dee N' A and take her leave, her hand brushed along the edge of the tabletop. There was a difference in texture to the left of where Pogodina would sit. Melissa's gloves made it hard to detect such things, but here there was a slight edge underneath the tabletop and a different friction for a few inches, like plastic.

She crawled under and looked. It was a laminated eight-by-four grid of Cyrillic words glued in place. She took a photo and let her Tile translate it.

Window	Rain	Speaker	Golf
Tundra	Glass	Pillow	Book
Marble	Candy	Music	Saw
Illness	Wood	Grass	Air
Moon	Church	Glove	Hair
Computer	Bill	School	Corn
Hemp	Cosmos	Gas	Dice
Paper	Dog	Cream	Vulture

Regardless of what this was, it was something.

She checked the time: 11:05. Better wait a little longer before she got out.

•

Melissa's feet landed on the roof of the low building between Kungsgatan 79 and 77, and a soaking wet, shivering Jitterbug hugged her.

They packed up, climbed down, and headed northeast toward Kungsbron, or King's Bridge.

The second to last building before the bridge was inset about ten feet compared to the other buildings along the street. It created a wider pedestrian space, like a minute square.

The last thing Melissa remembered walking into the square was her entire body tensing up in a big cramp combined with heavy beating along her back.

Jitterbug later described it as a lightning bolt of pain and losing his balance as if someone pulled a wire between his forehead and the base of his neck.

Chapter Fifty-Seven

Zhiveye Na Pokriva

The soreness after a full-body workout combined with something like a blistering hangover greeted Melissa as she squinted into a bright light in front of her.

She was sitting on a chair, and her hands were tied behind her back with what felt like a plastic cable tie. There was a chemical smell in the air, like sweet, lemon-scented cleaner or wood varnish.

As her eyes adjusted, she saw Jitterbug sitting tied a couple of feet to her right, still passed out, head hanging forward.

"Sorry to go all mafia on you."

The female voice came from close in front of her. Slight Eastern accent. Melissa recognized it, but she couldn't see who it was because of the light.

"You have been in somewhat of a delirium the last hour or so. We're not in the business of taking hostages and will set you free as soon as we've had a chat about Pogodina."

"Is that you, Naturelle?"

The woman delayed. "Yes."

It sounded like Naturelle. Melissa rolled her shoulders and tilted her neck left and right. "Did you shoot us with a Taser or something?"

"It's called a Red Devil, but the effect is the same."

"Fuuuck." Melissa sucked in dribble from the corner of her mouth.

"We are sorry." It was a second, deeper voice. Male, with a heavier Russian accent. "We had little time."

"Have you checked that Ji...my friend is okay?"

"His vitals are fine." It was the man again.

"What do you want from us?"

"If you give us all information you got from your search through Nord Stream's office, you can be on your way."

"I don't know what you're talking about."

"Access to your Tile will work."

Melissa chuckled in pain. "Yeah, right."

"Any other suggestion?"

"I suggest you go fuck yourselves."

The woman got back in the driver's seat. "We are not your enemy. I meant what I said up there. We can help each other. It's just that things took a different path than expected."

"Why don't you show yourself so I can see if you're Naturelle?" As Melissa said that, she realized she didn't actually know what Naturelle looked like.

A woman with Naturelle's height, posture, and movement came forward. It was the first time Melissa saw her without a mask. Pitch-black hair parted in the middle, falling down in large, untidy waves. Pale complexion with intense, black eyebrows, and deep red lips in a slightly sad expression. She wore a tight, black leather necklace with a diamond-shaped metal pendant, an orange fold top, and black pleated pants.

"If you're not Russian authority, how did you get away from Pogodina?" Melissa asked.

"I leveraged some intel on Nord Stream, stuff that she can't afford public light on. To build those huge gas pipes, Russia relied on Swedish ports and infrastructure."

"Bribes?"

"Swedish politicians are very reluctant to receive dirty money. Instead, they want you to make investments in their cities or communities to help them get reelected. Russia generously upgraded the port of a city called Karlshamn to create jobs and all that good stuff. Russian internal documents make it very clear that this was a bribe. Leak those documents and you'd cause a significant stink in Swedish politics and tangible risk to Nord Stream's business. Pogodina proposed a deal before we reached the embassy."

Melissa's body was booting up. "Can I get some water?"

Naturelle obliged, and Melissa gulped with Naturelle holding the glass to her mouth.

Melissa wasn't done digging into Naturelle's connection to Russian authorities. "Who gave you access to documents on the bribe?"

Naturelle got back behind the lamp. "The Russian Ministry of Internal Affairs."

"So you work for the Russian government after all?"

"We have good and deep connections. But no, we are not part of the government. We are Zhiveye Na Pokriva."

"Shiveh Nah Pockriva?"

"It means having fun, living by thievery, hacking for the lulz." Naturelle pulled a chair over and sat down in the light. "But those days are gone. We're much more serious now. You have probably heard of Russian oligarchs."

Melissa nodded.

"The most famous of them is Vladimir Petrov, a guy with a net worth of fifteen billion US dollars. His money comes from acquiring one of Russia's most successful businesses—Nornickel—for a fraction of its real value. It's a mining and smelting company in North Siberia that was built up with forced labor during Stalin's reign."

"Stalin, the businessman."

"Stalin won World War II and modernized our country, but nothing can justify the sacrifices he demanded of the people. Russia needs to pay its dues to the descendants of the ones who died building Nornickel. We're hackers, and we're going to funnel Petrov's money to the people who deserve it."

Melissa recognized the approach—hack society instead of changing it through regular means.

"So where does Pogodina come in?"

"Ah, right. New taxes have been announced in Russia, comprising expatriated money in tax havens. This got things moving quickly among the oligarchs. When people move quickly, they make mistakes. We got a tip that Petrov is paying Pogodina to help him make an exit before these taxes kick in. Help as in smuggling. That's why we need to get into Pogodina's computer."

"A noble goal but risky as hell. Why would someone like you care so much about atrocities Stalin committed a hundred years ago?"

"One of those dead Gulag workers was my great-grandfather, Ivan." Naturelle's voice was low-pitched and resolute. "He was forced to work, then shot."

"I'm sorry about that," Melissa said. She bit her lower lip. "Do you have anything to back that story?"

Naturelle got up and looked piercingly at her for a few seconds.

"There's a Russian civil rights society called Memorial. They have records of politically persecuted citizens and their relatives. My family line is in there. Mikhail, untie her and give her back her Tile. You can have a look yourself on their website. Search for Veschitsky Ivan Adolfovich."

Melissa found the Memorial site and did the search.

```
Veschitsky Ivan Adolfovich
Born 1919, Oryol, Oryol Oblast.
Russian.

Journalist, Kaliningrad Printing House,
corrector.

Arrested on August 7, 1947, by The Ministry
of Internal Affairs (MVD).

Sentenced according to Article 58-10 for
active counter-revolutionary agitation.

Verdict: 25 years.

Shot May 19, 1953, Norilsk, Krasnoyarsk
Krai.

Place of burial: Norilsk, Krasnoyarsk Krai.
```

Among the names listed as Ivan's family was a Naturelle Tatyana Veschitskaya.

Either Naturelle was telling the truth, or she had prepared her lies well. If she was telling the truth, she had also given Melissa her real name up on the roof.

"I'm sorry about your great-grandfather."

"Don't be. Instead, help us. I've shared our mission. It's time for you to share yours."

Melissa hesitated. She knew she could not blow the full story, but she had to give Naturelle enough to be set free and to keep the door open to cooperate with Zhiveye Na Pokriva. This vigilante group obviously had key intel and help inside Russia. Help that would be very welcome in the pursuit of an entry to Russian G20S systems.

Melissa looked up. "We are the Survivors."

Chapter Fifty-Eight

G20S: A Favor

"Hi, Dr. Kawasaki! This is Manoel Ferreira with Brazilian G20S. How are you today?"

She looked at the phone's screen, which confirmed that the person on the other side had authenticated as Manoel Ferreira, head of G20S in Brazil.

"Hello again, Mr. Ferreira. Doing well over here. What can I do for you?"

"We understand this is not really something you deal with on a daily basis, but at our meeting back in November you mentioned that you were willing to help personally should we find ourselves in a tight spot."

"Absolutely. What is this tight spot of yours?"

"We have detected strange activity on one of our agent's accounts, and traces lead us to believe we might have been subject to a cyberattack on US soil. At one of our consulates to be specific."

Kawasaki paused for a few seconds, contemplating.

"This wouldn't happen to be your consulate at the Wilshire Grand in Los Angeles, would it?" she asked.

"Well … yes actually. Is this something you are aware of?"

"We have an ongoing investigation."

"I would have thought you'd reach out to us if you were investigating adversarial activity against one of Brazil's consulates."

"We didn't know it was Brazil's, just the rough location and that G20S was the target. So thank you for this puzzle piece."

"I see. We'd like to resolve this."

"Of course. I'll have my people share with you what we have."

"Excellent."

"Might I ask if Brazil has given any further thought to the upcoming vote on G20S leadership?"

Chapter Fifty-Nine

Parallel Execution

Seven hackers sat around Robert's office kitchen table—two Russians, four Americans, and one Swede. Robert had removed a lot of gear and looked cautiously excited.

West had heard descriptions of Naturelle and her colleague Mikhail, both from Melissa and the impromptu FRA vetting Robert had insisted on. But he couldn't help but stare at them in the flesh—Naturelle with her black, wavy hair and colorful clothes; Mikhail with plenty of muscle and a square face. Kiss seemed fond of their looks too.

Melissa's chin was bruised, and she shrugged slowly and massaged the back of her neck before she started talking.

"I want to get everyone's agreement here, face-to-face. We've got two separate goals. ZNP ... I looked it up and Shiveh Nah Pockriva is spelled with a 'Z' so I'm gonna call you ZNP. Shiveh Nah Pockriva is too damn long."

Naturelle smiled in confirmation.

"ZNP is going to take back a ton of money from an oligarch who stole it from the Russian people. If we help them, they will share some of that money with us and will help us get access to Russian G20S. Are y'all cool with a co-op on this?"

"You're paranoid enough for all of us, so I'm good," Kiss said.

Melissa looked around. No one objected.

"Okay, I'll share what we have on Pogodina." Melissa commenced. "She receives a digitally signed, encrypted, four-kilobyte file three times a week. We believe the file holds the G20S access codes for the coming forty-eight to seventy-two hours. If we are correct, the content of that file will allow us to tap into and even hijack her communication with Moscow."

"Russian G20S end-to-end encryption," Mikhail said in a confident tone. "It goes by name Fraktal, with k, and uses 358-bit secret key, generated on receiver's device and communicated in Moscow." He stopped himself. "Communicated *to* Moscow. The sender uses it once to encrypt single data delivery, then throws it away."

"I got a photo of the MCST model she uses." Melissa beamed a red-tinted photo of a sticker from the back of Pogodina's PC onto the room's big screen.

West leaned over in the direction of Mikhail. "Do you know what operating system she's running on that thing?" he asked in a lower tone, as if they were only talking to each other.

"Astra Linux."

Robert filled in. "The community version is called Astra Linux Oryol and is fully open source. We looked at it a couple of years ago. Smolensk—the special purpose flavor for Russian intelligence—has closed source additions on top."

Mikhail reacted when Oryol and Smolensk were mentioned. "The 358-bit key generation can be done on community edition. But Fraktal encryption and decryption is closed source. I may be able to set up link in decryption service in Kaliningrad, where you can test keys. But you need file to decrypt."

Melissa gave the Russian a nod. "Today is Thursday, which means the next file arrives tomorrow morning. Jit and West, you investigate Fraktal; Kiss and Mikhail, you figure out how to snatch a copy of the file; and Naturelle and I focus on Petrov's smuggling business. Rob, you'll have to help us with anything Swedish. Sounds good?"

Naturelle approved. "Pogodina caught me in there, so she'll be replacing equipment and searching the place for microphones and cameras. However, the SORM has special hooks to Moscow, so it'll take a few days for her to get a new one."

"What's a sorm?" Melissa asked.

"*Systema Operativno-Rozysknikh Meropriatiy*. Network surveillance. Basic building block of the Red Web. It looks like a Wi-Fi router. I compromised it to get us access to the office Wi-Fi. Did you connect the piece of hardware I gave you?"

Melissa looked puzzled for a second. "Oh, the thing with the JTAG? Yes."

"The JTAG port on the microLED driver chip allows us to take screenshots from Pogodina's monitor by dumping the display buffer and piping it out over Wi-Fi. But when we do so, her computer screen freezes for a second or two, so we can't afford to do it too often or she'll notice. Let's hope she doesn't replace her monitor. She would never use Western gear, and the subpar Russian supply chain should be working in our favor."

"How would we know when there's something interesting on the screen?" Kiss asked.

"The SORM in Pogodina's office has metadata on everything that goes in and out of her PC," Naturelle said. "All official activities abroad are surveilled by Moscow—embassies, our offices within the UN, our office at the World Bank, and so on. It's done by terminating network transport security at the government-issued SORM and feeding metadata back to the central authority. They actually repurposed an old anti-spam feature to do it."

Melissa connected the dots. "We look at Pogodina's metadata through the SORM you tampered with and use that to decide when to capture a screenshot of her monitor?"

"Yes. We can see exactly when she receives a message, when she opens it, who sent it, and so on."

"Sweet. That SORM router could also be a place to grab the file."

"But 358 bits to decrypt it though, that's brutal," West said. He started typing on his Tile and then remembered he could just ask it. "What is the search space for a 358-bit key?"

"The number of possible combinations of a 358-bit key is a six with 107 zeroes behind."

Melissa nodded. "We have to find a *weakness* in Fraktal if it's going to be our way in." She gave West a mischievous smile. "Sounds like your cup of tea."

Everyone looked at him. He glanced at Kiss. "I need someone to discuss with."

Melissa responded before Kiss had a chance. "I already decided you work with Jit."

"I can do it," Kiss said, winking her left eye at West.

Melissa looked at her. "Jit does this one."

Jitterbug intervened. "Sure, I'll do it."

Melissa looked at Kiss. "Can I talk to you for a moment? Alone."

Chapter Sixty

Rule Number Three

Melissa pulled Kiss down into the basement of Robert's office complex.

"What's rule number three?" Melissa asked, fuming.

"What do you mean?"

"The Survivors have three basic rules. The third?"

"No romance."

"Exactly. And how would you describe your relationship with West?"

"We're not dating or anything."

"Oh, come on. You're fucking him."

"We've had sex, yes. I didn't think you were into him anymore."

"I'm not. That's not the issue here."

"Is celibacy the fourth rule?"

"Fuck you, Kiss. I didn't make that rule for funzies. I'm trying to protect the integrity of the team. We all have to make levelheaded decisions, and we need to be able to trust each other. I was hoping you two would come to your senses. But instead you flirt openly and behave like I'm stupid."

"You know what? I don't like your leadership. You make us miserable, and you have no manners."

"I. Don't. Fucking. Care. You have two choices. Either you terminate whatever it is you and West have going, or you leave the team."

Tens of seconds ticked away as the two women stared each other down.

"Are you going to have a similar talk with West?" Kiss asked.

"No. He's fragile, and I'm afraid this fling of yours is something he's clinging on to. If I push him, he might make the wrong choice. Besides, I have a better use for your flirting skills."

Kiss jerked her head back and frowned.

Melissa glanced toward the stairs to the ground floor. "I don't trust these Russians."

CHAPTER SIXTY-ONE

Entropy

"Oh my!" Kiss erupted from the other side of the room.

West looked over. She was sitting close to Mikhail.

"This is the real deal," she continued and put an arm around the Russian's wide shoulders. In a friendly way, West decided.

Kiss and Mikhail were repurposing the anti-spam and malware feature built in to the SORM Wi-Fi router in Pogodina's office to get access to the four-kilobyte files before those morning calls with Moscow, files they hoped would contain encrypted G20S access codes. They had tried to treat all incoming correspondence as spam and quarantine any attachment just long enough to make a copy, but somehow important emails slipped through.

He walked over to see what the fuss was about and found them staring at a list of sender domain names preconfigured to never be introspected for spam or malware:

```
президент.рф
правительство.рф
fsb.ru
government.ru
kremlin.ru
mil.ru
g20s.ru
```

These were the senders slipping through. It was the real deal.

•

By midnight, Jitterbug and West had a reasonable understanding of how Pogodina's Linux PC generated the crypto key used to decrypt the four-kilobyte file she received three times a week.

Astra Linux used six sources of entropy to produce the key's 358 random bits—128 bits from the device's IP address and 48 bits from its MAC address. Then 64 bits from the current timestamp in seconds, called epoch, and 32 bits from microseconds at process startup. Finally, 22 bits from the process ID and 64 bits from the PC's entropy pool called /dev/urandom.

```
IPv6 address
0011111111111110 0001100100000000
0100010101000101 0000000000000011
0000001000000000 1111100011111111
1111111000100001 0110011111001111

MAC address
0011100011001001 1000011000011110
1101100010101010

Unix Epoch, seconds since 1970
0000000000000000 0000000000000000
0101100110001111 1111101100010101

Microseconds since process start
0000000000001110 0000010111101011

Process ID
0001000011110111 100101

/dev/urandom
1000110110010111 1111010001100010
1000010110111000 0010010011101110
```

"Mikhail said his server can test about ten million keys a second once we have a file to decrypt. We need to bring this down from 358 to about 40 unknown bits before we can brute force it in a day," West said.

In the back of his head, he kept thinking of Kiss and Mikhail, who both had gone to bed half an hour ago. She really seemed to enjoy the Russian's company and had barely said goodnight to West and Jitterbug.

Jitterbug yawned. "I'm ready to go to bed. But let's at least do the obvious ones. We own their Wi-Fi router, which will give us both the IP and MAC address of Pogodina's PC. That brings us down to 182 bits if my math is correct."

"Sounds right," West said and went into the time part of the puzzle. "Microseconds are stored in a 32-bit variable, but there are only a million possible microseconds, which means there's only 20 bits of real entropy, so 170 bits left."

Jitterbug asked his Tile how many seconds there are in a month.

"Two million, five hundred and ninety-two thousand."

"Okay, so if Pogodina restarts her PC at least once a month, we're down to 126 bits."

"What if we could reboot the computer for her?" West suggested. "That would mean we control the process start time."

"That'd be pretty radical. It would probably make the process ID predictable too. That would put us at 84 bits, which would be sweet but still years' worth of brute force tests."

"We don't have a way to reboot her computer anyway. But it would solve a big chunk of the problem."

"Mhm." Jitterbug yawned again. "Man, I really need to hit the hay."

"I'll stay up a little longer. Haven't had my first cup of coffee yet, so I have that card to play."

"God bless, my friend." Jitterbug stood up and gave West's shoulder a friendly squeeze.

West was now alone on the ground floor. Alone with the insurmountable task of breaking a Russian custom crypto.

Stockholm's winter weather kept the windows wet with gentle rain. The office space where Robert's employees had their desks was a glowing pool of screen savers.

West brewed himself five cups of coffee and poured it all into one of Robert's giant merchandise mugs labeled "Sec-T 0x0Anniversary."

Even if we find a way to reboot her machine, we still have to shave off another 44 bits.

Hours later, he crashed on his bed, still dressed, having just sent a burst of texts to Jitterbug.

Hey, J!t! If we can pull off
that reboot, I think I've
brought this sucker home.

To provide enough entropy
at system startup, Astra
Linux leaves the /dev/
urandom pool uninitialized
in the hope that it will
contain garbage data.

But Pogodina's MCST uses
error-correcting memory
which makes the pool all
zeroes at startup. One
technology killing another. :)

/dev/urandom will provide
20 bits of entropy tops after
a reboot. Add microseconds
and you are down to just
40 bits. That's one trillion
possible keys. Not easy, but
brute forceable.

·

West didn't get up until two p.m. He emerged from the basement and strolled over to Kiss. She was laughing at something in the company of Mikhail.

"Hey, guys," West said loudly.

"Oh, good morning, West." Kiss kept her focus on the screen in front of her. "I heard you figured out the entropy hack. Good job."

"Thanks. Did you get the file?"

"Oh, yeah." Kiss threw the Russian a high five. "We had a brief look, and it seems like an encrypted blob all right."

"Lunch?" he asked, putting his hands in his pockets and faking a yawn.

"There's a nice sandwich place called Drama Triangle two blocks away. You should check it out," Kiss said.

West stood silent for an awkward minute or so.

"I was thinking we should try some local beers," he said.

Jitterbug called him over. "Hey, West. Awesome work on urandom. I've been driving myself bonkers over how to reboot Pogodina's machine. My best idea so far has been to cause a power outage, but Naturelle is dead certain she saw an emergency power rig up in that office."

West slumped into his chair.

"What's the matter, friend? You da man."

West gave him half a smile. "We have to time the reboot with one of the file transfers anyway. That's when the key is generated. Next chance is Monday."

"Maybe this can cheer you up. I've written a script that feeds Mikhail's server with keys to try and then checks if the decrypted output is plaintext, Russian or English. I'm about to run it on the file Kiss and Mikhail got us even though we still have 126 unknown bits. Who knows, we might get lucky."

West watched Jitterbug execute his script.

```
Exhaustive search through 126 bits


85,070,591,730,234,615,865,843,651,857,9
42,052,864 keys to test


Testing key 1 ...
```

Chapter Sixty-Two

Screen Grab Coming In

It was ten in the evening, and everyone but Melissa was watching a new sci-fi movie called *Vertebrae* on the big screen, starring Marilyn Monroe. West had tried to sit next to Kiss, but she somehow got Mikhail to sit between them.

"Hey, pause that thing and come over, y'all," Melissa yelled. "Pogodina just replied to an email conversation we're following. Screen grab coming in."

The team gathered to see what was captured and translated.

```
> To: pogodina@nordstream.com
> From: sdvornikov@promgaz.com
> Subject: Pipe delivery 26/1
>
> Dear Director Pogodina,
>
> We are happy to inform you that
> pipe delivery NS3-552 is
> expected to leave Kaliningrad on
> 25/1 and arrive to Karlshamn on
> 26/1.
>
> Pd-15 is included, finally.
>
> Yours, Stanislav Dvornikov

Thanks! That completes the set.
Should make Xin happy.
```

We've been assigned temporary storage
in Warehouse 6 (canvas). Specify in the
unloading and storage plan that Pd-15
should remain on the cargo ship. We're
about to close the deal. No need to move
it.

--DirP

West checked today's date. "The shipment left Kaliningrad today. There has to be records of what was loaded, including the Pd-15 thing."

"Records of what they *believe* was loaded," Naturelle inserted.

"Maybe they're smuggling something inside a pipe?" West suggested.

"Pogodina's going down there, right?" Jitterbug said. "Can I see the message thread we snagged earlier?"

Melissa pulled up the relevant screenshot.

The SR committee would
very much like to meet you
on-site. Are you able to
make it to Karlshamn on
Monday?

P is there. He can handle it.

I'm afraid not. The Chinese
specifically asked for you.
They're nervous, you know.
And they have never met
you. They need a face.

Damn it. I have to be in
Stockholm for my call with
Moscow.

Can't you take the call from
here?

Not with such short notice.
You know how sensitive the
protocol is.

Actually, I don't. :)

The call needs to be taken in
my office, that's all I can say.
Xin will have to meet me
Sunday.

Should work. They stay at
some hotel here.

I'll be at Ronneby Airport at
09:20. Have a car pick me
up.

Everyone stood still around Melissa's monitor, trying to make sense of it all.

"A Chinese 'SR committee' and a male named P is in Karlshamn," Jitterbug said.

Melissa's Tile lit up with a notification. She snapped it off the table and read intensely, shielding the screen.

"Wassup?" West asked her.

"Nothing."

She put her Tile away and shifted to her characteristic doer mode. "Whatever Pogodina's emails and messages are trying to tell us, there's an imminent business transaction, and it could very well be the liquidation of what Petrov is smuggling. Let's all get some sleep and then start moving. Kiss, you work with Mikhail and see if we can get access to Karlshamn port systems and find out more about what's on that ship."

West saw Kiss smile, but not at him.

Melissa continued. "Naturelle, you and I head down to Karlshamn proper to scout the port and be in place when Pogodina meets this Chinese committee. West and Jitterbug, you've got two things on your plate—search for what could be behind the abbreviations 'SR' and 'PD,' and figure out how to reboot Pogodina's PC so that we can brute force the next crypto key. We can't afford to lose time, since she may receive a replacement SORM and monitor any day."

Chapter Sixty-Three

A Bug Under the Rug

West listened in on Kiss and Mikhail as they took on the Karlshamn port software system. If they were to help ZNP steal whatever Petrov was smuggling, they had to get hard info on the shipment.

"Not a single CVE entry for Tegia or TegTerminal," Kiss said after asking her Tile to search the Common Vulnerabilities and Exposures database for the software system Karlshamn port was running. "Wow, that's zero published security vulnerabilities in like fifty years. This Tegia company is either flying under the radar or we're talking Fort Knox here."

"I'll check Russian databases," Mikhail said.

"Cool, can I see?"

"It's all in Cyrillic, so you'll have to use some translation thing," he told Kiss.

West got nothing useful done in the three hours it took for Mikhail and Kiss to get a hit for Tegia in the Russian data sources.

"They have couple of security issues in their XML import," Mikhail said.

The Russian's accent irritated West. *It's Ex ML, not Ix ML.*

"XML—the original sin," Kiss said in a narrator voice.

Mikhail sifted through the vulnerability description. "Ha. This was found in Nord Stream original security audit. That's irony. Patched long ago, I guess."

West walked over to have a look at the find.

"My translator says that's a reference to some systems documentation." Kiss pointed to a section on Mikhail's screen.

Mikhail scrolled and stopped. "Even better, here are the credentials for account Tegia set up for security auditors. And a link in login page."

```
Username:
karlshamn_audit@nordstream.com

Password:
osihnr56(GGue4u5s

Login:
https://customerportal.tegia.se
```

The TegTerminal customer portal was a barren webpage. Email and password, a checkbox for "Remember me," and a link to reset your password through email.

Mikhail hesitated.

"Go for it," Kiss said.

He copy-pasted the credentials and hit "Log in."

```
This account has been disabled due to
inactivity. A link has been sent to your
email address for password reset.
```

"Oops. I hope mailbox is inactive."

West snuck back to his corner, where he was supposed to be monitoring Pogodina's inbox. Schadenfreude bubbled up inside him when he saw the metadata of a new message coming in.

"Mikhail, did you just try to reset a password? Pogodina got an email for a 'Karlshamn underscore audit' account."

"Let's hope she's not working on Saturday," Mikhail said.

"She's at her desk all right. It just got marked as opened."

"Quick, grab screenshot."

Kiss and Mikhail rolled their chairs over and sat on either side of West to read the password reset email.

Dear Karlshamn Audit,

You need to set a new password to
reactivate your account. Please use the
enclosed QR code to access the account
reactivation page.

Thanks!
The Tegia Team

"Use the link before Pogodina consumes it."

West blipped the QR code, and seconds later they had activated the account.

A convoluted and confusing user interface filled the screen. Labels and options were in English, whereas entries and menu choices were in Swedish. The wide center pane had a drop-down menu named "Job List Clients." It featured four obviously made-up test businesses.

"Check import function," Mikhail said, leaning over, pointing at the screen. "That's probably where XML security problems were happening."

West noticed Mikhail's aftershave.

He checked the import function as Mikhail suggested, and there were only two options—HTS and EDIFACT. "No *Ex* ML import."

He switched to Export. Here there were *three* options—JSON, EDIFACT, and XML.

Kiss smiled. "XML and JSON. We will die before those formats do."

"Važno ne to, kak dolgo ty prožil, a kak horošo žil."

"That's beautiful. What does it mean?" she asked.

"The important thing is not how many years in your life, but how much life in your years."

"True dat."

"Platitude," West muttered.

"Let's get back to our corner, Mikhail. West seems to need some space," Kiss said.

She stroked West across his shoulders as she got up from her chair. A condescending gesture, he decided.

He felt hot. "Hey, Jit, can you keep an eye on Pogodina's traffic, please? I'm going to take a walk."

"It's been raining on and off the whole day," Jitterbug replied.

"Sure, but I need to get out of here."

West got up and took his jacket. Just as his hand was going to open the door to the outside, he had an idea that could help Kiss and Mikhail. He pushed the door open. A gust of rainy wind splashed his face.

He closed the door again, still inside. "You said the TegTerminal security bug you found in the Russian database was in XML import, right?" he said loud enough for Kiss and Mikhail to hear it. "Why do they still have an export function if they no longer support import? Maybe they simply *hid* XML import in the user interface instead of fixing the security problem?"

He headed out without waiting for their reaction.

Chapter Sixty-Four

G20S: Walk the Walk

A Canadian Bid for Less US Power Over G20S

Commander Emelie Pelletier of Canadian G20S today proposed a new direction for the international security agency in a bid to win the upcoming election of global director.

"The initial promise of G20S was to empower the global community to fight terrorism, manipulation of political processes, and cybercrime. Given where we are today, I think we can do better," Pelletier said in a prepared statement.

"Both the conflicts that drive terrorism and the cracks in the system that allow for cybercrime are symptoms of mistrust and lack of collaboration. I want to resolve the conflicts and solidify our joint intelligence so that we can reach the goals we set up years ago."

She went on to propose a change in voting power and an international expansion of the agency.

"This involves two major shifts. One is to equalize the power between the G8 countries and the rest of the G20. I support voting power based on population size as proposed by Brazil last year. The other shift is to invite countries beyond G20 to the core network. I know both these ideas may sound strange coming from a country on the inside; one of the privileged powers. But I truly believe that the security and safety of citizens in G8 can only be ensured through less of superpowers and more of shared responsibilities."

Experts say this is Pelletier differentiating herself from her contender, Dr. Akiko Kawasaki of US G20S, and betting on all the non-G8 votes plus at least two of the G8 ones to win the day. The power structure within G20S has been challenged ever since its inception with comparisons to unhealthy classification of common stock into Class A shares carrying more voting rights than Class B.

Europe, which has the most countries in G8 but also many small countries, could see this as an opening for less North American dominance in the intelligence community.

This article's sources are GPI-validated.

•

BestBye and her aunt were on a Saturday morning walk. They were met by a trickle of runners with everything but their faces covered in polyester, doing one-mile laps around the Parade Field in Fort Meade in just below freezing temperature.

Dr. Kawasaki was moody and gestured to the left to take a turn onto a more secluded path.

"This is where they launch fireworks," she said, pointing forward.

She had said the same thing last time they walked here, almost half a year ago, and followed up with details on Commander Pelletier from Canada, Agent Espinoza from Brazil, and Dr. López from Mexico, and a plausible story on how BestBye had spotted them in New York, lurking outside the G20S meeting. Out of those three, Kawasaki had urged BestBye to make the Survivors go after Pelletier. BestBye hadn't known about the upcoming appointment of a North American director of G20S back then.

It seemed like her aunt had something to share this time too. BestBye didn't mind waiting.

"My agency not only protects lives," Kawasaki started off, "we protect the American *way* of life. Before we all got self-driving cars, people on the left used to point out that more people died in traffic accidents than from terrorist attacks, questioning the powers my agency was given. But car crashes are different losses."

Dr. Kawasaki stopped and looked into the distance between the sparse, leafless trees lining the path.

Even though her aunt didn't make a move for it, BestBye knew she was yearning for a pull on the pocket flask in her coat.

Dr. Kawasaki sighed. "The public isn't willing to give up its constitutional rights because of traffic accidents. But confronted with terrorist attacks and acts of war, they want protection. I've been assigned to provide that protection, and it is a heavy burden, I tell you."

She started walking again. "We've received intel indicating that Russia …"

Icy gravel creaked under their shoes.

"Never mind," Kawasaki said. "We need to make Melissa go *into* Russia."

Chapter Sixty-Five

A Pipe Dream

Melissa and Naturelle took a high-speed train south toward Karlshamn to figure out what Petrov was smuggling and how to steal it on behalf of ZNP.

Jitterbug's list of potential meanings to the abbreviations "PD" and "SR" came in during the ride.

```
Hey, here's what I got.

PD-15:
Aviadvigatel PD-15, a new Russian jet
engine. There are other meanings to PD
such as a Positive Displacement pump that
can be used in pipes, but the jet engine
is a direct hit. Top secret project.

SR committee:
1) SR-5, a Chinese rocket launching
system.
2) Socialist Revolutionary Party, key
player in the Russian Revolution.
3) Serbian.
4) Slovak Republic.
5) Swedish Radio, public service thing.

/J!T
```

"Military tech. Always a prime suspect in smuggling," Melissa said.

They reached Karlshamn around lunch. The coastal winter air was chill and damp, and they were hit by a strange, foul smell, like sweaty feet or rancid butter.

Between them and the station house there were six parallel tracks without platform access, which indicated a lot of freight.

Melissa felt out of place. This smalltown part of Sweden wasn't something you'd visit as a tourist, at least not during winter.

Melissa and Naturelle followed the handful of locals toward the station house—a brick, one-story building with a gray upper floor mounted on top as an afterthought. It appeared vacant, blinds down.

"Maybe we can catch a bus to the port," Melissa said, seeing Naturelle approach the waiting hall's doorway. "I see a couple of bus stops."

"You can only take the bus to the port in the morning." The male voice startled Melissa.

She swiveled around and saw a man standing between two blue dumpsters about twenty feet away.

"Or you can run. Twenty minutes if you run fast." His Swedish accent was heavy.

He wore a blue workwear overall and a baseball cap with a logo that read "Karlshamn Energi AB." It almost looked as if he were hiding, the way he stood between the containers.

"Do you run there often?" Melissa asked.

"I did once. The other way. My A tractor was broken, and I almost missed a train I wanted to see."

"Missed a train?"

The man nodded.

"Oh, you're a trainspotter. You come here to watch the trains?"

The man nodded the exact same way again, like in a looped video clip.

Naturelle walked up next to Melissa. "What is an A tractor?" she asked the man.

He pointed out a blue metallic micro-pickup in the nearby parking lot.

"Perhaps you can drive us to the port?" Naturelle asked. "We can pay you."

"The train leaves in one minute. Then we can go."

The three of them squeezed into the pickup's single row of seats.

Apparently, the speed of an A tractor was capped at a dreadfully slow twenty miles an hour, but that gave Naturelle time to tap into the man's knowledge of the port.

"I guess you see a lot of Russian ships these days?"

"They deliver concrete-coated steel pipes weighing twenty-three metric tons each," the man replied. "One comma two meters in diameter. It's for the pipeline. The pipes used to come from Germany, but now they come from Kaliningrad."

"Do you watch them being unloaded?"

"Stripped. It's called stripping. I talk to the workers, and they tell me what things are called."

"Got ya. Do you watch them being stripped?"

"Stripping takes twelve hours. They store 76,000 pipes here, and the pipe supply vessel takes ninety pipes at a time out to the laying barge. It's called laying barge. Stuffing the supply vessel takes seven hours, sometimes six hours and forty-five minutes."

Naturelle pulled in air to try to say something but was interrupted by the man.

"But they don't lay pipes during winter."

"Interesting. Do you know if they do special treatment of some of the pipes?" Naturelle asked.

"What is special treatment?"

"I don't know. Maybe put them aside or store them in a special place?"

"They have an extra storage of six thousand pipes off the port property in case of an interruption in the supply."

The two women looked at each other.

"Could you take us to this off-site storage? We can buy you lunch if you're hungry."

"I like kebab pizza."

"Kabob pizza it is."

Their driver devoured his thin-crust pizza stuffed with strips of meat and drizzled in two sauces in under ten minutes.

They drove westward out of central Karlshamn and ended up on a small side road. Trees paved the right side, but she could make out a fence behind them and what looked like a storage lot.

"You can see the six thousand pipes through here. I don't want to drive all the way to the gate. The security guard doesn't like me."

"Thank you so much. We really appreciate it. We'll find our way out of here once we're done checking it out." Naturelle put a friendly hand on his shoulder. "Just don't tell anyone we're here, okay?"

"I will come back for you in one hour and thirty-five minutes when I have watched the oil tanker delivery from Ust-Luga."

"That's very nice of you. Hey, you don't happen to have tools in your truck that we can borrow?"

He proudly handed over a stuffed toolbox and was off.

The fence behind a few feet of trees and bushes was not high security, probably because twenty-ton pipes the length of a freight truck were not easy to steal.

The pipes were stacked four layers high in three rows, with huge, white weight sacks along the sides of the lowest tier to stop them from rolling. The ends of the pipes were covered with black cloth plugs carrying yellow tape labels. Dirty snow lay packed against the shady side of the stacks.

There was no human movement in sight.

The wired fence had "No Trespassing" signs with "Creab Security" logos every twenty feet.

Naturelle cut the fence open with a large pair of diagonal pliers. "Let's take a row each. Look for anything labeled PD."

As Melissa reached her stack and was about to start her meticulous inspection of the labels, she realized the size of it all. Each pipe's diameter was well above half her height.

The yellow tape labels on the ends were hand-written with two letters and five digits. The fastest way to read them was to snap photos of five by four pipes and zoom.

Half an hour went by, and the tedious work was getting on Melissa's nerves. There was no apparent order to the labels and definitely no "PD." Then, a vibration from her wristband: a message from Naturelle.

Ppl coming your side. Hide!

Melissa's head flinched left and right. Instinctively it felt like her left was the most probable direction people would come from.

The distance to the end of the row on the right was too far, so she couldn't run to the other side.

She looked backward toward the fence. It would just take a few seconds to run there, but she didn't know exactly where the cut hole was. Moving against the pattern of the wire would make her easy to spot.

She squatted and punched full force, straight into the end of the pipe in front of her. The synthetic cloth tore. A few additional rips and she had an opening large enough to squeeze in, feet first.

The inside was coated in a thick, oily substance smelling of petroleum. Streams of light shone through the torn cloth onto the pristine, silvery inner surface. The sound of the outside was dampened.

She texted Naturelle.

> I hid in one of the pipes.
> Lowest tier.

They're on your side now.

From which direction?

> From the port.
> Your left when you face the
> pipes.

Can you tail them and let
me know if they get super
close? I'm around the middle
of the pile.

> I'll try.

Melissa had to breathe through the opening in the cloth to not get lightheaded from the chemical fumes.

They're getting close.

I took some pictures and
zoomed in. The white guy
is Petrov himself!

The other four look
Chinese.

Melissa put her ear through the cloth. Voices. English with two different accents.

"Ladies and gentlemen, just few more meters," said Petrov with a voice similar to Mikhail's.

Half a minute passed. The footsteps in the gravel were right next to her pipe now.

"Let me see. Ah! Here we go," Petrov continued. "It's these fourteen here. See, they look exactly the same as the steel ones. Just a little thicker concrete coating to make the weight the same. Nothing to worry about."

One of the Asians replied. "Can we see?"

"See what?"

"The inside."

"That would require us to tear the protection open, and we don't want to do that."

"There is one here that is already open."

Melissa held her breath.

A hand came in through the pipe's open cloth, and she jerked back as fast as she could without making too much noise.

The air this far inside was thick with petroleum gases, and she knew she couldn't stay here for long.

"I'm sorry, but I have no idea why the seal is broken," Petrov said.

The voices were harder to hear this far in.

"So, can we do acid test?" It was the Asian man again. The fumes made Melissa feel sick.

A loud sigh from the oligarch. "Da."

The hand came back in, this time holding a short metal rod. The person scraped the bottom of the pipe firmly with the tip of the rod, then took it out again.

The last words Melissa remembered hearing was the Asian man saying "Confirmed. We can do business."

She passed out.

Chapter Sixty-Six

We Own the Night

West stood in Robert's office space with rosy cheeks, jacket still on, hair damp. He'd been out walking in the drizzle for an hour.

"Kiss, can I talk to you for a moment?" he said.

The words didn't really come out right, but he had to get straight to it.

"We're kind of in the middle of something here. You were right about the XML import, by the way. XML is still there, just not available from the menu."

"I just need to talk to you alone."

She looked at him. "Okay, okay."

They walked downstairs in silence.

Kiss sat down on one of the bunk beds.

He swallowed, feeling nauseous. "I'm sorry for being testy earlier. There was no need to go after Mikhail. He seems like a great guy."

"He is. Was that all?"

He looked down at the floor, took a breath, and moved his eyes up to look into hers. "I want to be your boyfriend."

Her facial expression changed. First a subtle, warm reaction with a hint of a smile, then restraint.

"I'm dependable," he added. "I mean, I can be dependable."

She tittered, then bit her lower lip and let her eyes wander.

Fuck. Why did I do this? Now everything's going to be awkward.

"I didn't know you had feelings for me," she said.

"It's okay. You don't have to say anything. It's just that I feel sick when you … when you're with him."

"Mikhail?"

He nodded.

Kiss got up and hugged him. "It's been a long time since someone I trusted had feelings for me."

West felt like peeing his pants.

She kept her arms around him. "I always felt a little guilty having sex with you." Her voice was muffled by the collar of his damp jacket. "But you seemed okay with it."

Seconds passed.

She pulled back and looked at him. "Remember, my relationships always end badly, so don't tell Melissa." She dried a tear from the corner of her eye.

A warm ease spread throughout West's body, making him feel floppy.

She took his hand and pulled him up the stairs.

Back on the ground floor she let go of him, picked up her coat, and headed for the door. "Hey, guys."

Mikhail and Jitterbug looked at her.

"West and I are going for a ride to clear our heads. Please keep the show running."

"Everything okay?" Jitterbug said.

"We're good. Just a little homesickness to iron out."

Stockholm was famous for its automated cabs, which were part of public transportation. A car was at Robert's office in five minutes.

As the car doors closed, Kiss blipped her GPI band against the car's scanner, and a soothing voice assistant came alive. "Hej, Amber Love! Vart vill ni åka?"

"Shit," Kiss said to herself. She started fiddling with her Tile. "I switched my GPI band to Swedish when I hacked the developer meetup waiting list. There we go."

She blipped again.

"Hi, Amber Love! Where would you like to go?" the voice assistant said.

"Just drive us around to beautiful places in Stockholm. We wanna see the sunset."

"I see you haven't visited any of Stockholm's landmarks," the car's voice said. "Would you like a guided tour?"

"Sure."

"Got it," said the car's voice. "I'll pick a good spot for the sunset at 3:50 p.m. You like hair metal and power ballads it seems. How about some soft Swedish hair metal?"

"Let's do it."

"Okay. Now playing 'We Own the Night, Live' by Treat."

Kiss reached out for his hand and pulled it to the middle seat between them. His hand was warmer than hers.

"Do you like traveling?" she asked.

"I was going to travel to Europe with my mom."

"I'm sorry."

"Don't be. We're in Europe now, and she would have loved for me to go."

•

The car took them past the City Hall where the annual Nobel Banquet was held, the parliament building, and the Royal Castle.

Before they knew it, the sun was setting, and the voice instructed them to walk the last bit to the "Evert Taube Terrasse." The car even provided them with blankets from its trunk for a small additional fee.

The stone-paved area was just next to the water, and in the corner there was a bronze statue of a man in a poncho and sombrero holding a lute. A set of curvy white benches faced west—all occupied by couples.

As they walked toward the waterline, a young man stood up from one of the benches. "Here, take ours. We're locals. We can come here anytime."

West and Kiss thanked the gracious couple and sat down. The view was stunning, featuring the city as a silhouette with a long bridge in a gentle arc at the far end of the basin of water, all below a blood-orange sun piercing through streaks of lofty clouds.

"Maybe it isn't just the drinking," West said. He put his arm around Kiss's shoulders. She leaned in. Her hair smelled like peach, a little synthetic but peachy.

She put her hand on his lower thigh and squeezed it. "I love how you said you want to be my boyfriend. Like an offer."

"I was going to say 'I want you to be my girlfriend,' but I thought it might sound needy or demanding."

"We're all needy and afraid. That's why I keep saying my relationships all end badly."

"I was thinking of that the other day," West said. "Almost all relationships end. Not badly, but each one of us can only have one relationship that lasts your whole life."

"Or zero."

"Come on."

"Sorry. You're very different from my earlier boyfriends."

"Not as good-looking?"

"Stop being stupid. I mean you're much more like me. Nerdy, caring about this G20S stuff."

"I may be like you, but I'm dependable." He patted her shoulder.

She laughed. "Do you ever want to have kids?"

"Mhm. I want to sing for them and build sandcastles with them and read bedtime stories."

"Names?"

"What?"

"Have you thought about names for the kids?"

"No, not really."

"Good. I have names."

CHAPTER SIXTY-SEVEN

Pd

Melissa woke up with a terrible headache. Something covered her mouth. She was wearing a plastic mask, breathing through some tube. In a raised bed.

She looked around in panic. It looked like a hospital.

"Are you awake?" The voice was familiar.

Melissa produced a mask-obstructed "Yes" followed by a nod.

Naturelle stood up to make herself visible. "I got you out as soon as I could. The physician said you'll be fine, but they want to properly ventilate your lungs. How are you feeling?"

Melissa reached for her Tile on the table next to the bed, dismissed a notification of a message, and typed "acid test pd" into the web browser's search field, and showed Naturelle the result page.

Did you mean to search for "acid test pdf?"
Showing results for "acid test pd."

Testing Palladium | Acid Testing for
Palladium Metal

Does anyone know a good way to test a
palladium ring?

How to Test Jewelry: Gold, Platinum, &
Palladium

Melissa spoke slowly through her breathing mask so Naturelle could hear what she said. "Pd is the chemical symbol for palladium. Petrov is not smuggling anything inside the pipes, he's smuggling palladium *as* pipes."

Naturelle's eyes widened. She started walking back and forth at the foot of the bed.

Melissa read the incoming message she'd dismissed earlier. It was a news link.

Frozen: Inside the G20S Backup Facility

Isolated, polluted, and above all cold, Norilsk is a city built on misery and blood, as part of Stalin's Corrective Labor Camps and Settlements, or Gulag. It's the chilliest city on earth with temperatures down to -67 F. But there's more than meets the body. Underground lies what has remained a secret until this day: the secret of Technical Note 1.

Read more: The Mythical Technical Note 1

Exclusive to *Wired*, we give you the inside story on Norilsk's most important gig to date: hosting and protecting G20S's only offline backup.

The US backup with its rolling window of thirty days of data has up until today been known as the only fallback solution G20S has. Independent security experts have blasted the agency for it, claiming that an offline, long-term backup is needed. It turns out that such a system has been in place all along.

But no permanent, offline backup can keep up with a fire-hose of information the likes of GPI, and so the data that lie dormant inside the volcanic rock mountains of the Siberian Traps is small in size, both technically and physically. "I can't tell you the medium we're using, but you could carry what we have so far in a large backpack," our source commented.

Internally referred to as "Technical Note 1," the Siberian facility was the compromise the G7 countries reached with Russia to get the Eastern superpower onboard with Global Personal Identities. Russian leadership accepted nothing less than a 50/50 split between the US and them on the responsibility for data backup.

Norilsk has no high-capacity wired connections to the rest of the world, and satellite transfer is both too risky and doesn't have the bandwidth. Instead, data is flown in weekly and transported by an uncrewed train into a fully automated space inside the mountain.

Security experts we've talked to say it's unclear how quickly such a backup can be used to resurrect a compromised GPI system, but it could take in the order of weeks. This means the Norilsk operation really is a passive last line of defense.

Secrecy is no stranger to G20S, and the disclosure of the existence and physical location of this facility comes at a sensitive time when North America is about to take over G20S leadership and the US and Canada continue to fight over whose candidate should have the privilege.

We've reached out to Russian and US G20S officials and will update this article if we hear back.

This article's sources are GPI-validated.

A nurse came in to check on Melissa as she finished reading the news piece. Naturelle took the chance to ask. "Can she remove the ventilation mask for a while? She's dying for a cup of coffee."

Melissa closed the *Wired* article on her Tile and gave Naturelle a discreet thumbs-up.

"Coffee is self-served out in the corridor. I can show you how to take off and put on your mask while your friend gets you a cup."

It wasn't great coffee by any stretch of the imagination, but Melissa needed it.

When the Russian hacker spoke again, she pulled close and lowered her voice. "Palladium fits right in. While waiting for you to wake up, I dug into Karlshamn and what this Chinese delegation could possibly be doing here. Have you heard about the Beijing-Moscow Alliance?"

Melissa shook her head.

"This is a two-year-old article." Naturelle started reading from her Tile. "The Beijing-Moscow Alliance and the currency Bancor was announced today with the aim to bypass the US dollar in the global economy. The package also involves anti-corruption measures and taxes on expatriated money to instill trust in the two countries' domestic markets. Bancor is a cryptocurrency backed by gold and palladium, two precious metals that will provide stability and trust."

"They need palladium," Melissa said.

"Remember I mentioned Nornickel? They're the world's top producer of palladium."

"So that's where Petrov and the pipes come in."

"He's smuggling palladium out of Russia with a little help from the Nord Stream project."

"What about the Chinese committee?"

"SR in the messages to Pogodina stands for Silk Road."

"The old Dark Web marketplace?"

"No, the physical Silk Road—China's new railway connection to Europe. The ferry connection between Klaipeda in Lithuania and Karlshamn is its last leg up north. It's how the Silk Road reaches Scandinavia. So Karlshamn turns out to be this magic point where Russian and Chinese businesses meet on neutral ground. You smuggle palladium out of Norilsk, take it to Karlshamn in the form of gas pipes, and sell it to China, who needs it for Bancor backing."

"You said out of Norilsk."

"Nornickel is in Norilsk. It used to be called Norilsk Nickel."

Melissa thought for a second. Was Norilsk as the site for both the palladium and the TN1 backup really a coincidence? She needed to discuss with the other Survivors.

"That's where your great-grandfather died," Melissa said.

Naturelle nodded, lips pursed, then lifted her head and pulled in air. "The Silk Road means China has the means to transport huge pipes back home via railway."

"And we're going to steal a palladium pipe."

"Yes. Which means we have to get into the TegTerminal system." She looked at all the equipment around Melissa's bed. "Pogodina is on her way down to Karlshamn to meet with Xin, and the trade will probably happen as soon as they have shaken hands. That's in sixteen hours. Before then, we need to change the strip order and have the dockworkers execute it to send PD-15 somewhere else."

Melissa pushed her medical equipment aside. "I'll just go take a piss, and then we'll be on our way."

It was a rather spacious bathroom fitted with handrails and large, ergonomic handles for everything, and emergency call buttons both high and low. The mirror image in front of her featured a bruised chin from Naturelle's punch three days earlier, a red line from where the mask had pressed into her skin, and the gaze of a warrior.

She sat down and got her Tile out to write a message to the Survivors' private channel:

> Sending y'all a link.
>
> TN1 is a GPI backup in Siberia. West, make up a plan for how to get us into Russia. I have to focus on this pipe heist. Kizz and J!t, you reluctantly agree to whatever West comes up with. Argue a little. I will too. ZNP must not think we're eager.

She stopped her index finger just millimeters short of tapping the Send button. Perhaps it was better for the others to discover the news themselves? She didn't want them asking where she got these links.

CHAPTER SIXTY-EIGHT

SAX vs DOM

Watching the sunset with Kiss had been the most beautiful and satisfying moment in West's adult life—just sitting there with her, savoring the warmth of her body close to his. The high kept him company as they got back to Robert's office.

Kiss joined Mikhail, who had made good progress on the TegTerminal XML import. The aim was to manipulate work orders in the Karlshamn port.

West walked over to Jitterbug and pointed both index fingers at him in a friendly gesture. "Any luck with your brute force script?"

Jitterbug rolled his eyes, then showed him the script running.

```
Exhaustive search through 126 bits

85,070,591,730,234,615,865,843,651,857,942,
052,864 keys to test

Testing key 937,070,124,888 ...
```

"This is getting us nowhere," West admitted. "But even if we don't have the right key, the decryption is still spitting out files. We could have a look at a few of those files to see if they reveal something about Fraktal."

They didn't actually know what a successfully decrypted file looked like. Jitterbug's script was looking for plaintext Russian or English as a signal of successful decryption, but maybe that wasn't it?

West took the server's decrypted output files from testing three keys and opened them in a hex editor.

```
Decrypted-1
0D0A1A0A01000000060000000000000100
000001AE000003FFFDFF02FEFEFE0000
001F0000001F3A52BFF6375BDA4EC4EB
035FA7ABFE1344FD27BD172276042C55
1BF44347E8F51214BDFAAA5ED827D83B
9D828F012D73801C3E63B5A4AF2D4C49
```

```
Decrypted-2
0D0A1A0A01000000020000000000000100
0000028B000003FFFDFF02FEFEFE0000
003F0000003F662157946E84B27DCD43
8A1F0499860515FE5BBB03D038E5F1D1
5ED212EA833D84DB18C779C78321B4AE
006B4AE8A90FB4A17812BCF2E00D3AED
```

```
Decrypted-3
0D0A1A0A01000000010000000000000100
000001EE000003FFFDFF02FEFEFE0000
000400000004138CF00644602DE4BF02
0075E8D3B9355EA18FE2DE2AF7BB3D01
5EED9F18EDB5C63F0C25B52E5A3302D6
A4064D6D0693DDD6E98A6BDA57880104
```

He and Jitterbug both stared at the screen.

"The first 32 bytes are the same in all three files, starting with 0D0A1A0A and ending with FEFE0000," West said.

"Has to be a file header."

They searched the FileFormat.info website for a match without any luck.

"There is something familiar with the leading set of four bytes, 0D0A1A0A," West mumbled.

Robert brought them a bottle of Beaujolais wine and joined their discussion on how to crack Fraktal. Glasses were emptied sip by sip, and all three were getting fuzzy when Kiss shouted from her and Mikhail's corner.

"TegTerminal is going *down*."

Everyone gathered around their screen.

"Mikhail and I have had our minds on this class of security bugs where input validation parses the document in one way, and the actual data ingestion parses it in another. It sometimes allows for the validated input and the used input to be two different things."

West lit up. "Are you saying that's the kind of bug they fixed by just hiding the XML import in the interface?"

"Hell yeah. What we're looking at here is confusion between SAX and DOM parsing. Please, Mikhail."

Mikhail scribbled a data structure on the whiteboard.

```
<Data>
  <Signature>
  </Signature>
  <Order>
      123
  </Order>
</Data>
<Order>
  abc
</Order>
```

He pointed at the top "Data" element. "A SAX parser will go through structure top to bottom, so first 'Order' it finds is '123.' However, DOM parser will look at structure as hierarchy, from left to right. So first 'Order' element *it* finds is 'abc.' TegTerminal uses SAX to verify the order but DOM when displaying it to workers. Classic mistake."

Kiss added the punch. "With this bug, we're able to take an already signed TegTerminal order and add our own bogus order at the end, which is the one the workers will see."

Chapter Sixty-Nine

Strike One

It was past eight and pitch dark when Melissa and Naturelle arrived at the gate to Karlshamn Port. They were back in the black suits and masks they had on when they'd first met. Melissa could already feel her limbs stiffening from the cold and pulled down her beanie to properly cover her ears.

Melissa had asked Kiss earlier to come up with something manipulative that could clear the port area of people in case they needed to operate alone. Kiss had immediately suggested a bomb threat, but Melissa wanted something less police worthy.

Naturelle and Melissa walked along the port's chain-link fence away from the road. Signs in Swedish with the Creab Security logo informed of the rules and dangers around this massive workplace.

Electric lighting throughout the area was bright but spotty, and the two women climbed the fence to disappear in the shadows and move in the direction of the waterside. Melissa wore her anti-X-ray glasses to help with night vision.

"The Stockholm team has found a way to change work orders in TegTerminal," Melissa whispered to Naturelle. "I just got a text."

"That's awesome."

"Yeah, but you and I need to get access to an actual TegTerminal account for it to work. They just have a test account."

"The Kaliningrad cargo ship has got to have one. That should get us direct access to their work order too."

They got close enough to see a tall crane slowly stripping pipes off a carrier vessel onto flatbed trucks, which transported them for storage.

The wind grew stronger further out on the pier, and the smell of the sea became even more present. They hid in the last patch of shadow on the inland side of the crane base. From there they had a clear view of the lit scene.

Three workers in orange work clothes and safety vests stood next to the ship's side, watching the automated crane lift pipes out of the cargo space and drop them two by two onto a waiting truck. Helmets shadowed all three of their faces, but their conversation revealed that they were locals, not Russians.

"Looks like another case of unions protecting jobs to accept automation," Naturelle whispered. "Happens a lot in Russia. They get paid to watch machines work."

The matte white-and-gray cargo vessel looked almost like a submarine. The top had four large openings but no structure or real deck for humans, only narrow walk paths to inspect the cargo.

There was a white gangplank with a green safety net underneath for boarding, but no visible staff on the ship.

Melissa whispered over the voice channel. "Kiss, there are workers here, so get your diversion attack ready. West, figure out what kind of a cargo ship this is. Its name is *Ocean Spirit*, and it has no bridge."

Kiss muttered something about politeness but said everything was good to go on her part.

West came back after a little while. "Here's what I got on the ship. It's a remote-controlled, automated thing built by Rolls-Royce. At sea it's either on autopilot or controlled by its owner over satellite link. A local control room takes over when it approaches a port."

"Is there a manual override?"

"Gotta check." A minute passed. "Yes, international maritime law mandates a manual override, but the owner is allowed to cancel it remotely to prohibit pirates from taking over the ship."

"But it's under *local* control right now, so it would have to be the dockworkers here canceling an override."

"Maybe. Such details aren't really in the documents I found."

Naturelle tapped Melissa's shoulder. "With no one on the ship, it's better *you* board it and figure this out. If Pogodina sends people here, I at least know Russian and can stall them if necessary."

Melissa gave Kiss the go signal for the diversion. "De-ass the area. Please."

While they waited, Melissa read the scoop on Norilsk and the TN1 backup again, making sure Naturelle didn't see her screen. Frustratingly, none of her team members seemed to have read it yet, or at least they hadn't pinged her about it. She went to the Survivors' private channel. Her draft message on the Norilsk backup was still there. She pressed Send and tucked her Tile away.

Eventually, and much to Melissa's and Naturelle's delight, Kiss's trick played out. One of the Swedish dockworkers by *Ocean Spirit* pulled out their Tile. Melissa streamed to the others a live translated transcription of what was said.

> Hey guys! Check this out.
> Says here we just went on
> strike.

> A news flash, or what?

> Yeah. It's on Aftonbladet.

> Maybe we'll get the night off,
> how about that?

> Come on. That has to
> be fake news. There's
> no conflict going on.

> You can stay if you want.
> I'm going home to fuck the
> missus.

> We can't just go home
> because some news
> site says so.

> Guys, hold on. I'll check
> with Christian.

The man who looked to be in charge made a phone call.

Hi Christian, it's Hugo.
Sorry to call you this late.
Have you seen the news? It
says we're on strike.

Yeah. Aftonbladet.

I just wanted to check with
you.

Oh, you got a text from
central? Well, that settles
it.

OK, then. The men'll be
happy.

Take care. Bye.

In no time, the workers had secured the crane, shut off the lights, blipped their GPI bands against the manager's Tile to check out from their shift, and left.

"No one knows people better than you," Melissa said to Kiss on the voice channel.

"People believe what they wanna believe."

Melissa boarded the *Ocean Spirit*.

CHAPTER SEVENTY

Fractal Encryption

"Is that really true, that workers are paid to watch machines work?" West asked Jitterbug.

"Not in America. Not that I know of. Maybe unionized workplaces tried it, but we're too focused on profit."

"Makes you think about the end goal. Is work just a necessary evil until we can hand it all over to robots?"

"Some of it. Who wants to do dishes?"

"Some inmates liked it. It was called OTW—Other-Than-Work."

"Would they rather read a book or play basketball though?"

They chatted for a while about freedom and what makes life feel meaningful. West realized that solving complicated hacking challenges had made him feel more alive than he had in years. Or maybe it was Kiss who made him feel alive? He thought about his mom and how she had found meaning in life through struggle and sacrifice. The smile on her face when he was released was the most pure, unrestricted joy he had ever seen. God, he missed her.

Eventually they got back to Fraktal, and West again reviewed the output of the brute force decryption script, which was still running.

"I can't shake that file header—0D0A1A0A," he said. "Where have I seen that pattern before?"

Before for West meant before prison; he was digging through teenage memories. Wasn't that file header something related to documents?

"There's a piece missing," he said to Jitterbug. "0D0A1A0A is only half of the pattern. Maybe they've stripped out a few bytes to obscure the files?"

"Man, this is your show. I have nothing on this thing," Jitterbug replied.

West downloaded a large set of old documents—.doc, .docx, .pdf, .rtf—and started scanning for the header pattern.

He finally got a hit in the middle of a pdf. It was an embedded two-tone image, compressed with a lossy algorithm. Right before 0D0A1A0A was the missing four bytes—974A4232—which when converted into text, revealed the missing piece "JB2."

West's eyes widened as he filled his lungs to yell his finding. "It's JBIG2! These decrypted Fraktal files are compressed images, not text. We're searching for plaintext but the decryption outputs images."

Jitterbug was perplexed. "JBIG2? That sounds like a nineties rapper."

"You're not wrong about the decade. JBIG was developed for fax machine compression of black-and-white images. JBIG2 is the second version."

"The nineties. Now we're talking." It was Robert. "Can you open such a file?"

"My Tile rejects it. I'll have to find some old pdf reader."

"Windows XP sound good? I haz stuff downstairs." Robert grinned.

Soon enough, they were looking at the desktop image of an old Windows machine. West's Tile sat in a dock, which allowed the PC to use it as an external drive.

They pulled down three of the decrypted JBIG2 files. As soon as West added the missing four bytes, the files showed up as image icons in the Windows file explorer.

Robert double-clicked on one of them with the PC mouse. The old plastic did not sound happy.

A black-and-white image appeared on the screen, featuring blocks of Latin numerals and scattered Cyrillic characters. The glyphs were not distinct as in a pristine digital document. Instead they shifted in appearance like in a terrible Xerox copy.

ю XXI XC V D д X д э з IV XXI DCCC XIV Cⅅ н D XII LXXX D л XII
CD XIII LXX п Ⅽ II н и XI LXX у XIII XIV LX XX XL ь к о I X XL Ⅽ
DCCC CCC ч CI чл XI Ⅽ т II V г к L р с LXXX р у CD с VII о з л
ф з ю XVIII **XIII** е LXXX о XIII IV LXXX CCC е у CI **IX XC LXX VII**
XXX ё б Ⅽ LX VI **е** с CI **XIII** CC г г Ⅽ р DCC **VII** ф **й** и DCC **IV CC** ц
XC XVI ё XX I **XXII** е XL **XXX** э CI D ж ц XXII DCCC XX ш LXXX XIX ф
IX Cⅅ в р ж й д VIII ф XVI CCC CC в н ы з XX D XI к ц ы VI к DCC
CD Ⅽ д э с C V XVII IX CI LXXX л CI XVI ё ц с я у п щ XVIII ю
XVIII I CCC ш ш XVI LXX LXXX LXX XII XV р в VI IX XIV CD VI ж ч щ
ш ь Ⅽ ф IV и XC в CI XVI III CI п L р DC щ я XI L XV IX в я д
XIV DCCC DCCC п и Ⅽ C III XV и ш в DCCC д ё XL LXXX м р XC LX Cⅅ
у и X е б л XI CCC XL XL L IV IV п э л щ м DC LXX ы VIII и XXII е
III XL в ц в о I н IX с ш LXXX г ю I I й ь д DCCC Ⅽ DCC LXXX о г
CD L CCC XC II ф XIII XXX XL XVI VIII о м VIII CD XVII н э D IV
LX LX C VI II CCC и X IX м DCC XII XIX DC Cⅅ CC XIV п XV ъ п х
DCCC CCC CC XIII CD п XIX к XXII ф LX XVI V л й ч м г DCC л я
XIII XL DCCC **XXII** XII CC VI ф IV щ у ь д X ц я LX д CI XX III D о
VIII с XIV DCC п Cⅅ LX XXX XVII XXI ё V щ ы у ж XV VIII CC ш CD
L а XIV CC XIX D у I I IX XII XVII ч XVII XIV IV Ⅽ д ь ж Cⅅ э
CCC Cⅅ я DCC я CC DCC и VII ь и VIII XC XII XXI VI щ Ⅽ й н CC т
XI IV ж **IV** е XII р м ф XI п у о п XXX з ш н ф CCC XV D XXII б V ж
й ы т C в CCC VI о к **XVI L ь** а ч XIX э т CD LXX б е в и и н LXXX
л V DCCC ъ II о XVIII LXX LXX XVII IV с VIII ё ы Ⅽ C XXI у й XV
ч е XIII CCC ё ы н LXXX XIX DCC я XVI CC IX л XV я п к CI ж XXX
XX DC т D й XIX XIII XIII XL Ⅽ CCC IV XIV I XL я ж ш о м ъ п L й
т XV XVIII с VI DC XXII XIII VI LX D у XC I III л CCC IX L XIX ж
э LXXX п XVIII D э й XVIII э н л х XX ё DCCC г б в XVII IV C XV в
г Cⅅ ц р XIV щ I LX XVII к й LXX CD ю ш XI б XVII CCC б щ XV х с
д н XXI XII XI XXX о XC б XX III м я ж XX е XVIII CI ц ъ VIII CCC
XX ц DCC IV ы XXX DCC DC CD г L ы х VII г **XV** III Cⅅ ф D XII Ⅽ
XIII XI ч о XVI м XIII XL ж г ш DC й в XC Ⅽ L VI к о XXI XIX
LXXX в ё IV D щ L ш X ъ DCC DC CCC **LXX VII XVII** Cⅅ **XIX** ь г LXXX
м XXX CC в XIII ю XIV XII XL н э р ю CI и к II р з CI DCCC VI XV
I с X й э ш XVI II CD Cⅅ щ р х XIII DCC Cⅅ LX э д с XIX п XVI ж
VIII DCCC о IV р л L й з XV XVIII у **XXII** Cⅅ г с г ь CD ж б XXX
XXX п XXX D IX Cⅅ XC е VI II ь б VII с ю XC з Ⅽ CCC CD II DC
XIII р с XIV CI ц в **XX XIX в** XIV Ⅽ XII я н XC п III д XXII XVIII
д **XIII** ф XIII с LXX **IX** щ **LXX** XL м LXX о XIII XIV XV XIV XI I х к
XX XVII ъ XXX X в ш **DCC CCC** к CD к XXII ё XV VII XVI DC XXII ы я
т **LXXX** ъ II е XVIII DCC L V у XC XC э е д у ю ю II у ф I д щ XXII
ч XIII CD а я ь а XC CD у ы ы XVI XVII XXII DC XXII ю Cⅅ V XXI
XVIII р р X DCCC II XIV а **X XC ж** ц ь VII р IX н XIII X л и ш а
III ж Ⅽ з XV C CCC C и CD **т XI ы XI т** я ё I т в III XX XXII XL
CCC щ DCCC C з IX ы з CCC D **DCCC VIII** X и CC ж XC р в D е С д XXX
ы Cⅅ VIII C л XIII XXII е CC Cⅅ к и XIX п ф XII ф **XXI** XV р CC II
м XIV XXX л ы XVII у ж CCC д **XI** н т ъ I ц XIII ы XV CI IV ю ч
VIII б в г ж ы III CC м Ⅽ ь CD о ё III ц ф XXX щ D VI LXX XXX п
LX я DCCC ю XI ж х XVIII б ш DCCC I ы CC CC VII IV II XV XX XV
XXX XIII ъ L х I ё о б II XII XIV XC VII м IX CD к XI VII я я X

"Is that an effect of the compression algorithm?" Robert asked. "I mean, fax machines were bad but not that bad."

The bulky CRT monitor hummed and flickered.

"Nah. This is something else," West said. "The noise in the image looks generated."

Just as he uttered the word *generated*, something dawned on him.

He slowly turned to Jitterbug and Robert. "I think I know what this is. Fraktal is not just a cool name for this crypto. This shit literally is *fractal encryption*. The Russians are using fractal compression. I bet the 358-bit key is used as a fractal seed to generate an image with access codes to the G20S system. That way, someone doing brute force decryption of it in search of something legible will fail. Just like we did."

"Wow. But how are we going to find the right one if every decryption output is a valid image with characters like these?"

West massaged his closed eyelids. "I don't know."

Chapter Seventy-One

Ocean Spirit

Ocean Spirit was a marvel of technology, and Melissa had to restrain herself not to poke around too much. The inside of the ship was devoid of cameras and surveillance as far as she could tell. It simply wasn't built for human presence. There wasn't even a bathroom.

News of West's breakthrough discovery in Fraktal decryption made her all the more interested in pulling this palladium heist off and to get moving toward Russia.

"Found the manual override control room on the ship and picked the lock," she said over the voice channel. "Still clear outside, Naturelle?"

"All clear."

Ocean Spirit's command room had a comfy white leather command chair in front of three curved, ten-foot-wide screens.

She sat down. Three control panels automatically lit up and moved in place in front of her to create an interactive desk together with a speed throttle, a joystick, and a huge trackball with buttons around it.

The big screens started streaming what was in front of the ship as if Melissa were looking out from a ship's bridge.

She inspected the desk's user interface. There was a map, a circular radar, and a schematic of the vessel with sensor data.

She moved the trackball, and an overlay menu came up on the map screen.

Autopilot | Assist | Joystick | Admin

She clicked "Admin."

Language | Prompt | System reset

A system reset sounded tempting, but she didn't want to get rid of data, she wanted access to data, so she chose "Prompt."

The midsection of the desk between the throttle and the joystick physically popped up a few millimeters with a click sound. She lifted it to reveal a small qwerty keyboard and three OmniPorts.

"It's a Unix system. I know this," she mumbled as she pulled out her Bunny drive and flipped the switch to "Shell."

The Bunny did its job, and she had soon dug up *Ocean Spirit*'s cargo orders on the file system.

There was one current order, number 0091.

She opened it in an editor and checked the details.

```
<Data>
  <Signature>
  </Signature>
  <Order>
       <Port>
         Karlshamn, Sweden
       </Port>
       <ServiceDetails>
         <StripInstruction>
           Warehouse 6.
           Store in numeric order.
         </StripInstruction>
       </ServiceDetails>
  </Order>
</Data>
```

This was ripe for the taking. She would add an instruction to move PD-15 somewhere else.

"There's a car coming." Naturelle's voice in Melissa's earpiece was tense.

"I just have to change the order, then I'm done."

"No time."

It wasn't likely that whoever was in that car would go on board. Melissa decided to stay put.

Half a minute later, Naturelle's voice came in sharp and whispering in her ear. "Russians getting out of a car right by *Ocean Spirit*. Probably

Pogodina's men. Some Swedish guy is with them. I'll patch you in over text."

The conversation among the men outside *Ocean Spirit* appeared on Melissa's Tile.

There's not a soul here.

You had specific orders,
Christian.

As I said, the men are
on strike.

There's no fucking workers'
conflict going on. We would
have been notified. This
ship needs to be stripped
and stuffed. It's leaving for
Klaipeda tomorrow.

We were not aware of
your tight schedule.

It was decided an hour
ago. Get your men here
within thirty minutes,
or we'll do the work
ourselves.

That's not how this
works. In Sweden we
have a system.

In Russia we have money,
and you seem to have been
very happy taking it so far.

I'll see what I can do.
But it's Saturday.

Make it fucking Monday.

Melissa's mouth dried up. Getting off *Ocean Spirit* had suddenly become nontrivial.

What was the recent decision that the Russians referred to?

She fired up *Ocean Spirit*'s terminal window again to have a look at the orders. A new one had been added; number 0092.

```
<Data>
   <Signature>
   </Signature>
   <Order>
        <Port>
           Klaipeda, Lithuania
        </Port>
        <ServiceDetails>
          <StripInstruction>
             Train CGTN-812 to Chengdu.
             Bancor payment address:
             A8CFBBD73726062DF0C68
             64DDA65DEFE58EF0CC52A
          </StripInstruction>
        </ServiceDetails>
   </Order>
</Data>
```

Melissa used the voice channel to the whole team. "This ship is headed to Lithuania, where it'll be stripped for transport by train to Chengdu, China. The Silk Road smuggling is on."

Naturelle responded. "You have to get off that ship. You and I can take down these two Russians. They're pretty big, but we can do it."

"And kiss our palladium goodbye? We have to come up with something better."

Kiss broke in. "It'll still be dark for many hours. You can get in the water on the other side and swim away from the ship, Melissa. The map shows a camping place across the water where you can get out."

"I have a better idea." It was West. "I read up on *Ocean Spirit*'s navigational system. Stay on the ship, Melissa."

CHAPTER SEVENTY-TWO

The Karlshamn Heist

West was nervous taking the lead. But Melissa needed him to help them get into Russia, and Kiss and Jitterbug put up a nice resistance theater as he got them to agree.

By midnight, all parts were in motion.

Kiss had experience in yachting from her youth in Juneau, which made her the best choice for the tasks to be executed in Klaipeda. West wanted to go with her, but she said Melissa would disapprove, so she and Jitterbug got tickets for a flight at seven a.m. from Stockholm, through Latvia, to Lithuania.

Melissa was busy reading the details of *Ocean Spirit*'s hardware support for automated and remote-controlled navigation, and Mikhail began hacking his way through Karlshamn's three hotels to figure out where the Chinese Silk Road committee stayed.

"I'm in the dock's cafeteria," Naturelle whispered through her mic. "Found some contractor clean-up bags. Says 'tear and puncture resistant.' What kind of food do you like, Liz?"

"Whoa. Don't call her Liz," West interjected.

"It's all right, West. I'll grant her temporary permission. What kind of food do they have, Naturelle? This boat has no fridge and no heating equipment."

"Graham crackers and some fruit. The rest is frozen stuff."

"Just make sure I have painkillers and water. Lots of water. And toilet paper."

They heard Naturelle stash things into plastic bags. "I'm going to wrap these bags in tape to make them sticky and put them inside the palladium pipe you tore open and hid in. That's one of the palladium pipes they're loading."

"If those water bottles don't get on here …"

"I'll get them to you. Gotta head out to the storage lot."

A couple of hours passed.

West relayed information from the Stockholm operation. "Mikhail has found out where the Chinese are staying in Karlshamn—Best Western, outside of the city center. Rooms 308–311. Room 308 is marked as a 'Sponsored Room' with a slightly higher rate. I bet that's where Xin stays."

"Mikhail always delivers," Naturelle said, catching her breath. "There's a truck on the lot moving pipes like there's no tomorrow. I just got Melissa's goody bag into the palladium pipe. West, find out how I get into that hotel room, preferably from the outside, please."

"Xin's room is on the third floor. You'll need a ladder."

"Or I rappel from the roof. If there's one thing I've seen a lot of around the port, it's rope."

"Let me look at some street-view photos," West said. Moments passed. "Eighth window pair from the left, facing the road. When you get close, get us a video feed."

•

At three in the morning, West, Mikhail, and Robert saw what Naturelle saw up on Best Western's flat roof. The streetlights across the hotel's lawn shone like beacons in the night. Gusts of wind were audible through her mic.

Naturelle muttered about some terrible smell in the air as she leaned her head over the roof's edge to count her way to the right window.

She found the right spot between rooms 308 and 309, got up, made sure her shoes were clean, anchored her rope to the base of a rooftop aircon unit, and descended.

No lights from inside bled through the blinds. One of her hands left the field of view and came back closed seconds later. She opened it slowly to show her spectators a handful of pebbles, then tossed the first one onto the window. Then a second, and a third.

A faint light came on inside, and the blinds opened. Naturelle waited until they closed again and threw another pebble.

This time the window opened. Naturelle yanked it fully open and jumped in.

The video feed wobbled like on a rollercoaster as Naturelle quickly scanned the room. An elderly Chinese man stood hunched in his underwear, protecting his head with his arms. As he got upright, Naturelle's hand shot out and covered his mouth.

"Shhh."

The man nodded intensely, eyes wide open.

The room was small, the king-size bed taking up most of its space. The wall above the bed was filled with a huge, glass-framed poster of five coffee beans in a neat line and a stylized word, *Fika*.

Naturelle started talking in a low voice, executing West's plan.

"I'm not here to hurt you, and I'm not here to steal anything. I'm here to cut a deal. If you scream or call for help, I will change my mind and indeed hurt you. Do you understand?"

The man nodded again, and Naturelle slowly removed her hand from his mouth. "Your name is Xin, right?"

"Yes. Who are you?" he asked.

"I work for the Russian Ministry of Internal Affairs in Kaliningrad."

She let him scan her GPI band, and he read it carefully.

Naturelle continued. "Large quantities of palladium have been stolen and smuggled of out of Russia with the intention to sell it to you here in Karlshamn. This is no doubt a delicate matter, since relations with China are important to us, not in the least around Bancor and palladium. A public scandal would likely hurt the value of our joint currency and cast doubt on our ability to cooperate. Thus, Russia will handle this with confidentiality. Do you follow?"

The man hesitated. "I don't know what you're talking about."

"Really? How about these photos of you walking with Vladimir Petrov on Nord Stream's storage lot?" She held up her Tile to his face.

"We're here to study the Nord Stream project."

"Is that why you did an acid test to check for palladium? Look, I'm going to give you this one chance to save your business deal and not make things worse. To settle this matter, Moscow has decided to honor the business transaction. However, the handoff will take place on Russian soil, in Kaliningrad, not Klaipeda, and the Bancor payment address is instead going to be this."

The Chinese man looked at the slip of paper he was handed.

Naturelle continued. "What is the payment setup with Petrov?"

Xin took his time. "Half … half when the pipes are loaded on the train, half when the train reaches China." His face was limp, eyelids drooping.

"Good. We will honor that and lend you the necessary trucks to get the pipes from Kaliningrad onto your CGTN-812 train to Chengdu. Do we have a deal?"

Xin looked as if he wanted to cry. Significant time passed in silence.

He finally ceded with a weak, "Yes."

"Perfect. Move your Klaipeda people to Kaliningrad and make contact with Irina Alexandrovna at the Ministry of Internal Affairs as soon as possible. Irina Alexandrovna, got it? She will provide instructions about the trucks. Your meeting with Pogodina is in a few hours. Where will you meet her?"

"Here. In the hotel restaurant."

"Just act as if everything is fine. We'll be watching you, so no monkey business. If you leak this information or try to trick us, we will blow your illegal business wide open, and you won't get the palladium."

"What happens when Petrov and Pogodina find out?"

"I assume the PRC, too, has a Ministry of Internal Affairs."

Xin nodded.

"Well, then you know you won't be hearing from them again."

•

Naturelle sent a couple of photos from Xin and Pogodina's meeting in the morning. The whole thing seemed to go smoothly with no sign of Xin flaking. But then again, they didn't know how Xin acted under normal circumstances.

West was just about to pour himself a second cup of coffee when a message from Jitterbug came in.

> West! We just landed in Lithuania and I figured it out. I figured out how to reboot Pogodina's machine!

> How?

What is the rule with the
JTAG screen grabber?

Rule?

What did Naturelle tell us?

Not to use it too often
because it freezes
Pogodina's monitor.

On the button. What if we
deliberately hit the screen
grabber over and over?

There's no way to tell
the difference between a
frozen screen and a frozen
computer. She will think
the computer has crashed
and ...

Reboot it.

That's genius.

:P

Now it's up to you to
figure out how we find the
right JBIG2 image out of
a trillion. We need G20S
access before going into
Russia.

Godspeed.

Chapter Seventy-Three

Mr. Vektor

"Something is off. Xin was nervous." Pogodina waited for a response from the man on the other side of the video call. He was clearly hung-over.

"What would you have us do?" he asked after a pause.

She sighed. All that these people ever did was ask for orders. She wanted to discuss the situation, reason about it. The only person with a brain in this operation was Petrov, but he wasn't responding, and this could quickly turn into an on-the-ground issue.

"Maybe the Chinese will pull something on arrival," she said. "This is a big shipment, and we can't afford any slipups. Make sure to run a capable welcoming committee and track *Ocean Spirit* closely as she docks."

"Mr. Vektor is always close at hand," the man said, showing teeth on her screen.

SR-1M Vektor. Same gun as hers.

CHAPTER SEVENTY-FOUR

Piracy

Kiss did not look forward to going to sea. The weather in Klaipeda was windy with a temperature just above freezing. Jitterbug mostly worried about seasickness.

They had rented a cruiser with a company called Vacation Boats. There was no ice on the Baltic Sea this far south except for patches further into the Curonian Lagoon, but it was not the season to rent yachts. They had to pay triple for their "scientific excursion."

Kiss spent some time convincing the owner she could handle the Bayliner Cuddy—an open-deck, compact cruiser by the name of *Carmen*—while Jitterbug went into the city to get them rain clothes, boots, and supplies.

After lunch, they received a message.

> Show a leg! Ye mighty pirate Melissa sails the Baltic Sea. Ocean Sprit is moving and ETA is around midnight. I uploaded my scheduled route to SurvivorNet. See you soon!

•

It took Melissa all afternoon to get ready for the planned transaction at sea later that night.

Her first order of business after leaving the Karlshamn port was to dismount *Ocean Spirit*'s AIS transponder, AIS as in Automatic Identification System.

If she were to fool whoever monitored *Ocean Spirit*, the AIS messages had to continue on to Klaipeda, and the way to achieve that was to make the transponder travel on Kiss and Jitterbug's cruiser using the transponder's own emergency battery power.

The AIS equipment weighed in at twenty pounds, and it took about an hour to get it removed and packaged with its power supply still connected.

Next duty was to make sure she wouldn't set off an alarm when she did her manual navigation override to change the course of the ship, and for this she didn't have a plan yet.

If she disabled the ship's network connection or antenna altogether, Pogodina and Petrov would be notified immediately that the ship's signal had gone missing.

Could she block only the off-route alarm from the ship's outgoing network traffic? Maybe. But she didn't know what that traffic looked like.

What about a combination—disable the antenna temporarily and deliberately trigger the alarm just to dump the traffic for analysis? Nah, even a short disruption in sync with headquarters could raise suspicion.

Wouldn't it be sweet to get the autopilot to work *for* her instead of against her? No manual override, no alarm.

She fired up the terminal in the command room.

Beside the current autopilot command files were old navigational orders in archives. *Ocean Spirit*'s destination before Karlshamn had been Kaliningrad.

This presented an opportunity.

She copied the old Kaliningrad order onto the work queue and changed the ship's system clock backward enough to match the old route to the Russian exclave.

The ship immediately started to turn south, and the navigational log spewed out reroute information.

She switched back to today's date in panic and flung her head back in the command chair. The ship corrected its course.

She got out on deck, all alone in the vastness of water. The sun had already set, and her surroundings were shifting to a beautiful moonlit night on the Baltic Sea. Now the wait until handoff.

•

Kiss sent a message to West at six p.m. as she and Jitterbug left the coast of Lithuania.

> Hey, gorgeous! We're about
> to lose carrier service. I'll let
> you know when we're back.
> XXX

Yo! Sounds good. Feels like
I'm putting all my friends
at risk here. Worried about
you.

> We got this. I think it's cool
> with you leading instead of
> Melissa.

It's not that I'm trying to
take over or anything.

> Mutiny. :D

Two and a half hours later, *Ocean Spirit* emerged right where it was supposed to on Kiss's radar. Even so, she and Jitterbug were freaked out by its size and speed, straight as an arrow.

They waited outside its safety zone for it to pass, then folded in behind it. Kiss pushed the Cuddy up to speed.

They got a peer-to-peer message from Melissa.

Ahoy! I hope that's you on
the radar.

I never thought we'd
meet under these
circumstances. As soon as
you have the loot, keep 25

knots straight to Klaipeda
along the route I gave you.
Confirm, and the drop will
be in 30 seconds.

Half a minute after their acknowledgment, a small object emerged on the radar between the yacht and *Ocean Spirit*.

Kiss slowed down as they approached. It was a lifebuoy.

Jitterbug fished it up to find a tightly sealed tear- and puncture-resistant clean-up bag filled with equipment. He swiftly unpacked *Ocean Spirit*'s transponder and connected it to their yacht's antenna system.

"There we go. We are officially *Ocean Spirit*."

Kiss brought them up to speed, took a deep breath, and looked into the endless, moon-reflecting sea, blending seamlessly into the starlit sky. It reminded her of the view of space just before a Star Wars ship would jump into lightspeed.

"Hope," she whispered to herself.

Chapter Seventy-Five

Bleeding

West decided to sleep off the anxiety of all his friends messing with Russian state property at sea.

Repeated new message chimes woke him up at 1:12 a.m. They were messages from Jitterbug to the Survivors.

> Kizz shot. Bleeding.

> Came out of nowhere. Boat approaching.

> Ppl yelling in Russian or something.

> Shutting down. God help us.

West's hands clutched his stomach as if he'd been stabbed.

He got out of bed and shuffled around a few steps. Where was he? The room was dark except for the light from his Tile and blue and green dots of light blinking in the corner.

He checked the chat room to see if Kiss's Tile was connected. It wasn't.

Same thing with Jitterbug's. Either their Tiles were shut off or they had no network connection.

He sat down on the bed, supported his elbows on his knees, and landed his forehead in his hands. Tears came pouring.

I should have gone with you. Now you're bleeding to death in some shitty port while I sit here.

He shouted "Hey" toward the stairs up to the ground floor even though he knew he was alone. Mikhail had left a few hours earlier to catch a train south and meet up with Naturelle. The two of them would take a morning flight from Copenhagen to Kaliningrad to pull off the final parts of the heist. Melissa was still off the radar completely, on board *Ocean Spirit.*

He texted Robert.

> You awake?

> Now I am. What's up?

> Kizz is shot. She and J!t
> may have been caught in
> Klaipeda. No one else is
> responding.

> Shot??

> I'll be there in 15 min.

Robert was there in ten.

"Here, this is the last message I got from Jit." West handed over his Tile and dried tears from his puffy cheeks.

Robert read the four short messages. "This has to be Pogodina's henchmen. Which means she now knows her ship is gone. How likely are Kiss and Jitterbug to talk?"

"Not very, I think."

A cold orb of anxiety moved around in West's guts. This whole plan was his idea.

Robert continued. "We have to assume Pogodina will find out where *Ocean Spirit* is headed. Update Naturelle and Mikhail on the situation. Things will have to move fast down in Kaliningrad."

West said nothing.

"Come here," Robert said in a soft voice. The two men hugged, and West let the tears flow again.

Robert comforted him for a good long while.

"I have to go to Klaipeda," West said.

Robert moved his head back and held West's shoulders. "Of course we're going to help her. But going there without intel would be suicide. We need to know where Pogodina is taking them and whether she plays this by herself or intends to bring in her whole agency. We need Russian G20S access—access as in breaking Fraktal. You are so close."

West nodded, sobbing. He had to find the strength and will to keep working. If nothing else, for Kiss.

"I'll help you," Robert said. "I think the FRA was right all along. First, Pogodina generates the 358-bit key on her PC which we can bring down to forty bits and brute force. Second, she takes the phone call from Moscow. Finally, the encrypted file arrives, which we're able to capture, but we don't know what to look for in the decrypted output. Something in that phone call has got to be the missing piece. A handshake of some sort."

West agreed, pressing his lips together to push back the tears and respond. "We have to tap into that phone call."

Robert nodded. "And we have …" He released West's shoulders and checked his analog wristwatch. "… six and a half hours to figure it out before the new file comes in."

Chapter Seventy-Six

No Service

After blowing his nose thoroughly, West started where he typically did—pencil and paper. He made a drawing of Pogodina's wedge-shaped office space based on Melissa's description.

"Can we listen in physically, through the windows?" he asked Robert.

"FRA tried that using laser microphones, but she has defeaters on all the windows that jam the sound spectrum of human voices."

It turned out FRA had also failed to listen through the ceiling of the floor below and to read Pogodina's lips through the windows.

Picking up sound through the compromised Wi-Fi router sounded promising but led them nowhere, and another break-in was deemed both unfeasible and too risky.

West let himself scroll through Kiss's and his private message thread. It made it all too obvious how recently they had become something more than friends with benefits.

He stopped at their latest conversation, when she was on the yacht.

> Hey, gorgeous! We're about
> to lose carrier service. I'll
> let you know when we're
> back. XXX

Robert leaned in without looking at West's Tile. "I know you worry about your friends, but we don't have much time," he said in a mellow tone.

West's brain made a warp, and something emerged from Kiss's message. "What do people do when they get poor cellular service on their phones?" he said.

"Move to a window."

"And if the service is still too poor?"

Robert's eyes widened. "They go outside."

"We take down just the right cellular antennas to make the signal weak inside Pogodina's office, and she will go out on the balcony where we can listen in on her part of the call."

Robert nodded. "We have to move fast. We need a way to record her at a distance. Maybe a parabolic microphone? As for taking down antennas, cell tower positions are not public information in Sweden. The carriers only provide vague heat maps of coverage."

"Can you get antenna information through your contacts at the FRA?"

"Not at one thirty in the morning on a Monday. They'll need clearance to give me that." He rubbed his stubble. "But I do recall a vigilante survey."

Robert searched a bunch of Swedish terms and names with his Tile. Something made him laugh. "You won't believe this. It is the Left Party, the old Swedish Communist Party, doing vigilante surveys of cell towers."

He started reading from a political manifesto on the matter, translating as he went. "The expansion of the sixth-generation mobile networks is upon us, and there is great concern for how radio frequency waves affect the human body. People with electromagnetic hypersensitivity risk worsened health due to exposure to these waves, both from mobile devices and from cell towers. The Left Party considers it every citizen's right to know one's surroundings and what electromagnetic equipment is in use there. Therefore, we do what the government and the carriers refuse to—we make this information public. Below you find detailed maps of where cell towers are located in Stockholm city. We thank our hard-working members for their time and effort to gather this information."

West leaned over and counted the antenna towers around Pogodina's office building on the Left Party's map. "Seven transceivers in six towers on top of four buildings."

CHAPTER SEVENTY-SEVEN

Åse

"I'm too old for running between buildings," Robert said. "But I can get Åse to help us. She's the only one on my team who's disclosed on our FRA intel."

"Should we really pull in more people?"

"Look, this is already taking forever. We don't have time. Trust me. Besides, you've met her—the sniper from Norway. You two take down the carrier service, and I'll make sure we can record Pogodina on the balcony."

Åse got to the office in half an hour. Her cheeks were rosy from the cold night, but at least her hair and jacket indicated that it wasn't raining.

"Sorry it took so long," she said. "I don't live as close as Robert. Housing prices downtown are nuts. But I'm glad I finally get to help out with this thing."

She pulled off her wool gloves, revealing rainbow-colored fingernails. West noted that the order of the colors was correct—red, orange, yellow, green, and blue.

"Thanks for coming, Åse," he said, shaking her hand. "You're the one who told us about the Dragunov rifle, right?"

"Correct. De-rah-goo-noff." She smiled. "As a matter of fact, I brought this little puppy with me."

She pulled a modern-looking handgun with a suppressor out of her backpack. On top of it was a scope sight that looked like a Maglite. "I can hit a human-sized target at 350 meters with this, and that's without assisted targeting."

West looked at the gun, then at Åse. "We are not going to shoot any human-sized targets."

"Of course not. But I have military training. If I'm going up against Russian G20S, I pack a gun."

Robert calmly said, "I only hire the best."

West shook his head. "It's your city. Just don't get anyone hurt, please." He pulled in air and switched gears. "We've got seven antennas— one at Kungsgatan 77, one at Pipersgatan 26, two at the nearby subway station, and three at Kungsbroplan. Robert, did you find out what the power setup is?"

"I did. Property owners rent out roof space for the antennas, and all contracts I read said they must inform carriers when there's a planned power outage. Ergo, the antennas use the buildings' power."

"Okay, let's find the circuit breakers in these four buildings. That's two buildings each for you and me, Åse. You know lock picking?"

She nodded.

West turned to Robert. "Final piece—how do we listen in on Pogodina?"

"I decided to skip the parabolic microphone and winch down a bug from a drone right onto her balcony well before she gets there in the morning." He held up a penny-sized device. "These suckers are so small, she won't notice."

•

Four hours of hard work later, everything was ready, and the team spread out in the city blocks neighboring Pogodina's office to not be seen lurking around. The elevator camera would tell them when the agent got in.

West saw the sign of a small coffee shop called Wilmer's Coffee Bar and decided to get something to eat. Just as he was crossing the street, his right foot skidded forward an inch. Dog shit.

"Fuck."

The inside of Wilmer's was warm and smelled of coffee and tea. Flush ceiling speakers were playing low-volume music with Swedish lyrics. There was a handful of other people here but no staff.

He walked up to the ordering system—a large screen presenting itself as Wilmer. As soon as he scanned his GPI band, the menu switched to English and pushed eggs and bacon, a BLT sandwich, and a vegan thing called facon up to the top. Defiantly he scrolled to the bottom and ordered a whole wheat egg sandwich.

A few bites in, he got a message from Melissa.

Hey, West. I just got
connected outside
Kaliningrad. What the fuck
happened to J!t and Kizz?

He lost his appetite instantly.

I haven't heard from
them since the distress
messages. :((

Anything from Naturelle or
Mikhail?

Nothing.

But they're on their way
down here, right?

Yes.

We've helped ZNP a ton.
They'll have to help us
enter mainland Russia and
find J & K.

What's up with the G20S
hack?

Robert, me, and one of
Robert's employees are on
it.

Who? The employee.

Her name is Ausseh. Don't
know the spelling.

I don't like bringing in more
people.

Robert vouches for her.

Don't talk to her about the
Survivors or anything. But
you know that.

I've got to find out how to
dock this ship. Keep me
posted.

West stared out of the coffee shop's windows into the glow of the streetlights. The sun wouldn't rise for another hour and a half.

His mind bounced between anxiety for Kiss and stress over the four-step hack that lay less than ninety minutes ahead of them: 1) get Pogodina to reboot her PC, 2) get her out on the balcony, 3) record her phone call, and 4) grab the incoming file through the SORM Wi-Fi router.

He was very tired.

Chapter Seventy-Eight

The Call

Pogodina got into the elevator on Kungsgatan 79 at seven thirty a.m. She looked sleep-deprived on the camera stream.

Having already turned off the cell towers at Kungsgatan and the subway station, West was stationed at the circuit breakers of Kungsbroplan and Åse at Pipersgatan.

His Tile buzzed with a message from their Wi-Fi monitor. Pogodina was at her PC, fetching her email.

He started sending repeated screen grab commands to the JTAG device in her monitor.

Screenshot after screenshot came in. He could see Pogodina move her mouse pointer ferociously but what *she* saw was just a frozen screen.

Finally, the PC's Wi-Fi traffic went dead.

He recorded a timestamp and told the voice channel, "She's rebooting."

Minutes passed. West heard his own breathing and felt his pulse in his temples. He watched the seconds tick on his Tile until 7:45:00.

"Åse , let's go."

He flipped the circuit breakers for the two towers on the roof of Kungsbroplan and watched the service indicator on his Tile go down from a hundred to 23%. If their math was right, below 25% at where he was would guarantee no service at all inside Pogodina's office.

"Robert, do you have a visual of the balcony?"

Robert whispered back. "Yep. I'm taking a slow stroll down Kungsholmsgatan, old man style."

7:50. Ten minutes to Pogodina's call.

Åse's voice spoke in West's ear. "Hey, I got full service again."

West checked his Tile. It too was back to full service. "What the f… Has someone turned the other cell towers back on?"

"I'm checking cell IDs," Åse said. She came back with results within seconds. "It's a totally new transceiver."

West saw the new ID too, and it was nothing he had seen on the Left Party's map. "We have nine minutes to find this sucker and shut it off."

Robert's voice came in as a forced whisper in their earpieces. "Guys, I think I know what this is. It's FRA's Hurricane IMSI-catcher. The phone surveillance I told you about. They only use it conservatively, which is probably why it came online now, right before Pogodina's call. That thing has emergency power."

"So, we're fucked. And Kiss is fucked. And Jitterbug is fucked," West replied.

Silence.

I knew I should have gone to Klaipeda instead of this folly.

"Hey!" It was Åse. "Share your exact geo positions and signal strength to FRA's Hurricane. Let's triangulate this thing."

"It's no …" West started.

"Do it."

At 07:56, Åse had triangulated the IMSI-catcher's position at inch precision. "Kungsgatan 92, right across the street from Pogodina's office. That antenna has gotta be on the roof."

"*Robban, kan du rygge längs Kungsholmsgatan tills du ser taket på 92an?*" Åse had switched to what sounded like the local language.

"*Jag kan försöka men van fan, min syn är ju kass alltså,*" Robert replied.

"*Men ta ett foto då och skicka över.*"

Åse was on the move judging by the labored sound of her voice. "West, sorry for switching to Swedish. Faster that way. Robert will get a photo of the roof while I go to the top floor and try to get roof access here on Pipersgatan. Hopefully there's just enough light to get a view of that thing."

"What's the plan?"

She changed her voice to almost a whisper while climbing stairs by the sound of it. "I can shoot the antenna down from here if I get a clear shot."

"What about ricochets?"

"Best in my class—one shot, one kill. No ricochet."

West checked the time: 07:57.

Åse came back with crackling noise through her microphone. "Okay, I've got air access, and I can see an antenna across the courtyard through my scope. It better be the one."

Seconds passed.

"Faan," she uttered in a much lower than usual voice. It sounded like a Swedish curse. The next moment her nasal voice was back. "I have to get my pulse down to take the shot."

More time passed. Half a minute. West could hear Åse's breathing slow down. Then silence and a dampened shot, like a click.

"Robert, don't tell the FRA, okay?" she said.

West checked his Tile—07:59—and his cellular service was back down at 23%.

Half a minute later, Robert whispered "She's coming out. She's taking the call on the balcony."

Chapter Seventy-Nine

Trust, But Verify

"Enough sleeping. It's noon already."

West looked up at Robert, who continued talking.

"Åse perfected the Russian translation of the call. You and Melissa have a copy on your Tiles."

West had had nightmares about Kiss being shot, Kiss dying in a hospital, and himself on the run from a bunch of thugs through a maze of city blocks he didn't know.

He stared into the bunk bed above him a good while before reaching out for his Tile and opening the translated text of the G20S call.

Obviously, they only had Pogodina's half of it.

> Agent Zabolotnaya, how are you?
>
> Fine, thanks! Although when the weather is like this in Stockholm, I do long for the tundra.
>
> Exactly. The pipe deliveries continue according to plan.
>
> Don't worry. He's just a medium-sized dog with a big dog attitude.
>
> Thank you! And say hi to the Norilsk tundra for me, will you?

They hoped this call contained the information they needed to instruct Mikhail's decryption server on what to look for in the generated JBIG2 files. But there was no code exchange, no spy-like handshake.

He listened to the original recording several times, and there was nothing indicating Pogodina was structuring her language in some intricate way, no hesitation or weird intonation, as far as his understanding of Russian intonation could carry him.

The only thing that stood out at a glance was the reference to Norilsk. Agent Zabolotnaya, whoever that was, was up there for some reason and not in Moscow. Maybe the meaning of "call from Moscow" was not literal but a reference to central power?

He showered, painfully remembering when he and Kiss had made love in Cuba. He put on a fresh set of clothes before going upstairs to sit down and analyze the transcript again.

The pencil in his hand scribbled notes as his thoughts wandered.

Things and places Pogodina mentions:
weather, Stockholm, tundra,
pipe, deliveries, plan, dog,
attitude, Norilsk

He shuffled the list a couple of times, but nothing surfaced. What could the missing sentences from Mrs. Zabolotnaya be? He wrote down some candidates, but it felt too speculative.

Maybe there are numbers hidden inside? Maybe it's not what she says but the length or order of the words?

Such an analysis would have to be done on the original in Russian.

Агент Заболотная, как дела?

Спасибо, хорошо! Но когда
такая погода в Стокгольме, я
хочу вернуться в тундру.

Отлично. Поставка труб идёт по
плану.

Не беспокойтесь. Он просто

собака среднего размера с
собачим характером.

Спасибо! И передай привет
норильской тундре за меня.

He wrote a script to do the counting for him.

```
Number of sentences: 9

Words per sentence: 4, 2, 11, 1, 5, 2, 8,
1, 7

Words per paragraph: 4, 13, 6, 10, 8
```

He put the Russian and the English versions beside each other. These were two very different languages. The word "tundra" even had two different spellings in the Russian text—тундру and тундре—probably because of grammar rules he didn't understand.

Hadn't he even seen a third spelling of that word recently—тундра?

He closed his eyes. Where was it? He drew a quick breath through his nose as the answer came to him—the matrix under Pogodina's desk! Seconds later, he was looking at the translation of it.

Window	Rain	Speaker	Golf
Tundra	Glass	Pillow	Book
Marble	Candy	Music	Saw
Illness	Wood	Grass	Air
Moon	Church	Glove	Hair
Computer	Bill	School	Corn
Hemp	Cosmos	Gas	Dice
Paper	Dog	Cream	Vulture

Could she be referencing X and Y positions in this matrix?
He texted Melissa.

You got Robert's text with
Pogodina's call, right?

For sure.

> I think I'm onto something
> with the code matrix you
> found in her office.

!!!

> She mentions tundra and
> dog twice in the call, and
> both are matrix hits. If you
> view the matrix as a 12-bit
> key, dog sets bit 1 and 11
> and tundra sets 0 and 5.

Looking now.

Too complicated. Ease of
use, West. They haven't
designed this thing to be
impossible to use.

She knows the words
from the matrix because
she picked them. What if
those words are visually
present in the generated
JBIG2 image as proof of a
trustworthy key?

West's brain lit up. Maybe this wasn't a complicated handshake after all. Maybe the phone call's real purpose was for verification, just like Melissa suggested.

Russian agents around the world would pick two words from their individual matrices and say them during the call. Central Russian G20S would then bake those two words into the JBIG2 file so that agents could verify that the key exchange wasn't broken or compromised.

He got working. He'd have to teach Mikhail's server to use optical character recognition to convert JBIG2 images into plaintext and make his search script look for tundra and dog.

Fourteen hours later he woke up in his chair. His Tile was beeping.

```
Exhaustive search through 40 bits

1,099,511,627,776 keys to test

Search hit for key 434,400,000,010
```

He ran down the stairs and loaded the search hit image on Robert's old Windows XP machine.

It looked just like all the other JBIG2 files they had inspected: the same blocks of Latin numerals and scattered Cyrillic characters. Except for two sequences; тундра and собака; tundra and dog.

в ц щ о CCC з IV щ III д XV XIX VII CC XIV в б к ц C⦶ XIX г м ш
C XXX CCC ё CCC XIX ш V г C п XV н IV ж CCC XVII к ы LXXX собака
a D XL п XVII XII XVII XVII ц п з CCC п DC IV LXXX IX ф III LXX
XXII CD ъ ф ё II п XIV D e XL т XIX LXXX o XVII XIX XX ц C XXX и
XIX ц щ с ж ж III у XIV XVIII III л VII ы IX C⦶ в X CC LXX XXX
XXX CI II р I у XXII л XVII и III ш XVIII XC ё o ц XIII XIII к x
C XL ъ CI XI р IX XV у XIX X д CCC ю III LX o в XC я ш IV э й
XVII o л ш VIII XL щ ю XII C⦶ ф XI ь VIII DCCC IX C⦶ V м VIII XL
ы x XVIII XIX п XC ж x VI б CI м XIII XIV CCC C XXII XVII у ю a
XIV н V й I LXXX IV л DCCC э XXX DCC в д р б и и у I IV VI э XXX
ш XL XVII ы т e C⦶ г LXXX XXII V т г ж л й II CC п IV LX XII I D
VI з п XIII o C XXI XV д XXX III ⦶ д у XVI ж V LXXX ⦶ ю д x CCC
п VIII VII XX VIII ъ у XVI ж CC CI ⦶ CD р м XXI a ф x I в в ф д
CI DCC DCCC щ ч XVII XXX щ IX ь э VI X р к XXX л р XC щ x II н ю
XXX XXII н II з т ф ъ o ⦶ ж XV ь CC LX XV LXXX г DCCC н DCC XXII
ь XC ю XX x ъ щ CD у XXX э x ц D л DC н X DC я ш CI XL XV XI ю
XVII д ю XVI LX б ⦶ DCC XL у ⦶ X C⦶ XVIII ь C⦶ e б e x й VI CI
н ш V XVI LXXX п a т XIV XVIII ы б e D ф DC н ъ C⦶ XXX XC д a x
й ю DCCC ж ю VII C XIV DCCC XC XXX V ы XV LXXX р ч XVII XI LX VII
C⦶ X ф ж ж XIV ю ч C⦶ XC ь CD IX ю III г CC ч XX CC C XIX э с a
я CC XXI IV III т VIII ф XVII у XXII XIX IV XVI X м г XII XX DCCC
XX XVI XVII x C CCC LX a с в XIV XVI б т XXX и CCC XVII D з ь CD
XL г з ъ a CC й л ш ы VII o ф DCCC VIII р e у ё XXI C⦶ у ф ж VII
CC DCCC a л у CC CCC ч a з у р DCCC XVI л DC I в н XVIII н ы и щ
LXXX ы ч к ы XVIII X a з XVIII LXX й г D ю г р DC LXXX ж й щ ж
VII CC CC ж н ч ь L D л л CD XXX XIV II р VIII ⦶ з ц a CCC ы щ V
CCC XI г XVII д XVI DCC г ю щ н LXXX CCC ч XVIII CD XXX C ъ II з
III м э e VII ⦶ I н C⦶ XVII ч XXI м e CI тундра x II CI X XX LXX
п в C⦶ к x LXXX р XIX XXX X DCCC DC XX б ы x и у LXXX o XXX ю г
L ё XXI LX e XVIII ч XVIII ь к й ы р н III C V XC ц C⦶ VII CC
XXX в в XV XII I LX XXII LX VI ъ у XX л x IV ч XL в ⦶ м XX п ш к
ы XVIII ч DC в XXII CC д DC и ь CD ч LX X ь e ф у XI н XIII ё VII
э L I CD XXX DC o в II DCCC ш п XXI LX ъ C LXXX XI II б ь ⦶ CI
III ж д ч LXX м р ж e CD г г IV в XXII ю XV и с V IV II ъ ч DCCC
C C⦶ ь IV XX ё к X CI e ю XIV XX ц D VI o XXII ъ ю I XXI я III
LXX ч IV в II XXX DCCC a XL XIV й б з б с ы й VI м a XVI CD XIV
VI CD з з a ё ы L у VI a ю II ю X к п I L VIII I x э CCC XXII XXI
д э XXII п VII C⦶ к x XII б a C⦶ ц C⦶ б CCC I IV ю ф ф IV ё o ш
я e XIII LXXX CI в VIII CD ё XII LXX г т XVI CI LX г ъ ⦶ ш й DC
м e X XXII ц CI XIII XXI б a VI XIII к ф L XL XIX XL ж ь л XXI г
ь VII з л XX CI г I ё V L ж н o C DCCC L DCCC XVII XXII ф э ы я
III X IV XVIII и LXXX ь ш у м ж LXXX ё ъ XI з e x C⦶ XI DCC щ DC
XL CI C д VIII II с н ы в DCC XL ц л ц XVII л з x п LXXX DC ф л э
XXI CI V ж DCCC и ё e XIX к XXII LXXX XXII XVI e XIV L XIV a DCC
л DCC DCC L XC IX XXII CC ⦶ ы XL x XIV XVII ш ъ XV CI ъ X XV CCC
XIX XIV X з г XC й e м X DCCC ⦶ ш II VII I IV XV э XXI з C ы C⦶
XC з XVIII VII D C⦶ LXXX л C I VI DCCC C э C ч VII ъ LXXX CC й л
т XVI т щ CC ъ й ц XXII XIII т с XII э IV б DC л IX XXX CC XC ш a
VII р C⦶ з x D e XXX э м XVI XVI C DCCC x e ю XC э й ф ы x XVII

CHAPTER EIGHTY

Priorities

West texted Melissa with hurried finger taps.

> You were right about the words being the markers to look for. I got the key.

That's fucking awesome. Imagine that. You hacked a Russian custom crypto. I told you I needed a pattern matcher.

> Thanks.

The pipes are offloaded as we speak. Xin will make his inspection tomorrow morning, transfer half the money, and leave.

Mikhail already uploaded a URL to a login portal you can use with Pogodina's key.

Set up at least two back
doors as soon as you're in.
That key you got expires in
two days.

Just start a download of
her email archive and leave
it for now. I don't want to
raise suspicion.

I'll use Kizz and J!t as an
excuse to keep ZNP on
board and help. From this
point it's all about the TN1
backup for the two of us.

> No it's not. It's all about Kizz
> and J!t!

Sure. Let's try to find them
first.

> Try? We have to find them!
> Are you saying the backup is
> more important?

Of course it is. Kizz and
J!t know what they signed
up for. This is about the
human species, West.
If G20S takes me out, I
totally expect you to carry
on yourself. We have to
figure out how to steal the
backup without a word to
ZNP.

West threw his Tile on to the table in front of him, cheeks burning. Their friends were in the hands of some thugs, Kiss possibly dying, and Melissa kept plotting.

Fuck Norilsk. I'm getting you back, Kiss, and then we're out.

He got the URL to Mikhail's Russian G20S login proxy and used the freshly decrypted key.

The screen greeted him as Agent Fedosia Pogodina.

Her remote desktop was well organized. Word processor, spreadsheet software, documents folder, email, and a proprietary instant messaging client.

He opened her inbox. The most recent email was unread, and he let his Tile translate it.

```
To: fedosia.pogodina@g20s.ru
From: alena.zabolotnaya@g20s.ru
Subject: Re: Americans


The American woman is in critical
condition. The man is not talking. We
don't really have anything on them.

I reached out to our US contacts,
and they offered help. Organizing the
meeting in Smolensk to avoid Moscow, as
requested.

--Z
```

Chapter Eighty-One

A Meeting in Smolensk

The inland Russian winter penetrated West's layers of clothes as he stood listening in on a guided tour in Glinka Garden, Smolensk. About an inch of snow covered the ground and trees. It was past noon, and this was the rendezvous point Naturelle had given him.

The guide wore moon boots, and the prints she left in the snow were small ovals with two dots in them, like pig snouts.

"Smolensk's famous bronze deer," the guide said, gesturing to a full-sized deer statue with huge horns in the square opening in front of West. "A gift to the city in 1945 from Soviet soldiers liberating Kaliningrad, Lithuania, and Poland from Nazi Germany. The deer was found outside General Hermann Göring's lodge on the lush hunting grounds of Rominter Heath. Deer in that region grow large, and the stags' horns feature excellent trophy qualities. Today this bronze deer is a favorite place for parents to photograph their children. Some say if you rub the genitals of the deer, you attract good luck."

The spectators lined up for a shot at good fortune, some removing their gloves.

A familiar female voice appeared from West's left. "I find the art of the deer much more captivating than its Nazi history."

A quick glance. It was Melissa.

"Look at the intensity of its eyes," she said. "That animal is sizing you up."

West moved into the eyesight of the motionless bronze deer.

"Huh." His breath was visible in the cold air.

"I take it you're here on business?" she said.

"Audio tech."

The FRA had helped him get his documents in order as a token of appreciation for the Pogodina hack. His alternate self Jonathan Ash was visiting Russia on a single entry, sixty-day visa, under the guise of a US expat market researcher for the Swedish music industry.

He turned his head to meet Melissa's eyes for the first time since she left for Karlshamn. It felt like weeks ago.

Seeing her close made the pent-up emotion around Kiss bubble up, and he had to double breathe. He extended his right hand. "Nice to meet you. I'm Jonathan."

She swallowed. "I'm Taylor. How about a bite and an expat chat at Russkiy Dvor?"

Russkiy Dvor was a popular fast-food place in the park. The interior was colorful and picturesque with brass handles, an ornamented ceiling, and playful pillars with matryoshka dolls watching the guests. And the chattery line was a perfect place to catch up.

"How are you?" Melissa looked genuinely worried.

"I've been better." He looked down. "A lot better."

Her pinky touched him. "We'll find them. And it's the perfect excuse for us to go …" She stopped herself.

"She's in critical condition," West said. "You saw the email."

"She's alive," Melissa replied quickly. She paused. "I worked with Naturelle on the G20S account you got for us. Thanks again, by the way, that was some kickass hacking you did."

He looked up. "Did everything work out with *Ocean Spirit* and the pipes?"

"A few mishaps, but we got paid in the end. Sounds crazy, but we're filthy rich right now."

She flashed him a smile. He didn't reciprocate.

"You said you and Naturelle had worked on Pogodina's account," he said.

"Pogodina is flying here directly on a government plane from Stockholm. Zabolotnaya will join over video link, and she shows no sign of knowing what was really on that ship, so maybe there is no connection there. The meeting will be held tomorrow morning in the G20S building along Krasno-something Sloboda street. From what I can tell, Jit will be there."

"Then we break him out."

"Careful. We're dealing with Russian G20S on their home turf, and you and I have to stay under the radar until we can get to the backup in Norilsk. Naturelle has a plan to tap into that meeting. We have rented an apartment for the week just a block away."

The idea was to do a person-in-the-middle attack on Zabolotnaya's video connection to Smolensk. Among Pogodina's emails was the meeting invitation to her colleague. It was a URL compressed with a link shortener, meaning Zabolotnaya had no idea where the link would actually take her.

Naturelle copied the webpage from the real link and set up a replica on a very similar domain name. She then created a new shortened link and sent out a meeting update to Zabolotnaya through Pogodina's account.

·

At 08:58 a.m. Moscow Standard Time, Zabolotnaya connected to the replica site and entered her credentials. A script copied them to the real site and logged the Survivors and ZNP in to the actual meeting. West noted that Zabolotnaya used some kind of two-factor login and that her password was fifteen characters long.

Is fifteen enough these days?

The video feed was forwarded to Zabolotnaya's device, and they stayed in the middle, seeing and hearing both sides and recording the whole thing.

The feed showed a bland, rectangular conference room with somewhat of a fish-eye effect on the camera. Four faces immediately caught their eyes—Jitterbug together with Pogodina on the right, and the pale Dr. Kawasaki with BestBye on the left.

"Kawasaki," Melissa said through her teeth.

West thought it peculiar that Melissa didn't comment on BestBye's presence, which was just as surprising. BestBye was dressed formally, whereas Jitterbug had ill-fitting clothes most likely issued to him.

There were ten people in total sitting at the meeting room table, and they all turned toward the camera, Pogodina taking the lead. "Welcome, Agent Zabolotnaya. How is Siberia?"

"Way ahead of you, as we say here in the Krasnoyarsk Time Zone."

"Always a pleasure. Let's have you introduce yourself first."

"I'm Agent Zabolotnaya, head of G20S operations in Krasnoyarsk Krai, the largest krai in the Russian Federation and the third largest subnational governing area in the world." The phrase sounded rehearsed, and there was pride in her voice. "I am in frequent contact with our US counterpart since we host one of the two GPI backup facilities. Normally, I would not mention that with undisclosed people in the room, but information on our operations leaked to the press a short while ago, as I'm sure you're aware of."

West couldn't help but look at Melissa. She didn't move.

Pogodina turned to Dr. Kawasaki and lowered her voice slightly. "I can assure you we are hunting down the sources of that leak."

She went back to conference phone tone. "I'm Agent Pogodina, head of Russia's Nordic G20S branch as well as our Nord Stream 3 project. To the left of me we have our American suspect. And to my right ..." She handed it over to the three men with a nod, and they introduced themselves as local Smolensk G20S staff.

"I'm Dr. Kawasaki, head of US G20S. The rest of my people need no introductions. You have their profiles in your GPI logs, so let's get on with business." She looked briefly at Jitterbug. "We were told you apprehended *two* of our citizens."

Pogodina was caught off guard by Kawasaki's haste but played it cool. "That is true. Unfortunately, the woman was wounded when she and her accomplice tried to escape in Klaipeda. I can assure you we provided world-class medical treatment, but her life could not be saved."

That freeze frame would stay in West's memory forever—he and three other hackers sitting on wooden dining chairs in a sparsely furnished Smolensk apartment, lights off, blinds down, the distress in Jitterbug's face through the video feed.

Melissa's arms caught West as he tipped forward.

CHAPTER EIGHTY-TWO

An Internal Russian Matter

Nightmares and turmoil had kept West company for ten hours. He couldn't sleep anymore, but his limbs wouldn't move.

Melissa sat beside his bed.

"The others went out to get some food. You should drink some water," she said.

He didn't respond.

She started talking to herself. "Kiss was a wonderful human being and friend. I'm forever in her debt, for many things."

"I'm out," West mumbled. His mouth was dry.

Melissa continued. "She saved me from myself so many times. She could even handle my trust issues."

He could see her head turn to him in the corner of his eye.

"I know you two were close," she said. "But we still have to save Jitterbug."

West wanted to say something but couldn't decide what.

"Can you at least watch the rest of the recorded video call so you know what's going on?"

"Don't pressure me, Melissa."

"Just listen. That's all you have to do."

She replayed the video feed from the meeting from a point where Kiss's death wasn't mentioned anymore. West could make out the distinct voices of Pogodina, Dr. Kawasaki, and Zabolotnaya without watching the feed.

Pogodina went first. "These two individuals were caught stealing GPS tracking equipment from a Russian cargo ship we use for pipe deliveries.

Since you had offered general assistance in exchange for Russia's vote on you as a candidate, we requested your help."

Dr. Kawasaki responded in a monotonous voice. "We have checked their identities. Kate Libby and Dade Murphy are correct. US intelligence has had its eyes on them for some time. I will make sure to share their files with you."

"And the accomplice they must have been working with?"

"We believe they worked alone."

"Then who took the ship to Kaliningrad? It was found there with its cargo gone."

"It's an automated ship, is it not?"

"Are you saying Libby and Murphy made the ship go to Kaliningrad by itself?"

"We'd have to inspect the ship's systems to draw solid conclusions, but that certainly is a possibility."

"What about the stolen pipes?"

"Our sources say they were sold to a Chinese government delegation. Unloading and land freight went through regular means. If this was not expected, I would assume illegal activities."

Melissa paused the video to add her thoughts. "I can't see how Kawasaki could make something like this up and hit the truth bull's-eye. How does she know about the Chinese? She even seems to know about the shipment along the Silk Road."

Melissa tapped play again, and Pogodina's voice came back. "China? What would China want with our gas pipes?"

"You tell me." Dr. Kawasaki sounded rhetorical.

Zabolotnaya interrupted the two. "We will look into these allegations. The People's Republic of China is an ally of ours, and we don't take lightly implied corruption or theft. But thank you for sharing the intel you have, Doctor."

"As far as our intelligence goes, it was a legitimate business transaction."

Pogodina snapped back. "A business transaction between these two Americans and the Chinese?"

Dr. Kawasaki took her time to respond. "That's not what I'm saying, Agent. Miss Libby and Mr. Murphy were probably hired to do the job. Hired by someone who orchestrated the deal with the Chinese in Kaliningrad. My assumption would be a Russian insider."

Melissa stopped the video briefly. "Here Kawasaki turns to Zabolot-naya, and the meeting is derailed."

Dr. Kawasaki continued, apparently talking to Zabolotnaya. "If you're looking for traces of the business transaction with the Chinese, I sug-gest you investigate Agent Pogodina's activities in Sweden the last few months."

There was a sound burst, as if something hit the wall in the meeting room. Pogodina's voice was now significantly louder. "This is preposter-ous! You come to our country as guests to discuss two of *your* citizens stealing one of our ships and its cargo. And you throw accusations at us? At me?"

Dr. Kawasaki remained calm. "You sold some pipes to the Chinese on the side. Maybe it's sanctioned, maybe it's not. We can take Murphy off your hands and say no more about the pipes."

"We have no intentions of handing you this criminal."

"He's an American. I suggest we follow the G20S treaty."

"Excuse me, but I believe the appropriate phrase is 'Fuck you.' Mur-phy is going to a correctional facility in Norilsk until we get those pipes back."

"I'm sure your superiors and I can work something out. Perhaps we can help you interrogate him?"

"Only people with special permission set foot in Norilsk, and I can assure you, you no longer have it."

"We helped you build the backup facility. We even helped you hire unique mining expertise as part of the whole deal. Norilsk would not be where it is without American help."

"Maybe we should send that 'help' home? This conversation is over. If Mr. Murphy doesn't talk in Norilsk, Zabolotnaya has got a permanent place for him in the Ice Dolphin Prison. You'd do best in forgetting he ever existed."

"I can tell you are very upset about these pipes. How about I pay you for them in exchange for Murphy?"

Pogodina replied, struggling with her self-control. "I can tell this Murphy is very important to you, which makes us even less inclined to ever release him. I told you this conversation is over. In fact, it never hap-pened. You can kiss Russia's support for your G20S candidacy goodbye. Take your stupid sword with you and go home."

The video ended. Melissa sat quietly for a while before commenting on what they had just listened to. "A lot to unpack there. Kawasaki surely knows all about the Survivors through BestBye. So why did she lie about Kiss and Jit working alone? And why does she want Jit for herself so desperately that she's willing to shell out tax dollars for a shipload of gas pipes? And why blow up Pogodina's smuggling operation?"

"BestBye just sat there," was West's first comment.

Melissa was quick to reply. "Dr. Kawasaki has something up her sleeve that's making her play hardball with the Russians. But the fact that they're taking Jit to Norilsk gives us an excuse to go there. I've already asked, and ZNP are on board."

West looked at the ceiling. The thoughts of Kiss dying stung from every possible angle. "I'm out."

CHAPTER EIGHTY-THREE

I Have Nothing

Melissa left him food and paid for the apartment for a few extra days before she and the two Russian hackers left Smolensk, headed to the riverside city of Dudinka, close to Norilsk.

He stayed in bed for two days, only drinking water and going to the bathroom. Stomach churn got indistinguishable from hunger.

Patches of sleep allowed him not to think at all, but every waking moment his psyche dug deeper, worsened by the lack of carbs.

Why was he made to suffer like this? Hadn't he endured enough? Or was he even allowed to feel sorry for himself? He hadn't died; his mom and Kiss had.

His promise to himself had been crystal clear—live a normal life and build a family. Instead he'd gone on a hacking spree, taking huge risks. What an idiot he was.

Kiss would still be alive if he hadn't come up with the idea to steal the ship. Or if he had gone to Klaipeda instead of her. Or if they had just stayed in Havana.

And his mom. He'd basically killed her too. He *should* be suffering.

His Tile lay on a chair beside the bed, and he asked it to describe the Ice Dolphin Prison.

It responded instantly. "The Ice Dolphin Prison is a maximum-security facility for enemies of the Russian state, known for its harsh conditions. It is located on the northern island of Severny, close to the Matochkin Strait of Novaya Zemlya in the Arctic Ocean. Transportation to Ice Dolphin Prison goes through the administrative center of Novaya Zemlya called Belushya Guba. From there, prisoners are transported by ship, 'Never to see civilization again,' as put by the Russian president."

Jit is on his way to that place, not me. Melissa'll probably end up there too.

His Tile buzzed. He reached out reluctantly and grabbed it. On the screen was a reminder for tomorrow:

```
Call parole officer.
```

It was a smack in the face. The world wasn't going to stop just because he had.

As he stared at the Tile's screen, it dimmed from inactivity. If he gave up now, everything he had strived for since he got out would be thrown in the dustbin. Kids were born into this surveillance nightmare this very moment, their newly minted identities put on the blockchain before they even left the hospital; kids like the ones he and Kiss were supposed to have.

Just before the screen went black, he touched it, and it came back to full brightness. He switched to the Survivors' messaging channel.

You there, Melissa?

You bet.

I know I will never get Kizz back. Maybe I'll never be happy again.

I'm devastated too.

But it's selfish to not help J!t get out.
I'm sorry.

Don't be. We need you.

How do I find you?

We're on the Trans-Siberian Railway with

another day to go before
Krasnoyarsk. From there
we'll fly up to Alykel Airport
and Dudinka.

> I'll figure out how to get
> there. I need a guide or
> something.

Dudinka is closed, just
like Norilsk, so you need
a Russian ID and a travel
permit. Naturelle can set
you up.

I'm Dina Kuznetsova btw.
An engineer from the
Moscow State Mining
University, specialized in
Automation and Computer
Science. (Yay, I got my
master's.)

> I also have to fake a video
> call from SF.

Parole thingy? Better use
my proxy for that. I'll send
you a link.

Welcome back, Survivor.
See you in the freezer.

West would need Russian-speaking help. The only one he could think of who he could trust was a former sniper in the Norwegian special forces.

CHAPTER EIGHTY-FOUR

North Siberia

West huddled in the arctic cold as he approached Your Guys Grill in west Dudinka. He couldn't believe he was in Siberia. How many Americans had been in this part of the world?

As if just being in this place wasn't enough, he was still blown away by the fact that Åse had been able to get him here, through train and airline tickets to simple things like ordering food. The hardest part had been airport security in Krasnoyarsk, where he had to surrender his Tile and couldn't have Åse as an in-ear prompter. Luckily, the airport people were just as uninterested in talking as he was, and Naturelle had cleverly created him the fake identity of Vadim Nikolaev—a shy, mumbling, self-taught programmer who grew up in the US, which gave him an excuse for a bad accent and occasional switches to English.

He spotted Melissa standing in the grill preorder line, just as promised. None of them said a word. They got their food in thick, insulated cardboard boxes, and West followed Melissa at a distance to the hotel where their operations apparently were set up.

Once in Melissa's hotel room, she gave him a long hug. "Thanks for coming back." She sniffled, maybe because of the cold outside.

"I keep thinking of her," he whispered back, "getting pulled down into this dark place where I just want it all to end."

"We had kind of a falling out, the last I saw of her," Melissa said. "I can't get over it."

He moved his head back from the hug and looked at Melissa. "You and Jit are all I have left now."

They sat down and opened their grilled-food boxes.

West hadn't had any appetite since Smolensk and looked down at the meat rolls in his box. His Tile had translated it to "Taiga meat," and the rolls supposedly contained mushrooms and bacon. Melissa had ordered a bean burger with fries.

Naturelle and Mikhail joined, and Melissa started talking business between bites. "Transport options. Let's hear it."

Naturelle had been investigating ways to get them into the forbidden mining city of Norilsk. "Commute buses leave in both directions every hour between six in the morning and midnight."

"What about the train?"

"It's a fifty-five-mile one-track railway connecting the two cities, but it is strictly for freight."

Melissa nodded at Mikhail and Naturelle. "You two speak Russian, so you'll have to keep doing the outside research. Check out the bus stop and the train station here in Dudinka. Talk to some locals if possible."

"I have idea." Mikhail held up a set of small clip cameras. "These can record twelve hours of video on battery. Clip them on one of buses and on train cart, collect them when they come back, and we get video footage of stations in Norilsk."

"Cool." Melissa folded a French fry and threw it into her mouth. "I will go through Pogodina's recent communications once I've secured a connection that can't be traced to our hotel. West, you get the honors of applying machine learning to her old emails and messages. The ones we've already downloaded. I've already massaged the data. Should be a case of unsupervised learning to reveal key people she works with and what they're up to. We need to understand the connection between Zabolotnaya and Pogodina, why they decided to take Jit to Norilsk, and who's in charge of things."

They finished eating and got moving. Naturelle and Mikhail headed out to scout the bus terminal and train station.

West took a deep breath. He hadn't done machine learning for a decade and a half.

Unsupervised learning was about finding hidden structures in data, which meant he had to give the machine learning algorithm somewhere to start.

He made his Tile ingest the communication data Melissa had already prepared and looked at Pogodina's stats.

```
92,001  incoming messages
54,603  messages sent
14,112  incoming emails
10,483  sent emails
 4,484  email threads
```

4.04 GB data

I wonder what's in there?

While his Tile was processing the data, he seized the opportunity to chat with Melissa while the Russians weren't around. "How are we going to steal the backup? I read the *Wired* article again, and it doesn't say much. Inside a mountain."

"I don't know. At some point we'll have to fork off from ZNP, but we need to get as far as possible with their help. Entering Norilsk is hard enough as it is."

This is ludicrous. We have no plan.

"Suppose we pull it off, the whole shebang; we compromise GPI. What do you think happens next?" he asked.

Melissa sighed.

"Aren't we going to talk about that?" he insisted.

She looked up from her screen and paused for a couple of seconds. "Three possible outcomes," she began. "Worst case, the G20 governments spin it as an 'attack on society' and argue for even more surveillance. We get called out as terrorists and serve lifetime sentences."

"I'd rather die than go to prison for the rest of my life."

"Normally I frown when people say they'd rather die than blank. But I guess in your case it's reasonable. Let's make sure we don't end up there. Middle of the road outcome, some significant agency heads roll, we get a public debate and protective legislation in the US, but G20S continues its operations. The Survivors are pardoned, but the deep state will come for us anyway. We live our lives as fugitives. Sad trombone."

"Best case?"

"Best case, people realize that digital information on everything they do and say, and the power to analyze it, is the ultimate weapon to oppress and dupe humans. Public outrage, G20S is disbanded, new laws are put in place throughout the world, and political parties who defend basic freedoms thrive. Bam!"

"You think we'll keep these?" West fingered his GPI band, which had started to feel familiar.

"Sure. They're too damn convenient. But they don't have to expose your identity all the time, and no central place should collect data on where and why you use it. You talk to an insurance company? That's between you and them."

She got a message notification and started typing aggressively on her Tile.

"News from Naturelle and Mikhail?" West asked.

"Nothing," she said, still typing.

"I just thought—"

"It's nothing."

"You keep saying that when you get text messages. In Havana, at the airport, in Robert's office. It makes me nervous."

She tapped her Tile's screen and held it up to him. It was the contact card of a skinny, smiling man. The name said Jeffrey Orr.

"It's Jeff. My old bf. He started texting me again, out of the blue."

West blushed. "Oh."

He returned sheepishly to his Tile. Its first machine learning pass was text mining for important words commonly used in Pogodina's correspondence.

The second pass grouped the messages into clusters based on similarity and context.

The last pass listed the most important contacts and words for the three main clusters.

Cluster one and two were clearly the Nord Stream business and the palladium smuggling, including deals with Xin. No news there.

But the third cluster looked like an unknown leg of Pogodina's work life, involving Zabolotnaya and Xin but on some different topic. It also involved an additional contact named Liu Jian.

```
Cluster 3

Contacts
0 Liu Jian
1 Zabolotnaya
2 Xin Ping
```

```
Words           Score
0 Hefei         0.044036
1 Norilsk       0.033229
2 Bao Gong      0.027058
3 LiveLearn     0.017350
4 data          0.016722
5 Bancor        0.014900
6 Mingjia       0.014824
7 Fa-Jia        0.012118
8 Mozi          0.009894
```

He fired up the service Melissa had told him about months earlier called Context Search. Instead of a regular web search, you provided a set of words or sentences, and the engine did a deep search for contexts where all of it made sense together.

The results came back as a computer-generated summary with links.

```
No context found in which all 10
words make sense. There is 1 strong
hit containing 4 of the words:

Chinese Justice & Moral Philosophy

Bao Gong, Mingjia, Fa-Jia, Mozi

Context score: 82%

Bao Zheng, commonly known as Bao
Gong or Lord Bao, was a government
officer during China's Song Dynasty.
In office, he gained the honorific
title Justice Bao due to his ability
to help peasants overcome corruption.

Mingjia, the Logicians or School
of Names, was a school of Chinese
philosophy that grew out of Mohism
during the Warring States period.
```

Fa-Jia or Legalism is one of Sima
Tan's six classical schools of
thought in Chinese philosophy,
and one of the main philosophical
currents of the Warring States
period.

Mozi (Latin as Micius), was a
Chinese philosopher during the
Hundred Schools of Thought period.
He founded the school of Mohism that
argued strongly against Confucianism
and Taoism. His philosophy emphasized
self-restraint, self-reflection, and
authenticity rather than obedience
to ritual.

Tap to see all results (1 more
available).

Why is Pogodina messaging about Chinese philosophy?
He pulled up three random emails from the Chinese philosophy cluster to have a look.

To: alena.zabolotnaya@g20s.ru
CC: pogodina@nordstream.com
From: Liu.Jian@hfut.edu.cn
Subject: Re: Bao Gong delay

Dear Agent Zabolotnaya,

As mentioned earlier, we are making
progress on Bao Gong. However, the
testing is particularly complex and
cannot be compared with Mingjia, which
was more of a prototype. I hope you
understand that we are working very hard.
My assistant on site in Norilsk, Dr.

Yiang, has been instructed to work double
shifts.

Best,
Jian

To: Liu.Jian@hfut.edu.cn
CC: pogodina@nordstream.com; xin.ping@
pbc.gov.cn
From: alena.zabolotnaya@g20s.ru
Subject: Trip to Hefei

Thanks! We appreciate your invitation,
and let me assure you we are no strangers
to restricted access and government
protection of sensitive projects.

--Z

> The Chinese Central Committee,
> the Chinese G20S, and our dear
> Principal of Hefei University of
> Technology have granted you the
> privilege to visit our
> facilities as part of our joint
> initiative.
>
> Hefei University of Technology
> is a national key university
> administrated directly by the
> Ministry of Education, and the
> Mingjia project is top secret.
> We therefore urge you to be
> discreet and let us manage your
> trip from Shanghai and onward.

```
To: alena.zabolotnaya@g20s.ru
CC: pogodina@nordstream.com
From: xin.ping@pbc.gov.cn
Subject: Re: Bancor Payment

China accepts the terms of payment and
will figure out the details with Director
Pogodina, as instructed.

Yours, Xin Ping
```

Huh. These Chinese philosophy things sound more like codenames.
He went back to the Context Search results page and tapped to see the remaining, lower-score result.

```
Chinese Quantum Computing
Hefei, Mozi

Context score: 29%

The National Laboratory for Quantum
Information Sciences, in Hefei, Anhui
Province, China, opened in 2020. It
has two major research goals: Quantum
metrology and building quantum
computers.

China's quantum satellite, nicknamed
Micius or Mozi after an ancient
Chinese scientist and philosopher,
was the first to successfully beam
pairs of entangled photons to
receiving stations on Earth.
```

"Hey, Melissa. Come check this out."

She read through all of West's results in silence, then looked at him. Her eyes were dark, and her jaw clenched.

"This is the race for quantum supremacy," she said. "Russia and China are colluding to beat the US on analyzing the G20S data set with quantum computing. Russia gets the data in Norilsk to be able to produce the offline backup, and China has the world's first large-scale quantum computer. What is LiveLearn?"

They queried Pogodina's message data for the top hits on LiveLearn and read them together.

LiveLearn was an alternate, more descriptive name for the project called Bao Gong. The Chinese solution was an extremely fast and power-hungry quantum memory bank that could hold about a week's worth of GPI data at a time. The Bao Gong system would be fed weekly increments of data as a secret side business to the extraction of core data for the lean Norilsk backup, learning things "live."

"This is what it's all about, isn't it?" West said, looking at Melissa.

She nodded. "World War Three–level conspiracy. Not a word to the others."

Chapter Eighty-Five

Entering the Forbidden City

West was worried that he couldn't keep his poker face, so he asked Melissa to tell the two Russians about his findings when they gathered for a roundup late that evening.

"West's statistical analysis of old data confirms what we know about Nord Stream, the smuggling, and Pogodina's good connections with Zabolotnaya," Melissa commenced. "The news is that Zabolotnaya seems to be involved in the dirty palladium business. That's probably why we didn't see any pushback from her on Pogodina's ousting of Dr. Kawasaki."

"Cash rules everything around me," Mikhail said with a tired smile.

Melissa continued. "As for Pogodina's correspondence since Smolensk, she seems to have handled most of it over voice. Only a few messages in text. But one of them is useful. She has a contact at the Norilsk Police, who she sent instructions to for the detainment of Jitterbug. We could forge new instructions, email them to that same Norilsk Police officer, and create a way in."

She showed the others a draft email to be sent from Pogodina's account.

```
Subject: Interrogate US captive

Dear Praporshchik,

Agent Zabolotnaya and I have appointed
three persons to interrogate the detained
Mr. Murphy:
```

Ms. Naturelle Veschitskaya
Mr. Mikhail Simonov
Ms. Dina Kuznetsova

They are all computer experts assigned to
help me understand what damage Murphy and
Libby have caused to our operations in
Sweden.

You are to escort Veschitskaya, Simonov,
and Kuznetsova to Murphy's cell, where
they will do their work undisturbed for
two hours at a time. Then you or your
staff check in on them.

Strip them of any technical equipment
that Murphy might steal, and provide them
with a standard-issue PC with internet
connection.

The regular guards on duty remain, of
course.

It is of utmost importance that you do
not talk to anyone about Murphy or of
this interrogation. Don't even talk to
Zabolotnaya or me about this unless we
bring it up.

--DirP

"What do y'all think? By the way, I'm totally counting on you two to translate this for me." She looked at Naturelle and Mikhail.

I'm not mentioned in the email. That can't be a lapse.

"The last part instructing them not to bring it up is a little telling," West said, rubbing his chin.

"Kiss taught me the trick, and she swears ... swore by it," Melissa replied. "People fear authority, and we don't care if they *eventually* talk, just that they don't talk when we're still in operation."

"It would be nice to tell the officer to remove the guards, and to let us keep our Tiles," Naturelle said.

"Nice for us, but I'm trying not to contradict Pogodina's earlier instructions. We'll be walking a thin line here." The rest of the team seemed to agree. "Good. Naturelle, what have you got on the buses? We need to get into the city before we can get to the police station."

"I was able to scan hundreds of commuter bands this morning through a reader I set up at the bus stop. Nothing stands out—it's just regular GPI. They blip it as they get on. I think we can set ours up to pass the check. The buses drive in convoys, at least during winter. But there's another problem." She beamed a set of short video clips onto the room's big screen. "This is from Mikhail's clip camera I put on one of the buses. It shows the arrival at the terminal in Norilsk at eight thirty."

It was still pitch dark outside, and the scene was lit with an eerie yellow glow from electric lights. People in the video walked through double revolving glass doors with a short air gap in between. They all stopped briefly in the gap.

Naturelle paused the video and pointed toward a black, large module above the second revolving door.

"I believe that's a facial recognition system. See how people stop for two, three seconds and look into that thing?"

Melissa walked up close to the screen and gestured to get a couple of replays of the sequence.

"You're right," she said.

Naturelle pointed out two figures behind the glass walls of the terminal. "The security guards look reasonably attentive."

West shook his head. "Facial recognition and manual guards." He turned to Mikhail. "Let me guess, the freight train scans your retina and takes a blood sample."

Mikhail chuckled. "Not really. I paid guy at train station to talk. I said I was looking for job in cargo. He even showed me locomotive so I could snap on cameras. They transport explosives for Norilsk mines. The train is loaded at eight in the morning in Dudinka and leaves for Norilsk at ten. But *main* purpose of the train is to transport mining products *back* from Norilsk in Dudinka Port."

"Let's see what the cameras got," Naturelle said.

Mikhail played two long, tiring video clips in parallel, taken from either side of the freight train. The only one who seemed to stay alert was Melissa.

She's probably on some chemicals.

West had dozed off, but then the videos stopped, and Melissa commented on them.

"I prefer the bus idea. We need to blend in," she said. "I'm so out of time zone right now I can work a few more hours. Tomorrow we figure out how to beat or skip that facial recognition camera and get everything in order. Friday morning we roll."

Mikhail shrugged. Naturelle nodded.

"I hate to bring it up, but am I part of this plan?" West asked.

"Ah, yes." Melissa turned to him. "Not to be rude, but you're more likely to crack under pressure after your prison time. Getting into Norilsk and getting Jit out of jail is going to require a lot of human interaction. You stay in Dudinka as a base of operations. If one or more of us are busted, you're our last hope. Once inside Norilsk, the cellular network is off-limits. We may be able to get sporadic Wi-Fi access, but we can't rely on it. I have set up a server where we can post and read messages anonymously. That's our emergency means of communication."

I can't believe she doesn't have a plan for the backup.

"One more question," West said. "How do we get out of here? If you break someone out of jail, we can't just travel out of this place like normal people. We need an exit."

"That's what we spent the first two days in Dudinka arranging. Sorry for not mentioning it," Melissa said. "Oleg Ivanovich, a Russian magnate in the mining business. He has a permanent travel permit to this region and agreed to fly us out of Alykel Airport on a three-hour notice. Agreed to as in accepted a large amount of Bancor, 10% down, 90 on fulfillment."

"We're doing business with oligarchs now?"

"Any better ideas?" Melissa forced a smile. "Once I ping Oleg, it's get on that plane or stay in the Arctic."

•

West went to bed around midnight. His hotel room was small and featured a twin-size bed, a wall-mounted TV, a small desk, and two glasses in holders made of metal. Each floor had a large, ornamented, metal container with a tap where you could get tea around the clock. There was a faint smell of cigarette smoke.

As he was about to fall asleep, his Tile lit up on the bedside table. It was a private message from Melissa.

> You alone?

> You mean from M and N?

> Duh.

> Yes.

> You've got to see this on the TV.

He looked up and saw the set come alive. Melissa must be sharing from the other side of the wall.

> Sorry for being paranoid. I don't want your Tile to carry any traces of this.

> That's why I'm beaming to your TV.

> Here's the plan.

> Tomorrow you buy really warm clothes, a comfy backpack, bottled water, something edible, and a thermos.

The message continued for a couple of screenfuls and outlined a solo mission so daring and open ended that he didn't know what to think.

CHAPTER EIGHTY-SIX

Driver's Seat

West was early enough at Dudinka train station to not see anyone else around. The pale electric lights outside the terminal made it clear that this place no longer welcomed human passengers. This station was a freight workplace.

He instinctively felt for his GPI band. It wasn't there. Good. It was already in its F pouch. From this point he was not supposed to meet anyone, log in to anything, or even exist in the eyes of the GPI system. He was entering an automated world where there were no humans or personal identities.

There was a modern, green freight train on the third track from the building. West had envisioned it as white, given how most machines looked these days, but its label was correct: 3P2T-7229.

The train was pointing south toward the harbor. He decided to go to the right, get to the other side of the train, and approach the locomotive from the back.

As he crossed the tracks, he looked into the darkness over the majestic Yenisey River. It was windy, cold, and frightening out there. He took a deep breath.

One small step for me …

He reached the front of the locomotive and let his half-empty backpack slide to the ground. It contained a large thermos of coffee, a water bottle, a cheese sandwich, and his Survivor Kit, leaving plenty of space for the backup.

The lock to the train's cab was electric, and it took West a couple of minutes to find the mechanical fallback keyhole and another few to pick it. Lock picking really was a hacker's best friend.

The pneumatic door actuation broke a thin layer of ice that had built up around the door's edge and slid it to the side. No lights came on.

He kicked the snow from his boots, climbed into the compartment, and closed the door.

Instinctively, he took his fur hat off, only to quickly put it back on again.

The space featured a large front window, three dark screens angled at the engineer, two large levers and one small, a keyboard with a Russian layout, and a stylized logo that read "V. Tikhomirov Scientific Research Institute of Instrument Design."

In the back there were two hangers, two mug holders (the right one with coffee stains), and a door to a tiny bathroom.

Four hours until sunrise.

CHAPTER EIGHTY-SEVEN

Tongue-In-Cheek

Melissa, Naturelle, and Mikhail's morning commute to Norilsk was an hour and a half's ride in darkness. Their bus was last in a convoy of eight.

It was a modern vehicle and highly adapted to the weather conditions with a mesh floor to drain melting snow from the passengers' boots, heated seats, and powerful lights not only in the front but on the sides.

Melissa casually eavesdropped on the conversation between two women in front of her with the use of in-ear translation. They were talking about an upcoming disco called Mechanika. It sounded like a popular event. They would stay with friends for the night. Unless they got lucky.

The bus stopped gently outside the glass-walled Norilsk terminal building with the double set of revolving doors they had seen in Naturelle's video. Yellow light flooded the scene.

The three hackers had not looked at each other for the whole trip. Instead, they were spread out inside the bus—Mikhail in the front, Naturelle in the midsection, and Melissa in the far back.

Mikhail got up early enough to catch a pole position to get off. Naturelle took it easy, as did most of the others. Melissa stayed seated, put on a bored, everyday face, and looked out the window toward the front of the bus.

The doors opened, and Mikhail got his large fur hat on. His breath plumed in the air as he walked slowly toward the doors through an inch of snow. The passenger behind waited politely as Mikhail entered the facial recognition vault.

Melissa saw him take off his hat just like they had practiced. He took his time, holding the hat in front of his chest. In his left hand, hidden up his coat sleeve, he held a 1.5W blue laser pointed straight into the camera lens, hitting the sensor.

Just as the situation was about to become awkward, he lowered his hands, hat off. An LED on the camera module had gone from green to red.

Both guards reacted to something. One of them communicated with Mikhail through the glass; the other one opened what looked like a control panel mounted on the back wall. More passengers lined up outside.

The guard closest to Mikhail gestured for him to come through, and Melissa could see Mikhail get questioned and blip his GPI band.

A sting hit her gut. The Russian phrases she had rehearsed for her Dina Kuznetsova identity would not stand up to arbitrary questioning.

She thought of solutions as the passengers in front of her exited the bus and went through the manual procedure one by one. Most of them got through much quicker than Mikhail, but Naturelle got the lengthy treatment too. The system probably detected that they were newcomers.

Melissa left the bus last and stood in the five-person line waiting. It was freezing cold, and the air had a toxic smell. She had about a minute to come up with something to pass the guard's questions. Mikhail had left the terminal long ago, but she thought she saw Naturelle waiting at the far end.

The last person in front of her entered the revolving doors. No more time.

She put her tongue between her front teeth and bit down halfway. The pain was intense. If she bit further, she would cut the tip off completely. Not good.

She moved the tongue to the right, in between her back teeth, braced herself, and bit through as far as her will would take her.

She quelled a scream of pain. Warm, iron-tasting blood flowed from the side of her tongue. She gently moved her tongue around in her mouth to convince herself it was still in one piece. Her spit stained the snowy ground red.

The first revolving door let her in without a sound. She looked up at the facial recognition camera. A buzz signaled that the inner door unlocked. She stepped through.

The inside was not room temperature but more pleasant than outside. The guard by the door looked at her and held out a badge reader. Melissa blipped her GPI.

"The third unrecognized person on the same bus," his translated voice said. He turned partially toward his coworker in the back. "Are we on a hiring spree?"

He turned back to Melissa. "Name and home address."

"Mmm gnn."

"Do you have a hearing problem? I'm asking for your name and address."

"Nnn." She pointed to her mouth.

The guard took a step forward.

Melissa tilted her head backward and swallowed a good deal of blood before opening her mouth.

He jolted backward. "Fuck. You're saying you can't speak?"

"I know this woman." The translated voice in Melissa's ear did a good job of mimicking Naturelle's. "She's a friend. Newly hired, just like me. It's our first day."

"Do you know her name and address?" He looked down at the tablet-sized device to confirm the right answer.

"Dina Kuznetsova, Sports Street 9, Dudinka."

Seconds passed with the guard still reading on his tablet.

Finally, he looked up without moving his head. "Why are you still here? Everyone's late because of this damn camera problem."

Chapter Eighty-Eight

The Ride Majestic

The first workers turned up at Dudinka train station about an hour after West got on board. From that point he had to stay low and rely on push-ups instead of jumping jacks to keep warm.

At ten, the train started rolling. Soon he was safely outside Dudinka and stood up for the first time in three hours.

The stunning landscape outside revealed itself in the rising sun and made him pay little attention to the stiffness in his knees and back.

Blindingly white snow covered the tundra with only low bushes and twigs shooting through. Snow fences kept the winter from drifting fully onto the tracks.

Halfway to his destination, he could see chimney smoke on the horizon.

The arrival at Norilsk train station was smooth. He ducked in the cabin and used his Tile's camera to look outside.

Through the left side mirrors, he saw forklifts commence unloading. He couldn't tell if the vehicles where automated, but at least two people oversaw the process.

He checked the right side of his train. No activity.

Further back, two tracks across, there was a freight train similar to his with just three cars. The side of it read "g20s.ru." This was the train Melissa had discovered in Mikhail's video clip; this was what they hoped would take West to where he needed to be.

Sneaking over to it would be risky with people working on the other side. Especially since he would need a few minutes to pick its lock.

Could he just wait? Who knew how long the G20S train would stay here? And who knew when the next opportunity would come?

He had to make those workers leave.

What would Kiss have done? She had always made people do what she wanted. Fake a strike like in Karlshamn? Trigger some alarm like the fire drill in LA?

Maybe the train had some alarm system? He looked at the engineer's instruments in front of him. There was a keyhole to the right of the three screens, and it looked identical to the lock on the door.

The cold air made fine motor skills hard, and it took him several minutes to pick the instrument lock, but eventually the screens came to life. Russian interface, of course.

He started navigating menus and reading onscreen buttons with the help of his Tile. The closest he could find to an alarm was "train horn."

That should get them startled.

He was just about to tap the horn button when his mind switched to the workers' perspective. What would make them most likely to leave? Not a sudden honk. What would scare them?

The train moving.

He pulled the brake handle all the way back toward himself. Hissing sounds reached him as air was pumped into the cylinders to release their pressure on the wheels.

A quick look in the mirror. The forklifts were backing off.

He inched the power lever forward and stumbled to regain his balance as the locomotive started pulling its cars. Loud yells from outside. Another check in the side mirror showed someone approaching, running.

West stopped the acceleration, applied the brakes, and crouched. The running person was shouting close by.

Still squatting, West pulled down the handle to the minute bathroom in the back. He swiveled inside on his left heel and closed the door just as he heard someone climb the locomotive's metal steps.

There was a thump against the side window and a raised male voice saying something. The cabin door was unlocked and opened. The man entered, cursing.

West could hear him move and breathe mere inches away on the other side of the bathroom's thin door.

Fuck. The control screens are still on.

West didn't have much space here to swing a punch. The only thing he would have to his advantage was the element of surprise.

He balled his hands.

The man talked to himself for a while. Then left.

West waited a good while before slowly opening the bathroom door.

The floor had patches of snow, and the control screens were black. The air was flavored with cold, polluted Norilsk air.

The left side mirror revealed that the forklifts were again unloading cargo. He grabbed his backpack and pushed the right-side cabin door handle to get everything ready for an escape.

He picked the lock to the train's dashboard a second time, disengaged the brakes, jolted the train set forward a few feet, stopped it, and got out with the train between him and the station.

A loud argument broke out on the other side.

He moved backward along the train, catching glimpses of the station side between cars.

The argument fizzled out, and the voices got more distant. He got far enough back to where they had been unloading. There was no longer a human in sight.

The forklifts stood idle with pallets in the air—pallets carrying boxes labeled Tovex and ANFO.

He remembered his prison friend Jeremy talk about ANFO, an industrial explosive: *"So many myths about ANFO. You have to use a booster with ANFO, not just a blasting cap. You need dynamite or Tovex to set that thing off."*

West stood still, biting his lower lip.

There are a lot of things worth blowing up. Who knows what I'll find?

Checking one more time for any human activity, he bent down and crossed the tracks under the coupling between two cars of the freight train.

His heart thundered as he got into one of the half-unloaded cars and checked its cargo. Soon enough, his backpack contained a mini sack of ANFO prills, a few inches of Tovex, which looked like a thin sausage, and a roll of detonation cord labeled "Pentaerythritol Tetranitrate."

As he got back to the other side of the freight train, the G20S train lit up … and started moving.

He ran across the two tracks between him and the G20S train, his now heavy backpack pounding his lower spine and hips.

The narrow gap between the G20S locomotive and the first car approached from his right as the train picked up speed. He would have to jump on.

Memories of the staged car accident in Detroit flashed by. This time there would be no one to save him if he missed.

His right shoulder hit the car as he jumped up onto the coupling in the gap. Three thick cables hung above the mechanical connection. He regained his balance and squeezed into a seated position with his feet against the locomotive and his backpack moved to his chest.

The metal against his back and bottom was ice cold, and swirls of snow swept in. If this trip was long, he would not be able to keep his body temperature up.

The train started out toward the southeast. To his left, West got a glimpse of what he assumed was downtown Norilsk before the train turned south past a small lake, which oddly enough wasn't frozen over. Then again southeast through what looked more like an Old Town, and finally into an unlit tunnel.

The sound of the electrical train bounced off stone walls. The darkness meant he had no point of reference, but it felt like he traveled in a downward slope. He had to apply pressure with his feet to keep his back against the freight car.

Minutes passed as he went further and further into whatever this was. Suddenly, the brakes kicked in and hurled him forward.

His reflexes weren't quick enough to get his hands up in front, but the cables and his backpack saved him from a faceplant. He struggled to keep his sideways balance.

The brakes kept decelerating the train, and West pushed and pushed with his legs to get back in place. His hands grabbed the cables for support as his thighs went numb with lactic acid.

He groaned up into the blackness above, eyes closed, teeth clenched. This would not hold much longer.

Chapter Eighty-Nine

Norilsk Police Station

Behind the commuter bus station in Norilsk there were four local buses waiting. Sheets of snow blew through to the yellow cones of streetlight.

Someone in a reflector vest waved and shouted, "Where to?" at Melissa and Naturelle.

"Police station," Naturelle replied.

They were dropped off outside the Norilsk District Court building, six stories high with a Russian flag top center. Mikhail emerged from the back of the bus and got off too.

According to the map Melissa had downloaded to her Tile, what they saw beyond this block was the small Lake Dolgoye. It wasn't frozen. Instead, steam hovered above its surface. In the distance, she saw layers of mountains whose precious metals fed the Russian economy.

The bus procession left, and Naturelle started talking. "That was close. By the way, Melissa can't speak because she bit her tongue to pass the guards."

They looked at Melissa. She shrugged.

Mikhail huddled under his thick coat. "Let's walk toward station while we go over plan."

Two white Toyota off-road trucks with monster-truck tires stood parked around the corner of the pale blue court building. Their red-and-blue labels read "Norilsk Police."

The station entrance was a gray box protruding from the building, with a window facing out and three-step stairs on either side. The window blinds were closed. A sign outside informed of metal detectors.

The smell of old linoleum, citrus cleaner, and musky, old cigarette smoke greeted them inside. After being scanned for metal, they walked up to a chest-high, long wooden front desk with metal-framed, laminated glass protecting the desks and people behind.

"Good morning. We're here to see Mr. Praporshchik on behalf of Agent Pogodina," Naturelle said, according to Melissa's in-ear translation.

"That would be me. Are you Naturelle?"

She nodded.

The officer had them sign in through a GPI scanner on the desk and took care of their Tiles and earpieces.

Melissa discreetly snatched a pen intended for customer signatures.

Soon enough they were being escorted two floors up. The young police officer carried a green metal briefcase with a computer symbol on it.

He avoided looking at them and mumbled something as they passed the elevator. Several of the walls had patched-up cracks in them, and the floor didn't feel fully horizontal.

At the end of the corridor of floor three, two guards were on duty. They put away their Tiles as soon as they saw the officer approaching.

Melissa noted the guards' equipment—pistols, dedicated radio devices, handcuffs, flashlights, and rubbered batons.

The officer gave the guards instructions in Russian.

Melissa also took a good look at the lock mechanism as they passed the first of two doors to enter the room where they supposedly held Jitterbug. She scanned the walls and ceiling for cameras. Nothing. The air had an acetonic smell. No windows or natural light.

The officer gestured for the three of them to stay put as he took the final steps inside. "Mr. Murphy, please stand up." His English was good.

There was movement inside. "There are three interrogators here, sent directly by Agent Zabolotnaya and Agent Pogodina. They will question you in segments of two hours. I suggest you behave and answer questions truthfully."

The officer turned around and gave Naturelle a faint smile. "This is not a regular cell or anything. It's a shared bedroom for when staff on late shifts cannot get home safely during winter. This is what we ended up with to keep it off the record. If the detainee gets violent, you'll have to call for the guards. They are right outside."

Chapter Ninety

I Know a Bot

West opened his eyes. Compact darkness. He was horizontal.

Cold, hard, jagged surface below, backpack on top of him. Electric and mechanical sounds came from above. The air was damp and smelled metallic.

He must have passed out and fell down below the train.

He moved his gloved hand to the left—joints and muscles complaining—and touched what felt like a train rail. The machine sounds from above continued.

He reached for his Tile. Covering its LED with his hand, he turned the red flashlight function on and carefully let light out between his fingers.

He found himself in the narrow crawl space under a railway platform. Above him to the left towered the G20S train. He remembered now—he had thrown himself to the side with his last strength to try to avoid being run over when he dropped down. Seeing where he had landed, he realized he could just as well have hit the platform.

He put his Tile snugly inside his jacket's front pocket with the top sticking out, red light freely flowing. The space between two cars created a gap for him to crawl up onto the platform.

The sounds were from a human-sized robot swiftly unloading the cars. It grabbed a box about the size of a sixty-four-gallon garbage cart and took it through an automated doorway in the back wall, cut out of the rock to fit the robot perfectly.

The door closed immediately after the robot entered, and no other passageways were in sight.

He turned to the train. All three freight cars were open, filled with boxes in perfect lines. The robot would be back for these.

He entered the last car and checked the box. It was almost chest high on him and locked. His hands followed the lid's edge on all four sides. No mechanical lock mechanism. He tried to move the box, but it was too heavy.

As he was stepping out, his eyes caught an asymmetry. The last box had shifted slightly out of place. He entered the car again and gave the stray box a gentle push. It moved easily. And the lid opened.

There was nothing inside except for a label—**Рециркулировать**. "Recycle" according to his Tile. He looked around, climbed in, and closed the lid.

Minute by minute he heard the robot work its way closer to his box. The sharp sounds made him aware of the fact that these boxes were not handled in a gentle manner; this was a machine managing nonliving materials.

The robot clamped his box with a bang and swung him in a sideways arc to an abrupt stop. The side of his head slammed hard into the side of the box, and he lost consciousness for a second or two.

He was now moving into whatever facility this was. Fear kicked in as he realized his head had been struck in the same spot he had hit during the staged car accident.

He pulled off his glove and felt the side of his head underneath the fur hat. Blood.

The robot's motors whirred. His fingers traced the scar where the stitches had been. It seemed intact, but exterior blood wasn't the problem. He pushed his elbows out to cushion any further violent movement.

The box swung left after just a short while and was put down on a hard floor. The robot let it loose, and he could hear it pick something else up before it left. The noises became faint, then dead silence.

He slowly opened the box's lid and lit up the space with his Tile. It was a small cubic room with concrete or stone walls. Straight ahead was a doorway.

His box was the only one in here. On the floor to his right, there was a marked square exactly the size of the box he was in.

He climbed out and moved to the doorway. The walls were thick and rugged. Outside the room was a narrow corridor, about four feet wide. Cool, dry air flowed from the left.

There was a matching "Recycle" label at the entrance of the room where his box was put.

To the right was a closed door, which had to be to the railway platform. He walked right up to it, but it didn't open. At the top were large ventilation holes.

He turned around to explore the inner parts. The walls had cat's-eye reflectors like California roads every five feet.

Probably guidance for the robot.

Thirty feet further in, the corridor ended in a T fork. The air flow came from both left and right, and he could hear the low-frequency noise of industrial fans. Cat's-eyes glimmered in the distance both ways, with a short break in the pattern about fifteen feet in on either side. The left corridor had a slight downward slope and the right one continued upward at the same angle.

His hand felt the side of his head. The blood was now sticky, gluing his hair to the fur hat. The weighty backpack's straps dug into his shoulders.

I should have stashed the ANFO in the recycle bin.

He took the left turn down the slope. Where the pattern of the cat's-eyes broke, there was a niche in the right-side wall, as deep as the corridor itself. He entered it to have a closer look.

A spinning, high-pitched sound came from far down the corridor, fast approaching.

West considered his options. Run back for the train platform exit, run up the right-hand side corridor in the T fork, or stay put in the niche.

He pushed himself back against the wall.

The robot from the platform rolled past him at high speed. The corridor was just the right size for it with mere inches to spare on the sides and top. Its kinetic energy would have easily knocked him out, possibly killed him, had he stood in its way.

What the fuck am I doing walking around in an automated cave facility? I don't know what I'm looking for. I don't even know how big this place is.

The sound of the robot disappeared in the distance of the upward corridor. West estimated it to be at least forty yards, given the robot's speed. He had to get out of here, back into the passageway to the train platform.

Slowly, he stuck his head out of the niche to make sure the coast was clear.

Nothing upward left, nothing downward right.

Or wait. Midstep he looked back right again with his Tile's red light pointing in another direction. A faint, blinking green spot of light was zigzagging its way toward him at floor level, and there was a hissing sound to whatever it was.

He stepped back into the niche. Minutes passed as the hissing thing meticulously worked its way closer. Just as West could make out what it was, the round, flat thing rolled into the niche and stopped moving.

The top read "Bot Ana 103," and it was a vacuum cleaner.

CHAPTER NINETY-ONE

Up and Down

Jitterbug didn't meet the eyes of his interrogators. He looked gloomy, sitting on one of two beds alongside the left wall.

Melissa waved her hands to catch his attention.

He lifted his head, and surprise and relief instantly broke through two weeks of despair. They all hugged and cried and laughed as quietly as they could. Melissa saw her friend look at the ceiling, nodding.

With a sudden movement, Jitterbug took hold of Melissa's shoulders and looked her deep in the eyes, tears still forming in his. "Kiss didn't make it. Her soul is with God now."

Naturelle moved in closely so that Jitterbug could hear her whisper. "We know. We tapped into the meeting in Smolensk."

His eyes widened. "I guess you know Kawasaki is involved then?"

Naturelle nodded.

"Melissa, speak to me," Jitterbug said. "Where's West?"

She opened her mouth and showed him her swollen, wounded tongue.

Jitterbug flinched, wrinkling his nose. "Who did this to you?"

Naturelle filled him in.

Jitterbug released his hold on Melissa and sat down on his bed. He turned to Naturelle. "How on earth did you find me?"

She sat down beside him to be able to keep her voice down. "West finally cracked Fraktal and got into Pogodina's email. From there we could follow what she planned for you."

"Where is West?"

"He is still in Dudinka. If we fail here, he'll try to get us out."

"Alone?"

"Yes. How are you?"

"Not great. They've been starving me. Lots of questioning."

Melissa looked at her friend. He did look as if he had lost a few pounds.

They heard the outer door move, then the inner door flung open. Agent Zabolotnaya stood in the doorway, handgun drawn.

She was shorter than Melissa had expected.

Behind her were the two guards and the officer that helped them earlier, the latter with a smug smile on his face.

Zabolotnaya's movements were jerky as she scanned Melissa, Naturelle, and Mikhail in quick succession.

"State your names," she commanded in English.

"Mikhail Simonov."

"Naturelle Veschitskaya."

Faced with Zabolotnaya's gun, Melissa didn't dare stay silent. "Gina Kufneschoba."

Naturelle clarified. "Dina Kuznetsova. She injured her tongue, so she can't speak."

"Spare me your lies. We know she's American. We'll find out what you are up to, who you're colluding with, and what your motives are," Zabolotnaya declared. "When I come back after my regular duties, you either answer my questions or you go straight to Ice Dolphin Prison."

Zabolotnaya leaned over her right shoulder while still watching the intruders and gave the guards instructions in Russian.

Melissa, Naturelle, and Mikhail were stripped down to their underwear, and the guards took their GPI bands before leaving with Zabolotnaya and the officer.

Melissa drew her first breath for several minutes, or at least it felt like it. She pointed toward the green PC briefcase. It had been left behind.

Mikhail pulled it out and opened it. It was full of books.

CHAPTER NINETY-TWO

Make It Stick

West looked at the automated vacuum cleaner as if he had found a friend. Its green LED kept blinking, but it didn't move; it stayed idle beside him in the niche.

The sound of the large robot emerged again up the corridor to the left. West peeked out and let his Tile light the scene. The robot carried a freight box and slowed down to take a turn into the passageway toward the recycle room and train platform. Shortly after, it returned and went back from where it came.

As soon as the sound of the big robot was gone, the vacuum cleaner left the niche and started zigzagging up the corridor again.

You were waiting for your turn. Which means there must be a synchronizing protocol between you and the big robot.

He jumped out of his hiding place and grabbed the cleaning bot by the sides. It wasn't too heavy.

He lifted it to his chest and ran for the passageway. The little bot's wheels spun frantically in the air.

He stopped inside the recycling room, panting. The bot had given up and was quiet. West placed it on the corner of his transportation box with both its main wheels in the air in case it tried to escape. He got his backpack off and rolled his aching shoulders in relief.

With his Tile's flashlight switched to white, he inspected Ana. On her top was an OLED screen showing a triangular, yellow warning sign and a message in Russian. It also displayed the current time, network connectivity, and battery status.

He got the tools out of his backpack and unscrewed Ana's bottom cover. The battery pack was easily accessible underneath. He pulled it to the side and disassembled further plastic parts to get to the bot's computer.

It was a dust-protected, dark gray circuit board with a single 4GB RAM module. West looked for a way to connect directly to Ana's storage unit, but those components were soldered on, so he would have to talk to her computer to be able to get to her storage.

There was a peculiar, two-by-two-inch daughterboard hovering ten millimeters above the main circuit board. It was green instead of gray and didn't look mass-produced.

West pinched and wobbled the daughterboard side to side until it came loose. Underneath was a connection port—a round, seven-pin, Mini-DIN.

Ana, that's freaking ancient. I don't have a Mini-DIN with me.

He connected the daughterboard again and had a closer look at it. There were four metal connection strands about a millimeter apart on one side.

Looks an awful lot like an old USB mount.

He connected his Survivor Kit's multimeter extension cords to his Tile and probed the four strands of metal. +5 Volts, nothing, nothing, ground. His USB theory seemed to hold up.

But how to connect? There was no socket. He could cut open one of his USB cables and expose its four wires, but he had no soldering equipment to connect them to the thin pieces of metal.

He instructed his Tile to turn off the light and sat down in the dark to think it through.

Could he use power from an outlet to heat up and snatch solder from some other part of Ana's circuit board? Nah, he hadn't seen any power outlets, and fiddling with AC power felt risky. He could blow a fuse and cause people to come and inspect. Also, removing solder from her circuitry might break something completely and cripple the bot all together.

The wires just need to stay connected. I don't need a solid solder solution.

He visualized the wires touching the USB connectors. Could he clamp them on? Nope, he had no coated paper clip or the like in his backpack. He had tape, but taping wires on there would be too fragile.

Glue. I have superglue.

Chapter Ninety-Three

Frenemies

Melissa kicked the green briefcase into the wall, books falling out. She picked up one of the books, slammed it on the table, and started writing ferociously on one of its blank pages. The rest pulled their clothes from the floor and got dressed.

Melissa showed the book page she'd been writing on to the others.

We have to break out of here before Z comes back. Let's figure out weak spots and make a plan.

My observations:
  - Regular office lock on the door.
  - No surveillance in here.
  - Two guards outside with comm radios, Tiles, handcuffs, batons, and guns. Take them out?
  - Building falling apart, cracks and stuff.

What else?

Melissa got dressed while they read it. No one said anything for a while.

"I …" Naturelle stopped herself and looked at Mikhail.

His eyes widened. "Нет!"

"We have to, Mikhail." She turned to Melissa. "Melissa, I have not been completely honest with you."

Melissa made a small change in her posture. Left foot forward, right foot back, left hand lifted an inch up in front of her chest.

Naturelle hurried her voice. "Almost everything I've told you is true. Zhiveye Na Pokriva, Ministry of Internal Affairs, Petrov and Pogodina's dirty business, and Mikhail's and my backgrounds. All of that is true."

Melissa saw Jitterbug straighten himself up in the corner of her eye. Mikhail looked tense behind Naturelle.

Melissa gave Naturelle an up-nod to continue.

"That American woman you saw at the meeting in Smolensk, we're working with her to take down Petrov."

It took Melissa a second to process what Naturelle had said. The two Russian hackers were working for Dr. Kawasaki.

Melissa's hands shot out and grabbed the right side of Naturelle's half-open fleece jacket chest high. She pulled the Russian down toward her hips.

Naturelle hurled her right hand forward to stop the fall if she was pulled further, then jerked back to regain balance.

Melissa leveraged her opponent's backward, upward motion to jump up, swinging one leg above Naturelle's left arm and the other under the right arm. She locked her legs behind Naturelle's neck and let her body weight pull them both to the floor.

Melissa landed on her back with Naturelle still on her feet, folded over. Melissa pushed Naturelle's legs back with her hands and locked a perfect triangle choke with her legs around the neck. It didn't take much pressure to get the Russian to yield.

She saw Jitterbug cut off Mikhail in the background, but he wouldn't be able to stop the well-built man. Luckily, Mikhail seemed to realize that Melissa had the upper hand and held off.

Melissa waited for the scene to calm down, then released the pressure on Naturelle's neck and arm. "Blease gontinue. An kell me why I chouldn'p gill yue."

Naturelle moved her head under Melissa's hold to ensure blood flow to her brain. "You seem to know more about her than we do. She is our ticket out of here," she said with a strained voice. "She knows where we are, and I'm supposed to ping her with my Tile by noon. If she can't get ahold of me by three, she puts things in motion."

"Melissa, I can help you ask the questions." It was Jitterbug, still on the floor between her and Mikhail. "Naturelle, in what way are you working with Dr. Kawasaki and for how long have you been doing so?"

"We've worked for almost a year with US people on the Petrov thing.

We didn't know anything about Kawasaki as a person until Smolensk. We've been working with anonymous contacts. But after the meeting, she made direct contact to convince us to go with you to Norilsk."

"She asked you to work with us?"

"We got a request for help in Stockholm three weeks ago."

"What request?"

"To place the JTAG in Pogodina's monitor and hack the SORM in the tower room. They had an insider who could arrange for the break-in, but he's just muscle, not a technical guy. That's why they needed us. In exchange, we would get intel on Pogodina's business with Petrov."

"And then Melissa found you on the roof," Jitterbug said.

"I had no idea who you were and had to improvise. We got pretty derailed when Pogodina pulled a gun on me. I synced up with our US contact as soon as I got out of Pogodina's car."

Naturelle winced under Melissa's lock, but continued. "Our contact said you worked with the Swedish FRA, targeting Pogodina. By owning Pogodina's monitor and SORM, they wanted to control what information you got out of there."

"I have a personal question for you," Jitterbug said. "Why the Taser attack?"

"Our US contact was adamant that we get you on track for Russia. But we couldn't just offer you our help for nothing, so we came up with the Karlshamn deal." Naturelle swallowed. "None of us anticipated the stolen ship."

Jitterbug looked at Melissa. "God requires faith and action. I had faith that someone would come for me, and you did. Now's the time for action." He turned back to Naturelle. "Talk to me about that ticket out of here."

"Kawasaki said she has had her eyes on Norilsk ever since the G20S backup was placed here. You know the thing they talked about in Smolensk. She has combat-trained people on site, at the ready, people working in the mining industry. I don't know the exact time, but if she can't get ahold of us within a few hours, she will get us out. She doesn't want us here as traces of her involvement."

"If Kawasaki indeed has people here helping her, she will have them kill us all in the end. You do realize that, right?" Jitterbug said.

"I said ticket out of here, not ticket home."

Chapter Ninety-Four

Laser Replay

West connected his Tile to the glued-on USB cable on Ana's daughter-board.

She was running an embedded Linux, and as one would expect, no security patches had been installed for more than a year.

He ran an exploit to make Ana reboot from his Tile and then mounted her disk as regular storage. The vacuum cleaner software was installed under /etc/ana.

A README document explained how to run Ana, how to do diagnostics, and—causing West's heart to race—the details of her mapping capabilities under something called SLAM.

In the SLAM directory, West found a file containing the laser measurements Ana had made to map out her work environment so that she could vacuum it.

Let's share, shall we?

He changed Ana's start sequence to replay the laser scan as if she'd discovered her workspace all over again, and with a little addition of his own, Ana drew a rudimentary map on his Tile's screen.

For the first time since Dudinka, he smiled.

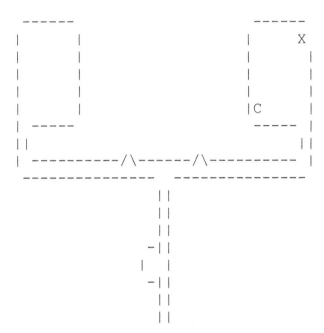

He checked the code to see what the letters represented. X was "restricted area," and C was Ana's charging station.

There was an algorithmic extension file called bank.alg. It contained a lot of source code, mostly for some wireless communication protocol.

A particular data structure caught his eye, especially the double slashes with trailing comments from the programmer. He translated the programmer's comments to English.

```
let availableResources =
    [
            false, // Sapphire
            false, // Corridor Left
            false, // Recess Left
            false, // Corridor Out
            false, // Garbage
            false, // Train
            false, // Recess Right
            false, // Corridor Right
            false  // Server
    ];
```

Corridor, Recess, Train, and Garbage sounded a lot like the parts of the compound he had seen so far.

Kind of funny how the developer went with "garbage" but the label maker went with "recycling." I wonder who's right?

Sapphire and Server were things he hadn't seen yet. "Available resources" sounded like something to be allocated.

He searched the source code and found a cluster of related functions: requestResource, releaseResource, and receiveMessage.

So you can request and release access to a corridor, a recess, or a room, and you're receiving messages back.

He scrolled back and forth, reading the source code and piecing it together in his head.

This is how you synchronize with the big bot, isn't it? You request and release parts of the cave as you move around vacuuming. That's how you two don't crash into each other.

We're going to talk to the big bot, Ana.

CHAPTER NINETY-FIVE

Prison, Prison, or Death

Melissa kept her legs at ease albeit ready around Naturelle's neck and armpit as she thought things through.

Being bailed out by Dr. Kawasaki's people would be super risky, if not fully out of the frying pan into the fire. They didn't even know if Kawasaki really had people in Norilsk, if those people were capable of a jailbreak, or if Naturelle's absent ping would indeed trigger a bailout. Lots of ifs.

Even so, Zabolotnaya might get back to the police station before Kawasaki's swat team arrived, in which case they'd have to fight her head-on. Death was the most probable outcome there.

The only other option was to kick down the doors right now and attack the guards outside, which at least would give them better odds than waiting for Zabolotnaya.

Melissa looked daggers at Naturelle before releasing her chokehold. She stood up, reached for the book and pen, and scribbled a question on the exact timing of Naturelle's contacts with Kawasaki.

Naturelle replied without hesitation. "My last message to her was on the bus here."

Melissa turned to a fresh page and wrote a long passage, then let them all read it.

I have to make contact with West. Let's bet on Kawasaki's swat team and do the following:
  - Somehow hide me in here.
  - Tell the swat team that Z has me.

- Swat team gets the 3 of you out.
- I get myself out and find a way to message West.
- If we make it, we meet again.

"I'm not in love with running into the arms of Kawasaki," Jitterbug said. "But I'll do it if you promise not to leave West behind."

Melissa nodded.

CHAPTER NINETY-SIX

Cyborg

The ANFO was out of West's backpack, and Ana was now in. The glued-on USB cable went from her, over his shoulder, and connected to the OmniPort of his Tile.

With this setup, he had impersonated the vacuum cleaner in the view of the central resource management system and was in full control of what spaces Ana requested and released.

His Tile displayed what the central system saw right now.

```
availableResources =
    [
            true,  // Sapphire
            false, // Corridor Left
            true,  // Recess Left
            true,  // Corridor Out
            true,  // Garbage
            true,  // Train
            true,  // Recess Right
            true,  // Corridor Right
            false  // Server
    ];
```

You are still in the corridor. I guess that's where I picked you up. Big bot is in the server room.

He requested access to Corridor Out and walked up to the door to the railway platform. Ana's map indicated she didn't vacuum the platform, which made sense, but it was worth a shot. He requested "Train."

The platform door opened for two seconds, enough for him to spot a reflection of the train in the distance, then closed.

This is my way out, by train or walking. Time to have a look at what Sapphire is.

He walked to the T fork, took a left, and stopped by the niche, facing the downward slope of Corridor Left.

Looking back up Corridor Right, he envisioned the big bot speeding toward him, knocking him out, crushing his limbs. Once he was far enough down Corridor Left, he would have nowhere to go but further in if the big bot came from behind.

He continued downward, counting his steps … eighteen, nineteen, twenty …

The cat's-eyes paved the way, and the industrial fan noise got more present the further he went.

Thirty-nine steps in total to the right bend.

As he turned, his Tile's light revealed a short, narrow entranceway, which ended in a closed metal door, like the one at the railway platform.

There were no handles and no visible lock mechanism. At the top were foot-wide ventilation holes.

He took a breath and made Ana request what was behind that door, called "Sapphire."

Nothing happened. He pushed the door. It didn't flex a millimeter.

He checked the logs and saw that Ana had been denied access. She was apparently holding too many resources at once.

Oh, this thing prevents deadlocks. She won't be granted access to new resources if she holds on to earlier ones. Ana needs to behave like a computer.

He made her release Train and Corridor Out.

A spinning, high-pitched sound emerged in the distance. The big bot had moved out of the server room, and the noise was getting louder.

He swept his Tile's light in an overhead arc to get a view of the narrow space around him. The only extra space was the gap above the door, and the ventilation holes up there wouldn't even fit his backpack with Ana in it. The rock walls were smooth to the touch.

He checked the resource list. Ana still held Corridor Left, and biggie had acquired Corridor Right and Corridor Out.

West held his breath as the big bot came closer, closer, slowed down, and took a turn.

He let out a sigh. *These are robots. They play by the rules.*

He requested "Sapphire." This time, the metal door opened, and he jumped in. A thud behind and he was enclosed.

The light from his Tile showed a room filled with white, shelved cabinets from floor to ceiling. On their sides, about waist-high, were rotating hand wheels with three handles and black, spherical knobs. Metal rails were fitted in the concrete floor.

Something glittered on the cabinet shelves closest to him.

West walked over and found pristine, shiny disks standing in perfect rows. They looked how he remembered Blu-ray discs, but larger, seven or eight inches in diameter and two millimeters thick.

He looked at the shelf labels. They were in ten languages, out of which West could identify English, Russian, and Spanish, and they read "Global Personal Identities" along with years, starting from when the ID system had been inaugurated.

This was the offline backup.

West noted that the labels were written using Helvetica.

A timeless font.

He pulled out the leftmost disk from last year's batch. Its description read "Afghanistan – Bahrain." The next one read "Bangladesh – Bulgaria."

The sensation of seeing and touching the disks was intense. In this cave room, the global surveillance apparatus was storing digital identities of virtually every human on earth.

He moved to the side and rotated the hand wheel. The shelf behind was empty. He went through all twelve, and except for the first one, they were all empty, waiting for centuries of backups to come.

This meant there really weren't too many disks yet.

"You can carry what we have so far in a large backpack."

West put his backpack down gently, opened it, and grabbed a handful of disks.

Chapter Ninety-Seven

Jailbreak

"Shhh. You hear that?"

Naturelle's whisper was sharp.

Seconds passed. Melissa could hear an upset discussion in Russian outside their room.

The voices stopped.

"The guards were called down but decided to follow previous orders," Naturelle whispered. "Kawasaki's team is here, I'm sure of it. Let's wrap up."

Suddenly, the guards started outright yelling. Dampened shots were fired. Screams and curses of pain. Two more shots. Silence.

Keys opened the outer door to their room.

Melissa had no visual of the room from her hiding place.

She heard footsteps of a person entering. Heavy boots.

A male, muffled, Russian voice uttered what sounded like a question. Naturelle presented herself, explained something, and ended with the names of her comrades in the room—Mikhail and Murphy.

Three more rapid questions and answers, and the boots started moving again. Rubbered soles walked to the bathroom and pulled the door open. There were slams and knocks as the man searched the small space. He even flushed the toilet.

The boots crossed the room toward the two beds, closer and closer to Melissa.

Rubber squeaked against the floor as the man squatted by the innermost bed. He was close enough for Melissa to hear him breathe under some kind of mask. He bent down and checked under the bed. She wasn't there.

The smell of him reached Melissa. Peppermint.

He moved to inspect the second bed, then stood up, uttered commands toward the hallway, and finally said in perfect American English: "Let's go."

·

Melissa lay still for what felt like an hour but was probably more like five minutes. Her neck sent pain signals from having been at a ninety-degree angle for too long.

The foam mattress was wet from her breath. Her butt cheeks were numb from being clamped between mattress coils. The bra band they had used to tie down her breasts cut her like a knife.

She rose from the foam cut-out of her body and pushed the blanket aside.

CHAPTER NINETY-EIGHT

Type Confusion

This is a damn lonely place, West thought. It was tempting to take the GPI backup disks with him and get out of here. But he wanted to figure out where Russia and China were in the race for quantum supremacy, so he left the Sapphire room and most of the disks behind and headed up Corridor Right.

The existence of an identical metal door outside the Server room and the fact that his requests for access to the room behind it were rejected didn't surprise him. Big bot was probably working in there. But Ana would have to charge too at some point, which should give him an opportunity to enter.

With all corridor resources released, he sat down in Recess Right with his legs pulled in.

His Tile said it was almost nine in the evening. He had been hungry for half a day, but the thought that whenever he ate might be his last meal had made him hold off. Now was the time for his sandwich.

The salesperson in Dudinka had raved about the cheese—a domestic, artisanal Tilsit. It was good.

Like a nice Havarti.

As he was chewing, he wondered if Melissa and the others had found Jitterbug. Would they ever get out of this mess? What would life be like if they succeeded?

He missed Kiss dearly. Something should be done to honor her death.

His Tile buzzed. The big bot had been granted access to Corridor Right and was leaving the Server room.

It passed him in deceleration and took a turn into the recycling room passageway. West and Ana made it into the Server room as he swallowed the last piece of bread and Tilsit cheese.

The first thing that caught his attention inside the room was the familiar blinking LEDs from rack-mounted servers. Beside the rack, on a shelf, there were neatly stacked disks like the ones in the Sapphire room.

He walked over to the disks. They glittered in the light from his Tile, unlabeled and in mint condition.

I take it this is where you process the backup data and eventually produce those labeled disks, big one.

The rest of the room contained the remaining boxes the robot had fetched from the train, with data still to be processed.

As he walked around, he found Ana's charging station in the corner. A bay with guard rails, and above it, stickers with a checkered pattern.

The opposite corner, the one marked X on Ana's map, had similar stickers and a large charging bay for the big robot.

He looked back at the racked servers.

This can't be LiveLearn. I don't know what a modern quantum computer looks like, but this is just a few regular blade servers.

He walked over to the server rack and pulled out its terminal with keyboard and monitor. The monitor flipped up, and a prompt came alive.

```
(*) Root
( ) Guest

Password:
```

Laying his hands on an old physical keyboard felt nice, almost comforting.

Time to guess the root password. His first test was always with an empty one. It didn't work. He pulled up a list of the twenty most used admin passwords on his Tile and started typing.

```
admin, PASSWORD, password, root, 1234,
0, 0000, installer, secret, changeme,
ChangeMe, operator, sysadmin, system,
access, administrator, linux, unix,
default, welcome
```

None of them worked either.

You're going to make this hard on ol' West?

He logged in as a password-less guest and ran a command to figure out exactly what operating system the servers were running—Debian GNU/Linux 15.0.

His local CVE database came back with zero results for known Linux 15.0 security vulnerabilities. This meant he would have to find a way in through the application layer.

Do you have a web browser, my friend?

The browser launch command spat out an error message.

```
This account has restricted network
access. You can only reach the loopback
interface.
```

Of course.

He set up a local server on the loopback interface just to see how the browser presented itself.

```
User-Agent: Lynx/5.0.1 (EcmaScript/7.0)
```

Lynx with JavaScript. Who would have thought?

He asked his Tile for known Lynx security vulnerabilities. It came back with just nine entries since 2008. None of them applicable to version 5.0.1.

But there was a tenth result in his Tile's search. A locally stored blog post which explored an old spectacular hack presented at the 2003 IEEE Symposium on Security and Privacy.

The Survivor database really is a historic archive of hacks. This is amazing.

Two Princeton researchers had used memory errors introduced by cosmic radiation to attack virtual machines, and according to the blog post, this hack could be abused to attack JavaScript virtual machines too.

The trick was to create a program with just two object types, A and B, and fill all the computer's memory with objects of type B except a single object of type A.

The B objects were created so that a bit flip in them would cause a "type confusion" between A and B, which was enough to compromise the virtual machine. All the hacker had to do was to wait for a cosmic ray to hit a memory circuit in the victim's computer and cause that bit flip.

"On average, a cosmic ray bit flip happens once a month," he read out loud.

He looked around. *Not inside this mountain, and I don't have a month.*

He would have to come up with another way to flip bits.

Getting the software part of the hack working took a solid four hours even with the steps outlined in the blog post. He desperately needed sleep. But there was no time for that.

He got the lid off the top blade server. The cooling fans made sure he knew their presence.

Inside were four blocks of metal coolers for the floating-point processing units, and a much smaller section where the central processing unit and main memory sat. Sixty-four gigabytes of memory.

West looked closely. The memory circuits were marked "ECC."

Shit.

Error correcting meant what it said on the tin: these circuits would self-correct a bit flip.

He checked the circuit board for a hardware setting to disable ECC. Nope.

He turned the server off with the main switch and booted it into Configuration mode.

```
SYSTEM MEMORY SIZE ...... 64.0 GB
SYSTEM MEMORY TYPE ...... ECC DDR5
SYSTEM MEMORY SPEED ..... 4266 MHz
SYSTEM MEMORY VOLTAGE ... 1.05V
SYSTEM MEMORY MODE ...... Adv. ECC
```

System memory mode. Gotcha.

He changed the mode to "No ECC."

```
SYSTEM PASSWORD:
```

"F.U.C.K."

He threw himself back against the wall and looked up into the ceiling. Hours of hacking for nothing.

Why not steal the Sapphire disks and blow up the server rack with his ANFO? He thought about the exit via the rail tracks and how to get to the airport; all the while his brain kept the server hack on the back burner.

Deep down, he wanted desperately to see the inside of this supposed rogue LiveLearn operation. What were the Russians and Chinese up to?

Attack the layer below, West.

Was there some way he could trick the error-correcting memory? Perhaps make the correction help him instead of foiling his attack? Or switch to another server that might not have ECC memory modules?

Wait. Ana has a memory module.

He pulled open his backpack and got Ana's blinking circuit board out. There it was, her four gigabyte RAM module. He checked the fine print. Not ECC.

He popped the server's four RAM modules and inserted Ana's single one. There was a piercing beep just a second after he hit the power switch.

A warning screen showed up.

```
SYSTEM MEMORY SIZE 4 GB IS BELOW THE
RECOMMENDED MINIMUM OF 8 GB.
CONTINUE?

(*) NO
( ) YES
```

His choice was obvious. A minute later he was back as Guest, running his local server with the exploit and loading the site in Lynx.

Time to turn these damn fans off.

Too much heat meant bits would start to flip. He waited, and waited, and waited; eyes fixed on the monitor.

Suddenly Lynx disappeared from the screen, and the top left corner displayed something else.

```
sh-5.2$
```

"Whoooho!" The bit flip hack had worked. He had a root shell; he was in.

Chapter Ninety-Nine

The Message

Melissa stretched and jumped to regain flexibility in her body after her stunt as a mattress.

She got all the pieces of ripped-out foam out of the green briefcase, stuck them back in the body-shaped void where they came from, and re-made the bed.

The door to the hallway was left open. No sounds.

Blood painted lines on the floor as she dragged the dead bodies of the two guards into the room to frisk them.

Both their Tiles were locked and of no use, but one of the guards was skinny enough for his belt to fit her. Keys, comms radio, baton, flashlight, and handcuffs came with it.

Before leaving the room, she stopped briefly and looked at the corpses. Two lives had ended here.

She listened carefully for sounds of activity and headed for the stairs. A glimpse toward a window told her that daylight was long gone.

The ground-floor ceiling lights were turned off, and none of the switches by the staircase worked. Light from the floor above created a lit island where she was standing, like a stage spotlight.

She moved into the shadows and turned on the flashlight from her belt. In the distance, she could see the laminated glass at the front desk. It glittered oddly, as if shattered but still in place.

"Кто здесь?"

It was a voice yelling from the direction of the desk.

Melissa studied the scene ahead, estimating distances, memorizing obstacles, and considering angles for cover.

She closed her eyes and covered them with her hand to fully adjust to darkness while keeping the flashlight pointed at the front desk to make sure whoever was there would be at a dark vision disadvantage.

Sixty seconds. A hundred and twenty seconds. More yelling. A hundred and eighty. She turned the flashlight off, clipped it onto her belt, opened her eyes, and started running diagonally across the hallway.

She skidded on the floor to decelerate as she reached the wall on the other side and ducked behind a stone pedestal with a bust on top.

There was a crack of a gunshot, and the ricochet twanged behind her in the direction of the staircase. Her opponent didn't know where she was, but crossing the hallway again would be too dangerous with guns involved.

She leaned against the pedestal and peeked beyond its corner. It moved; the whole pedestal moved. She knocked the painted surface. Hollow. Probably plywood.

She stood halfway up, pushing her back to the wall, and reached for the bust. It wasn't fixed to the pedestal. Her hands cradled its chin and back of the neck and lifted it down to the floor. Now she could easily push the hollow, wooden pedestal along the wall.

It sounded like dragging a cabinet made of board on a hard floor. She made steady progress toward the desk in the dark. Just a few more paces. A small stone screeched as it got stuck and dragged in the push.

"Покажи себя!"

The gun whipped again, much closer this time, hitting the pedestal midway up, easily ripping through the two layers of processed wood. If this person was wise, they would shoot lower next time. She had to run for it, now!

Melissa pushed her hands in between the pedestal and the wall and got her legs into starting position as if at a race. She heaved the pedestal into the hallway and launched herself forward. The gun fired twice rapidly. She could see the muzzle flash, which gave her a rough distance to her adversary.

Three full thrust strides later, she erected her body and lifted her left hand chest-high—opened and ready to grip. The two-inch-thick wooden front desk hit her palm slightly high, but she was able to clamp it, spring up using her left foot, and rotate her hip and shoulder over the desk.

Her body rammed the glass center, bending it further before it came loose. Plastic film kept the fractured pieces together just like a smashed car window.

She hit what felt like a person, then a computer screen, and slid off a small desk onto the floor with office material flying everywhere.

Things were still falling as she got up into a squatting position, grabbed the baton, and started beating down on where her instincts told her the other person was. What she was hitting felt soft and ejected cries of pain.

She slammed herself on top of the other body. Her hands found a head, and she pushed a forearm against the other person's throat. Her other hand grabbed the flashlight and lit up the man's face. He looked ready to die, squinting at the direct light and wincing.

Melissa scanned the area around them and secured the gun from the floor. He had no other weapons on him. She got up and threw her handcuffs to him.

He cuffed himself behind his back and scooted over to show her it was properly done.

She waved the flashlight to make him get up, then moved into his desk space, got the monitor upright again, and hit the spacebar. The computer requested a fingerprint read. Another wave of the flashlight and he complied, fumbling with his hands behind his back. It reminded Melissa of a party trick Kiss used to do—typing behind her back.

The computer unlocked, and its interface was in Russian.

Faint memories of Pogodina's G20S desktop gave her a hint of how to switch applications and do a local search. The keyboard had Cyrillic letters but Latin sublabels. She entered "Kuznetsova." No hits. And nothing for "Naturelle" or "Simonov" either. "Dina" and "Mikhail" had in total seventeen hits for different people with tons of information. "Dade Murphy" came up as empty.

She scanned the office landscape with the flashlight. The back wall had shelves with clothes, lots of binders, and a grid of unlabeled metal drawers with locks. Her Tile and earpiece might be in one of those drawers, but breaking into and searching each one would take far too long.

Pogodina's emails to the police officer about Jitterbug had said "off the record." Maybe they've put everything under *Pogodina's* name?

A single search entry came back for "Fedosia Pogodina." Almost all fields were empty, but one of them read "Б-01."

She pointed at "Б-01" and looked at her prisoner. The man walked her over to the set of unlabeled drawers and knocked his head against one of them. It was unlocked, and inside were Melissa's and the others' equipment plus some of Kiss's and Jitterbug's belongings.

The last thing to do before bailing out was to signal West through her anonymous server, and she sat down by the computer to formulate something.

```
We found J but things went south. N and M
fucked us. They're working for Dr K.

Dr K's people got them + J out and I
believe they're headed for the airport.

I stayed behind to get this message to
you. Don't give up. I have one more little
surprise up my sleeve.

Figure out how to steal that thing. I know
you can—you're the best.

You'll find me at the airport. O still has
his promise to fulfill. Just turn on your
Tile's radio chips when you get there and
text me.
```

Chapter One Hundred

Elevated

West reenabled the rack-mounted server's cooling fans to not induce more bit flip errors, then set up an additional root-level account named "we$t" and rebooted with the 64GB ECC memory back in place.

Logged in as we$t, he now had a Lynx web browser with full network access.

He entered the IP address to Melissa's server and found her message, reading it at an aggressive speed.

We've been played all this time?

He sat down against the wall to think. How deep did this go? Was the message true, or had someone pressured the server details out of Melissa and written this message on her behalf? Were they all effectively working for the US government? Was *Melissa* working with Kawasaki?

His brain was too tired to figure it out, his stomach too empty, and his options too few. The only thing sure was that their chances of freedom were now slim to none. He made his decision back in Smolensk, and there was no use in even contemplating an out. He had a task at hand—the physical here and now.

How did this server rack get internet access anyway? And power? How was this automated cave facility connected to the outer world?

He got up and walked around the rack in search of cables but found none. Lying flat on the floor, he managed to see with one eye into the gap under the lowermost server. A thick bundle of cables went down through a circular hole in the stone floor.

He inspected both robot charging bays, and they too had cables going down.

Back at the server's terminal, he browsed through existing files and soon found an interesting file system mounted. It was named "Bao Gong."

The ping time to Bao Gong was a minuscule 0.1 microseconds. Maybe it was just a regular server named Bao Gong sitting in this rack? He disconnected the remaining active servers in the rack one by one, checking in between if Bao Gong was still available. The conclusion was that Bao Gong was not a server in this room.

But with a ping time of just a tenth of a microsecond, it must be close.

He did the math on his Tile. Bao Gong was just thirty feet away.

There has to be a part of this cave I haven't found yet. Is that where you've been, big bot, when you've claimed to be here in the Server room?

He checked the resource management system. The large robot was idling in the niche, probably waiting for Ana to go to her charging bay and give it access to the Server room.

Maybe I can figure it out if I can watch the big bot working?

He got the server rack back in order, switched his Tile to red light, and placed his backpack and himself in the corner with Ana's charging bay before releasing the Server room resource.

The big bot entered within seconds and went straight for its charging bay. West couldn't see it from where he was standing because the server rack was in the way. He walked closer, hiding behind the rack, and peeked out at what the robot was up to.

Two large symbols lit up on the wall in front of it—an S in the middle and a down arrow below—giving the bot an eerie backlight. It was just standing there.

First there was a humming sound. Then another sound took over, and the robot started to move downward, through the floor.

West jumped out from behind the server rack and sped toward the descending machine.

Too late for him to stop, the faint light from his Tile revealed matte, thick bars sticking up around the robot like a cage. His right knee crashed into one of them just before his shoulders hit one bar each and his head was slung in an arc, ending with his chin in his sternum. Pain signals blared in his tired body.

When he managed to open his eyes, only the robot's head remained on his floor's level. The charging bay was an elevator!

He squeezed in between the rods and dropped down onto the moving platform, taking the brunt of the fall on his left foot. The platform bounced back slightly.

His face was just an inch from the metal housing of the big bot, and he had no space to move as they traveled down.

The air got noticeably cooler the further they went.

After what felt like a minute, the elevator came to a stop and the metal bars started to retract back into the platform. His foot reached out into the unknown to check what lay beyond the bars. Floor.

He squeezed out, right knee throbbing, and turned around to make his Tile lighten the room. The only reflection he got back was from something shiny far away. Either the space was painted matte black or he was in a huge void.

The robot started moving.

West threw his back up against the wall to get out of the way. Something protruded where he had landed his left palm. A light switch. An honest-to-God, one-gang light switch.

He flipped it and was blinded by the first proper light he'd seen in fifteen hours.

Slowly, as his eyes adjusted, a mind-blowing scene revealed itself.

The space was majestic in size, like a mountain hall.

In the middle stood a huge round pot made of high-gloss metal, like a crucible. Above it, encased in inch-thick glass and hanging from the ceiling far up, was an intricate metal apparatus looking like a giant chandelier with wires, tubes, and framing.

High up on the walls were enormous printed textiles with traditional images and ornate text, two in Mandarin and two in Cyrillic.

Further along the wall where he was standing were two scissor lifts.

This was China's state-of-the-art quantum computer; this was Bao Gong.

Chapter One Hundred One

Fasten Seatbelts

West turned on the radio chips on his Tile and texted Melissa as soon as the airport's cellular network accepted his connection.

I'm here. Where to?

You idiot! Why didn't you reply on the server?

Cooler this way.

Do you know how close I was to giving up on your ass?

Glad you didn't. :)

Did you get the work done?

Yes.

Awesome.

I'm in Oleg's private little lounge. He said he and his pilot can get here within an hour after we ping him.

Let's meet on his plane in
the private hangar once
he's here.

Sending you directions.

Thx.

BTW, I can't speak. My
tongue is destroyed.

Destroyed? What happened?

I'll explain later.

Melissa's instructions took West on a detour. Mentioning Oleg's name and apparently being on some list opened many back doors.

Oleg's plane was a white-and-blue Gulfstream. The man himself greeted West on the few steps up to the cabin door. Oleg was a wide, tanned man in a white suit and a captain's hat. His hand was warm.

To the left, West saw into the cockpit, where a woman greeted him, holding a large Tile.

"She's the real pilot," Oleg said with a smile. "Let me take your coat. Then get yourself a whisky, and we'll be on our way." He turned to the cabin and raised his voice. "Your friend's here. We'll get airborne as soon as you transfer the Bancor. The Wi-Fi password is Volgograd with capital V."

West entered the cabin limping, favoring his left leg. Melissa was the only person there, holding up a whisky glass in a salute. There were six single seats along the sides—four facing each other and an extra row behind. The aisle in the middle was narrow.

One of Melissa's cheeks was bruised, which together with her smug smile made her look badass.

He smiled back at her, slowly shaking his head. "In a million years, I never thought anyone would make me a hacker again."

Her smile turned impish.

West poured himself a Glenlivet from the small alcohol collection

Oleg had pointed him to and held up his glass, too, as he got seated facing forward on the opposite side of the aisle.

"You gig ik yourchelf," she said.

"Ouch. Tell me about the tongue."

Melissa scribbled something on her Tile and showed him.

Can I see it? The backup.

She nodded at his backpack.

"Later," West replied, discreetly pointing at cameras on the side walls of the cabin.

•

The small jet plane took to the Siberian skies just as the whisky nudged West into a slumber.

A loudspeaker voice woke him up. They were no longer the only passengers in the cabin. Dr. Kawasaki and BestBye had joined them, and in the background, by the door to the cockpit, Oleg was pointing a gun in their direction.

West cursed himself for not having checked the rest of the plane, as if discovering Kawasaki earlier would have made a difference.

BestBye avoided eye contact as she cable-tied West's and Melissa's hands and took a seat in front of West. A subtle communication between Kawasaki and Oleg made the Russian return to the cockpit and close the door.

Melissa looked harried but still composed. Kawasaki looked indifferent.

"I take no pleasure in this," the director of US G20S commenced. "The last time you and I met, Melissa, I was a different woman, still fighting my way up, still relishing the rush of power."

"She can't speak because of her tongue," West said in a thin voice. His mouth was dry.

"I know," Kawasaki said without moving her eyes off Melissa. "A shame we can't talk. Might be our only chance." She slowly turned to West, showcasing her calm and deliberation.

She reached over and started pulling West's backpack from the narrow space between him and BestBye. "Thank you," she said in his direction.

"No one should have that data," West hissed as the backpack slid into the aisle.

Kawasaki stopped her move and looked up at him with a sly smile. "So why did you steal it?"

"It should be destroyed and made illegal to collect," he spat out.

She completed the move with finesse and sat down again. "You tried that fifteen years ago and lost half your life as a result. The question of surveillance data's existence is moot. Banning it now would be like constructing the A-bomb and then throwing away the plans. Nation states don't do that. The question that remains is who controls the data, and more importantly, the models derived from it. Do you want to live in a world where the Russians or the Chinese know the most about how humans function and use that knowledge against us?"

"You're using it against your own people."

"Domestic terrorism." She paused for a sardonic smile. "You should read about it."

"My mom was no terrorist!"

A shadow came over Kawasaki's face. Her cheek muscles worked in waves. "I apologize for the uncouth Agent Timothy. His insurance stunt was a terrible overstep, and he is now in early, dishonorable retirement."

"She wasn't the only American you framed." West saw Melissa look his way for a split second, and the exchange did not go unnoticed by Kawasaki. The Survivors' knowledge of manipulation of the blockchain would be a critical piece of evidence to ever get out of this. If they'd get their day in court, that was.

The doctor waited patiently for something more to come, then sighed loudly and focused on West once again. "I'm the first to admit that the fight for freedom causes casualties. As any large organization, we have a few bad apples. But I challenge you." She pointed at him. "Look at the big picture. Look at the last hundred-plus years. Which country on earth has stood up for freedom? Huh? Which people?"

West's face wrinkled. "America marches to a different drummer," he quoted, murmuring.

"I didn't know prison libraries had literature of that quality. Then you know it's our mission to bring liberty and democracy to the world."

"Surveillance isn't going to get us liberty."

She shook her head fidgety. "This is what you zealots get wrong. You think we take an interest in ordinary people; you think we're after the average person. We don't care what you eat or think or jerk off to." Kawasaki's voice got intense, stressing every important word in her sentences. "We are looking for the needle in the haystack; we are looking for actual adversaries. Our work is risky, disheartening, and soul crushing. We doubt ourselves all the time; we question our motives and constantly deal with the fear of impostors, hackers, and spies. If communists and authoritarians would fold, we could live in actual peace. But they're at our doorstep twenty-four seven. A single exposed vulnerability, and they'll thrust the knife in to the hilt."

"So why is the US working with them? We signed the G20S treaty," West retorted.

"Well, that's the downside of democracy, isn't it? Vigilance doesn't get the vote when the perceived world order is peace. During such times, the people elect softies who either can't see or don't want to see. That's how this international data sharing came to be. I hate it as much as you do. We should have used our advantage. The US *owned* the Information Age, and we could have used it to defend our values."

"If the backup is so important to the US, why didn't your agency take it?" He nodded to the backpack in Kawasaki's possession.

"West. You really are a boy still. Dismantling the treaty won't happen without proof of a viable attack—an outsider attack. An attack from the inside would cause more harm than good. It wouldn't prove that there was a real threat and instead could turn the Cyber Cold War hot. So it had to be an outsider—an outsider with the United States as saviors."

Kawasaki got up and walked the aisle over to the latched lockers. She poked around inside them for a while and muttered "No ice." Eventually she poured herself a generous glass. She walked back slowly while indulging, then stopped and massaged the creamy white leather headrest of BestBye's seat with her free hand.

She looked back and forth between Melissa and West and brought gravitas to her voice. "You two are American heroes, you know that? You have proven that the GPI system is vulnerable, which is exactly what the US needs. For that I am thankful. But your heroism is going to have to stay between us."

She sat down, balancing her whisky glass between a thumb and middle finger, and looked Melissa straight in the eye. "The US live backup has thirty days of correct data, remember? And thirty days have not passed since you achieved full GPI control. There will be zero disruption to our operations."

Kawasaki loosened the backpack's straps and got out a Sapphire disk while elegantly managing the glass of whisky in the other hand.

The disk's composition of precious materials and West's fresh memories of the cave complex and all the trouble the Survivors had gone through to snatch the backup—the hacks, the travel, the risks, the death—it made him realize the weight of it all. That disk represented the pinnacle of power in the age of the internet.

"What were you thinking, Liz?" Kawasaki said while admiring the reflections of the disk. "Pogodina and Zabolotnaya, are they the ones you want calling the shots? Or perhaps Espinoza, with his attitude toward women? Or the cockeyed optimist Pelletier, who sings Kumbaya while we all get fucked?"

She put the disk back in the backpack. "I'm going to be the last-minute savior of the American people, and you are going to be locked up for life, unsung and deprived of your legacy." She looked deep into the golden liquid in her glass. "That is sad, but it is necessary."

BestBye's movement came suddenly.

In the blink of an eye, she had smacked the whisky glass into Kawasaki's face. Her aunt screamed as the alcohol burned her eyes.

BestBye jumped an inch to pull the handle of the overhead bin and grabbed what looked like an ornamented scabbard. A second later, a pristine steel blade presented itself to the cabin, and its tip landed on Kawasaki's bare neck at a speed that made West close his eyes.

When he opened them again, Melissa was in the narrow aisle, sliding her cable tie along the length of the sword's edge, then throwing her arms above her head and blasting her hands down, elbows out. "Hiyaa!"

The scream was muffled by her injured tongue, but there was no deficiency in the force. The weakened cable tie snapped the instant her hands hit her thighs.

Kawasaki was still struggling with the sting in her eyes but had seen enough to grasp her precarious situation. "What are you doing, Hoshi?" she shrilled, frozen still, making sure her throat didn't engage the blade.

West saw Melissa squeeze by BestBye and move swiftly but quietly to position herself on the hinge side of the cockpit door. Sure enough, it swung open into the cabin with Oleg's stretched-out arm pointing a gun at the scene in the back. Melissa put the weight of her upper body behind a downward blow to Oleg's underarm and secured the gun before he had fully landed on the floor. She walked back toward West and the other two, paying no attention to the moaning pile she left behind.

"I know you like long plays," BestBye hissed to Kawasaki, cheeks blushing.

"You're not capable of killing a person," Dr. Kawasaki said, looking down on the slender piece of metal touching her skin. She twitched, making the blade drop down half an inch like a razorblade shaving her neck.

"Ay am," Melissa interjected and pulled the trigger of Oleg's gun, blasting a bullet into the back of her own seat.

West's ears rang. BestBye moved back into her seat and nodded to West to cut his cable tie on the sword. The smell of gunpowder reached him as he worked to get his hands loose.

"Please, no shooting," Oleg blared from the front. He was holding his palms in the air. "I will get you to Krasnoyarsk and you can kill each other there, okay?"

Melissa sat down hard in her seat and rested the gun's butt on the table, barrel pointed at her opponent.

Kawasaki's nostrils flared as her eyes moved back and forth between BestBye and Melissa. "How did the two of you …"

"Melissa's old boyfriend turned out to be useful," BestBye said, "or rather his Tile."

So that was Melissa's remaining surprise. So much for trust.

BestBye reached for the backpack and pulled it back to her and West's side. "Soon your thirty days of backup will have passed," she said.

Kawasaki gave her a poisonous look, then turned to the muzzle at point-blank range. "You're going to have to kill me."

"I'm recording," BestBye said, pointing at one of the cabin cameras. She looked to Melissa, who picked up her Tile in her free hand, thumbed down a long message, and gave the device to West. He read her message loud and clear.

"Killing is for governments, not for us. You'll send orders to free Jitterbug in Krasnoyarsk in exchange for your life. What you do with Naturelle and Mikhail is none of our business. An email from Agent Pogodina's account will get you jailed, and we can only assume Pogodina will want to keep you in custody for a while after we tell her what you've been up to. As for any future in the US, either we and the American public never hear from Akiko Kawasaki again, or you'll be charged with treason. If you play along, there will be a cabin by Deep Creek Lake waiting for you under a new US identity—Kumori Irezumi."

Dr. Kawasaki's jaw was clenched to the point of breaking her teeth. She gave the backpack another look. "G20S will hunt you to the end of the world for that thing," she said with distinct, minimal mouth movement.

"We'll make a copy and destroy the original," BestBye said.

Kawasaki chuckled like a pressure valve letting off steam. "The data is in a proprietary format. It'll take you months to read those disks."

"West and Jit broke Fraktal in a week. I'm sure they can manage," BestBye replied.

West knew it was the highest accolade he'd ever get from her.

"No one will believe you if you can't show the disks," Kawasaki said, "and if you have the disks, G20S will get them."

"There is a third way," West said, pulling out his own Tile. He was trembling.

Melissa turned to him in a twitch.

He opened the web browser and typed twelve characters on the Tile before putting it screen-down on the table.

Seconds passed.

"I never stole the backup," he said. "Those disks are blank."

Melissa's eyes narrowed and her head tilted.

He swallowed as he made eye contact with her. "When I saw your message and learned that Naturelle and Mikhail were working with Kawasaki, I figured we were being used against Russia and China."

Melissa closed her eyes slowly.

"The empty disks are proof that we *could* have stolen the backup. That's all we need," West said desperately.

"If you didn't steal it, Russia still has it," BestBye pointed out.

"True." He had to control his hand to not drop his Tile as he picked it up. He carefully positioned his index finger above the webpage's Send button before showing the screen to the others.

"The risk to humanity was not created by the race between three superpowers. The risk was created by collecting the data," he said, barely keeping his voice steady. "Today, we the people, correct that mistake. Some things are worth blowing up."

As the small jet plane pierced through the Russian sky, the fate of the Global Personal Identity system and humans' right to their own fate was in the hands of an ex-convict with little to lose and a newfound belief in his own agency. His mind touched upon liberty, and the right of resistance and self-preservation. It was a profound moment, true and epic.

His finger touched the screen.

•

Deep inside the Siberian basement rock, down under Nornickel's headquarters, a compromised rack-mounted blade server had been reloading West's remote webpage over and over for hours on end in search of a particular string of characters. Finally, it got a hit and sent out a signal through a USB cable.

A few feet away, the automated vacuum cleaner Bot Ana 103 woke up in her charging bay, detached herself, and started off on her newly programmed route.

She requested and was granted Corridor Right, Corridor Out, and Garbage. The journey took her just under four minutes, since she didn't have to vacuum.

In the Garbage room, there was a metal box where the big robot normally put her used dust bags. Now it was full of sapphire disks and ANFO.

Ana did as her new program told her and drove up to the side of the box where two copper cables stretched out and touched plus and minus on her exposed battery pack.

The electrical discharge was violent and lit the end of a flexible plastic tube filled with pentaerythritol tetranitrate. It took the fuse 0.47 milliseconds to travel through the tube and into the metal box, ending in a Tovex blasting cap embedded in the bag of ANFO prills.

As boom, smoke, and dust billowed up in the cave's underground corridors, the screen attached to the compromised blade server was still displaying West's triggering string.

4 Kizz & Mom

CHAPTER ONE HUNDRED TWO

Epilogue

Congress Repeals the PITA

A bipartisan majority of both chambers of Congress today repealed the Personal Information Transparency Act, or PITA, which has been the linchpin of G20 Security's data collection and processing practices. This sweeping legislative change follows months of debate and outrage over vast violations of Americans' rights, ranging from oversteps in surveillance to full-fledged framing of citizens deemed to be troublemakers.

Speaker of the House of Representatives, Mrs. Cortez, summarized her position with references to the past. "We need to find a better solution to safety than omniscient, persistent surveillance of our citizens. We have to offer people the freedom to think, act, and pursue their dreams without supercomputers constantly meddling with their lives. That is the promise of this great nation, and that is the highest priority we have as elected officials. As you know, I prefer to quote historic women, but at a time like this I find no better words than those of Benjamin Franklin: 'Those who would give up essential Liberty, to purchase a little temporary Safety, deserve neither Liberty nor Safety.'"

On the other side of the debate, the message was more mixed. Senator Gait lamented "throwing the baby out with the bathwater" without concrete details on the merits he saw in PITA. Representative Daniels, on the other hand, was "aghast about our politicians' ignorance and lack of backbone. We are playing directly into the hands of our enemies, who have zero intent to curb their own use of personal data."

The future of Global Personal Identities in America is still up in the air, with proponents hailing their convenience and usefulness in everyday commercial life. The European Union already has proposals and is likely to restrict the use of GPI in the market space long before Capitol Hill can make up its mind.

This article's sources may or may not be GPI-validated.

•

West admired the little copper pot on his table at Cafe Istanbul in downtown San Francisco. He'd never had Turkish coffee before. What an experience it was—intense, sweet, cardamom-infused, and perfectly paired with the citrusy Turkish delight he had chosen.

He had promised himself to try one new thing per day, and this totally fit the bill. He needed things to get his mind off the heavy memories he carried.

Jitterbug had helped him track down Kiss's family in Juneau a couple of months ago, and he had eventually gathered strength to deliver the heartbreaking news. It took a while for them to believe him, although they had not heard from their daughter in a long time and had considered reporting her missing, against her repeated instructions never to do so. Her parents decided they'd first try to get Russia to release Kiss's body before arranging a funeral.

Melissa had said she'd disappear for half a year or so until she felt safe coming back. West had no clue where she was, and he didn't blame her given the political scandals the EFF set in motion once GPI was fully compromised. BestBye never said where she'd go.

West helped out at Jitterbug's church once a week, which was more than enough of a social life for the time being. The rest of the weeks he spent watching the world. It felt good being an observer, a free agent collecting experiences and forming opinions.

He paid for his coffee plus a generous tip and started walking west, past City Hall toward Golden Gate Park. Today he would find a nice spot in the shade on one of the lawns and start reading Chelsea Manning's new book, *Miss Gender*.

Just as he got on Fulton Street, his right foot skidded forward an inch. Dog shit.

He smiled.

I have to find a dog to pet. Or get a puppy.

He scraped the poop off on the curb and continued walking.

This novel is dedicated to my daughter Judith Wilander.

ACKNOWLEDGMENTS

This novel took me years to write, edit, and publish. Many helped me along the way. Thank you so much!

Development editor: Georgia Lin Sundling
Development editor: Marissa Frosch, ravensquillpublishing.com
Copyeditor: Lisa Gilliam, lisagilliam.com
Marketing coach: Marius Wenneson

Alpha readers, the truly daring ones: Jonathan Davis, Joseph Pecoraro, Megan Gardner, Keith Rollin, and Devin Rousso.

Beta readers providing invaluable, structured feedback: Björn Löndahl, Anna Wetterbom, Erik Ihrén Ebeling, Marcus Ossiann, Adrienne Porter Felt, Erlend Oftedal, Mikael Sahrling, Anna Moritz, Christofer Lindqvist, Eric Lawrence, Marion Daly, Krister Svartström, Sarah Baso, Åsa Boge, Bo Svangård, Linus Engback, and Hans Rahmqvist.

Made in United States
North Haven, CT
16 July 2022

21473077R00215